Praise for the novels [illegible]

"Woods really knows what readers have come to expect from her stories, and she always gives them what they want. Here, she pens another great love story...written with great care."

—*RT Book Reviews* on *Where Azaleas Bloom*

"Sherryl Woods always delights her readers—including me!"

—#1 *New York Times* bestselling author Debbie Macomber

"Woods is a master heartstring puller."

—*Publishers Weekly* on *Seaview Inn*

"Woods...is noted for appealing character-driven stories that are often infused with the flavor and fragrance of the South."

—*Library Journal*

"A reunion story punctuated by family drama, Woods' first novel in her new Ocean Breeze series is touching, tense and tantalizing."

—*RT Book Reviews* on *Sand Castle Bay*

"Woods imbues her characters with determination and humanity, deftly shedding light on real-life dramas."

—*Booklist* on *Seaview Inn*

Also by #1 New York Times *bestselling author*
Sherryl Woods

The Sweet Magnolias

Stealing Home
A Slice of Heaven
Feels Like Family
Welcome to Serenity
Home in Carolina
Sweet Tea at Sunrise
Honeysuckle Summer
Midnight Promises
Catching Fireflies
Where Azaleas Bloom
Swan Point
The Sweet Magnolias Cookbook

Seaview Key

Seaview Inn
Home to Seaview Key

Adams Dynasty

Christmas at White Pines
Winter's Proposal
The Heart of Hill Country
White Pines Summer
Wildflower Ridge
West Texas Nights
Winter Vows
Texas Ever After
Starlit Secrets

Ocean Breeze Trilogy

Sand Castle Bay
Wind Chime Point
Sea Glass Island

Whispering Wind

After Tex
Angel Mine

Chesapeake Shores

The Inn at Eagle Point
Flowers on Main
Harbor Lights
A Chesapeake Shores Christmas
Driftwood Cottage
Moonlight Cove
Beach Lane
An O'Brien Family Christmas
The Summer Garden
A Seaside Christmas
The Christmas Bouquet
Dogwood Hill
Willow Brook Road
Lilac Lane

Nonfiction

A Small Town Love Story:
Colonial Beach, Virginia

For a complete list of all titles by Sherryl Woods,
visit www.sherrylwoods.com.

SHERRYL WOODS

Home to Seaview Key

MIRA

MIRA™

Recycling programs for this product may not exist in your area.

ISBN-13: 978-0-7783-0557-6

Home to Seaview Key

First published in 2014. This edition published in 2024.

For questions and comments about the quality of this book, please contact us at CustomerService@Harlequin.com.

TM is a trademark of Harlequin Enterprises ULC.

Mira
22 Adelaide St. West, 41st Floor
Toronto, Ontario M5H 4E3, Canada
www.Harlequin.com

Printed in U.S.A.

Home to Seaview Key

One

Abby stirred at the unmistakable pressure of a man's mouth on hers, coaxing, tantalizing. The kind of yearning she'd buried for years awakened with a vengeance. Whether this was a dream or reality hardly seemed to matter as her breath caught and her pulse raced. It had been so long since she'd felt like this.

She sighed when the man drew back, then slowly opened her eyes to find a soaking wet, bare-chested, incredibly gorgeous stranger kneeling in the sand beside her, his expression every bit as startled as her own must have been.

"Looks like you're going to be okay," he said, a hitch in his voice and a surprising hint of color in his sexily stubbled cheeks.

"Okay?" she echoed, bemused. There had been nothing wrong about the past couple of minutes. They'd been enchanted, in fact. Spectacular, even. Definitely well beyond okay.

"I pulled you out of the water just now," he reminded her, worry darkening his blue eyes. "You don't remember going under? Calling out for help?"

Suddenly the panic came rushing back, the sensation of water closing over her head, her feet unable to touch the sandy bottom of the Gulf of Mexico. One second she'd been standing in waist-deep water, the next a wave had caught her and the floor of the Gulf had fallen away.

Memories of another near drowning right here in these waters years ago had arisen, right along with a bubble of hysteria. Then the memories had faded and a harsh present-day reality had set in. She'd been fighting her way to the surface, gasping for air, screaming for help. She'd choked on water before going under again and again.

"I was drowning, just like before," she whispered, shaking, the potent effect of what she'd thought to be a kiss vanishing. He'd been doing mouth-to-mouth resuscitation, she realized, embarrassed that she'd thought otherwise, wondering if she had, in fact, tried to kiss him. She had an awful feeling that she had. A very powerful memory of tongues tangling in a shockingly sensual way tugged at her. Humiliated, she knew her cheeks must be flaming.

Years ago in a similar situation, Luke Stevens had been close by. He'd saved her, become her hero. They'd been inseparable after that along with her best friend, Hannah, but she and Luke had been a couple, right up until the day they'd left for college and gone their separate ways. Though they'd both claimed to be brokenhearted, they'd been resolute about not standing in the way of each other's hopes and dreams—his to be a doctor, hers to be *something.* She'd wanted to excel at anything that would get her away from this dead-end island life.

As immature as they'd been, somehow they'd known

they weren't meant to last forever. And while she and Luke had deliberately separated, she and Hannah had simply drifted apart.

It was ironic really that now, after so much time had passed, all three of them were back on Seaview Key. Now, though, Luke and Hannah were married and Abby was the third wheel…or would be if she reached out to them. She wasn't sure she wanted to be cast in the role that she'd forced Hannah into back then. Life had taught her that being witness to someone else's happiness could be incredibly painful.

Besides, for the moment she was content just to be on her own, getting her feet back under her. Not that this morning had turned out to be a very good start on that front, she thought with a touch of the wry humor she counted on to get her through tough times. For a woman who'd been swimming since before she could walk, she was surprisingly inept in the water, apparently.

The man kneeling next to her was still studying her with concern. "Maybe we should get you over to the clinic, have you checked out," he said. "You seem to be a little fuzzy about what happened."

Abby shook her head, fully aware that going to the clinic meant seeing Luke again under awkward circumstances. "No, really. I'm fine. Just a little dazed, I think. That will pass."

"You swallowed a lot of water."

"And surely coughed up most of it," she recalled, embarrassed yet again by the pitiful spectacle she must have made of herself.

"I'd feel better if Doc Stevens took a look at you. My car's right up there on the road. I can have you there in a couple of minutes."

"Seriously, no," she said more forcefully. This wasn't the way she wanted to see Luke again, bedraggled and half-drowned. Maybe he hadn't been put off by that twenty-some years ago, but she still had a little pride left. She wanted to look her best when she finally crossed paths with Luke and Hannah. She needed them to know that coming home had been a choice, not a necessity.

"I live right over there," she said, gesturing toward the house where she'd grown up.

The sad sight was almost as much of a mess as she was—the yard overgrown with weeds and the house itself in desperate need of a lot of tender loving care. While she'd been planning her return for a while and had made several quick trips to the island, she'd only been physically back to stay in Seaview Key for a few days. So far she'd tackled the dust and cleaning inside to make the house habitable again. She'd get to the rest eventually. For reasons not entirely clear to her, she was determined to do the work herself. Maybe she simply needed to get back to basics, remind herself of how little some of the luxuries she'd gotten used to really mattered.

The man stood up and held out his hand to help her up. "Then I'll make sure you get to the house okay. I can check you out myself, take your pulse, listen to your lungs. I have a medical kit in my car."

Abby regarded him skeptically. Since when had Seaview Key required two physicians to keep up with the small population of locals? "You're a doctor, too?" she inquired doubtfully.

"Paramedic," he corrected. "I'm Seth Landry. I worked with Doc Stevens in Iraq. After my discharge, I came here for a visit. He told me the town could use a volunteer rescue squad. He got me hired to organize it." He grinned at her. "See, I'm totally respectable. I'm not just trying to get my hands on you."

Too bad, Abby thought to herself. For a few minutes there, she'd actually felt desirable again, not like the pale shadow of the woman she'd once been before her marriage had sucked the life out of her.

Seth slowed his steps to match hers as they walked across the sand and up the path to her house. At the bottom of the porch steps, worn smooth by decades of sandy feet, she stopped and lifted her gaze to his, noting with delight that though she was tall at five-ten, he was taller, at least six-one or -two.

"See?" she said lightly. "Perfectly steady. Thanks for rescuing me."

"All in a day's work," he told her. "But if you're from around here, you should already know how the bottom out there drops away unexpectedly. If you're not a strong swimmer, stay closer to shore. Stick to wading, even."

"You're absolutely right. It won't happen again," she assured him. In fact, she shuddered just thinking about how differently her morning and that innocent dip she'd taken in the Gulf could have turned out.

"I'll see you around, then," he said, giving her a casual wave before jogging off down the beach.

Abby watched him go, admiring the well-muscled shoulders, the narrow hips, the long legs. He was younger, too, if she was any judge of age. That made that flicker of awareness that had passed between them just a little more alluring. Maybe she still had it, after all, whatever that *it* was that could catch a man's eye.

Too bad that kiss hadn't been real, she thought with genuine regret. Seth was definitely the kind of hunk who'd been made to awaken any sleeping beauty's senses, hers included.

Hannah sat on the porch facing the gently lapping water, a cup of coffee in hand. She smiled when her husband slipped up behind her, kissed the back of her neck, then sat down in the chair beside her. The few minutes they had together like this each morning set the tone for their days. She reached for Luke's hand, twined her fingers with his.

"What's on your schedule for today?" she asked.

"I need to track down Seth to talk about a possible rescue boat I've found. I thought I'd stop by Seaview Inn to try to catch him before I open the clinic."

She gave him a long look, amused by his attempt at innocence. "Nice try. We both know you're dropping by because Grandma Jenny bakes every Wednesday. She'll have the treats that are never on the menu here."

He grinned, his expression boyish and unrepentant. "You caught me. I'm hoping for blueberry muffins. How about you? How's the new book coming?"

Hannah felt a little shiver of excitement at the question. Little more than a year ago she'd been an ambitious, driven public-relations executive in New York. Now she was not only surrounded by the tranquility of Seaview Key and married, but she was writing children's books. The first was due for publication in a few months, the second six months later. She'd been working on the third for a couple of months now.

She grinned at Luke. "I'm putting the finishing touches on it today," she told him, then frowned. "At least I think I am. I can't wait till Kelsey and Jeff get back to town, so I can read it to the baby. Isabella's my favorite test audience."

"You do realize she's not even a year old," Luke said. "Maybe you should call my kids. They always have uncensored advice for you. And my daughter was the first to recognize your talent. You captivated her with your story when she was injured on our boating trip. She was so caught up in it, she forgot all about being in pain from a broken arm. You provided the best medicine she could have had before we got back to shore."

She laughed. "I don't know about that, but your kids can be a little too uncensored at times," she admitted. "I like the gurgles of delight. After that, I can take whatever your kids have to say."

Her stepchildren, who lived in Atlanta with their mother and her new husband, were regular visitors to Seaview Key. After a rocky beginning, they'd accepted Hannah into their lives…and forgiven their father for moving so far away. They'd even accepted the fact that he wasn't the one who'd caused the divorce, that it was their mom who'd moved on while their father was serving overseas in a war zone.

Even at their young ages, they'd learned that assigning blame was a waste of energy. They could all thank Grandma Jenny for imparting that lesson, Hannah thought, grateful to her grandmother for smoothing out the rough spots in the relationship. That had allowed Luke to remain in Seaview Key with a clear conscience. He traveled to Atlanta at least once a month to see them and was always available for special events like class plays or soccer championships. They'd made it work.

Hannah gazed at the early morning sunlight filtering through the trees and sparkling on the water, then drew in a deep breath of the cool morning air. "Luke, do you realize how lucky we are?"

"Every minute," he said, his gaze on hers. "Being here, with you, is exactly what I needed."

"No regrets?"

"Not a one. You?"

She thought about the life she'd left behind to come home, the life she'd been so certain was exactly the one she was meant to live. There were things she missed about New York. Being able to order any food imaginable at midnight was one of them. Her best friend. Beyond that, though? This house already felt more like a home than her apartment in New York ever had, even when Kelsey had been filling it with clutter and noise. And her marriage? Being with Luke on an ordinary day surpassed anything she'd had with Kelsey's father, a perfectly nice man who'd been totally unsuitable for her, for marriage and for parenthood.

"I'm happier than I ever dreamed possible," she told him honestly.

Luke studied her, his expression filled with concern. "Then why that frown?"

"I wasn't frowning," she insisted. Surely she was better at disguising her feelings than that.

"It's because you have another cancer screening coming up, isn't it?" he said, not letting her off the hook. "You're going to be fine, Hannah. I know it. You're religious about the self-exams. I've backed you up. Your report is going to be clean."

"I want to believe that, too, but sometimes I panic."

"Because?"

She gestured to him, then to the serene setting around

them. "All of this," she said. "You, Kelsey, Jeff and my granddaughter. Grandma Jenny's in good health for someone her age. It's all so amazing, more than I ever expected."

He regarded her with understanding. "And you're afraid it's too good to be true, that it's going to be snatched away?"

"Sometimes, yes."

Luke squeezed her hand. "No way, sweetheart. You and me, all of this? It's forever."

"You sound so sure," she said, envying him.

"I am," he said with unwavering confidence. "One of these days, you're going to believe that, too."

Hannah truly hoped so. She wanted to live the kind of optimistic life her husband lived, but doubts crept up on her. She'd spent too many years facing challenges, rather than counting blessings. She couldn't seem to stop the doubts, not since her mother had died of breast cancer just months after she'd been diagnosed herself. Sure, she was in remission now, but who knew better than she that things could change in an instant? The very minute she started taking this wonderful life for granted, who knew what perverse twist of fate could take it from her?

After his run and a hot shower, Seth wandered into the kitchen at Seaview Inn and found the owner at the kitchen table, a cup of coffee and a batch of stained recipe cards in front of her. The aroma of blueberry muffins came from the oven. Another batch was cooling on a rack on top of the stove. He noted that one was missing and barely contained a grin. Luke had been by. He'd bet money on it.

"What sort of feast are you thinking of preparing for tonight?" he asked, gesturing to the well-worn cards in her hand.

Grandma Jenny glanced up, laughing. "I'm not sure yet. Whenever I get tired of fixing the same old things, I drag out my mother's recipe cards and look for inspiration." She gave him a chiding look. "I was wondering when you were going to turn up. We stopped serving breakfast an hour ago."

Seth leaned down and dropped a kiss on her forehead. "Could I have one of those muffins and a couple of eggs, if I fix them myself?"

"And mess this place up when I finally have it all tidied up?" she asked. "I don't think so. I'll make an exception this morning and get those eggs for you. Scrambled, maybe with a little cheese thrown in?"

It was their morning ritual. Grandma Jenny, who was actually Doc Stevens's grandmother-in-law, feigned annoyance at Seth's failure to observe the inn's schedule, then made sure he left with a full stomach. He'd noticed that she thrived on mothering anyone who crossed her path, family or not.

"Luke was over here looking for you earlier," she reported.

Seth chuckled. "You sure he wasn't here for the muffins? I've noticed he shows up a lot on Wednesday mornings."

"Well, of course he was, but he made a convincing show of needing to speak to you right away. He wants you to stop by the clinic, says he has a lead on a rescue boat that might do for getting folks over to the mainland to a hospital."

That was good news, and worthy of an early morning visit, Seth thought.

"A rescue boat is just what we need," Seth said as Grandma Jenny placed a plate of steaming eggs in front of him along with one of those still-warm muffins. "I'll head over to the clinic as soon as I've eaten. After that, I'm going to start looking for a place of my own. I can't keep occupying one of your guest rooms, especially since you refuse to let me pay for it."

Disappointment flashed in her eyes. "There's no rush to do that," she said, clearly trying to discourage him. "It's the off-season. We're not booked solid, so it's not costing me a dime to have you here. And with my great-granddaughter, her husband and the baby off on a little vacation, I'm glad of the company, to tell you the truth."

As soon as the admission crossed her lips, though, she scowled at him. "Don't be telling Hannah that or she'll be over here pestering me about going into some assisted-living place over on the mainland, even though I've told her that subject is dead and should be buried."

"This inn wouldn't be the same without you," Seth said honestly.

Her eyes sparkled at that. "Nonsense, but thank you for saying it. My great-granddaughter has this place running more efficiently than I ever did. Kelsey and Jeff are doing ninety percent of the work these days. We even have a website, for goodness' sake. I'm just around for window dressing. It makes some of our old regulars feel more comfortable to see I'm still alive and kicking."

Seth laughed. He knew better. Grandma Jenny was the heart of Seaview Inn. Kelsey might have inherited her love of the crazy, haphazardly put together beachfront inn, but Grandma Jenny knew what it took to make people feel welcome. She'd certainly done that with him once he'd been hired and had insisted on moving out of Luke and Hannah's guest room.

From the moment Luke had brought him here two months ago and introduced him, Grandma Jenny had made him a part of the family, the same way she did all of their guests. For a man with little family of his own remaining, it had been a wonder to find himself surrounded by people who treated him as if he belonged. Given the contentious nature of his relationship with his siblings, who'd been battling over their inheritance ever since their parents had died, it was a welcome and eye-opening change.

"You were even later than usual this morning," Grandma Jenny said, regarding him curiously. "Something come up while you were on your run?"

Since he knew she was always eager for news, he filled her in. "As a matter of fact, I ran into a woman on the beach."

Her eyes lit up. "Is that so? Sounds like just what you need."

"It wasn't like that," he insisted, though the way her mouth had felt under his had been exactly like that. The unprofessional thought and the memory of her sensual responsiveness had his face flaming.

"Don't try telling me that," she scolded. "That blush says otherwise."

"The woman was floundering in the water, in real trouble," he corrected. "She'd lost her footing and was going under. I just got her back to shore. That's it. A routine rescue."

Worry immediately replaced the teasing glint in her eyes. "She was okay?"

"Seemed to be. She refused to let me take her to the clinic and didn't want me to check her out. Looked embarrassed, to tell you the truth. I walked her home. She seemed fine by then."

"Who was she?"

"I didn't get her name."

Grandma Jenny regarded him with feigned disgust. "You let an attractive woman get away without getting her name? What am I going to do with you?"

Seth laughed. "I never said she was attractive."

"You might not have said the words, but I know better. Where does she live?"

"Back in that Blue Heron Cove gated community, though her house doesn't look like any of those big new places they're supposed to be putting up in there in the next few months. Looks as if it's been around for years."

"Abby Dawson," Grandma Jenny said at once, looking startled. "Dark hair? Green eyes?"

"As a matter of fact, yes," Seth said, recalling the way her eyes had sparkled like bits of jade-colored sea glass.

"What's she doing back, I wonder? Last I heard she was living up in Pensacola or some small town thereabouts. I've forgotten her married name. Miller, perhaps."

"Maybe she's just in town for a visit," Seth suggested, surprised by her reaction and even more startled by the mention of marriage. He hadn't noticed a ring, but then he hadn't been looking. He'd been a little too focused on her lips. All in the line of duty, he assured himself, even though the scrambling of his pulse said otherwise.

"Is there something upsetting about her being back?"

he asked, finishing the last of the muffin and pushing aside his plate to concentrate on what Grandma Jenny had to say.

"No, I suppose not," she said, though the worry didn't fade from her expression.

"You're not a very good liar," he said. "You listen to me go on and on about my troubles. It's my turn to return the favor. What worries you about Abby Dawson being back?"

"It's just that once upon a time she and Luke, well, they were like two peas in a pod. That girl had a real hold on him." She met his gaze. "Luke saved her from drowning. Did she mention that?"

"No, but she did say something about it not being the first time she'd gotten in trouble in the water," he recalled. "Luke rescued her?"

"He did, and fell for her on the spot," Grandma Jenny confirmed.

"I thought he hung out with Hannah back then," Seth said, beginning to understand her concern.

"He did. It was the three of them, day and night, but there was no question that Hannah was just tagging along. To give Abby credit, she wasn't one of those girls who ditched her best friend when she got involved with a boy, though it might have been easier on Hannah if she had been."

"Because?"

"Hannah had had a crush on that boy for years."

Oh, brother, Seth thought, envisioning a bitter teen rivalry. "Did Abby know that?" he asked, his attraction to the woman he'd met dimming just a little at the thought that she'd deliberately set out to steal the affections of Hannah's guy.

"I can't say for sure, but they were best friends. Don't girls that age tell each other everything?"

Seth shook his head. "I have a couple of sisters, but the workings of their minds are way beyond my pay grade."

"Well, it was a difficult time around here watching Hannah on the sidelines, her heart obviously aching, but trying so hard to act like it didn't matter that Luke was dating Abby. As bad as I felt for Hannah, it was hard to blame Abby and Luke. They were good kids and it wasn't as if Luke and Hannah had been a couple. I doubt he'd noticed she was alive before he got involved with Abby. Then the three of them were underfoot around here all the time. I sometimes wondered if Abby didn't even go a little overboard to be extra nice out of guilt because she knew Hannah was hurting."

"In that case, surely you don't think that after all this time, Abby might want to rekindle things with Luke," Seth said. "Would she come back just to stir up trouble for them?"

"I have no idea why she's come back," Grandma Jenny said with a touch of impatience, then sighed. "Hopefully it's just for a visit, but if not..." Her voice trailed off.

"Come on," Seth protested. "Luke and Hannah are solid. I've never seen two people more in love. And you said this Abby is married."

"That's what I'd heard. I'm just saying her being back could stir up some old memories, good and bad." Her jaw set with determination as she stood up. "I'd better warn Hannah."

"Or maybe you should leave it alone," Seth suggested mildly, even though he was out of his depth when it came to marital relationships. His one serious relationship had ended tragically. Before that it had been all heat and intensity. There hadn't been a lot of complex issues to resolve.

"For all we know this woman could be gone by morning," he said. "You'd have upset Hannah for no reason."

"Spoken exactly like a man," she muttered.

"Which I am," Seth replied, amused.

"Which just means you don't know how women's minds work. You admitted that yourself, not more than a minute ago," she reminded him. "Wash up those dishes when you're done. I'm going to see my granddaughter."

"But we don't even know for sure if Abby Dawson was the woman I met this morning," he argued, hating that he seemed to have set off alarms.

"Oh, it was Abby," Grandma Jenny said with conviction. "I can feel it in my bones. Trouble's coming."

Before he could think of a thing to keep her from leaving, she was gone, and Seth was left to wonder whether Seaview Key was quite the tranquil, boring little town he'd thought it to be. It sounded almost as if the return of Abby Dawson—if that's who she was—could stir up a whole boatload of pain for his friends. Which, come to think of it, was too darn bad given the feelings she'd stirred up in him.

Two

Hannah finished the latest draft of the story about a puppy named Jasper who'd befriended a lonely little boy, typed *The End* on the last page and shut off the computer just as she heard the front door downstairs open and then close.

"Hannah?" her grandmother called out. "You up there?"

"On my way down," she responded at once, startled by her grandmother's midmorning visit. She was usually rigidly respectful of Hannah's writing schedule, never dropping in before afternoon. Something serious must be going on for her to violate her self-imposed rule.

Hannah found Grandma Jenny in the kitchen placing several freshly baked blueberry muffins on a plate. "I was sure my husband already ate his share of those today," she commented.

"Nothing makes me happier than a man who appreciates my baking," Grandma Jenny replied. "Luke knows that, bless his heart. I thought you might want one, too, or are you dieting?"

Hannah smiled. "I could eat one. I'll make tea."

"Iced tea, please. It's hotter than blazes out there already. You'd think it would be cooling off by now. It's almost Thanksgiving, for goodness' sake."

Hannah poured two tall glasses of iced tea, then sat down at the kitchen table and regarded her grandmother expectantly. "What's on your mind?"

"Do I have to have something on my mind? Can't I just drop by for a visit?"

"Of course you can," Hannah responded patiently, "but you usually wait until afternoon in case I'm working. I figure something must be important for you to show up at this hour."

"Obviously I need to start being more unpredictable."

Hannah merely lifted a brow at her irritated tone. "Are you lonely with Kelsey and Jeff away? Heaven knows, I'm missing my daily fix of seeing Isabella. It must be even harder for you, though I thought having Seth underfoot would help."

"I'm not lonely. I'm worried," Grandma Jenny said candidly, startling Hannah.

"Worried? Why?"

"Seth met a woman this morning."

Hannah regarded her blankly. "Why is that worrisome? Given your matchmaking tendencies, I would have thought you'd be thrilled. You've been muttering that he needs a woman ever since he got to town."

"Well, I may have been thrilled, but if this is who I think it is, it might be for the best if she just went back to wherever she came from."

Since Hannah had never before heard her grandmother use that disparaging tone about anyone, she stared at her with shock. "How so? Who on earth is she? I didn't think there was anyone in Seaview Key, past or present, with whom you had any issues."

Looking thoroughly uncomfortable, Grandma Jenny announced, "I'm pretty sure the woman is Abby Dawson, or whatever her married name is. And it's not me who has issues with her."

The news hit Hannah like a blow. It shouldn't have. Abby's return shouldn't matter to her at all. She and Abby had never had a falling-out, not really. They'd just left town and lost touch. Truthfully, though, the friendship had been fractured long before that when Abby and Luke had gotten together. As determinedly as Abby and Hannah had both tried to keep up the pretense that things between them were fine, they'd both known that the relationship had been changed forever.

Working hard to keep her tone neutral, Hannah said, "Abby's back? Are you sure? No one in town has mentioned it. I might not hear the latest gossip, but Luke hears everything."

"Would he tell you something like this?" her grandmother asked. "You know how he hates upsetting you."

"He would have told me," Hannah insisted, though she wondered if that was true.

"Maybe so." Grandma Jenny shrugged. "Maybe she's been keeping a low profile. Maybe she just got to town. I don't know. I just thought I ought to tell you." She gave her a pointed look. "You know, because..."

"Because of her past relationship with Luke," Hannah said flatly. She didn't want her grandmother to see how shaken she was, so she tried to keep her worry out of her voice. "That was a long time ago."

"I know, but that doesn't mean you shouldn't be prepared."

Rather than accepting the well-meant concern in the spirit in which it had been intended, Hannah fought annoyance. "Prepared for what? Luke to fall head over heels for her all over again? I can't start thinking like that. Besides, Abby's married now. So is he. Life goes on."

"And every now and then the past rears its head and shakes up the status quo," Grandma Jenny said direly. "I have a bad feeling about this, Hannah."

"Thanks for your confidence in my marriage," Hannah muttered, regretting that she was in her own kitchen and couldn't just get up and walk away and pretend that this conversation had never happened.

"I didn't mean it like that," her grandmother said hurriedly, looking genuinely shocked. "Luke adores you. I believe that with everything in me. The bond between the two of you is strong."

Hannah responded to the vehemence in Grandma Jenny's voice, her nerves quieting. "Then what did you mean?" she inquired more calmly.

"I'm not sure *you* believe it," her grandmother said gently, her worried gaze holding Hannah's. "And when you start having those doubts that plague you, things can get twisted around."

Hannah bit back a sigh. It was true. Hadn't she admitted the same thing to Luke this morning, that she was prone to doubts about everything good in her life? Who knew that better than this woman who'd helped to raise her, who'd witnessed her devastation when Luke had fallen in love with Abby way back when, who'd seen the impact her mother's death had had on her own confidence that she could win her battle against breast cancer? It seemed doubts popped up like dandelions, unwelcome but hardy. Even in her early forties, she'd never outgrown that tendency to let doubt overrule logic.

"I don't want you to go borrowing trouble," Grandma Jenny told her. "That's what you do, you know. This happiness you've found with Luke is exactly what you deserve. Don't let anything or anybody make you question that."

Hannah forced a smile. "So you're really here to give me a pep talk?"

Her grandmother covered her hand and gave it a squeeze. "Something like that."

"Okay. I'll make you a deal. I won't panic over Abby's sudden return until and unless there's a reason to."

"A *real* reason," Grandma Jenny amended. "Not something you start imagining to make yourself crazy."

"How am I supposed to know the difference?" Hannah inquired curiously.

"I'll be watching," her grandmother promised. "I'll be the first to let you know."

Hannah laughed. "Then since you're on the case, I won't give Abby's return another thought," she promised, hoping it was a promise she could keep for her own sake. Some people took comfort from knowing God was looking out for them. Hannah had Grandma Jenny in her corner. God, too, she knew, but her grandmother was a force to be reckoned with in her own right.

Grandma Jenny looked doubtful, but she nodded. "Okay, then. By the way, as unsuitable as I think she might be and as much as I might like her gone, I'm fairly certain that Seth is attracted to her. Could be he's the answer to our prayers, especially if her marriage is over and she's on the prowl."

"On the prowl?" Hannah echoed, laughing.

"Well, isn't that what those cougars do? You know, the older women who go after younger men? Seth is definitely younger than she is by quite a bit. She's your age, for goodness' sake."

"Ancient, then," Hannah said wryly.

"Stop putting words in my mouth. I was just commenting that there's an age difference. That's a fact, not a judgment."

"Ah, so you *have* decided to do a little matchmaking if the circumstances warrant it?" Hannah concluded. "Does Seth know what you're up to? Has he already figured out how sneaky you can be?"

"I hope not. I won't be half as successful if he's already on to me," Grandma Jenny replied with an unrepentant gleam in her eyes. "Besides, if I was reading the situation correctly—and I usually do—he's not going to need much encouragement from me. Something happened between them on that beach this morning, and it was a whole lot more than the simple rescue he wanted me to believe it was."

"Seth rescued Abby?"

Her grandmother nodded. "Said she was close to drowning."

Unfortunately Hannah recalled all too vividly that a rescue had brought Luke and Abby together, as well. Was history repeating itself? And, if it was, was it good or bad that Seth had been the hero? She tried to assure herself that it was good. She plastered a smile on her face and injected an upbeat note into her voice.

"In that case, it actually might be fun to watch you in action, now that I'm not the one in your crosshairs," she said. "Maybe Abby's the one who needs a warning."

"Take my advice and stay away from her," her grandmother said flatly.

"It's Seaview Key. You know that's not going to be possible. If she's here to stay, I will run into her. So will Luke."

"Well, just don't make her your bosom buddy, not until we know what she's up to, or until Seth has made his move."

Hannah shook her head at the hint of drama in Grandma Jenny's voice. At the same time, it helped to know that her grandmother's plotting might keep Abby far, far away from Luke. Despite Hannah's brave talk, she couldn't seem to ignore the tiny flutter of worry that had come right along with her grandmother's announcement.

Abby had kept mostly to herself since moving back to Seaview Key. She'd even loaded her car with groceries and cleaning supplies on the mainland before taking the ferry across to the island, just to cut down on gossip before she was ready to deal with it. After this morning's incident on the beach, she had a hunch her solitude was likely to be disrupted. She might as well suck it up and head into town.

Lunch at The Fish Tale seemed like the perfect way to let the locals—at least anyone who remembered her—know she was back. It might also be a good way to get some feedback on her plans for Blue Heron Cove. Given the way the locals had responded to the threat of any sort of development over the years, she imagined there would be plenty of opinions about the new houses she was planning for the land her folks had owned and deeded to her.

Though she would have preferred a table in a dark corner in the back where she could observe people without being noticed, it seemed the only available booth in the busy restaurant was right up front by the window. Abby slid in, then pulled a menu from the rack at the edge of the table and hid behind it, hoping for at least a few more minutes of anonymity.

She recognized Jack Ferguson behind the bar, same as always. His daughter, Lesley Ann, who'd been a classmate of hers, was waiting tables, though every so often she paused to pick up a baby from a playpen positioned at the end of the bar and show him off. She still held the baby when she came over to Abby's table.

"Can I take your drink order?" she asked, bouncing the baby in her arms. "I'll be right back with that and take the rest of your order."

Before Abby could respond, Lesley Ann's eyes widened. "Abby? Is that you? Oh my goodness! It's been years. You look fantastic!"

Abby grinned at her exuberance, which hadn't changed a bit since they'd been cheerleaders together. "And you look like you're very adept at being a mom, bouncing a baby on your hip while waiting tables. You must have learned that from your mom. She could always multitask."

A shadow passed over Lesley Ann's expressive face. "She was an expert, that's for sure."

"Was?" Abby said softly. "She's gone?"

Lesley Ann nodded. "For a while now. Not a day goes by that I don't miss her. Dad's been lost without her. Thank goodness for this place. It's kept him going. He knows the locals count on him and he loves meeting the tourists who come to town during the season."

"I'm so sorry for your loss," Abby said sincerely. "I always liked your mom. She was unflappable, no matter how rowdy we got."

"I aspire to be just like her, but I'm not there yet. I am pretty good at the multitasking, though. This little angel is number four and the very last one," she said emphatically. "If another baby sneaks up on us, I swear I'm suing our doctors for malpractice. I made Bobby get a vasectomy. I've had my tubes tied for good measure. I'm thinking I should probably stock up on condoms while I'm at it."

"That surely ought to do it," Abby said, laughing.

"Hey, would you mind holding the baby for just a minute while I get your drink and place this other order? Little Adam Jackson here—we call him A.J.—is getting fussy. It's almost time for his bottle. Dad's good with him as long as he's on his best behavior, but tears shake him up. And I don't entirely trust him not to grab the nearest bottle to try to calm him down. Since there are a few too many beers behind the bar, that's a potential problem."

Without waiting for a reply, she placed the baby in Abby's arms. "Iced tea, right? Unsweetened, no lemon?"

Abby was impressed. "Good memory."

"Not that difficult. We used to drink the stuff by the gallon all year long. That sort of habit doesn't wear off. Back in a sec."

She dashed off, leaving Abby to gaze down into the wide blue-gray eyes staring back at her. The weight of the baby in her arms set off a maternal tug that she'd assured herself was long-since dead and buried now that she'd passed forty. She'd wanted children so badly, but it simply wasn't meant to be. That's what her husband had told her, his tone so blasted accepting.

Sure, it made sense that her minister husband had taken God's will at face value, but she'd desperately wanted answers, real, scientific proof that there was a physical reason why they'd had no babies after so many years of trying. Marshall had refused to consider testing, and that had been that. For a man who'd preached about tolerance, commitment and compromise in a healthy marriage, he'd been surprisingly rigid about getting his own way.

Not that their marriage had been loveless or abusive. They'd had a lot of good times, moments of real tenderness. She'd been a better person for having known him, for trying to live up to his ideals. In the end, though, trying to be good, to be the perfect role model and mentor for their parishioners, to do everything in her power to keep from seeing that flash of disappointment in his eyes when she failed, all of it had worn her out. It had sapped the life right out of her.

So, here she was, back in Seaview Key, hoping to find the other Abby, the one who'd laughed freely, who'd dreamed, who'd known passion and embraced life.

She just prayed that it wasn't too late.

Seth had responded to two emergency calls in a row, something that rarely happened on Seaview Key.

The first had been an amateur fisherman who'd gotten tangled up with a hook. It had taken only a few minutes to remove the hook and treat the man. It had taken longer to calm his hysterical wife who was sure they needed to be seen by a "real" doctor on the mainland.

The second call had taken both time and patience.

Eighty-two-year-old Ella Mae Monroe had called in complaining of chest pains. Since this happened at least once a week, Seth had known she was more in need of calming and companionship than medical treatment. Luke had filled him in on the pattern his first week on the job.

This morning he'd spent over an hour with her, assuring her that her vital signs were strong, that her symptoms were related to anxiety, not a heart attack.

What Ella Mae really needed were friends who'd stop by or activities she could enjoy. He reminded himself to speak to Grandma Jenny about dropping in to visit and maybe inviting her to join some of the other older women in their church groups.

By the time he left Ella Mae's, it was after noon. Since The Fish Tale was on his way to see Luke, he decided to grab a couple of their excellent grilled grouper sandwiches and take them to the clinic.

He was halfway to the bar to order, when he spotted the woman from the beach sitting in a booth, holding a baby and looking a little shell-shocked. Drawn by some force he didn't entirely understand after Grandma Jenny's earlier revelations, he crossed the room.

"Yours?" he asked, earning a startled look.

When she recognized him, her expression brightened. "Hardly. This is Lesley Ann's little boy, A.J."

"Ah," he said, recognizing the baby then. "You were drafted into duty. Lesley Ann's very clever. Be careful. If you're good at keeping A.J. calm, you'll have him for hours."

She laughed. "Voice of experience?"

"I've put in my share of time as impromptu babysitter," he admitted. "A.J. and I have a deal, though, a pact between guys, so to speak. Twenty minutes and he lets out a scream of disapproval that has his mama flying across the restaurant. He looks pretty content with you. You could be in for a long haul."

He studied her intently. "You don't look as if you'd mind that."

"Not entirely," she admitted.

"You have kids of your own?"

She shook her head and there was no mistaking the hint of sorrow in her eyes.

"I'm sorry," he said at once.

"So am I," she said quietly. "How about you? Do you have children?"

"Never married," he said, then realized that wasn't necessarily an answer. "And no children out there, either."

A smile played on her lips. "I'm glad you clarified."

"Well, it's not always the case," he admitted. "I've known plenty of men who are a lot more reckless and casual than I am. By the way, I didn't get your name this morning."

"Abby," she told him.

Despite his certainty that Grandma Jenny had gotten it right, he had to admit he was a little disappointed. Abby Dawson obviously brought a lot of baggage with her. "Dawson?" he asked to be sure.

She regarded him with puzzlement. "Actually it's Miller now, but yes. How did you know that?"

"I'm staying at Seaview Inn. When I mentioned to the owner that I'd run into a woman on the beach, she thought it might have been you."

Her expression brightened. "Grandma Jenny's still alive?"

"And going strong," he confirmed.

"I thought I'd heard something about her great-granddaughter running the inn these days."

"Kelsey and her husband have taken over the day-to-day operation, but make no mistake, Grandma Jenny is still in charge of the place," he told her.

She smiled. "I'm so glad. I must have eaten about a million of her cookies over the years."

"I'm closing in on that many and I've only been here a couple of months," Seth confided. "That's why I swim and run and go to the gym every day."

"You told me this morning that you ended up here because of Luke. So you must know Hannah, too."

"I do. She's incredible." Recalling his earlier conversation with Grandma Jenny, he felt compelled to add, "Luke and Hannah are amazing together."

"I can imagine," Abby said. "Nobody is more deserving of happiness than those two." Her expression turned nostalgic. "We were all good friends once. Did you know that?"

"I'd heard."

"I hope we can be again," she said, a wistful note in her voice.

"Really?" he asked, unable to hide his skepticism.

Her gaze narrowed. "Did you hear that Luke and I were involved at one time? Is that why you felt the need to tell me how good they are together? And why you sounded just now as if us being friends would be impossible?"

"Grandma Jenny mentioned something about you and Luke being a couple," he said. "As for me, I was just making conversation."

"Really?" she replied doubtfully, then added, "It was

a long time ago, Seth. Believe me, I didn't come back to town with ulterior motives where Luke's concerned."

"Glad to hear it," he said solemnly.

"I meant what I said, though. I do hope we can all be friends again. Seaview Key is a small town. I certainly don't want things to be awkward for any of us."

Since that decision certainly wasn't up to him, Seth changed the subject. "You mentioned your name is Miller now. You're married?"

"Divorced, actually. For about a year now, so well past the stage of crying myself to sleep."

He was startled by her candor. "But earlier I got the sense that you were running away from the past."

The baby whimpered in her arms. She instinctively rocked A.J. until he fell back to sleep, then met Seth's gaze. "I prefer to think that I'm running *toward* something," she countered. "Without boring you with the details, my marriage changed me. I came back here to see if there was any of the old me left." She gave him a wry look. "It's ironic, really, since I couldn't wait to get away from Seaview Key and the old me and become a totally new person."

"That didn't turn out as well as you'd expected?"

"In many ways it did," she contradicted. "In others, not so much."

Just then Lesley Ann rushed over to the table with a glass of iced tea and a large soda for Seth.

"Sorry about the wait," she apologized to Abby. "We had a tiny crisis in the kitchen." She grinned at Seth. "I saw you come in and brought your usual. You work fast. How do you know Abby already? I know for a fact she just got back to town."

He winked at Abby. "We met on the beach this morning. I was trespassing."

"But I imagine you sweet-talked her into not calling the cops," Lesley Ann said. She grinned at Abby. "Watch him. He's a very smooth talker."

Abby laughed. "I've already figured out that much."

"So, two fish sandwiches?" Lesley Ann asked.

"Sure," Seth said, then met Abby's gaze. "If you don't mind the company."

"I'd love it," Abby said.

"And I'll take A.J. now, so you can relax," Lesley Ann said, sweeping the baby into her arms. "Back in a flash with your food."

"Did she always have that kind of energy?" Seth asked when she was gone.

"Head cheerleader, student council president and homecoming queen," Abby said. "Lesley Ann was always a dynamo. Of course, I would have predicted she'd take on running the entire state of Florida, not become a mother of four."

Seth laughed. "Who knows? Maybe one of these days she'll do both. How about you? What did you do after you left Seaview Key?"

"College, then marriage," she said. "I had a business in a small town outside of Pensacola."

"What kind of business?"

"A restaurant," she said, "which is why I know just how talented Lesley Ann and her father are. A lot of the things that made my restaurant successful I learned from watching them. It takes more than good food to become an indispensable part of the community the way this place is."

"Do you still have the restaurant?"

She shook her head. "I sold it a few months ago, right after the divorce."

"Wow! That's a lot of life changes all at once."

She shrugged. "It was time. I needed a clean break. What about you, though? Seaview Key must be quite a change from being on the front lines in Iraq."

"And then Afghanistan," he said. "It's a welcome change. Just what I needed. I imagine Luke would tell you the same thing."

"Is this permanent or just a stopover?" she asked.

Seth had asked himself the same thing. When he'd first arrived in Seaview Key and Luke had offered him the opportunity, he'd seen it as a transition to something else. Lately, though, he realized the community and the people were growing on him. He liked the pace of life here. The only thing missing was someone with whom he could share his life.

He'd been telling himself he was in no hurry, that he could wait for the right relationship to come along, but every time he was with Luke and Hannah he felt envy stirring. Trips to the mainland, hanging out in bars, hooking up on occasion, it wasn't the answer, not for the short term and certainly not for finding the kind of woman he wanted forever.

He met Abby's interested gaze. "I'm not sure," he said honestly. "I've fallen in love with Seaview Key, but I don't know if that's enough."

"Are you feeling restless already?" she asked.

He thought he read worry in her eyes. Since he doubted it was meant for him, he asked. "You worried it won't be enough for you?"

"It wasn't before," she said.

"But you're not the same person you were back then,"

he reminded her. "That is what you said. You want different things now."

"That's what brought me back here," she agreed. "I guess we'll see if I've gotten it right."

"Isn't that life?" he asked. "Taking it day by day, seeing how things go? Last I heard planning only gives God a good laugh."

Lesley Ann set their sandwiches and fries on the table just then. Abby's eyes widened.

"Now this is exactly the way I remember it," she said before taking a bite, then sighing. "Heavenly."

Watching her, Seth covered a sigh. Despite all the potential complications Abby represented, he couldn't help thinking that *heavenly* just about nailed it. For the first time since he'd arrived in Seaview Key, he thought he might have found more than a job to keep him here.

Three

Even after the lunch crowd at The Fish Tale had drifted away and Seth had left for an appointment, Abby stayed where she was, sipping iced tea and thinking about the way Seth had reacted to the prospect of her being back in Hannah and Luke's lives. There'd been a hint of worry there, no question about it. How was she supposed to prove that the last thing she wanted was to cause trouble for them?

Even as she pondered that, Jack Ferguson slid into the booth opposite her.

"What happened to the girl I remember coming in here in pigtails with her mama and daddy?" he asked, a grin spreading across his weather-beaten face. "It's been way too long, Abby. You're all grown up."

Abby laughed. "That's what happens when more than twenty years go by. And believe me, the pigtails are in the distant past, thank goodness."

He shook his head. "Hard to believe it's been that long, even though I have Lesley Ann and her passel of youngsters to prove that time has marched on."

"She seems happy," Abby said.

"Bobby's been good to her. I think she really lucked out in that department. Of course, I'm the really lucky one. Unlike my son, Lesley Ann wanted to stick around and help out here." His expression turned wry. "Well, what she really enjoys is bossing me around, but I'm willing to go along with that to keep this place in the hands of family."

"I'm sorry about Mrs. Ferguson," Abby told him.

He nodded. "Me, too."

Silence fell for a minute, but then he leaned forward. "Okay, I'm going to get into something, even though Lesley Ann told me I should stay out of it. She reminded me we're supposed to make a practice of not deliberately riling up our customers."

Abby braced herself. She had a hunch she knew what was coming. "And you think whatever you have to say will rile me up?"

"It's a possibility," he replied.

"Go ahead. Questions from old friends are never out of line."

He nodded. "Okay, then. What's this I hear about you selling out to some developer who's going to destroy Blue Heron Cove?" he asked. "Is that true? If it is, your mama and daddy must be turning over in their graves, if you don't mind me being blunt."

Abby wasn't surprised by the direct question or by the implied criticism. "I haven't sold out," she said quietly.

He was clearly taken aback. "You haven't?"

"No, but I am developing Blue Heron Cove myself."

Jack sat back, his expression shocked. "I can't believe it. *You're* the one who's going to ruin our tranquility?

What would your parents think? You must know how they felt about this island."

"I hope they'd think that I'm a smart businesswoman who loves this island as much as they did," she said, refusing to take offense. She'd expected precisely this reaction before people heard all the facts. "I'm not going to ruin anything, Jack. I give you my word."

He didn't look as if he thought that was good enough.

"What exactly have you heard?" she asked. "Maybe I can put your mind at ease."

"Not an hour ago I heard that you'll be starting to clear-cut that land any day now, as soon as the town signs off on the permits," he said accusingly. "Then you plan to put up a bunch of fancy houses that will be making all sorts of demands on our resources out here. I've seen the signs and ads for Blue Heron Cove myself. No question those places are going to be big, too big for a town this size. You denying that, too? Seems to me a picture is worth a thousand words."

"One thing at a time. We won't be clear-cutting," she assured him. "That's the truth. As many trees and shrubs as possible will remain in place. Others will be salvaged and replanted once the houses are built. There wouldn't be much point in enticing people to live in a serene seaside setting like this and then destroying it."

Jack's gaze narrowed. "Gospel truth?"

"Gospel truth," she confirmed. "It's also true that the houses will be larger than some out here, but there won't be that many of them. There will be one-acre lots, so only ten houses, maximum. A couple of people have even inquired about larger lots, so that would mean even fewer houses. They'll be very high-end, so the people who buy them will contribute to the economy here. They won't be a drain on it. Blue Heron Cove isn't going to damage this island, Jack. I'll make sure of it. That's why I made the decision to oversee this myself, start to finish. I may not wield a hammer or put in the electrical wiring, but I'll see to it that every detail is done right. So will the contractor I've been talking to. His reputation is sterling. He won't mess this up."

There was no mistaking the relief in Jack's eyes. "How'd this get so twisted around?" he asked, then shook his head. "Never mind. Gossip usually spreads fastest when it's negative."

"Do you suppose you could help me get the truth out there?" she appealed. "There's a council meeting coming up for the final approvals. I could use some backing. People may not remember me or trust me, but they know and respect you."

He nodded. "I'll do my best. You bring your plans by and show them to me. You do that and if everything looks like you've described it, I'll be right there at that meeting to back you up."

"That would mean a lot to me."

"Just don't make a liar out of me, you hear," he said.

"Not a chance," she promised. "I always keep my word."

It had always been true, but being married to a minister had reinforced for her that honesty and integrity were traits never to be compromised. She certainly didn't intend to start messing with them now. If she was going to stay in Seaview Key and make it home, she needed to start out on the right foot, not with lies and deceptions. And if an old-timer like Jack Ferguson put his faith in her, there was no way she'd let him down.

* * *

Seth caught up with Luke between patients, which wasn't all that difficult to do. Seaview Key had a tiny, exceptionally healthy year-round population, which grew in winter with a lot of senior snowbirds. This time of year, though, there were mostly locals around and the occasional day-trippers from the mainland enjoying the shops and galleries that had sprung up in what had once been little more than a fishing village. Come January, according to Luke, that would all change and the town would be packed with strangers.

"Hannah's grandmother told me you have a lead on a boat we might be able to outfit for emergency runs to the mainland," Seth said, settling into a chair in Luke's office and propping his feet up on one of the boxes of medical books that Luke had yet to unpack. For a man who practiced medicine with demanding precision, he didn't seem to mind doing it amid chaos. That had served him well in Iraq.

Luke dug through the piles of paper on his desk, his expression triumphant when he finally found what he'd been looking for. He handed the fancy color flyer from a nearby seaside community to Seth.

He gave Seth a couple of minutes to look it over, then asked, "What do you think? I made a couple of calls. It's got a few years on it, but the rescue squad chief says it runs well. He had a mechanic call me to confirm that. Best of all, it's already outfitted for what we want."

"If it's so great, why are they getting rid of it?" Seth asked, glancing over the specifications, then whistling when he saw the asking price. "And why is it priced so high?"

"They're selling it because a grateful patient is underwriting a new boat. They have another backup, newer than this one. And the price is that high because that's what this sort of specially equipped boat can command. If we had to start from scratch to outfit a boat with all that emergency medical equipment at today's prices, it would cost even more."

"Can we afford it?" Seth asked doubtfully.

"The bigger question is can we afford not to buy it?" Luke responded. "We can't keep relying on finding a volunteer to take our emergencies to the mainland. I'm equipped to handle a lot of minor things right here, but some people need to be in a major ICU and they need to get there in a hurry."

Seth nodded. "Agreed. And the cost for using a medical evacuation helicopter is prohibitive."

"To say nothing of the fact that there's no really good place to land it other than the school ball field, which seems to be swarming with kids even when there are no games going on."

"You do know the budget can barely squeeze out enough for my salary, bandages and emergency supplies, right?" Seth said, though he couldn't seem to tear his gaze away from the boat pictured on the flyer.

Luke nodded. "I've been thinking about that."

"Have you come up with anything? A fairy godmother, for instance?"

"Nope. I'm thinking we ought to start organizing some fund-raisers, make this a real community effort. I can put Hannah and Grandma Jenny on that, maybe get Lesley Ann over at The Fish Tale involved. She could sweet-talk a saint into donating a halo. I'll kick-start the drive with enough to get them to hold the boat for us. The community can do the rest."

"That could work," Seth said thoughtfully. Unfortunately Seaview Key was small and filled with hardworking middle-class families who didn't have a lot of spare cash. He couldn't begin to imagine how many bingo games or spaghetti dinners it would take to raise enough.

"It could take a while," he told Luke realistically. "What about going to the developer who's building those houses at Blue Heron Cove? I imagine the folks who buy those pricey houses are going to want ready access to top-notch medical care before they buy on an island that relies on ferry service to the mainland."

Luke's eyes lit up at once. "Great idea. The final vote on that deal is coming up in the next week. Maybe we could get the donation worked into the approval."

"Or maybe we could just ask the developer," Seth said. "It would be a terrific public-relations gesture."

Luke nodded. "Good point."

Seth drew in a deep breath, still weighing whether he should mention anything about his encounter with Abby Dawson. He opted to put the news out there. "And since we're talking about Blue Heron Cove, that brings up something else I need to mention."

"Oh?" Luke said.

"I fished a woman from that area out of the water this morning."

"But there aren't any houses in there yet," Luke said, his expression perplexed. "The beach along there is posted with No Trespassing signs."

Seth grinned. "Which I've been ignoring. The point is that the original house is still in there." He watched Luke's face closely and saw the instant when understanding dawned.

"Abby Dawson?"

"Grandma Jenny seemed to think so. I ran into the woman again at The Fish Tale just now and she confirmed it. Her married name's Miller."

"Well, I'll be," Luke said. "Abby couldn't wait to put Seaview Key behind her. I'm surprised she's back."

"Grandma Jenny mentioned that the two of you used to be pretty tight," he said casually, watching closely for a reaction.

"Ancient history," Luke said a little too quickly.

"You sure about that?" Seth asked. "You look almost as worried as Grandma Jenny did. Is this woman being back going to cause problems for you and Hannah?"

"Absolutely not," Luke said firmly, then sighed. "I'm not sure Hannah will see it that way, though. Back then, Abby and I were..."

"Let's just leave it at 'close,'" Seth suggested.

"Oh, yeah," Luke said. "And then some. But we were over a long time ago."

"But that's not going to stop all of Hannah's old insecurities from rising to the surface," Seth guessed.

"Under normal conditions, she probably wouldn't give it a second thought," Luke replied. "But now? She might be in remission from her breast cancer, but it's always in the back of her mind. And the scar is a constant reminder. No matter how many times I tell her it doesn't matter, that she's a beautiful woman, on some level she doesn't buy it. And just today I realized that she's already worrying about the next screening. This is a stress she doesn't need right now."

He gave Seth a hopeful look. "I don't suppose Abby has aged badly, maybe gained, like, a hundred pounds or something?"

Seth laughed, thinking of the slender woman he'd held in his arms, the woman with curves in all the right place. "Afraid not."

Luke sighed, his expression troubled. "Maybe Abby's just passing through. Last I heard she was settled up in north Florida and happily married. She probably just came down to take care of some paperwork with the developer or something. All that land back in there belonged to her family."

"I don't think so," Seth said. "I mean, she told me herself that she's divorced and that she's back to stay."

Luke studied him curiously. "You sound surprisingly happy about that. What happened on that beach this morning?"

"I hauled her out of the water. That's it," Seth said, downplaying the effect the rescue had had on his libido.

"Which makes you her hero," Luke commented, then added wryly, "I recall what that was like."

Seth avoided Luke's knowing gaze. It was ironic really that she and Luke had apparently fallen for each other all those years ago after Luke had rescued her from the waters off Seaview Key. Was it possible that the same sort of connection would happen between himself and Abby? Was she the kind of woman who made a habit of falling for men who bailed her out of jams?

Earlier he might have dismissed the possibility of anything happening between them, but after running into Abby at The Fish Tale, he wasn't so sure. He'd felt another surge of electricity the instant he'd spotted her. The sight of her with a baby in her arms had been a little too appealing, as well, reminding him of the future he'd once envisioned for himself.

That vision had come back to him with increasing

frequency since he'd been in Seaview Key. Somehow all of the resolve he'd mustered after the tragic end of his last relationship was fading these days, replaced by a yearning he'd never expected to feel again. It didn't make the least bit of sense to put a virtual stranger like Abby Miller in the middle of that vision, but she seemed to have landed there just the same.

He could only hope that wouldn't cause a conflict that could ruin his friendship with Luke.

"Seth? You okay?" Luke asked, concern on his face. "I recognize that shell-shocked look. It worries me."

"Why is that?" Seth asked defensively. "Because you still have feelings for Abby, after all?"

"Not a one," Luke insisted. "But the Abby I recall wasn't interested in a life on Seaview Key. It's hard to imagine she's changed that much. She'll get restless, Seth. Then where will you be? And aside from that, she's my age, so that makes her several years older than you."

Seth didn't even try to hide a smile at that. "And that's some kind of a crime in your book?"

"Not a crime, a concern. I feel responsible for you."

Seth laughed. "Last time I checked, I was a grown man, Luke. I've even been through the same life-altering situations you have."

His words didn't seem to allay Luke's concerns. If anything, he looked more worried than ever. "And you lost a woman you loved," Luke said quietly.

"It's not as if I need to be reminded about what happened," Seth said angrily.

"Of course not, but you're vulnerable, Seth."

"And therefore easy prey for a devious older woman?" Seth asked, getting to his feet. "Thanks for the concern,

Luke, but I can handle this. Maybe you should focus on your own problems."

He headed for the door, then turned back. "Keep me posted on that boat. From now on, why don't we keep our conversations professional and leave the personal stuff out of it."

He saw the dismay on Luke's face just as he closed the door and even managed a moment's regret for his words. Luke had been a mentor in Iraq, a good friend, almost a big brother. He'd been an even more supportive friend since Seth had mustered out of the military and come home. What Seth had said to him just now shouldn't have been said between friends.

He stood outside, sucked in a deep breath, then forced himself to open the office door.

"Sorry," he said quietly. "You didn't deserve that."

"It's okay," Luke assured him, looking relieved. "You were right. Your personal life is none of my business."

"But I made yours my business," Seth said. "I'm the one who came in here all worked up about the impact Abby's return might have on your marriage."

"And, if I'm being entirely honest, I resented it," Luke said. "I guess we both crossed a line, but we both did it out of concern."

"No question about it," Seth said. "Then we're good?"

"We're good," Luke agreed.

But there was little question, Seth thought with regret, that the possibility of Abby coming between them in one way or another already existed.

Luke was more shaken by the entire encounter with Seth than he wanted to admit. It wasn't just concern for the young man he considered a kid brother. He was more worried than he'd acknowledged about Hannah's reaction when she found out that Abby was back. He knew it wouldn't take long before she heard the news, if she hadn't already. Truthfully, if Grandma Jenny knew, then there was a good chance she'd already told Hannah. He figured he had several choices, none of them pleasant.

He could head home and get into this with Hannah. He could check in with her grandmother and see if she'd broken the news and ask how Hannah had reacted, so he'd be prepared to deal with any fallout. Or he could track down Abby and gather a few facts before going home to see his wife.

He didn't stop to question why he chose the third option. He just headed to Blue Heron Cove and the house where he'd spent so much of his time back in high school. The Dawson home had never been as welcoming as Seaview Inn, but he'd spent countless hours there with Abby under the watchful gazes of her protective parents. After her near drowning, they'd been worse than ever, rarely wanting her out of their sight unless they knew she was at Seaview Inn with Hannah's mother and Jenny looking out for her.

Though he'd glimpsed the house during walks on the beach with Hannah, he was still taken aback by its neglect. If Abby was back, the house showed few signs of it. He went around back and approached from the beach. He found Abby sitting on the porch, her feet propped on the railing. She didn't seem all that surprised to see him.

"I wondered how long it would be before you turned up," she said, a half smile on her lips.

Luke stopped where he was, studying the woman he hadn't seen in so long. There were a few lines around her eyes, but otherwise, she looked almost the same with her hair scooped into a ponytail, her long legs bared by a pair of cut-off jeans, her toenails painted the same shade of kick-ass red, if he wasn't mistaken.

"I heard you were back. I had to see it with my own eyes," he told her. "You look good, Abby."

"So do you, though I thought I noticed a limp. I heard you were injured in Iraq."

He nodded. "I'm almost as good as new. Most of the time I don't even think about it."

"Then I'm sorry I brought it up," she apologized. She drew in a deep breath, then asked, "How's Hannah?"

"Great," he said, relaxing now that he knew she was aware that he and Hannah were together. "She's writing children's books, you know."

She laughed. "Seriously? I hadn't heard that. She was always the best at making up ghost stories when we had bonfires on the beach."

Luke was startled by that. "I'd forgotten that. She was, wasn't she? I guess we all should have known she'd wind up writing someday."

"I'm glad you're together, Luke. I really am." She held his gaze. "Can you stay and visit? There's iced tea. I'm afraid I don't have anything stronger in the house."

"Iced tea would be great," he said. "I can get it, if you want. I think I remember where things are."

"That's okay. The inside is still a work in progress. The dishes are all spotless, but I can't say the same for every other nook and cranny. It might offend your preference for a sterile environment."

He laughed. "I might like a sterile O.R., but I can tolerate a little mess everywhere else. Otherwise I'd never leave the house."

"Still, I'll get the tea," she said, heading inside.

Luke sat on the top step and awaited her return, thinking how comfortable he felt here—with Abby—despite all the years that had passed. He told himself there was nothing dangerous about that feeling. After all, feeling comfortable wasn't the same as feeling a spark of the old attraction. He certainly hadn't felt that. Hannah was it for him. Nothing about that had changed with Abby's return, he was relieved to say.

Abby came back outside, the screen door slapping shut behind her with a once-familiar creak, and handed him the ice-cold glass. "Does Hannah know you're here?" she asked.

He shook his head. "I wanted to hear for myself what you're doing back," he told her.

"I'm the one who's planning to develop Blue Heron Cove, and before you get all riled up about that, you need to know I'm doing it responsibly with as little impact on the environment as possible."

He smiled. "Ah, so you've heard all the rumors and have rehearsed that speech?"

"I've heard the rumors," she confirmed. "So, about Hannah, is she going to hate it that I'm in town and intend to stick around?"

"I don't see why she should," Luke said, though of course he knew exactly why she might.

Abby smiled. "Then you really are naive, my dear old friend."

"Okay, she'll probably be thrown at first," he conceded. "But you were friends, Abby. Good friends."

"And I'd like to have that back again," she admitted. "But I have no illusions about Hannah. She may not feel the same way. She could feel threatened, though I swear to you, Luke, I have no ulterior motives where you're concerned." She smiled. "You're not the first person I've had to explain that to today. Your friend Seth was worried, too."

"So he told me. You still haven't said why you're back. You were pretty determined to leave Seaview Key behind forever."

"I came back here for me, to start over again, just the way you and Hannah did."

"Where does Seth fit in?"

She laughed at the question. "I met him a few hours ago, papa bear. I have no designs on him, either. What did he tell you?"

Luke winced, unwilling to get into his conversation with Seth. "Never mind. He's had a tough year. I worry about him, that's all."

Her gaze narrowed. "A tough year in what way?"

He shook his head. "His story to tell, not mine."

"Okay, then, I am duly warned to tread carefully."

"Sorry. I've put my foot into it again. I'm really lousy at the whole advice thing."

"Ah, so you had this talk with Seth, too?" she asked, clearly amused. "And he's already told you to butt out?"

Luke nodded. "Pretty much."

"Then maybe that's what you should do."

He stood up and set his glass on the table beside her. "I think you're right. I'm glad you're back, Abby. I hope you find what you want here."

"As long as it's not you," she said dryly.

"Goes without saying," he said, smiling. "Nice to see you're still smart and direct."

"Will you tell Hannah you stopped by?"

"Of course."

"Would you tell her that I'm looking forward to seeing her?" she said. "But I'll leave that ball in her court."

Luke nodded. "I'll tell her."

As he walked back to his car, he couldn't help wondering, though, how Hannah would respond. As well as he thought he knew her, they'd never really talked about his old relationship with Abby except in passing. Now, out of the blue, it appeared they might be forced to deal with it. He had to admit he wasn't looking forward to it.

Four

Hannah went through the motions of getting dinner ready, but she was so distracted she burned the chicken and overcooked the pasta. She tossed both in the garbage and started over, this time with baked potatoes and steaks that could be thrown on the grill whenever Luke got home. At least she hadn't destroyed the salad, too. She put the bowl on the table.

She glanced at the clock and realized Luke was running late. There must have been some sort of emergency that kept him at the clinic. Just as well, since that would give the kitchen time to air out before he got here to ask questions about the ruined meal.

Hannah didn't want anyone, least of all Luke, to get the idea that she was intimidated by having her childhood best friend—and Luke's old love—back home again. Yet the instant her grandmother had told her of Abby's return about a million insecurities had crowded in, followed by a cascade of memories from the summer that Luke and Abby had fallen in love and Hannah had had to sit by on the sidelines while the teen romance flourished right in front of her.

The three of them had spent countless hours on the porch at Seaview Inn, playing games and talking into the night. She'd been forced to turn a blind eye as Abby snuggled against Luke's side in the old swing. On too many nights, as they walked off hand in hand, tears had leaked from Hannah's eyes and she'd gone to bed crying. The only thing saving her from complete humiliation was knowing that Luke hadn't realized just how miserable she was. Abby might have guessed, but she'd pretended otherwise, either to soothe her own conscience or to protect Hannah's secret.

But they were all grown up now. Hannah was the one who was married to Luke, and she had not a single reason to believe he would ever be unfaithful. Once he made a commitment, he kept it. After he'd come home from Iraq, he would have gone back to his wife, if she hadn't already started divorce proceedings so she could marry the partner in his medical practice.

That faith in Luke, of course, belonged to the strong, confident Hannah, not the one whose body had been disfigured by breast cancer and ravaged by chemotherapy. That woman had enough self-doubts to keep a psychologist busy for years.

She stiffened her resolve to keep those doubts to herself. She didn't want her grandmother or Luke watching her constantly to see if she was on edge about Abby's return. How did the saying go, "Fake it till you make it?" Well, she was going to fake being thrilled about Abby's return or die trying.

"Sorry I'm late," Luke called out, startling her as he jogged up the porch steps, then joining her in the kitchen.

"Last-minute emergency?" she asked, turning her face up for his kiss.

"Not exactly. I'll explain later," he said, a guilty flush in his cheeks. "I see you have the grill ready to go. Are we having steak?"

She nodded.

He sniffed the air. "Then why do I smell something that reminds me of scorched chicken?"

"Blast," she murmured. "I thought I'd aired the place out. I need to get some of that stuff that wipes out odors."

Luke frowned. "Something up? You never ruin a meal."

She forced a grin. "That's what you think. Maybe I'm just very good at hiding the evidence. After all, when I lived in New York, I excelled at takeout, not cooking. Ask Kelsey. She'll testify to that."

"If you say so. Let me get those steaks on the grill. I'm starving."

Hannah thought he was awfully eager to escape the kitchen and she was pretty sure it wasn't because he was hungry. Something was going on. The knot in the pit of her stomach—or maybe sheer paranoia—told her it had something to do with Abby. So did his strained efforts at making small-talk during their meal.

Still she couldn't seem to bring herself to mention Abby's return. Once she opened her mouth, she'd have to pull off that pretense that her world hadn't been turned upside down.

After dinner, when she and Luke sat on the deck, watching the sun set in a blaze of color over the water, a kind of calm settled over them. She finally drew in a deep breath. This conversation couldn't be put off another second.

"Have you heard that Abby might be back in town?" she asked Luke, keeping a close eye on his face as she spoke.

"Seth mentioned it this morning," he said, his tone as casual as hers had been. The only thing that betrayed his nervousness was the searching look he gave her. He was obviously worried that she might overreact. "How'd you hear?"

"Grandma Jenny came by."

"I figured she would." He held her gaze. "You should know that I paid Abby a visit on my way home."

Hannah's heart seemed to stop. He'd heard Abby was back and had immediately gone rushing over to see her? That wasn't good. "Really? How is she?" Her calm words belied her panic.

"She's good. She says she's back here to make a fresh start for herself. Apparently she's divorced. And she's the one who's developing Blue Heron Cove."

"I see," Hannah said, a shiver of dismay chilling her. She reminded herself that she couldn't let Luke see how that news terrified her. She forced herself to look directly into his eyes. "I think we should invite her to dinner. It will be great to catch up." She managed to get the words out without choking on them.

"If that's what you want," he said oh-so-carefully, unmistakable worry in his eyes. "Are you sure, Hannah? It would be understandable if you wanted to keep some distance between you."

"Understandable, why? Because you two have a history? That's the very reason we need to reach out to her," Hannah said. "Seaview Key is too small to start trying to avoid people. And you know how people talk.

They'll be speculating about what's going on with us. Why give them any reason to gossip?"

Luke looked relieved by her response, which told her she'd managed just the right tone, casual and breezy.

"Okay, then," he said. "Maybe we should include Seth."

"Why?" she asked. Recalling what her grandmother had said earlier, a thought occurred to her, one that actually eased her mind just a little. "Luke Stevens, are you playing matchmaker? I thought that was Grandma Jenny's domain."

Luke chuckled, clearly more relaxed now that he was convinced that she'd taken the news of Abby's return in stride. She gave herself a pat on the back for the successful deception.

"Hardly," he said. "But Seth is the one who rescued Abby from drowning today. Maybe they should cross paths under more favorable circumstances."

Unsaid, she knew, was that he hoped Seth would provide a buffer if things among the three old friends got awkward. Since she couldn't deny that a buffer would be good, she nodded.

"Sounds great, but you don't have to worry. I'm not going to freak out and start imagining things about the two of you," she told her husband, deciding to be open about the elephant in the room. "We'll just have a nice evening catching up. Asking Seth to join us makes sense. He needs to do more socializing. I worry sometimes that if he gets too lonely here, he'll decide to move on."

"I worry about that, too," Luke admitted. "As much as I love Seaview Key, it's not right for everybody. Since I'm the one who encouraged Seth to stick around, I want to do what I can to make sure he made the right decision."

"You really do think of him as a kid brother, don't you?"

"Sure. The bond we formed in Iraq will last forever. I'll always worry about him. Of course, he'd tell you I worry a little too much."

Hannah chuckled. "Have you been butting into his personal life?"

"Maybe a little. That's why I think this dinner is a good thing."

"A win-win all around," Hannah said.

Luke nodded.

But despite the cheery optimism they were both expressing, Hannah couldn't help wondering if she wasn't deluding herself about the wisdom of this dinner party. In her attempt to appear unaffected by Abby's return, it was entirely possible she'd gone too far. She might well be opening up a can of worms that would have been better left locked tight. Too late now, she thought wearily, pressing forward.

"Will Saturday work for you?" she asked her husband.

"Sure."

"And you'll talk to Seth or would you prefer it if I invited him?"

"I'll mention it to him tomorrow. Seven o'clock?"

"Perfect," she said. "I'll check in with Abby and make sure she's available."

It all sounded so ordinary, just another dinner with friends, something they did on a regular basis. Unfortunately, if Hannah's already-jittery nerves were anything to go by, this gathering was going to be anything but ordinary.

* * *

The unexpected knock on her door startled Abby so badly she upended the pail of already-filthy, soapy water she'd been using to scrub windowsills throughout the house. When she opened the door and spotted Hannah, she was even more stunned.

"Hannah!" she said, delight warring with caution. "I should have known word would get around that I'm here."

"Since my husband was one of the people who knew, it was almost a certainty," Hannah said, an edge to her voice that belied the even expression she managed to keep on her face.

The barbed remark left Abby momentarily speechless. Was Luke's visit the reason Hannah was here? Abby wondered. Had she come to protect her turf?

Hannah flushed, clearly embarrassed. "Sorry," she apologized. "What I should have said is that it's impossible to keep secrets in Seaview Key. Word spreads faster here than weeds."

Abby accepted the attempt to smooth over the awkwardness. "I remember," she said. "But I got through the better part of a week before anyone knew. If I hadn't come close to drowning yesterday, I'm convinced my secret would have been safe a little longer."

"Any particular reason you didn't want anyone to know you were around?" Hannah asked.

Abby studied her old friend, regretting all the years they hadn't been in touch, wishing there weren't this huge wall between them because of Luke. Hannah had always been the best kind of friend, one who'd listen without passing judgment. It was too soon to test if she could be that kind of friend again.

"No, not really," Abby said evasively, not wanting to get into all of the reasons she'd wanted privacy. "Come on in. Do you have some time? This place is a mess, but I'm making progress. We can sit in the kitchen. I finished cleaning in there this morning and I have iced tea."

Hannah laughed then, easing the tension between them. "Of course you do. I'll bet it's in your mom's old pitcher with fruit painted on it."

"It is," Abby confirmed. "That pitcher probably qualifies as some sort of antique by now."

Hannah held up a bag that Abby hadn't noticed before. She should have, since the aroma of freshly baked cookies was wafting from it. "Grandma Jenny's chocolate chip cookies," she guessed eagerly.

"Fresh from the oven not fifteen minutes ago," Hannah told her.

"Now it does feel like old times," Abby said, leading the way to the big oak table in the kitchen where they'd spent so many hours doing homework way back when, at least before she'd gotten involved with Luke and Hannah had started making excuses not to join them. The surface of the table gleamed and the wood smelled of lemon polish.

"So how are you?" Hannah asked when they were settled at the table with tea and cookies. "You look good."

"If you can say that with a straight face when you've caught me in ancient cut-offs and a faded tank top with my hair a mess and my nails in desperate need of a manicure, you're better at spin than anyone I know."

Hannah laughed. "That's exactly why they paid me big bucks in New York for a lot of years. But you do look good, Abby. A little tired, maybe, but otherwise not a gray hair or a wrinkle in sight. I wish I could say the same."

"Don't go fishing for compliments. You look wonderful, too. Must be that marriage agrees with you. I heard about you and Luke not long after the wedding. I meant to send a note, but I was clearing the decks to move back here myself and time got away from me. I'm so glad that worked out for you, Hannah."

"Do you really mean that?" Hannah asked, an unmistakable hint of vulnerability in her voice.

"Of course I do," Abby assured her. "Even though you kept your lips sealed about it, I knew you had a crush on him back in high school. I always felt a little guilty that he chose me."

Hannah regarded her with a surprisingly direct look. "I tried not to hate you for it," she said, her tone serious, but a glint of real humor in her eyes.

"Didn't always succeed, though, did you? I know things weren't really the same between us after Luke and I hooked up." She gave Hannah a hesitant smile. "I'm hoping it will be different now. I'd like to have my old friend back in my life again, especially since we're both living here."

"Then you really are home to stay? Luke told me you were."

Abby nodded. "That's the plan."

"He also mentioned you're divorced."

"For almost a year," Abby confirmed. "I took some time to reevaluate my life before deciding to come back to Seaview Key. I could have stayed where I was. I had a thriving restaurant just outside of Pensacola." She shrugged. "It wouldn't have worked. My ex has a lot of influence in that community and I needed a clean break."

"You were married to a minister, I heard," Hannah said, then added dryly, "*That* was a surprise."

"To me, too," Abby acknowledged with a chuckle. "Marshall is a great guy, one of the best, but being married to a paragon of virtue wore me out."

"Not compatible with your wild streak?" Hannah teased.

"Something like that," Abby said, her own tone turning serious. "I've missed this, Hannah. You and me. Just having someone to talk to who knows everything about me, good and bad. We shared so much history. Back then I felt like we were sisters, not just best friends."

"Me, too," Hannah admitted. "But sisters would probably have made more of an effort to get past what happened, instead of drifting apart the way we did."

"Maybe," Abby said. "Maybe not. I've learned a lot about family dynamics these past couple of decades. Sometimes friends get along better than family, at least it looked that way to me. Sadly, I didn't have a lot of experience with either one."

Hannah frowned. "Surely there were friends. You were always so outgoing."

Abby shook her head. "Not really. I had acquaintances, a ton of them, but I was discouraged from getting too close to the other women in the congregation. Marshall didn't want anyone knowing our business. And at the restaurant, I was the boss. I had to be careful with everyone there, too. As for the customers, I had to turn on the charm, be immune to the complaints. Turning the other cheek was so not me."

Hannah couldn't possibly imagine how isolating that

had been, Abby thought, remembering the loneliness, the longing for someone she could open up to.

"I'm sorry," Hannah said.

"Don't be," Abby said, her tone deliberately upbeat. "I'm leaving all that in the past. Somewhere around here there has to be some glimmer of the old me. I intend to find it."

"Maybe you can start by having dinner with me and Luke," Hannah said. "That's why I came by. To see if you're free on Saturday."

It wasn't just the invitation that startled Abby, but the warmth with which it was uttered. Taking it at face value, she said, "I really would love that."

"Luke wants to include Seth, if that's okay. He thought maybe you'd want to thank him for dragging you out of the water. Personally I think you need to find a safer way of getting a man's attention, but what do I know?"

Abby thought of that moment when her senses had stirred in a stranger's arms. It had been such a long time since she'd reacted to anyone like that. Did that make it something to be pursued or avoided at all costs? Seeing Seth again at The Fish Tale, feeling that same spark of attraction, had only added to her conflicted feelings. Unfortunately, with Hannah regarding her expectantly, she didn't have a lot of time to decide.

"Sure," she said finally, avoiding her old friend's assessing gaze.

Hannah studied her curiously for a moment longer, then grinned. "Oh my God, you're interested, aren't you? I recognize the signs. For one thing, you're blushing like a teenager."

"Don't be crazy. I barely know the man."

"If you say so," Hannah said. "But dinner's going to be a lot more interesting than I was anticipating."

Abby suddenly found herself hoping that Hannah was right.

Seth, Luke and a few of the other men in Seaview Key had been getting together for a while now to play poker on Friday nights. Seth's discord with Luke the day before was no reason to stay away, he decided, not when he usually managed to take a few bucks from his friend before most nights were over.

Jack Ferguson was hosting tonight's game in his apartment above The Fish Tale. He gave Seth an assessing look when he arrived.

"Saw you with Abby Miller yesterday," Jack said, his knowing gaze shifting from Seth to Luke and back again.

Seth nodded. "Just getting acquainted," he said, leaving it at that.

"Have you seen her since she's been back?" Jack asked Luke.

"I stopped by last night," Luke admitted.

Seth regarded him with surprise. "Really?" he said, not sure what that implied. Had Luke been lying when he'd claimed he was long over the woman? He sure hadn't wasted any time in going to see her.

"Just a quick stop to say hello and see what brought her back," Luke said, his gaze steady as if daring Seth or anyone else to question his motives.

"I'll tell you what brought her back," Jack said, pouring beers all around. "She's behind this whole Blue Heron Cove development."

Luke frowned. "What do you mean, behind it? She

sold them the land, right? I thought that's what she meant when she told me she was developing it."

Jack shook his head. "No, it's her deal, start to finish. She brought the plans by today for me to take a look. It's nothing like the disaster some folks were painting it to be, myself included, I have to admit."

"You're backing it now?" Luke said, his surprise plain. "I thought you were dead set against it. You've been grumbling to anyone who'd listen since the word first leaked out that the land was going to be developed."

"Well, I'm over it now," Jack replied defensively. "I've seen for myself what she has in mind. Only a few houses, all high-end. She intends to keep most of the trees, wherever she can."

"What happens if the builder points out it's going to cost more to do it that way?" Luke asked. In his experience watching developments take a turn for the worse, money trumped ideals at every turn.

"She'll stand her ground," Jack said confidently. "If you'd heard her, you'd believe that."

"Does Abby have any experience as a developer?" Luke asked, trying to imagine her in that role.

Jack shrugged. "Not that I know of, but I trust her to keep her word. I told her I'd back her up at the council meeting when she goes in for the final approvals."

Seth was impressed. If she'd convinced Jack, a diehard opponent of the island being overdeveloped, then Abby must have done quite a sales job. Her involvement might also make it easier for him and Luke to ask for a little backing for that rescue boat, too.

Nate Wilson looked at the three of them impatiently. "Are we here to play poker or are you guys going to chatter like a bunch of women all night?"

Jack gave him an amused look. "Forgive me. I thought you might be interested in the future of our community."

Nate merely growled. "I'm more interested in winning back that money you stole from me in last week's game."

"Then you'll have to play a whole lot better than you did last week. I'm feeling lucky again," Jack told him, just as Tom Jenkins, their fifth regular, finally showed up. Jack pushed a beer in Tom's direction, then nodded toward Seth. "Deal the cards."

From that point on, they stayed focused on poker, beer and the snacks Jack had put out for them. Seth had the feeling there was something on Luke's mind, but he kept silent until they were outside at midnight, both of them a little poorer. Jack had had a good night, just as he'd predicted.

"I was hoping to see you today," Luke told him as they walked toward their cars.

"Something on your mind?"

"Hannah's planning a dinner party for tomorrow night. She'd like you to be there. Are you free?"

"Sure, I can be there." His suspicions kicked in. "If you don't mind me asking, who else is on the guest list?"

"Just one other person, as far as I know," Luke said. "Abby."

Seth's mouth gaped. "Seriously?"

Luke nodded. "Frankly, I thought it was a bad idea, but Hannah insisted. I think she's trying to prove something."

"To you?"

"Maybe. More likely, to herself. She wants to believe she's not the least bit threatened by Abby's return.

I think your presence will help with that. Thanks for agreeing to come, especially after all the things I said to you yesterday."

Seth considered his assigned role as buffer in a very tricky situation, then shrugged off whatever discomfort he was feeling. "If nothing else, it will give us a chance to talk to Abby about the rescue boat. It sounded to me back at Jack's as if you didn't have any idea that she was developing that property herself."

"Not a clue," Luke confirmed. "I'm shocked, frankly. Her folks were always the first to speak out against development on the island. They liked that it still felt like a small fishing village. She swears she'll see that this is done responsibly and Jack's backing her up, but I'm skeptical."

"Abby's been living in a bigger community," Seth suggested. "She may need this place to change so she can feel better about being back. You certainly seemed to think she wouldn't be satisfied living here as it is."

Luke chuckled. "If Jack was right and she's only planning on a dozen or fewer new houses, Seaview Key still won't resemble that area around Pensacola. We'd have to grow a lot before we could support a mall or movie theaters or one of those big box stores."

"Maybe she just needs a project, then," Seth suggested. "She told me she gave up a business. She's clearly not used to being idle."

"And that's why I have trouble believing she's back to stay," Luke responded.

There was no mistaking the hint of warning in his voice. Seth smiled. "Still looking out for me?"

Luke sighed. "I just don't want you to get blindsided if she ups and leaves in a few months. She told me herself what her intentions were about staying, but that doesn't mean I buy that she'll be here for the long haul. What's she going to do once she's developed Blue Heron Cove?"

Seth gave him a long look. Luke held up his hands.

"Okay, backing off now. You're a big boy."

"Thank you. And thanks for the dinner invitation. I'm looking forward to it."

"I wish I were," Luke said.

"Are you thinking you could wind up skewered right along with the kabobs?"

"Something like that," Luke said.

Seth laughed. "Maybe you're the one who needs protection here, not me."

"Entirely possible, my friend. Entirely possible."

Five

"Please tell me I did not hear this right," Grandma Jenny said to Hannah when she marched into the house on Saturday morning. "You've invited Abby here for dinner?"

Hannah regarded her with amusement. "Since you obviously heard this from Seth, then you know I have."

"What happened to keeping some distance between the two of you?"

"It didn't seem practical," Hannah said.

Her grandmother regarded her with dismay. "Have you seen her? Is this fiasco a done deal?"

"I went by yesterday to ask her to dinner, if that's what you're asking," Hannah said. "She accepted. So has Seth." She felt compelled to add, "Abby looks fantastic, by the way."

"Do you think I give two figs about how she looks?" Grandma Jenny grumbled. "What's she up to? That's what I want to know."

"She came back for a fresh start," Hannah said, finding herself in the odd position of trying to defend Abby, when she had her own doubts about her motives running through her head. "You were supportive enough of Luke doing that. Me, too, as I recall. In fact, you were downright eager to get me to move back here."

"That was different," her grandmother declared.

"How so?"

"I was being selfish. I wanted you close by and I knew Luke would keep you here and make you happy. Abby's just going to stir up trouble."

"Not if I don't let her," Hannah insisted. "I honestly don't believe Luke has anything to do with her coming back. I really don't. And let's not forget about Seth. You were the first to say there was something there. Luke seems to think so, too. I'm counting on that. A hot and heavy romance between those two is the answer for everyone."

Grandma Jenny sighed. "I'm a big believer in romance, but I still don't like this."

Hannah leaned down and gave her a fierce hug. "Be glad that I'm making the best of the situation. Isn't that what you wanted? Not a panic attack yet."

"Okay, then," her grandmother said, looking relieved. "But I have half a mind to go to the council meeting next week and speak out against that whole Blue Heron Cove thing just to get Abby out of town. If she doesn't get those permits, trust me, she'll be gone soon enough."

"And that would be selfish and spiteful," Hannah scolded. "The Seaview Key economy needs that development. You've said so yourself. There were plenty of people who were skeptical, but you were all for it when you first heard about it."

"I might have been wrong."

Hannah laughed. "When were you ever wrong?"

Her grandmother gave her a triumphant look. "Never,

and that's something you might want to remember. I'm probably not wrong about Abby, either."

Hannah's expression sobered. "I'm hoping that's the exception that proves the rule. I want this to be okay," she said softly. "For all of us. I've only had one other friend as close as Abby and I once were. Unfortunately, Susie's in New York and phone calls aren't nearly enough. I realized when she came for the wedding just how much I miss that closeness. It would be nice to have a best friend here again."

Though her grandmother continued to look skeptical, she nodded slowly. "Then I'll hope it works out that way, but I'm going to keep my eyes wide open. You should, too."

"Will do," Hannah promised.

After she'd gone, Hannah spent an hour planning the menu for tonight's dinner. She wanted everything to be perfect, especially now that she knew Abby had run a successful restaurant. While entertaining on Seaview Key was usually casual, she'd put together her share of fancy dinner parties in New York. Of course, then she'd had the food catered. This dinner was going to be all on her.

After crossing off half a dozen options, none of which seemed appetizing or sophisticated enough, she put her head down and moaned. "What have I done?" she muttered. "This is going to be a disaster."

Luke walked in just in time to overhear her. He knelt down and put his arms around her. "I figured reality was going to set in sooner or later," he said, stroking her back. "Grab your purse."

"Why?"

"We're going food shopping on the mainland. The

way I hear it, there's a place that sells everything from hors d'oeuvres to decadent desserts already prepared. You can go wild."

"But it won't be the same as if I fixed everything myself," she protested.

He laughed, then sobered. "No, sweetheart, but it will be edible."

She frowned at him. "I think you just insulted my cooking."

"Your cooking hasn't killed me yet, but you told me yourself the night before last that it's not your strong suit. Since tonight seems to be all about impressing at least one of our guests, I recommend we give this a try."

She looked into his eyes. A grin spread across her face. "Thank you."

"For offering to spend a fortune on gourmet food?"

"No, for understanding why this dinner party being perfect matters to me."

"I'll always do anything in my power to make you happy," he promised her.

"I believe that," Hannah said. And at that moment, with nothing and no one around to challenge her faith in Luke's love, she believed it with absolute certainty.

Whether he was merely to serve as a buffer to keep the gathering on an even keel or whether dinner was a setup for him and Abby, Seth was surprisingly eager for Luke and Hannah's dinner party. It had been a long time since he'd taken such care getting ready for an evening out. Apparently his time had been well spent.

"You look great," Hannah said, grinning when she greeted him at the door. "I love your aftershave."

Seth flinched, fighting a desire to run home for a shower. "Too much?"

"Not at all. Come on in. Abby's already here. She and Luke are on the porch out back. You can grab a beer before you join them. Or would you rather have wine? I opened a bottle of red for Abby."

"A beer's good," he said, following her through the house.

So far, Hannah seemed surprisingly at ease. He hoped that boded well for the evening. He accepted the beer she offered, then went outside with her.

His gaze immediately went to Abby. He was pretty sure his eyes glazed over the instant he saw her. She looked drop-dead gorgeous, nothing at all like the bedraggled woman he'd dragged to shore or even the casually attired woman he'd joined for lunch at The Fish Tale. This woman looked as if she'd just returned from a shopping trip in some exclusive mall in Naples, over on the mainland. She was put together with elegance and care, though he suspected her linen slacks and silk blouse were meant to be beach casual. Every highlighted hair was in place, too. She was a jaw-dropping sight, that's for sure, just like those images his sisters had envied in their piles of fashion magazines.

Truthfully, though, he'd liked her better half-naked and soaking wet. She'd seemed approachable then.

He felt Hannah nudge him in the side.

"Say hello," she encouraged, grinning.

"Nice to see you again," he said, then took a chair as far from Abby as he could get. This Abby was not only intimidating, she was evidently way, way out of his league. Whatever fantasies he'd been spinning suddenly seemed wildly out of reach, the differences between them emphasized by salon styling and designer duds.

Judging by his expression, Luke was almost as amused as Hannah by Seth's dumbfounded reaction.

"Abby was just telling me about how she ended up starting a restaurant," Luke said. "She got tired of eating fried fish all the time."

"You have no idea," she confirmed, her gaze on Seth. "I mean, I love seafood. How could I not, growing up here? But The Fish Tale doesn't cook every single thing in a deep fryer."

"So you went into the restaurant business out of desperation?" Hannah asked.

"Something like that," Abby said. "I worked in a couple of very nice places in Pensacola to learn how to run a restaurant, took some cooking classes so I'd know more about what really good food could be, then found an inventive chef who was interested in the same sort of restaurant I'd been envisioning. Seemed to us there was no reason a small town couldn't have excellent food."

"Were you equal partners?" Seth asked.

She shook her head. "I was able to scrape together the start-up money," she said modestly. "He had the ideas. We made it a sixty-forty arrangement. We were one of the lucky ones. The restaurant caught on. By the time I left, we were so successful he was able to buy me out."

"Did you start the restaurant before or after you met your husband?" Hannah asked.

"Before," Abby said, a frown passing across her face. "Marshall wouldn't have approved of me opening it after, but he could hardly complain since I was already in business when we met. In fact, we met right there when one of the members of his vestry at the church brought him in for dinner."

Seth nearly choked on his beer. "You were married to a minister?"

She nodded, clearly amused by his reaction. "That's been a shocker to a lot of people, me included."

"Since I have a hunch there's a long story behind that courtship, maybe we should have dinner before we get into it," Hannah suggested.

"Great idea," Abby agreed a little too eagerly. "Let me help get everything on the table."

As the two women went inside, Luke gestured for Seth to remain behind. "You okay? You look a little dazed."

"She's not exactly the woman I thought she was," he admitted.

"Meaning?"

"Remember she was in a bathing suit when we met. Her house is a mess. Then I find out she's developing Blue Heron Cove herself and that she was a successful businesswoman, who was married to a minister, for heaven's sake. Does that sound like anybody who'd ever look twice at a guy like me?"

"Seemed to me she was looking at you with interest," Luke said. "She directed just about everything she said toward you. Hannah and I might as well not have been here."

"You're crazy."

"I don't think so," Luke said. "Settle down. This is just about dinner. Nobody, least of all Abby, is looking for anything more tonight."

Seth gave him a wry look. "You sure about that? I think there are at least a couple of people around hoping this will turn into something else. Are you denying that you and Hannah have an agenda?"

"Not me. I've already told you I have reservations about you jumping into a relationship with Abby. It doesn't really matter what Hannah or anyone else might be after," Luke insisted. "You and Abby are the only ones who get to decide what, if anything, comes next."

"I suppose," Seth conceded. The problem was, as intimidated as he'd been feeling for the past half hour or so, he was still attracted. And that, given the obstacles he saw ahead, was more disconcerting than all the other expectations combined.

Over a delicious dinner that Hannah sheepishly admitted she'd bought at a specialty store on the mainland, Seth finally relaxed, especially once the conversation turned to old memories. Shared right along with laughter and plentiful wine—beer for him—the evening ended on an upbeat note.

As things were winding down, he and Abby agreed that neither of them had any business driving home. Once again, he found himself walking her back to her house in Blue Heron Cove.

"You do know those two just hoodwinked us," Abby said as they strolled along the beachfront.

"You mean naming us co-chairs to raise the money for that rescue boat?" Seth asked, laughing at the very neat trap that had been laid, some of it his own doing since he'd suggested getting Abby involved in the first place.

"Exactly."

"Well, I hope you know something about fund-raising because it's a long way out of my area of expertise."

"But you know why the boat's a critical necessity for the community," she countered. "And I can plan bingo nights and bake sales with the best of them. A minister's wife excels at creative ways to raise money."

"You do know how much that boat costs, right? It'll take a lot of bingo and baked goods to raise that much," he said, his skepticism plain.

She winked at him. "Not the way I do it," she said.

They walked along in silence for a few minutes before she turned to him again. "Were you the one who came up with the idea for asking the developer of Blue Heron Cove for a major donation?"

He nodded. "At the time I had no idea that might be you."

"But isn't it lucky that it is me?" she said. "And all your arguments were completely valid. The people who buy those houses are going to expect reliable access to medical care on the mainland. Plus it will be wonderful PR for me to support this. I'll need that going for me when those permits come up for review."

Seth wasn't sure how he felt about her pragmatic thinking. It seemed a little sneaky to him. At the same time, a donation might mean the difference between getting that boat and not. He had to remember the goal. And he'd been well aware of those benefits to the developer when he'd first suggested the idea to Luke. It hadn't bothered him until that person turned out to be Abby. Why was that? It was something he needed to think about.

"So you're in?" he asked now.

"I'll get you a check by the beginning of the week to kick off the drive to raise the money," she promised, then held his gaze. "Will it offend you if I do it in a very public way? Maybe hold a little press conference?"

"That is the way the game is played, isn't it?" he said.

She studied him. "But you don't like it, do you?"

He sighed. "Actually I totally get it. The community needs that boat. I'm not going to do or say anything that might undermine the prospects for that happening."

They reached her front porch then.

"Would you like some coffee or a glass of tea before you head home?" she asked.

Seth told himself he ought to leave, ought to avoid anything that might lead to the two of them getting any more involved. Despite the stern mental lecture, though, he said, "I wouldn't mind a cup of coffee, if you're sure you're not anxious to get to sleep."

"I'm a night owl," she assured him. "That's what it takes to run a restaurant and I'm still not out of the habit. But I'll make the coffee decaf, in case you're not."

"Decaf's probably a good idea," he said, following her inside.

Though she'd made good progress in airing out the house and cleaning it up, there were still enough signs of the years of neglect for him to guess that the task had been monumental. That she'd been tackling it on her own didn't seem to fit with the woman wearing those expensive linen slacks, a silk blouse and diamond stud earrings, and shoes that no doubt cost as much as his weekly take-home pay.

"Can I ask you something?" he said when they had their coffee and were back on the porch with a light breeze coming in off the water.

"Sure."

"Why didn't you hire a cleaning crew to tackle this place? It would have been finished in a day."

"I needed a project," she said simply. "More important, I think maybe I needed to remember who I used to be."

"Since I doubt you were ever a maid, you need to explain that one."

"You asking for a history lesson?" she quipped.

He nodded. "I'm trying to figure you out," he admitted.

"Okay, here's the short version. When I was a kid, my parents owned this land, but we didn't have a lot of money. My grandfather had settled on Seaview Key when it was still just a mostly inaccessible fishing village. He fished, but he also invested in land, which my parents inherited. They were determined to keep it, to keep the island as unspoiled as it had been. Back then I didn't fully appreciate that, especially since I had to get a job in high school to help out and needed scholarships for college."

"If that's true, where'd you get the money to start that restaurant? Did you sell off an acre or two back then?"

"No way. The land wasn't mine then and my parents would never have agreed to sell. I'd worked hard and saved every extra penny. It turned out I had a head for business. I made a few investments with my savings and they paid off. It gave me enough of a nest egg to start the restaurant."

"How old were you then?"

"Twenty-four."

"Holy mackerel!" he said, impressed.

She smiled at his reaction. "Step one in the evolution of Abby Dawson," she agreed. "Then I got married.

My husband was pastor to a very wealthy congregation. I told you earlier that my restaurant caught on. It catered to a very upscale clientele. I got used to keeping up appearances. That completed the evolution to Abby Miller." She wrinkled her nose as if she found that Abby distasteful.

"What was so terrible about her?" he asked. He knew that having money could change people and not always for the better, but she still seemed pretty down-to-earth to him. In fact, that's why he remained so intrigued. If she'd been a rich snob sporting a moneyed, entitled attitude, it would be easier to ignore these sparks that kept flaring between them.

"I don't want to come off trying to sound like some poor little rich girl, but that wasn't who I am," she explained simply. "I had a lot of time on my hands after the divorce to think about that. I realized I'd truly been happier back here with a family that didn't have much except the land around us."

"In that case, I'm surprised you want to develop it," Seth told her.

"Believe me, I gave it a lot of thought. Seaview Key needs something if it's going to thrive. I'm in a position to make that something happen in a responsible way." She regarded him earnestly. "I'm going to do this right, Seth. There wouldn't be much point in coming back for the serenity I remembered and then seeing it ruined."

"So, scrubbing floors has gotten you back to basics," he suggested, trying to put what she'd said in perspective.

She nodded. "And I'm hoping that raising the money for this rescue boat will be one way to be part of this community again. A donation might be great public relations, but putting in an effort will probably do more for me in the long haul. I want to be accepted, Seth, not as some benevolent outsider, but as a local who cares about what happens around here."

He was surprised by the hint of yearning in her voice. "Being accepted really matters to you, then?"

"Sure. Doesn't it matter to everybody, when you get right down to it? Don't you care about being a part of the community?"

Seth honestly hadn't thought about it. He'd come for a visit. Luke had persuaded him to stay. The town had been eager to hire someone with his background as a medic. He'd felt accepted from the beginning.

"I guess I thought if I did my job, that would be enough," he said.

"That's because you didn't burn a lot of bridges when you left," she said, a rueful expression on her face. "I need to make up for some of the things I said about this town. I couldn't wait to get away. Other than Luke and my friendship with Hannah, this place held nothing but bad memories for me."

"And yet you came back."

"Perspective," she said. "Maturity. I'm the first to admit I didn't see the big picture back then."

He admired her honesty, but he wondered if she wasn't deluding herself, just as Luke had warned. Had she really changed so much?

"Are you sure Seaview Key is what you're looking for?" he asked, trying to reconcile it with the sophisticated woman sitting beside him. Was it possible for her to forego the lifestyle she'd obviously had in the Florida Panhandle?

"Can I say it with absolute certainty?" she asked.

"No, but I'm hoping I've gotten it right this time. I liked the person I was back then a whole lot more than the person I've become."

"You seem just fine to me now," he told her in all honesty.

She smiled at that. "You're sweet to say that."

Sweet? Seth nearly groaned at that. Women didn't call men they were interested in *sweet.* Recognizing that made this desire he had to seduce her about as wildly inappropriate as anything that had ever occurred to him before. He really, really needed another one of those annoying lectures from Luke before he did something incredibly stupid.

Abby saw the expression in Seth's eyes and immediately regretted her candor. She could practically see the distance growing between them. Maybe it had been a mistake to admit the truth to him. She'd gotten used to having money. Marshall had had oodles of it, thanks to family investments, and she'd made more when she'd sold the successful restaurant she'd started before she'd met him, enough to invest in developing Blue Heron Cove.

In her opinion, money was nice, but she'd realized very recently that other things mattered more. Not everyone saw it that way, though, especially men whose pride kicked in and wouldn't let them see past the dollar signs that separated them. She'd really hoped that Seth wouldn't be one of those men. Based on his shocked expression, though, it seemed that he was.

Of course, the alternative, which she'd experienced a time or two, was worse. She'd known men who were interested in her only because of her money. Right after the divorce, a few had hovered, hoping to get her attention. Some had even been audacious enough to mention investment schemes on the first or second date, pretty much giving away the reason for their interest.

"I should be going," Seth said, getting to his feet.

"Already?" she said, disappointed and not doing a very good job of hiding it.

"I'm on call first thing in the morning." He gave her a grin that emphasized an appealing dimple. "Never know when someone might take an early morning dip in the water and find herself in over her head."

"It won't be me," Abby assured him. "Lesson learned. Two near drownings in one lifetime have convinced me that my swimming should be confined to a pool."

"Still, maybe I will see you on the beach. I usually run about the same time every morning. Of course, now that I know the owner's around, maybe I ought to be avoiding this area. It is posted with No Trespassing signs."

"Those are meant to keep the kids away, though I doubt they pay much attention. I certainly wouldn't have, back in the day," Abby said. "You're welcome anytime."

He nodded. "Okay, then. I enjoyed tonight, Abby. Welcome back to Seaview Key."

She watched him take off, his pace slower than the jog a few days before, but the view every bit as excellent. He was a man who looked as sexy in khakis as he did in swim trunks, a claim too few men could make, in her opinion. She sighed as he disappeared from sight.

"Stop it," she ordered herself as she went inside to wash their cups and shut off the coffeemaker.

Working with him was going to be incredibly uncomfortable if she kept thinking about hauling him off to her bed. And if there was one thing she knew with absolute certainty about Seaview Key, it was that it was no place to have a careless fling. Gossip was plentiful and the ramifications could last for years.

"Abby looks great, don't you think so?" Hannah asked Luke as they cleaned up the kitchen after their dinner party.

"I suppose," Luke replied distractedly.

"I don't think she's aged a bit," Hannah persisted, determined to press the point, though she wasn't certain why she felt compelled to get an honest reaction from her husband.

He put the last of the leftovers into the refrigerator, then turned slowly. "Hannah, what's going on? Are you thinking I'll say something and give away some secret lust that Abby's stirred in me?"

She winced at the direct hit. He'd voiced the fear that nagged at her. "Well, it's always possible," she said defensively.

Luke stepped closer, put his hands on her shoulders and gazed directly into her eyes. "No, it's not. You're the woman I love. Abby's an old memory."

"Who's very much back in our lives."

"As a friend," Luke said. "But if even that's going to worry you, we can keep some distance between us. You've done your duty. You've had her over. We can let it go at that."

She frowned at his reasonable, accommodating tone. "And have everyone think I'm an insecure, mean-spirited shrew?"

He had the audacity to laugh at that. "Name one single person who'd ever think that about you. Everyone in this town loves you."

"*I'd* think it," she admitted. "That's exactly what I'd think of me if I cut Abby out of our lives." She sighed. "I'm such a mess."

"But you're my beautiful mess," he said, pulling her close. "We're solid, Hannah. What we've found is real and good and lasting, okay?"

She rested her forehead against his chest. "Okay," she murmured softly, relieved to have it all out in the open, even if her insecurities didn't speak well of her. "I love you, Luke. And though at times like this I can't imagine why, I do know you love me."

"Just hang on to that."

She really intended to try. She pictured Abby with her perfect body, her stylish clothes and gorgeous hair and regretted that God had given her quite such a test of faith.

Six

During the off-season when things were quieter, having Sunday lunch at The Fish Tale after church had gotten to be a habit for Luke, Hannah, Grandma Jenny and Seth. When Kelsey and Jeff were around, they came along with the baby. This week, with the three of them still on vacation, Seth escorted Grandma Jenny to the restaurant.

He'd deliberately skipped his run that morning, though he couldn't say for sure why. Had he wanted to avoid Abby or had he wanted to see her a little too much? The latter was scary under the circumstances, scary enough to disrupt his routine.

Unfortunately, the first person he saw when he walked into The Fish Tale was Abby, all alone in a booth again. She was making notes on a legal pad, but gave him a distracted smile when she looked up. Beside him, Grandma Jenny frowned.

"We should say hello," Seth said.

"Probably," she conceded grudgingly.

"And maybe ask her to join us."

The suggestion was greeted with a scowl. "Why

would we do that?" Jenny asked, then met his gaze. Something she saw there must have given away his feelings, because she gave a curt nod. "Never mind. Ask her, if it's what you want."

He thought about why issuing the invitation mattered to him. Was it about the undeniable attraction? Or was it about everything Abby had told him the night before about wanting to be accepted? That was the safe reasoning. Leaving her at that table all alone would be cruel, or at least that's what he told himself as they walked over to greet her.

Even with the decision made, he kept right on arguing with himself. Avoiding the beach had been one thing, he reasoned. Avoiding her in public would send an entirely different message, one he didn't intend. Of course he could have left the decision up to Luke and Hannah, but that would have been the cowardly way out.

He led the way to her table, fully aware of his companion's reluctance. Yet it was Jenny who spoke first, surprisingly without any hint of awkwardness. Whatever her reservations about Abby's return, she was innately gracious.

"Abby, it's been a long time," she said, her tone friendly enough.

Abby's expression brightened with unmistakable delight. "Grandma Jenny!" She looked hesitant. "Is it still okay if I call you that?"

"Of course," Jenny said, her expression softening.

"It's wonderful to see you. I've been wanting to drop by, but..." She faltered. "Well, I wasn't sure how you'd feel about that. There was the situation with Luke and me, and then Hannah and I lost touch." She shrugged. "You know what I'm talking about."

Seth noted that Jenny flushed with guilt, clearly aware that she hadn't hidden her displeasure over Abby's return well enough from everyone. Word had apparently gotten around. She straightened her shoulders and managed a smile.

"You'd have been welcome, of course," she told Abby, her good manners saving the day. "Are you expecting someone? If not, why don't you join us? Hannah and Luke will be along any minute. Jack holds one of the big tables for us."

The invitation, coming from her rather than left to him, surprised Seth almost as much as it evidently surprised Abby.

"I'd love to, if you're sure it would be okay," she said at once, looking from Jenny to Seth and back again.

"No reason it wouldn't be," Jenny said. "I want to hear more about these plans of yours for Blue Heron Cove. I like getting information straight from the horse's mouth. It's easier to make up my own mind that way, though I'll tell you straight out, I think it's just what Seaview Key needs."

Abby grinned. "And I'm always eager to talk about Blue Heron Cove, especially to a supporter," she said, then winked at Seth. "And I'm even more eager to get you involved in this project that Seth and I have been given."

Jenny looked startled. "What project is that?"

"The rescue boat Luke and I have been talking about," Seth reminded her. "We need to raise the money for it, and we need to do it quickly. Last night Luke coerced Abby and me into chairing a committee to make it happen."

Jenny rolled her eyes. "I imagine what you know about raising money would fit on the head of a pin," she said to Seth.

"Exactly, which is why Abby needs your help," he said. "You game?"

"I'm always willing to get involved in a good cause," Jenny said, regarding Abby with a more favorable expression as they made their way to the table Jack always reserved for them. "Any thoughts about what you want to do?"

"A few," Abby told her.

Seth sat back and listened with amazement as Abby rattled off half a dozen ideas that she'd apparently come up with overnight. It seemed to him she probably hadn't slept any better than he had if she'd been busy making all those notes. Even Jenny looked pleasantly surprised.

"You've given this some thought," she said approvingly. "And you were just given this assignment last night? I'm impressed."

Abby shrugged. "Sometimes I do my best thinking in the middle of the night when I can't sleep," she said, casting a pointed look in Seth's direction.

Jenny's gaze narrowed suspiciously as she looked between the two of them, but just then Luke and Hannah arrived. If Hannah was taken aback by Abby's presence, it didn't show. And once she heard about Abby's ideas for raising money for the boat, she joined in eagerly, offering to take charge of the press conference on Monday to kick things off. Luke sat back, looking satisfied with himself.

Seth regarded him with amusement. He leaned close and whispered, “Mission accomplished?”

Luke looked startled. “What?”

“Seems like peace and cooperation reign. Wasn’t that your intention?”

Luke laughed. “One of them, anyway. Getting the money for that boat trumps everything, though. It sounds as if Abby has that under control already.”

“You heard her ideas. She’s like some kind of fund-raising dynamo. And she says she’ll make a contribution on Monday at that press conference to kick off the drive.”

“That makes sense to me. Creating a big public hoopla will get people involved and excited.”

Seth shook his head at Luke’s seeming naïveté. “It will also help her when she goes to the council for those permits.”

Luke must have heard the note of disapproval in his voice because he merely lifted a brow. “That’s the way of the world, Seth. Nothing wrong with a win-win for everybody. You said that yourself, so why the cynical reaction now?”

“Double standard,” Seth suggested, hoping Luke would leave it at that since he hadn’t figured out his reaction. “Then again, you’ve made a sizable contribution and you’re not looking to be in the limelight.”

“Entirely different,” Luke replied. “I don’t need to build community support for me or the clinic. Plus, my backing for a rescue boat is expected.”

Seth still struggled to make peace with Abby’s public approach. Or maybe he was struggling to make peace with the fact that she was in a position to make such a magnanimous gesture in the first place. Her obviously healthy bank account nagged at him like a particularly aggravating gnat. He had a hunch that was the real issue—and one that wouldn't go away.

Abby's hand instinctively settled on top of Seth's as she leaned in to make a point to Luke and Hannah. She wasn't even aware of the gesture until she noted three pairs of eyes—Luke's, Hannah's and Grandma Jenny's—focused on her hand atop Seth's, rather than paying attention to what she was saying. She glanced at Seth and saw that he looked equally startled.

Embarrassed, she withdrew her hand, and tried to cover the awkward moment with a rapid-fire list of suggestions for their fund-raising efforts beyond the already agreed-to kick-off press conference on Monday.

"I'm leaning toward a big fish fry in January, at the height of tourist season, if we can get Jack to cooperate and maybe donate his time," she said. "We should consider doing it in the park to accommodate more people, but we could move it here if the weather's bad."

Lesley Ann overheard her. "I know Dad will want to help, no matter where you hold it," she said at once. "And I think all the fishermen who supply us will want to pitch in, too, especially Dave Hawkins. Ever since his heart attack when Luke kept him alive while one of his buddies raced them over to the mainland in his speedboat, Dave has been trying to figure out a way to help get a rescue boat. He'll rally all the other fishermen."

Abby regarded her with gratitude. "That would be fantastic. Would you be willing to work on that, getting all those guys on board?"

"Absolutely," Lesley Ann said.

Abby turned to find Seth regarding her with amusement. "What?"

"Neatly done," he said approvingly.

"Hey, when somebody's eager to help, you seize the opportunity to put them in charge of something," she told him. "That's lesson one."

"Exactly right," Jenny said. "Now tell me what I can do."

"How about rallying a group of people who can sell tickets in advance and take the money when we have the event?" Abby said at once. "The more people we get involved, the better. Not only will that guarantee a crowd of volunteers, but they'll all be sure their friends and neighbors show up."

"And I know someone you should ask," Seth said, recalling his visit to Ella Mae Monroe and his resolve to get her more active in the community.

"Who's that?" Jenny asked.

"Ella Mae."

Jenny regarded him with surprise. "Ella Mae's never been one to get involved with community activities, not since she retired from teaching," she argued. "She stays mostly to herself."

"Which is exactly why she needs someone to reach out to her," Seth argued. "She's lonely."

"I'm not trying to be contrary, but is she physically up to helping out?" Jenny asked worriedly. "The doctor used to be over there at least once a week. Luke, I know you've seen her a few times, as well. What do you think? Is she up to this?"

Abby noted that Seth was watching Luke closely to see if his reaction would kill the idea. Interesting that a man as confident and as experienced as Seth would be seeking Luke's approval in such an obvious way. It reminded her that Seth looked up to Luke, that whatever bond had formed between them in Iraq was strong and lasting.

Luke nodded slowly, his expression thoughtful. "I think she could use the distraction," he said. "If you keep in mind her age and don't assign her anything too demanding, I think it would be good for her to be involved. Seth's right. With no family that I'm aware of, she has too much time on her hands for sitting around worrying."

"So those spells of hers are mostly in her head?" Jenny asked.

"You didn't hear that from me," Luke said at once.

"Me, either," Seth said.

Abby grinned at the quick denials. So, they were writing a prescription for a patient that had nothing to do with medicine. It was just more proof of how much they cared. She hoped the residents of Seaview Key appreciated that. It would make this fund-raising drive even more successful.

She was especially impressed that Seth had picked up on what was really going on with Ella Mae so quickly. Another man might have dismissed her as being a hypochondriac, rather than realizing she was simply lonely and had too much time on her hands. And he'd picked the perfect person to reach out to her, too—Jenny.

As they all left The Fish Tale and headed for their cars, once more Seth fell into step beside Abby. She felt the way she had back in high school when Luke had walked her home every afternoon.

"If I had books, would you offer to carry them?" she teased Seth.

He stared at her blankly for a second, then chuckled. "I do seem to have developed the habit of walking you home," he said.

"It was sweet what you did back there for Ella Mae," she told him.

He frowned. "There it is again," he muttered irritably.

"What?"

"Sweet."

Abby laughed. "Too much of a sissy word for you?"

"Not a sissy word," he said. "But no man likes to be called sweet."

She resisted laughing again at his obvious discomfort. "How about thoughtful? Or generous? Or observant?"

"Better," he confirmed. "I just saw a need and thought of a way to address it. I'm relieved that Luke agreed and that Grandma Jenny's going along with it."

"What struck me was that Luke hadn't noticed what Ella Mae really needed or at least hadn't pinpointed a solution for it. Neither had Doc, and he'd been dealing with her crises for years. You took the time to assess what was really going on with her and found a way to make a difference."

He seemed uncomfortable with her praise. "Maybe I'm wrong. Maybe Grandma Jenny was right and Ella Mae will want no part of helping with the fish fry or anything else going on in town. She can be pretty cantankerous."

"And maybe she just needs to be asked," Abby said quietly, thinking of how many older people she'd known at the church who had sat on the sidelines desperately in need of a project, of a way to feel useful again. "Did you know that she taught school here for thirty-five years? She'd retired by the time I was in high school, but my parents both took her history class."

"No wonder she talks about the past with such enthusiasm," Seth said. "She made a career of making history come alive."

"That's certainly what my folks thought. Our house is filled with books about the Seminole Wars here in Florida and biographies of people important to the state's history. They had a lifelong interest in that because of Ella Mae."

"I'd like to borrow some of those books sometime," Seth said. "It'll give me something to discuss the next time I see her. I know she thinks my education is severely lacking because I was raised in the Midwest."

Abby regarded him with surprise. "You enjoy visiting her, don't you?"

"Sure. She reminds me of my grandmother, rest her soul. She could tell stories like no one else."

"Sounds as if you were close."

"She took care of me a lot. My mom and dad both worked by the time I came along. My sisters were already in high school and too obsessed with boys to be trusted to look after me."

"That explains why you get along so well with Grandma Jenny, too," Abby guessed. "You're comfortable with seniors. Too many people shy away from them, as if age were contagious or something."

Seth laughed. "I don't know about that. I think it's more about the pace at which everyone lives these days. Older folks have time on their hands. They like to spin out a story while younger people want them to get to the point. I think that's one of the reasons I like Seaview Key. People here aren't in such a rush."

"That's definitely one of the reasons I was anxious to get back here," Abby said.

"But you haven't really slowed down since you got here," Seth argued. "You didn't waste a minute jumping all over this rescue boat project, even though you already have a full plate between getting your place cleaned up and the Blue Heron Cove development."

"Force of habit," she agreed. "But I'll mellow eventually. I'm counting on it."

He didn't look as if he believed her. "Mellow how? You'll sit on your porch every afternoon with a book? Maybe wander into town for ice cream after dinner? Sit outside and enjoy the sunrise?"

"Exactly," she said. "Maybe I'll take up quilting, so my hands won't be idle while I laze around enjoying the view from the porch."

"Ah-ha," he said, laughing. "There you go, already thinking of productive ways to occupy yourself. The view should be more than enough on its own. That's the mellow lifestyle."

"Are you there yet?" she asked curiously, trying to imagine him being still for more than a few minutes at a time.

"I'm working on it," he said. "Want to give me a test?"

"How?"

"Pour a couple of glasses of iced tea, join me on your porch and we'll see which one of us gets bored first."

Abby held his gaze. "You're on," she said, accepting the challenge.

And as long as Seth was right there in plain view, she was pretty sure boredom would not be a problem.

Seth had no idea why he'd uttered a dare to Abby, even one as innocuous as this. Maybe it was because she'd looked so certain that she could attain some sort of Zen status eventually. He'd had his own share of troubles adapting to a more laid-back lifestyle, but the living-on-the-edge experiences of Iraq and Afghanistan had made him determined to succeed. He thought he'd made excellent progress since coming to Seaview Key. Abby still looked fidgety at the prospect of being unoccupied for more than a minute at a time.

He set the rocker he'd chosen into slow motion, closed his eyes and felt himself relax. Beside him, he could hear Abby's rocker going at an impatient, rapid-fire clip as if she had places to go and things to do and couldn't wait to get started. He bit his lip to keep from smiling.

"You'll wear a hole in the porch floor if you keep that up," he chided eventually.

"What?"

He glanced over and caught a guilty blush in her cheeks. "What were you thinking about?"

The blush deepened. "All the things I ought to be doing," she admitted. "You?"

"Absolutely nothing," he said, though the truth was he'd been envisioning taking the woman next to him inside, then tumbling around in her bed with her.

"Seriously?" she said. "You were actually able to empty your mind of everything? How?"

She sounded so eager to figure it out, Seth smiled. "Take a deep breath. Count slowly. Envision yourself all alone on a beach. Given there's not a soul in sight from where we are right now, it shouldn't be that difficult."

Her gaze narrowed. "And that works?"

"Try it."

She closed her eyes. He could almost hear the deliberate counting going on in her head. Her eyes blinked open and she frowned at him.

"Hogwash!" she said. "You made that up."

He laughed. "It works for me. I swear. You must have been counting chores on your to-do list, instead of letting your mind empty of everything going on in your life."

"Well, there's a lot to do," she grumbled. "It isn't going to get done if I'm just sitting around out here staring at the water."

"I knew it!" he said triumphantly. "You are incapable of total relaxation."

"And that pleases you why?"

He shrugged. "Something to hold over your head, I suppose. Or maybe because it suggests that I'm beginning to understand you."

She looked startled by that. "Is there some reason you want to understand me?"

He held her gaze, letting awareness sizzle between them. "I think it's best if people aren't strangers the first time they sleep together," he said quietly.

She swallowed hard at that. "And you think we're going to sleep together?" she asked, her voice choked.

"I know we are," he said evenly. "The more important question is whether or not it's going to be a mistake. Any thoughts about that, Abby?"

She looked completely flustered by the question, or maybe it was the topic. "Are you always so direct?"

"Always," he said. "There are fewer regrets if everything's on the table from the beginning. I've been attracted to you from the moment we met. I've spent a lot of time the past couple of days thinking I was probably crazy, but here we are. I still want you. I guess what I'm asking is whether *you* think it's crazy."

She seemed to be at war with herself. He could read the desire in her eyes, the precise moment when logic overruled passion.

"It would be a mistake," she said, though she was unable to keep a wistful note from her voice.

"Because?" Not that he hadn't thought so, too, but he wanted to know why she felt so strongly about it.

"You're younger than I am, Seth."

He actually smiled at that. "Try again. We're adults. We both know the age difference doesn't make it wrong or crazy."

"It's Seaview Key," she said, as if things might be different in another community—in a big, anonymous city.

"You're afraid of the gossip?" he asked.

"Aren't you?" she challenged. "You have a job that depends on community support. Doesn't it bother you that you could be fired if people disapprove of your personal behavior?"

"I guess I'm giving the people of Seaview Key more credit than that," he said. "And I'm thinking we'd be discreet."

"There's no such thing as adequate discretion in a town this size. Somebody always finds out. I imagine half a dozen people already know exactly how much time we've been spending together."

"In plain sight," he countered. "Not even a kiss in

public, although I've been desperate to get another taste of you, one that didn't involve seawater. What could be more discreet behavior than that?"

She choked on a laugh. "I really did kiss you when you were giving me mouth-to-mouth, didn't I? I was hoping I'd been wrong about that."

"You weren't wrong," he said. "It got my attention, that's for sure."

"Then that's what this is really about, just a crazy impulse I wasn't even aware of," she said earnestly. "Chemistry kicked in. Curiosity. It's perfectly natural."

"And none of that kicked in for you? I was the only one affected because, what? I'm a guy?"

"Okay, no. I was affected, too, but it was a heat of the moment thing. Nothing more."

"Not like it was with you and Luke?" he asked pointedly.

"That was different," she said at once.

"Because it was Luke?"

"Because we were kids. Adrenaline and hormones got all mixed up together. As you just pointed out, you and I are adults. We know when something is just a fluke."

"A fluke? That's what you're calling it?" he asked, feeling a sudden urge to prove her wrong. Unfortunately, it was evident that she was scared to death of the truth. For whatever reason, she wanted him to be wrong about the heat simmering between them even now.

He looked at her until she met his gaze. "I think I could prove to you it wasn't any fluke," he said softly.

She refused to look away, but he could tell by the desire in her eyes that she was waiting for him to do just that. He was the one who broke eye contact.

"And one of these days, I will," he told her. "Just not today."

He stood up, bent down and pressed a brotherly peck to her forehead. "See you around, Abby. Work on that relaxation thing, okay? Your pulse seems to be racing."

He hid his smile as he walked away yet again without claiming what he really wanted. There was time. That was one of the lessons of Seaview Key—that there wasn't any rush. Good things happened in their own sweet time. And something told him that once he and Abby made it as far as a bed, it was going to be very, very good. After that? Well, maybe just this once he didn't need to be looking too far into the future or examining all their differences. Maybe he needed to live in the moment.

Seven

Seth flinched when Luke told him that Ella Mae wanted him to come to her place right away on Monday morning.

"She's not feeling well?" he asked Luke worriedly.

"I don't think that's it. She didn't call the emergency line. She called the clinic directly and asked for you. She sounded more annoyed than sick."

Seth relaxed and allowed himself a satisfied grin. "Oh, boy. I'll bet I know what that's about. Jenny was going by to see her this morning. I'm guessing my name came up."

Luke laughed. "No question about it. I'm sure Jenny told her that you were behind this scheme to get her involved in raising money for the rescue boat. You'd better get going. You don't want to be responsible for one of those spells of Ella Mae's."

"I'm supposed to be at the press conference with Abby in an hour," Seth reminded him.

"Then you'd better hurry," Luke advised, a glint of humor in his eyes. "Bring Ella Mae along with you. She could probably use an outing."

"Something tells me she's barely going to be speaking to me once she's said her piece," Seth said. "I doubt she'll want to go out in public with me."

"Only one way to find out."

"You're taking entirely too much pleasure in this," he accused his friend. "Next time I'll just keep my prescriptions restricted to medications."

Luke's expression sobered at once. "Don't do that, Seth. You have good instincts. This plan of yours, no matter what Ella Mae might say to you, was exactly right."

The praise bolstered Seth as he headed for the older woman's two-bedroom home set on a small lot with little more than a glimpse of the water through the overgrown shrubs and trees. He couldn't help noting how much nicer it would be if some of that were trimmed back and cleared away. Maybe next spring, when the island was quiet again, he could get a few people to help with that.

Ella Mae was waiting for him on her porch, her expression sour. "Took you long enough," she grumbled.

"Luke said it wasn't an emergency," he responded, taking a seat next to her. "What's on your mind?"

"You were the one behind Jenny's visit this morning," she said. "Don't even think about denying it. She admitted as much."

"Then you don't need me to confirm it."

"I thought you were a paramedic, not a meddler."

"Sometimes the cure for what ails a person has nothing to do with medicine," he said. "I thought you might enjoy doing a good deed, instead of sitting around here all by yourself."

"I like being by myself," she claimed. "I have my books."

"And, of course, those can't talk back," he said.

She gave him a sharp look. "I worked hard all my life," she told him. "You think trying to cram a little knowledge into the heads of kids who resist at every turn is easy?"

"Absolutely not."

"Then you can understand why I think I've earned a little peace and quiet," she said.

Seth leaned toward her and took her frail hand in his. Hers was trembling just a little. "There's such a thing as too much peace and quiet," he suggested gently. "And this rescue-boat fund-raiser isn't all about you. Seaview Key needs this. Wouldn't you like being part of making sure it happens?"

"It's not as if I can go around town knocking on doors," she grumbled. "No matter what you think, I'm old."

"And not half as frail as you'd like everyone to believe," he countered. "Besides, is knocking on doors what Jenny asked you to do?"

"No," she admitted. "She said something about calling some of the people I had as students, telling them about the fish fry and selling them tickets. Since I taught most of the people on this island at one time or another, she seemed to think I'd have some influence."

"The way I hear it, a lot of them idolized you."

She waved off the comment. "More of them were terrified of me. That's exactly the way I wanted it."

"Either way works for our purposes, don't you think? They'll scoop up those tickets out of respect or fear."

A sound escaped that might have been a bark of laughter. "You think you're smart, don't you?"

Seth ignored the question. "What did you tell Jenny?"

"That I'd do it, of course." She frowned at him. "Doesn't mean I'm happy about being bamboozled into it or that I'm going to jump on the bandwagon for every cause the people around here dream up."

"Of course not," he said solemnly, feeling triumphant.

"I doubt I'll even go to that fish fry thing," she said.

"Not even as my date?" Seth said, determined to get her there.

Pink tinted her cheeks. "Don't try to sweet-talk me, young man. You've gotten your way. I'm going to help. Be satisfied with that." She gave him a sly look. "Besides, the way I hear it, you have your eye on Abby Dawson."

"Who told you that?"

"I may be leading a life that seems isolated to you, but I still have my sources around this town," she told him. "You'd do well to remember that. There are very few secrets in Seaview Key." She studied him curiously. "Is it true? About you and Abby, I mean?"

"We just met," Seth equivocated.

"That's not an answer. If you were one of my students, I'd take off points for evasiveness."

Seth laughed. "Then it's a good thing you're not grading me," he said. "Now, I need to run. The press conference to kick off the drive to raise money for the boat is starting any minute."

Ella Mae struggled to her feet. "Then we'd better hurry."

"You're coming with me?" he asked innocently, hiding yet another triumphant smile.

"Might as well. It's not as if I have a lot to do," she said, a twinkle in her eyes. "Besides, Abby's going to be there. I can get the lay of the land with you two for myself. I was always the first person in town to figure out when two young people were sweet on each other. I was the most hated chaperone at the high school dances because they couldn't put anything over on me. I never let them sneak off together," she said proudly.

"I'm going to regret dragging you out of your shell, aren't I?" Seth said with an exaggerated sigh.

She gave him a surprisingly impish look. "You know what they say about awakening a sleeping beast. Do so at your own peril."

Seth laughed. "I'll keep that in mind."

"Too late," she told him.

Seth tucked her arm through his and helped her down the front steps. She walked gingerly to his car and settled in, her shoulders squared regally. She patted the purse in her lap. "I've already started my list," she told him. "I imagine I can sell a few tickets before Abby even finishes making her pitch. I think I'll make a contest of it. Jenny thinks she can outsell me, but I have other ideas."

Seth could only hope she didn't put that same level of determination behind any meddling she decided to do into his life.

It seemed perfectly natural to Abby that Hannah had taken over making the arrangements for the press conference to announce the town's drive to raise money for a much-needed rescue boat. She obviously had the public-relations expertise that the rest of them lacked. Based on a series of phone calls Hannah made to clarify a few details, Abby was a little in awe of the full-throttle way Hannah tackled the assignment, especially with so little advance notice. She must have been working the phone all Sunday afternoon and into the night.

Abby was even more in awe when she showed up at town hall for the kickoff and found a crowd milling around out front.

Luke and Seth were both there, of course, along with Seaview Key's part-time mayor, Sandra Whittier, who was in her seventies and a member of one of the village's founding families. The editor of the local weekly was there with his camera. Hannah had even lured someone from a TV station on the mainland with the promise of an exclusive about what this rescue boat would mean to the island community and how many lives it might save.

There were several other people on the steps at town hall, too.

"Who are they?" Abby asked Hannah, imagining them to be town officials.

"People who came close to losing their lives because we didn't have a rescue boat," Hannah explained. "Their testimonials will stress the importance of this."

"And you pulled all of this together overnight?" Abby said, amazed.

Hannah grinned. "I was motivated. My husband really, really wants this boat and the community needs it. You've got a lot of money to raise, my friend. Just doing my part."

Hannah orchestrated the press conference like the pro she was, with a brief speech from Luke, comments from the people whose lives had once been in jeopardy, and then the presentation of Abby's check to kick off the fund-raising drive. The crowd applauded enthusiastically, with a number of people coming up afterward to thank Abby and to welcome her back to town. A few people even put bills and loose change into the donation jar that Jenny had thought to make for the occasion. It was filled to the brim by the end of the event.

Abby was so caught up in the aftermath of the press conference that it was a while before she noticed that Seth was nowhere around. She turned to Hannah.

"What happened to Seth? Did he get a rescue squad call?"

"I don't think so," Hannah said. "He was here a minute ago."

Abby tried to shrug off his absence, but once again she couldn't help wondering if it had something to do with that check she'd turned over to Luke. Though she might have imagined Seth's reaction to her financial situation on Saturday night, there was little question about what had happened just now. He was pulling back on a personal level. She'd bet money on it, she thought wryly.

Well, she couldn't worry about that now, she thought, forcing herself to focus on all the people who were volunteering to help out with various activities. The committee sign-up sheets were filling up rapidly. Ella Mae seemed to be as energized as Jenny. It was going exactly as Abby had hoped it would.

"Why do you look so disappointed?" Hannah inquired as people started to drift away. "This was a huge success."

"It was, wasn't it?" Abby said, forcing a smile. "Thanks to you."

"No, we made a good team. You're the one who gave me something to talk about to get all these people here." Hannah drew in a deep breath, then asked, "Want to celebrate over lunch? We can catch up a little more."

It was yet another overture Abby hadn't expected. "I'd love to," she said at once, pushing aside her worries about Seth and his untimely disappearance.

She and Hannah walked to The Fish Tale and secured a booth.

"You're upset because Seth took off," Hannah guessed as soon as they were seated.

"A little bit," Abby acknowledged. "I thought we were supposed to be doing this together."

"And now you're thinking…" Hannah frowned. "What are you thinking?"

"That all this emphasis on my money has scared him off," Abby admitted, then grinned ruefully. "Crazy, huh? It shouldn't matter to me what he's thinking. We're co-chairing a committee. That's not exactly a personal connection."

"But you want it to be, don't you?" Hannah said.

Abby shook her head in denial. "Seth and me together? It would be crazy."

"Sometimes logic doesn't enter into it," Hannah said.

Abby voiced the same concern she'd expressed to Seth the day before. "He's way too young for me."

"A nonissue," Hannah declared, waving it off.

"Well, if I'm right about the money thing, then he's too insecure."

"Maybe he just needs to figure out who you really are and that none of that matters," Hannah suggested reasonably. "Give him time, that is if you're really interested. Are you, Abby? Or are you just trying to fill some empty place in your life? Or to prove to me that it's not Luke you want?"

Abby was surprised by the plain talk. Years ago Hannah would never have tackled a subject like her relationship with Luke head-on. The proof of that was that she'd never once admitted that she had feelings for Luke back then. Of course, once he and Abby had hooked up, her pride would have kept her quiet. Now, though, her blunt question forced Abby to put some thought into her response.

"Maybe it's all of the things you mentioned," she admitted. "At least a little bit. I felt this amazing sizzle the second Seth and I met. I should be old enough to know that chemistry doesn't matter, right?"

"Chemistry can be a great starting point," Hannah corrected, "but sure, there has to be more."

"How am I supposed to find out if there's more if he's not willing?" she asked in frustration.

"Try giving it time," Hannah said, regarding her with unmistakable amusement. "Not every relationship gets a jump-start from a rescue on the beach. Some take a little longer."

"If you're referring to me and Luke all those years ago, I recognize that it was probably a heady mix of adrenaline and hormones that brought us together. I told Seth that just the other night."

Hannah looked surprised by her admission. "It's a possibility, though at the time you seemed to be pretty serious."

"If we'd really been serious, it wouldn't have been so easy to say goodbye," Abby told her, viewing the relationship through the lens of time and maturity.

Hannah's relieved expression couldn't have been

more revealing. Abby touched her hand. "I mean that, Hannah. I know Luke and I weren't meant to be. I knew it back then, too." She sighed. "Maybe it's the same between Seth and me."

"Maybe," Hannah agreed. "But if I were you, I wouldn't give up on Seth just yet. He seems awfully interested. And though you haven't asked, I know for a fact he hasn't dated anyone since he's been here."

Abby leaned forward. She could feel heat climbing into her cheeks even before she revealed, "Well, he did say he thinks we're destined to sleep together."

Hannah's eyes widened. "He did not!"

"Oh, yeah," Abby confirmed, grinning. "It makes me shiver just repeating it."

"Well, there you go. That's definitely a hopeful sign. You have to hang in there."

"You do know that patience was never one of my virtues. I've always gone after what I wanted."

"Oh, I remember," Hannah said. "But trust me, some things are worth waiting for."

Abby smiled. "Some things or some people? Like Luke, maybe?"

"I did wait a very long time," Hannah said. "And it was worth it."

Abby smiled. "Lucky you."

"Lucky me, indeed."

But even as Hannah echoed Abby's words, a shadow passed over her face.

"Hannah, what's wrong?" Abby asked.

Hannah forced a smile. "Nothing's wrong," she insisted. "Didn't I just say how lucky I am?"

"Not like you meant it, though," Abby said. "We used to be able to tell each other everything."

"That was a long time ago," Hannah said.

"You must know that you can still trust me," Abby reminded her. "I want us to have that kind of friendship again."

"I want that, too," Hannah replied. "I really do." Her expression turned sad. "I just don't know if it's possible."

It was late afternoon after a busy day of minor emergencies, when Seth headed toward Blue Heron Cove. He'd dressed for the run he'd missed in the morning, but what he really wanted was to see Abby. He didn't even try to pretend otherwise.

She was wading along the shoreline, wearing a long, flowing skirt that she held up in a vain attempt to keep the hem from getting soaked. Her tank top revealed skin that had already been gently bronzed by the sun. Seth jogged up beside her, drawing a startled look.

"I didn't hear you," she said.

"You looked as if you were lost in thought."

"Just seeking that Zen-like serenity you talked about," she claimed. "What happened to you after the press conference this morning? One minute you were there, the next you'd vanished."

"You noticed, huh?" he said, oddly pleased.

"Well, sure. I thought we were in this together."

"Duty called," he said. "I had back-to-back squad calls."

"Did I see Ella Mae with you?"

He smiled. "You did. After she delivered a firm lecture to chastise me for interfering in her peaceful life, she insisted on coming along to the press conference.

She figured it would be a good place to start selling those fish fry tickets."

"How'd she do?"

He shrugged. "No idea, but she was highly motivated. I think she and Jenny have some sort of competitive thing going on."

Abby laughed. "Well, that can only work to our advantage."

She regarded him curiously. "How did you think it went this morning?"

"I'm no judge, but it sounded as if there was a lot of enthusiasm. People seemed to be overwhelmed by your generosity."

She frowned at the comment, apparently aware of the edge he hadn't been able to keep from his voice.

"Well, they were," Seth said defensively.

"But that check made you uncomfortable, didn't it?" she prodded, surprising him with her insightfulness.

"Getting a donation from the developer of Blue Heron Cove was my idea, remember?"

"That was before you knew it was me."

"Can't I just say I'm grateful for the support and leave it at that?" he asked irritably. "What else is there to say?" She looked as if she wanted to argue, but to his relief she remained silent. He seized the chance to change the subject. "What about you? Were you happy with the turnout?"

She held his gaze a moment longer, then shrugged. "The turnout was incredible," she said, injecting a note of genuine enthusiasm into her voice. "Hannah really did a pretty amazing job, especially with such short notice. She's vowed to get more media coverage in the next week or two. She's already talking to some reporters on the mainland. The testimonials from patients whose lives once hung in the balance because we don't have a fully equipped rescue boat really triggered a lot of interest."

"Seems as if you two work well together," he said. "Any sign of friction?"

"Not on my part," she said at once. "If Hannah has any doubts about me, she's keeping them well hidden." She frowned.

Seth studied her expression. "Okay, what's wrong? Something's on your mind."

"She's keeping something from me. I'd lay odds on it. I asked her about it, but she blew me off, claimed I was imagining things."

"There's bound to be a little lingering tension," Seth suggested. "You were hot and heavy with her husband once upon a time."

Abby shook her head. "It's not that. It has nothing to do with Luke. We've both been pretty open about what happened in the past. I'm convinced we've resolved that or close to it." She turned to him. "Do you have any idea what else it could be?"

Seth thought of the breast cancer screening Luke had mentioned. That wasn't his news to share. He did know that it was likely that Hannah could use a friend in her corner. He just wasn't sure if Abby was the right friend. There was a whole lot of baggage in that relationship. In the end, though, it wasn't up to him to decide.

"Ask her," he suggested.

"I did," she reminded him with evident frustration.

"Ask again."

She studied him closely. "You know something, don't

you? I just want to be a good friend to her again, Seth. How can I do that if she won't let me in?"

"You keep trying," he said. "It could take time, Abby. It might never happen."

Her expression turned sad at that harsh reality. "I hope you're wrong about that."

He smiled and took her hand. "I hope so, too."

Because he knew that recapturing that friendship mattered more to Abby than being accepted by the entire population of Seaview Key.

With Seth's advice still ringing in her ears, Abby headed for Hannah's on Tuesday morning. She could have made a million excuses for putting off the confrontation, but on her list of priorities for this new life of hers, mending fences with Hannah had moved to the top of the list.

She waited until she was sure Luke would have left for the clinic. She knew she might be interrupting Hannah's work schedule, but she thought this was too important to be put off. And she was more likely to catch her home if she was working than she would be once she'd quit for the day.

"Hold on, hold on," Hannah shouted as Abby knocked on the door for a fourth time.

Abby winced. Hannah's tone didn't bode well for a casual conversation between friends. Nor did Hannah's aggravated expression when she finally opened the door.

"You were working," Abby guessed. "I'm sorry to interrupt, but I came by to thank you for yesterday." She held up the hamper she'd brought. "I come bearing gifts—those cranberry-orange scones made from my grandmother's recipe. I got up early and baked them this morning. You used to love those. And when I stocked up on my way out here, I found some Devon cream at a specialty store on the mainland."

Hannah's expression didn't mellow, but she did step aside.

"I guess I could take a break."

"I won't make a habit of interrupting your work," Abby promised, following her into the kitchen. "I'm sure it must drive you nuts when people assume they can drop by unannounced just because you happen to work at home."

"Sometimes," Hannah admitted. She busied herself making a pot of tea, then poured it. She gave Abby a probing look. "This isn't just about thanking me, is it?" she asked.

"Of course it is. You did a magnificent job yesterday. The press conference couldn't have gone any better."

"Which you told me at the time, and again over lunch," Hannah reminded her. "Spill it, Abby. What's really on your mind?"

Abby drew in a deep breath. "Actually it's more about what's going on with you. Something is, and I don't think it's worry about me and Luke. I know I said this yesterday, but I intend to keep on saying it until you believe me. You can talk to me. Even though we weren't in touch, I never stopped caring about you. You were like my sister, Hannah. When we drifted apart, it made me sad, especially since I knew I was mostly to blame."

Hannah looked away. For the longest time, Abby was sure she wasn't going to open up, but she finally turned back.

"I have a cancer check coming up," she admitted at last.

"Cancer check?" Abby repeated, taken aback. "You mean an annual mammogram?"

"More than that," Hannah said. "I've had breast cancer. I've had a mastectomy."

Abby absorbed the shocking news. Why hadn't she heard about this? She reached for Hannah's hand, held it tightly. "How long ago?"

"Almost two years now. I was diagnosed right before my mom died from a recurrence of her breast cancer."

"Oh my God!" Abby whispered. "You must have been terrified."

"You have no idea," Hannah told her. "To be honest, every screening freaks me out. I don't like to talk about them, because it doesn't really help."

"Oh, Hannah, I'm sorry," Abby said, feeling for her. The screenings could be scary enough without the reminder of what had happened to her mom in the back of her mind. "I had no idea. If you don't want to talk, I'll drop it right now. If you decide you need someone to listen, though, I'm here."

A faint smile touched Hannah's lips. "That makes it worse," she said. "Having you here, I mean."

Abby blinked at her candor. How could she have been so wrong about Hannah starting to accept her presence on Seaview Key? "I don't understand. I thought we'd resolved your worries about me and Luke."

"It's not about that, at least not exactly. You're beautiful. You're whole. Everything I'm not."

Abby regarded her with dismay. "Stop that this minute!" she said fiercely. "You're as beautiful as you ever were. More important, you're a survivor. Do you know how much I admire you for that? You won the fight, Hannah. And I may not have gone through it myself, but I *know* it's an outright war. Believe me, I've been around a lot of women who haven't faced it with such courage. I've been around a few who haven't won. You should be so proud of yourself. You should be counting every day as a victory."

A tear leaked out and spilled down Hannah's cheek. "Most of the time, I do, but I get so darn scared. Luke's a saint. He tries to keep my spirits up, but when these screenings come around, there's only so much he can do."

Abby reached for her hand. "He's a guy, for one thing. Look, Hannah, I know it's not the same for me, but every woman faces a momentary panic when it comes time for that annual mammogram. I have been through that more than once. I know how much harder it must be once you've had breast cancer."

"It's hell," Hannah said simply. "Because I know what lies ahead if something turns up on those tests."

"And I'm making it harder for you," Abby said.

"Not on purpose," Hannah said quickly. "It's just that you're you."

"And Luke and I have a history and I haven't had cancer," Abby surmised.

Hannah nodded. "And I'm glad you haven't had it. I wouldn't wish it on anyone."

"I can't change the past," Abby said. "And I can't change the fact that I've been lucky so far. I can promise you that you have nothing to fear from me. I thought we'd put that to rest, Hannah, but I'll keep saying it as long as it takes. What Luke and I had, it was so long ago. We're not the same people anymore. And even if we were, he's your guy. Period. I wouldn't dream of even trying to mess with that." She gave her old friend a long look. "Any more than you would have tried to get between us back then."

"You sound as if you mean that," Hannah said. "And I really need to believe it."

"Then choose to take it at face value," Abby said. She smiled. "Besides, Luke would tell me to get lost if I even tried anything. You know how loyal he is. He takes commitment seriously and he made his commitment to you."

Relief washed over Hannah's face.

Abby squeezed her hand. "Besides, there's Seth."

"Yes, there is Seth," Hannah echoed, her lips curving into a smile at last. "How's that going? Any updates since we spoke yesterday?"

Abby thought of their conversation the day before. "I'm more convinced than ever that he's been scared off by the fact that I have money," she admitted, then added wryly, "I should be grateful he's not attracted to me because of it, huh?"

"He's not that kind of a guy," Hannah said with certainty. "Just give him some time. He'll put the whole money thing in perspective."

"I hope you're right," Abby said. "It's not as if I'm going to burn it just to make him feel better."

Hannah laughed. "I think we can agree that would be crazy."

Unfortunately, short of using her cash to start a bonfire, Abby wasn't entirely sure what else might make Seth feel more comfortable. He just might be one of those men who saw money as the tipping point on a scale weighing the balance of power in a relationship. And if that was the case, they were pretty much doomed.

Eight

"The woman apparently has money to burn," Seth lamented to Luke. It was the first chance they'd had to talk since the press conference. Luke had been on the mainland with a patient for much of that time. "I know you saw the size of her donation."

"With her twenty-five thousand, we're well on our way to getting that boat," Luke said slowly. "Why do I sense that you're not entirely happy about that? You should be ecstatic. I know I am."

Rationally, Seth knew he ought to be, but his gut still churned when he thought about the reminder of the vast differences between him and Abby. "I don't know many people who can write a check for that amount without batting an eye."

"People? Or women you're interested in?" Luke asked perceptively.

Seth regarded him sourly. "Okay, yes. For about a nanosecond I thought about asking Abby out. I enjoy her company. I'm attracted to her. Now this? Come on. Why would a woman who could buy every one of my assets several times over be interested in spending time with me?"

"Maybe because you're a decent man with a sense of humor, at least about most things, and a respectable member of the community." Luke gave him an assessing once-over. "And some women think you're not bad to look at."

"Gee, that makes me feel all warm and fuzzy."

"If you want warm and fuzzy, see my wife. Personally I don't see the whole sexy-as-sin thing she talks about."

Seth stared at him, startled. "Hannah thinks I'm sexy as sin?"

"She does, and from what I gather, there's a consensus on this among the female population of Seaview Key. It apparently isn't limited to any particular age group, either. Grandma Jenny is one of your biggest admirers, along with Kelsey. And we know Kelsey's baby is completely gaga over you."

"I don't think we can really count Isabella," Seth said, but his mood was improving.

"How about my preteen daughter? Gracie is suddenly far more interested in coming down from Atlanta for a visit. She asks about you every time I talk to her, usually in the same breath with asking me to talk to her mom about letting her wear a bra. Frankly, I don't think that's coincidental."

Seth chuckled at Luke's discomfort. "A bra, huh? That must rattle you."

"Scares the daylights out of me," Luke admitted. "She's still a baby."

"No, she's eleven going on twenty," Seth corrected. "But that's not the point. And as thrilled as my ego might be by your pep talk, we were talking about me and Abby. You have to admit it's an entirely different situation."

"Okay, then," Luke said, getting back on topic. "What is the point? That you suddenly don't think you're good enough to ask Abby on a date? Do you even know Abby's background?"

"That she's from here, that her parents didn't have a lot, that she worked to pay her way through school? Yeah, she told me about all that."

"And you don't think that gives you something in common? Her background's not much different from yours."

"Not exactly," Seth said. His parents hadn't been working class or even middle class. They'd chased the almighty dollar with a vengeance. Their estate might be modest by some standards, but it was sufficient to have his sisters waging war with each other over their shares right now. He'd seen something crazy in their whole value system and joined the army to get away from it. So, maybe he was a little touchy about financial stuff, but not entirely for the reasons Luke thought.

"Then explain it to me," Luke said.

"Money changes people, and not always for the better." He gave Luke an earnest look. "The Abby you knew, she was hardworking, grounded, ambitious, right?"

"Sure."

"Do you really know her now?"

Luke looked momentarily taken aback. "I suppose not, but she's already anxious to get involved in the community. That's what this donation was about."

"It's a check, Luke. Apparently one she can easily afford. She's buying goodwill. She's admitted as much."

"And I can't entirely fault her for that. Why do you? I still say this is your pride talking. Since I've never known you to display a lack of confidence around women, I don't get it."

Seth knew Luke was right. Abby was the first woman maybe ever who'd thrown him so completely. He'd drawn them in all shapes and sizes and from a whole range of income levels, too.

Luke studied him. "Okay, let's get to the root of this. What's with the hang-up about money, anyway? I know you're not particularly materialistic."

"I told you I've seen the way money affects some people," Seth said. "It certainly has caused a huge rift between my sisters, and they're not even battling over a mega-fortune, just the relatively modest inheritance from our folks."

"Have you seen any evidence that Abby is greedy?" Luke asked.

"No, but she is ambitious," Seth said. "She started a restaurant from scratch and made it a success. Now she's tackling this development."

Luke was starting to look increasingly amused. "Now you're opposed to ambition, too? What next? Does it bother you that she's smart? How about beautiful? Any objections to that?"

Seth frowned at his attempt at humor. "You think I'm being ridiculous. I get it."

"I think you're scared because you have feelings for her and don't want to," Luke corrected. His expression turned serious. "Look, after what happened with Cara, it makes sense that you want to take your time before getting involved with someone new. But don't start manufacturing excuses to avoid someone who could be the right woman. Not that I'm saying Abby is," he added hurriedly. "Just as you said, I don't know her that well anymore. I can't say if you're well suited or not. Time will answer that."

Seth took the advice to heart. Luke knew the pain he'd been through when Cara had been killed in Afghanistan. Maybe his hesitance with Abby was about that and not about money at all. Maybe the whole money thing was just the excuse he'd needed to avoid getting involved. He couldn't be sure.

"Okay, let's say I go for it and ask her out," he said. "Where would I take her? She's obviously used to nice places. It's not as if I can afford some fancy restaurant."

"Which works in your favor, since fancy is in short supply on Seaview Key," Luke replied. "Maybe you should just worry about getting to know her. You have the perfect opportunity with this fund-raising drive. You'll be together all the time."

"Yeah, thanks for that, by the way. Real subtle."

Luke laughed. "After listening to you yammering on just now, I'm thinking you need all the help you can get."

"Bite me," Seth retorted, getting to his feet and heading out.

Why he'd expected understanding from the one man on earth he'd always trusted to have his back was beyond him. Then, again, maybe he'd gotten exactly what he'd come here for, a much-needed kick in the butt, and a reminder that he was making excuses for not going after Abby, rather than seizing an opportunity that had unexpectedly come his way.

Seth was on his way to The Fish Tale to grab lunch and hopefully a glimpse of Abby when his cell phone rang. He glanced at the caller ID, then sighed.

"What's up, Meredith?" he asked his oldest sister, thinking the timing couldn't have been more apt given his conversation with Luke just now.

"It's Laura," she said predictably, referring to their middle sister. "You have to talk to her, Seth. She's going to drag me into court over Mom and Dad's estate."

"Not my fight," he stated quietly. In fact, he was determined to stay out of it. It had gotten ugly the minute Laura had realized that his parents had left Meredith in charge of doling out their inheritances. They'd done it wisely, in his opinion, since Laura tended to squander every penny that came her way.

"Please, Seth. I need you to make her see reason," Meredith pleaded.

"Can't be done," he told her. "You know Laura when she thinks she's being mistreated."

"You mean when she's being greedy," Meredith corrected. "You get why Mom and Dad did what they did. Why can't she?"

"Because it was aimed directly at her," Seth suggested. "I don't need a dime from the estate. I figure anything that comes my way is a bonus. Laura is convinced that she's entitled to every penny and she wants her share now. It's ironic in a way. Mom and Dad raised her to feel entitled, then did this when they saw how she turned out."

"I can't cave in on this. She'll blow everything before the end of the year," Meredith said in frustration.

"You can't stop her from living her life the way she wants to," Seth reminded her. "I'm not sure why Mom and Dad thought they could control her from the grave, even though they had the best intentions. All they did was put you in the middle."

"If we go to court, the lawyers will end up with more money than any of us."

"Remind Laura of that," he suggested. "Maybe that will get through to her."

"You do it," she said. "She won't listen to me. If I say the sky is blue, she'll argue with me even with the evidence right over her head."

Seth chuckled, knowing it was true. "I'm not the best peacemaker," he told her, then gave in. "But I'll try."

"Thank you."

"You could just defy Mom and Dad," he suggested. "Give her the money."

"And have our parents haunt me from the grave? They would, you know."

Seth smiled. "Entirely possible," he agreed. "I suppose I wouldn't take any chances, either."

"So you will call Laura?"

"Yes," he agreed reluctantly.

"Now, before she gets a lawyer involved?"

"As soon as I hang up with you," he promised.

"And you'll let me know what she says?"

"I'll give you the censored version," he told her. He suspected Laura was going to give him quite an earful.

It took calls to Laura's house, her office and then her cell phone, but he finally caught up with her. She was the middle child and he sometimes wondered if that wasn't why she had all these issues with Meredith and, at times, with him.

"I suppose you're calling to tell me why I shouldn't

sue the pants off of Meredith to get what's coming to me," she said as soon as she picked up.

"Lovely to speak to you, too," Seth said.

It took a minute for his sarcasm to sink in. "Sorry," she said eventually. "It's just that she makes me so darn mad."

"You do know she didn't make these rules," he suggested.

"Yeah, Mom and Dad were looking out for me, yada-yada-yada."

"You do have a nasty habit of spending beyond your means," Seth suggested. "Isn't that why Jason divorced you, because you kept piling up credit card bills he couldn't pay and refused to listen when he told you it had to stop?"

"Is that what he said?" she demanded furiously. "Of course he'd want to get you on his side. Men always stick together. Crazy me for thinking my brother might back me up."

"Was he lying?" Seth asked patiently, knowing perfectly well that he hadn't been. Jason had shown the bills to Seth when Seth had tried to mediate before the talk of divorce had gone too far. He'd been completely thrown by his sister's lack of control.

"Okay, no, he probably had a valid point," Laura admitted. "But he'd told me he wanted me to be happy. Shopping makes me happy."

Seth nearly groaned. *That* was precisely the attitude about money that made him crazy. "Look, that's over and done with. Surely you can understand, though, why Mom and Dad wanted Meredith to manage the estate? You can't be trusted to handle money."

"What about you? Do you think it's fair that she's

in charge of your inheritance, too? You could join in this suit with me."

"I've never cared about the money," Seth told her. "It's nice knowing it's there. It's a good little nest egg. I'm living okay on what I earn now."

"Well, it's my chance to get out of debt and maybe make things right with Jason," Laura said, a hitch in her voice. "It could be the only chance I have."

Seth was startled by her admission that she wanted her husband back. It was yet another of her delusions. After talking to his former brother-in-law, he knew the likelihood of that was practically nil. It wasn't up to him, though, to tell his sister that.

"Have you told Meredith that?" he asked instead. "Maybe she'd give you an advance, maybe help you pay off the bills, if you explained why that matters. Otherwise, you're risking spending more on an attorney than you'll ever see from the estate."

"You don't think I stand a prayer of contesting the will, do you?"

"I don't," he said gently. "Mom and Dad had valid reasons for their concerns. I think any judge will understand that."

"And you'll side with Meredith in court, won't you?" she said accusingly.

"If it comes to that, I'd have to," he agreed.

"You are so blasted saintly and self-righteous," she accused, but she was starting to sound resigned.

"Will you at least think about what I said?" he asked.

"Yeah, sure. How can I not? The two of you always did gang up against me."

Seth smiled at that. "Meredith and I never ganged up against you," he said. "I was so much younger, neither of you wanted a thing to do with me. I was just a nuisance and, worse, an embarrassment."

She finally chuckled. "Yeah, that's true. What teenager wants to think about her parents having sex. Yet you were the living proof that ours did. Ugh!"

"I love you just the same," he teased.

"I suppose I love you, too," she conceded grudgingly.

"Call Meredith," he prodded. "Work this out."

"I'll think about it," she said again.

Seth figured that was the best he could hope for. He hung up before she took back her promise.

The two conversations, though, had been stark reminders that money could tear people—even families—apart. It made his hesitance to get involved with Abby seem more reasonable than ever. He glanced over at The Fish Tale, spotted Abby once again in that same booth by the window, and turned right around and walked away.

Abby had been watching Seth pace up and down the sidewalk outside The Fish Tale. She'd also been aware of the precise moment when he'd spotted her. The fact that he'd taken off, rather than coming inside, was just more evidence of how they were drifting apart, rather than getting closer. It seemed odd behavior from a man who'd declared only days ago that he envisioned them sleeping together.

"You still waiting for someone to join you?" Lesley Ann asked, stopping by the table with a refill of Abby's iced tea.

"Nope," Abby said, regretting that she'd even hinted

that she was waiting for someone. "I'll go ahead and order."

Lesley Ann took her order to the kitchen, then came back.

"If you'd like some company, I can take a break," Lesley Ann offered hesitantly. "I wouldn't mind getting off my feet for a little while. A.J.'s napping, so I might even be able to get through my lunch in peace."

Abby smiled. "I'd love the company. And, if you don't mind me saying so, you look exhausted. Maybe you should take the afternoon off and grab a nap."

Lesley Ann immediately looked wistful. "I could get out of here, but by the time I get A.J. home, he'll be wide awake and looking for attention."

"Leave him with me," Abby suggested impulsively.

"But you have work to do," Lesley Ann protested. "Aren't you trying to get everything together for tomorrow night's council meeting."

"I've been over everything so many times, I'm practically cross-eyed," Abby said. "I could use the break, too. You'll have to bring him over to my place, since I don't have a car seat, but he can stay as long as you like."

"Are you sure? I have to admit that sounds heavenly."

"Then take me up on it."

"Right after we've eaten," Lesley Ann agreed. "Let me grab those orders from the kitchen. I put mine in at the same time I gave Dad yours. And I'll tell him the plan. He'll probably be relieved to have a break from babysitting himself."

When she returned to the table, she uttered a sigh as she slid into the booth. "This feels so good," she said, moaning with pleasure. She took a bite of her sandwich. "And this is amazing."

Abby chuckled. "For a woman who's probably eaten more of those fish sandwiches than anyone else in town, you sound surprisingly impressed."

"I don't usually get to savor it like this. When it's hopping in here, I just grab a bite on the run. I barely get to taste it." She met Abby's gaze. "Don't get me wrong. I enjoy working in here. Always have. Unlike my brother, who couldn't wait to get away, I love this place. And I like being able to keep an eye on Dad, especially with Mom gone."

"What about a part-time schedule?" Abby asked.

"No such thing, not with me," Lesley Ann said. "I'm probably more like you than you can imagine. If I'm going to take over this place someday, I need to know how to handle every single crisis. And I need to be willing to put in the hours."

"But wearing yourself out can't be good," Abby argued.

"That's what Bobby says. He'd love it if I just quit, or took a leave for a couple of years, but there's no way I'm doing that. It would be too hard on Dad, for one thing. It would drive me crazy for another. I like being busy."

"And those kids don't keep you busy enough?" Abby asked, trying to imagine the chaos.

"It's not the same," Lesley Ann countered. "Both things are fulfilling, but not in the same way. I need the balance."

Abby nodded slowly. Balance was something to which she'd aspired, too. "You're lucky to have figured that out. Most of us go the all or nothing route in one direction or another, and forget how important it is to have balance in our lives."

"Are you one of those people?" Lesley Ann asked.

Abby nodded. "Surprisingly, I thought I had it for the longest time. I had my restaurant and my marriage, after all. What more could I possibly want?"

"What happened?"

"I realized my marriage was a one-sided empty shell of a relationship," Abby said with candor. "Not my husband's fault, by the way. I hadn't known enough to ask for more. After I inherited my parents' land back here and came back for a visit to check on things, I started remembering the old me, all the hopes and dreams I'd had, the fun I'd had. Do you know, I don't think I'd had a really good laugh in years? Life was always so serious with Marshall."

Lesley Ann gave her a commiserating look. "We all need to laugh," she said quietly. She hesitated, then said, "I've seen you laugh a time or two with Seth."

Abby smiled. "I have, haven't I?"

And that, even more than Hannah's encouragement, was why she was determined not to give up on him just yet.

It was nearly dusk by the time Seth went for his run. He could have avoided Blue Heron Cove entirely, but wasn't quite ready to pin the label of coward on himself. He simply hoped that Abby would be inside and he wouldn't have to face all these crazy, conflicted feelings of his.

Instead, she was on the porch, a soft light coming from inside to wash over her and what appeared to be a baby. He heard the baby talk she was using as she lifted the child up and drew giggles. He doubted she knew he was there observing her, so he stepped out of the shadows and walked toward the house.

"Have you borrowed A.J. again?" he teased.

"I have," she said, laughing as the baby gurgled with delight above her head. She lowered him, blew kisses on his belly, then lifted him into the air again.

Seth shook his head at the sight. Abby had been born to be a mother, that was clear. He wondered why she wasn't one. The question, though, was far too personal to ask outright.

"I didn't expect to see you tonight," she said as A.J. quieted down in her arms.

"I try to get in a run every day. If I miss it in the morning, I usually make up for it at night."

"I thought you might be avoiding me."

Seth grimaced at having been so obvious. "Why would I do that?" he asked, trying to seem as if avoiding her had been the furthest thing from his mind.

"A question I've been asking myself," she said, her gaze directed straight into his eyes. "Especially after what you said to me the other day."

"What I said?"

"About sleeping with me," she replied.

He gave her a startled look, then gazed at the baby. "We shouldn't be talking about this now."

Her lips curved. "I doubt we're scarring the baby. He's a little young to have a clue what we're talking about."

"Why is he here with you, anyway?"

"Lesley Ann was exhausted. I offered to help out for a couple of hours so she could catch a nap. She called a while ago and asked if I'd mind keeping A.J. till she can finish her evening shift at the restaurant." She tickled the baby till he was giggling. "So, A.J. and I are entertaining each other for a little while longer."

She directed a look into his eyes. “You ducked my question a minute ago.”

“I did,” he admitted.

“Any particular reason? Do you regret telling me that?”

“It was probably a little premature,” he said. “Or arrogant. I don’t usually go around telling women I plan to sleep with them.”

“Did I seem to be offended?”

“No, but…” He studied her serene expression and wondered how she could discuss this so calmly. Talking about sex wasn’t something he usually did. It either happened or it didn’t. He didn’t sit down with someone and reason out the pros and cons. Abby seemed intent on doing just that. “Why are you so determined to talk about this?”

She grinned, apparently amused by his discomfort. “Hey, you were the one who introduced the subject the other day. I’m just following up, trying to figure out if something’s changed. Has it?”

“I can’t tell you how uncomfortable I am discussing this while you’re holding a baby in your arms,” he said.

She laughed aloud at that. “Admit it. You’re uncomfortable talking about it at all. A.J. here is just a convenient excuse.”

Seth bristled at the accusation. “Like you said, I was the one who brought it up in the first place. Why would I have done that if the topic embarrassed me?”

She held his gaze. “You tell me. To be honest, you didn’t seem all that embarrassed the other day. It’s only now that I’ve called you on it. Are you one of those guys who’s all talk, Seth?”

“Excuse me?” he said, shocked. The desire to drag her out of that rocker and kiss the stuffing out of her was almost overwhelming. The presence of the baby precluded that, so he was left with his blood pounding through his veins and no way to express his annoyance at the unfair accusation.

She smiled, proving that she'd intentionally provoked him. She winked. "Two can play at that game."

His gaze narrowed suspiciously. "Are you flirting with me?"

Her expression was all innocence. "Could be."

"It's a dangerous game," he warned her.

"So is making promises you don't intend to keep," she replied.

They were back to his claim that they were inevitably going to sleep together, apparently. Given the way his pulse was pounding right now and desire was slamming through him, it seemed he'd gotten it exactly right. Sooner or later, for better or worse, they were going to wind up in bed.

Sadly, with A.J. present, it wasn't going to be tonight.

Nine

Abby felt a little guilty as she watched the emotions playing across Seth's face. She'd been using A.J. as a shield, knowing that she could taunt Seth about his confusing behavior without any risk that he'd call her on it. She discovered it was fun rattling him so easily.

Just when she thought he might take off, though, he stepped onto the porch and settled into the chair beside her, an odd expression on his face.

"What are you doing?"

"Calling your bluff," he said, a smile tugging at his lips.

"What?" she said, suddenly nervous.

"A.J. won't be here forever." He glanced at his watch. "Lesley Ann should be picking him up anytime now."

"And then what?"

He grinned. "I guess we'll see."

Her pulse took a hop, skip and jump. "Seth," she said, but the protest died on her lips as his grin spread. "What?"

"Just trying to see how brave you really are," he said. "Now who's all talk?"

She stared at him for a heartbeat, then chuckled. "We really are a pair, aren't we?"

"Mind telling me why you decided to get into this tonight?"

"Because you're here, because you confuse me and I don't like being confused," she admitted.

"You prefer being in control," he guessed.

She nodded readily. "Always, but especially these days."

"Why especially now?"

"Because for way too long I ceded control over much of my life to my husband. I want to reclaim what I lost."

"Then this thing with us is going to get interesting," he said. "I'm pretty unmanageable, or so I'm told."

"There you go again," she said in frustration.

"What?"

"Talking as if it's a foregone conclusion that there will be something between us," she said. "Your actions don't go along with your words."

"Because I keeping having second thoughts, then third thoughts," he said. "Much as it pains me to admit it, I'm probably every bit as confused about this as you are."

"Then maybe you should get back to me once you've decided whether you want to pursue this or not," she said.

He seemed amused by her exasperation. "You really, really don't like uncertainty, do you? Or letting someone else have the upper hand. I guess that's understandable given what you've told me about your marriage."

Abby scowled at him. "You certainly don't have the upper hand," she protested, not even attempting to keep a hint of indignation from her voice.

"I think I do," he countered.

"Now you really are being arrogant."

"Okay, how about we make a deal?" he suggested. "We'll work on this fish fry thing and the whole fund-raising effort, hang out together with no pressure, and see what happens. The way I hear it, really solid relationships are always founded on friendship. We could give that a try."

Abby fought to hide her disappointment. Agreeing to that really would give him the upper hand. He'd be setting the pace, if not predetermining the outcome.

"That's what you want, just to hang out?" she pressed, hoping he'd see the disadvantages to that. "Be friends?"

"Yep, no games. No expectations." He grinned. "No more talk of sex."

"So, you're not talking friends with benefits?"

"Afraid not. We'll be buddies. Pals."

She frowned at him. "And you can do that?"

"I guess we'll see."

To Abby's frustration, what he was proposing made sense, even if it did sound incredibly boring. "If that's what you want," she agreed, though she had a hunch it was going to be impossible. In fact, she couldn't help wondering which one of them would be the first to break the rules.

Seth sat in the back of the meeting room listening to Abby make her presentation about Blue Heron Cove to the town council. He couldn't help being impressed with how prepared she was, how passionate her arguments were. He didn't doubt for a second that she'd convince the council to give her everything she wanted.

When the discussion ensued, though, it was evident that the project still had its detractors, including the mayor. Sandra Whittier clearly didn't want Seaview Key to grow, even in the modest way that Abby was proposing. Two other members of the council backed her. With a three-three tie among the members present, there was no way to move forward, only to stall a final vote until next month's meeting.

Seth could read the disappointment in Abby's face. He waited at the back of the room until the crowd dispersed, then went to join her. She seemed to be fighting tears.

"I'm sorry," he said quietly. "I know you were counting on this going your way tonight."

She looked up at him. "I don't know why I was so surprised," she admitted. "Sandra's never been reticent about her anti-growth view. This is such a modest proposal, though. I was sure she'd see that it's a responsible way to improve the economy out here. And the other two votes to delay? I didn't see those coming, either. How did I misjudge things so badly?"

Jack Ferguson joined them then. "Those two follow Sandra's lead," he said disparagingly. "They haven't had an independent thought in ten years. I should have warned you."

"What am I going to do to convince them?" Abby asked in frustration. "I've already laid out all of my best arguments in favor of this."

"Come on back to the restaurant and have a drink on me," Jack suggested. "We'll talk about it."

Seth nodded, ignoring Abby's obvious reluctance. "Come on. You'll feel better once you have a plan. This is a setback, not the end of the road."

She gave him a grateful look, then nodded. "Okay, lead the way."

She gathered up all of her papers, but Seth took them from her. "Let's put these in your car, then walk to The Fish Tale. The fresh air will clear your head." He glanced at Jack. "We'll be there in a few minutes."

Jack nodded. "I'll have the drinks ready for you. Beer okay?"

"Sure," Abby said.

"Works for me," Seth agreed.

Once they'd deposited all of Abby's presentation materials in the car, he reached for her hand and gave it a comforting squeeze. "You're going to be just fine," he said. "They'll come around, and even if they don't, you're set financially, right?"

"It's not about the money, Seth."

He thought he'd figured that out. "You wanted something to justify leaving your old life and coming back to Seaview Key, didn't you?"

Her startled look told him he'd hit the nail on the head.

"That's certainly part of it," she confirmed. "More important, though, this project was supposed to be my way of making a difference here. I guess I had this grandiose vision of myself riding into town to save the day."

"Or maybe you wanted people to see you in a new light," he suggested. "You wanted to prove to everyone you'd gone away and made something of yourself."

She studied him with a narrowed gaze. "You're digging around in my head now?"

"Am I right?"

She nodded. "Pretty much."

"Well, there's something you missed. It's not about

you at all. Obviously, there are some people like the mayor and her backers who are against change of any kind. They don't see your proposal as the positive thing that you want it to be."

"I get that, but why not?" she asked. "It's not as if I'm planning to put up dozens of little houses and bring in so many people that it will tax the schools or infrastructure out here."

Seth thought about what he'd heard at the meeting, not only from the council, but the murmurings of the people around him in the room. "I don't think it's the scale of the project that's the problem."

"What then?"

"This town started as a humble fishing village, right? It's slowly grown to accommodate tourists during the winter season. They come here because it's quaint and charming."

"Yes," she agreed, looking bewildered. "I'm not going to change that. In fact, I'm doing everything I can think of not to change that. If I'd sold the land, which I easily could have done, I imagine any other developer would be proposing something on a much bigger scale."

"Fair enough, but who do you think will buy the houses in this exclusive development of yours?"

"People with money," she conceded. "Snowbirds, more than likely."

He held her gaze. "Can you see why that might worry the locals? They have modest incomes. What if these people expect all sorts of new amenities that the current tax base can't afford? I imagine there are some people who are barely making it, as it is. If taxes go up, they could be forced to leave Seaview Key."

She looked dismayed by the suggestion. "That's not going to happen," she insisted.

"Can you guarantee that?"

"There won't be that many people. They wouldn't be able to influence the council to vote for something that's not in the best interests of the whole population," she said with certainty. "If I'm right in my assessment of who'll buy the houses, most of them won't even be living here full-time. They won't have a vote."

"Maybe not, but money talks," Seth countered. "Once their friends start to visit, they could start buying other properties. Next thing you know, the island is completely changed. Locals can no longer afford to live here or don't feel comfortable if they do manage to stay. If you study the effects of gentrification in other communities, you see it all the time."

She clearly seemed to be weighing his theory. "You really think that's the root of the problem?" she asked eventually. "People are afraid they'll no longer fit in or be able to afford to stay here?"

He nodded. "I overheard a lot of people complaining about outsiders changing the way of life here. They feel threatened, Abby."

"Tell me the truth, Seth," she said. "How do you feel about Blue Heron Cove? Am I heading in the wrong direction?"

"Personally, I think it will be an asset in the long term," he said. "But I'm new here. I have a different perspective. For people who've built a life here, change is scary. You have to find some way to allay those fears."

He put an arm around her shoulder. "Don't look so defeated. You'll come up with something. You have Jack on your side and Jenny. They wouldn't be supporting you if they didn't see the positive side of this. Let them help you figure out an approach to win over the holdouts before next month's meeting. You didn't lose tonight. The vote was just delayed."

His sentiment was echoed by Jack when they sat at the bar. To Seth's surprise, Jenny was there, too.

"I thought you might be feeling kind of blue," she told Abby. "Don't. Those old stick-in-the-muds will come around. Jack did, once he learned the truth instead of listening to distortions."

"Exactly," Jack said.

"But I used the same arguments on them that convinced you. I don't have anything left in my arsenal," Abby protested. "And Seth just made a good point as we were walking over here. If people are afraid of growth, I don't have any real way to convince them there's nothing to fear."

"Let's focus on the council," Jenny said. "I think the answer is to divide and conquer. I've already invited Sandra to lunch here tomorrow. Told her it was about the fish fry, which is true enough, but we can ease into a few other things while we're at it."

Seth planted an approving kiss on Jenny's cheek. "You're very sneaky," he said.

"It comes in handy from time to time," she agreed, her tone unapologetic. She looked at Abby. "You'll be here?"

"Of course," Abby said. "Thank you so much."

Jenny shrugged. "Don't thank me just yet. Sandra could get up and walk out if she thinks she's been hoodwinked. I'm counting on the manners her mama ingrained in her to prevent that."

* * *

Abby was grateful to Seth for insisting on going back to her place after they left The Fish Tale. She wasn't quite ready to be alone with her disappointment over the way the council meeting had gone. Though she was encouraged by Jenny and Jack's determination to help, she still felt defeated, at least for the moment.

"Tell me something," Seth said, when they were on the porch, coffee in hand. "Why is Blue Heron Cove so important to you? The real reason. I've heard everything you've been telling other people, even me, about making a difference, but I sense there's something more personal at stake, even beyond providing an excuse to come back here."

She gave him a startled look, surprised by his insight. She thought about the past few years, all the doubts that had crept up on her about the person she was. Could she reveal all of that to this man she'd just met? She looked into his eyes as he waited patiently for her answer.

"I need to prove something to myself," she admitted quietly.

"What?" he asked, clearly perplexed.

"That I have something to offer."

"I don't understand. You've already proven that you can be successful in business. Even as little as I know about you, I imagine you gave back plenty when you were in the Panhandle."

She nodded. "I tried, in a lot of ways, as a matter of fact. But to hear my husband tell it, it was never enough."

"I don't get it," Seth said.

"I've already told you that Marshall wasn't overjoyed that I owned a restaurant and refused to give it up. So, he took every opportunity to diminish my accomplishments. If I gave a generous donation to charity, it was never quite enough. If I raised funds for something at the church, it could have been more if I'd devoted a little more time to it. I disappointed him at every turn. Eventually that constant message sinks in. I lost faith in the sort of person I was."

"I probably shouldn't say this about a minister, but he sounds like a jerk," Seth said.

Abby smiled at the heat in his voice. "I thought so, too, at the end, but it took me a long time to get there. I respected him, so I took everything he said to heart. It sapped all the joy out of every accomplishment and, eventually, it sapped the life out of me."

"And that's why you divorced him?"

She nodded. "I had to, before I lost myself forever."

"Good for you."

She smiled. "I was pretty proud of myself, too. I'm not a huge fan of divorce. I think it's too often the first choice and the easy way out. People should at least make an effort to work through their problems."

"Did you try?"

"Marshall didn't think we had any problems to work out," she said with regret. "When he told me that, I knew it was over. You can't fight denial."

"He must have been shocked when you made the decision."

"I think it was just one more time that I disappointed him. He almost seemed to expect it."

"Definitely a jerk," Seth repeated.

She smiled. "No, just a little self-absorbed and demanding. He was good in so many ways. The parishioners loved him. He was always there for them with a kind word or whatever comfort they needed."

"But he wasn't a very good husband," Seth argued.

Abby sighed. "Certainly not the right husband for me," she agreed.

Seth studied her. "So am I getting this right, that it's your self-esteem that's tied up in the success of Blue Heron Cove?"

"Something like that."

"You do know that even if it fails that doesn't make you a failure, right?"

"I'm not sure I can see it that way," she admitted.

"It could be just an idea that's ahead of its time," he said. "It might not be about you at all."

She let his words sink in. "Thank you for reminding me of that," she said. "I think you could turn out to be very good for me, Seth Landry."

"Happy to oblige, but you'd have come to that conclusion on your own eventually. You're a smart woman."

"Smart enough to appreciate a good man when I come across one," she said. "I think I might actually be able to sleep now."

He stood up. "I'll take that as my cue to leave."

Abby stood up and met his gaze. "I'll have to work on coming up with better cues," she teased. "I had something else entirely in mind."

The look that passed over his face was priceless. His expression went from confusion to understanding to unmistakable desire in a heartbeat. And then he chuckled.

"Watch yourself," he warned. "One of these days I'm going to take you up on what you're offering."

Rather than feeling the least bit threatened or looking away as he obviously anticipated, she held her gaze steady. "I'll look forward to it," she said solemnly. "Good night, Seth."

She walked quickly inside and closed the door, then leaned against it and released a sigh. She was playing with fire, no question about it. Then she grinned. She was enjoying every minute of it, too. Maybe the flirting that seemed to go hand in hand with this friendship business was just what she needed, after all.

When Luke finally got home, Hannah looked up from the book she'd been reading. "You look beat. I wasn't sure you'd get the last ferry home tonight. How's Marcia doing?"

He sank down next to her on the sofa. "She'll make it, I think. She's still in the intensive care unit, but her fever finally broke. The antibiotics seem to be working."

"That's great!" she said. "Have you had anything to eat? Want me to fix you something?"

He shook his head. "I just want to take a shower and crawl into bed. How are things around here?"

"Things with me are fine. Your kids called tonight. I told them you'd call back in the morning." She hesitated then added, "And Abby's project didn't get approved at the council meeting."

Luke sat up a little straighter. "Why not? Were you at the meeting?"

"No, but Grandma Jenny called me after it was over. Sandra held out and two others backed her, so they postponed the final vote till next month. With Christmas coming at that point, what are the odds they'll even have a December meeting? They almost always wind up canceling it. I wonder if anyone warned Abby about that?"

"Have you spoken to her?"

Hannah shook her head. "I gather she, Seth, Grandmother and Jack were commiserating and working on a strategy at The Fish Tale after the meeting."

Luke gave her a penetrating look. "Hannah, are you happy about what happened?"

"No, of course not," she said a little too quickly, then winced. "Okay, maybe on some level, I am."

"Why? Are you still hoping Abby will pack up and leave Seaview Key? I thought you'd gotten past that. I thought you were willing to give her a chance, maybe even be friends again."

She gave him a wry look. "That's on my sane and rational days," she said. "This wasn't one of those days."

"Because?"

"I made my reservation to go to New York for the tests," she said.

"Just one reservation? What about me?"

"You've been swamped lately and with Marcia so sick and the kids coming for Thanksgiving, it didn't make sense to ask you to fly up and back while I take a few routine tests. Sue will be around."

Luke frowned. "I'm the one who should be there. I want to be there."

She squeezed his hand. "I know you want to be supportive, but at some point I have to be able to go through these tests on my own without freaking out."

"Why? Surely you're not preparing for some day that's never going to come when I'll abandon you and you'll be left to deal with everything on your own?"

Hannah didn't want to admit that in a moment of desperate insecurity that's exactly what she'd told herself.

"Hannah?" he prodded, then shook his head in obvious frustration. "How am I supposed to convince you that we're solid, that when it comes to this we're a team?"

"We can't be a team, not really," she argued. "I'm the one who's had cancer."

"And I'm your husband," he replied impatiently. "What affects you affects me. If you don't get that, then how can we call this a marriage?" He stood up. "I'm going to bed."

He paused only to give her a lingering, disappointed look, then headed for the stairs.

Hannah stared after him in dismay. What was wrong with her? He wasn't going to abandon her. He wasn't going to turn to Abby. She was driving him away. This was all on her. And if one of these days he did look at Abby or any other woman, she'd have only herself to blame.

She picked up the phone and called Sue. "I'm an idiot," she announced without preamble.

"Could be," Sue said sleepily.

Since having a late-in-life baby, Sue was asleep by ten these days. It was after that now. Still, she didn't scold Hannah for disrupting her rest. Hannah could hear the covers rustling, as she sat up in bed, then her murmured comment to her husband to go back to sleep.

"What makes you think you're an idiot?" she asked Hannah.

Hannah explained what had just happened with Luke.

"Okay, idiot seems a little harsh, but you don't seem to be thinking too clearly. Luke loves you to pieces. If he's free to come to New York, you should let him."

"But you've been my support system from the beginning," Hannah argued, clinging to the sole rational claim she had for what she'd just done.

"And now you have a husband, one who knows a lot more about all the medical mumbo jumbo than I do," Sue reminded her. "Even if he weren't crazy in love with you, he's a better interpreter of all that than I am, so why the reluctance?"

"It's just such a reminder than I'm sick," Hannah said. "I hate having Luke view me as sick or weak."

"First, you're not sick. You've been cancer-free and there's no reason to think that's changed, correct?"

"Yes."

"And, second, do you think there's any way at all that Luke might be unaware of these tests and their implications? He knows they're coming up. If I understand anything at all about him, they were probably on his calendar as well as yours. You're not protecting him, Hannah. You're shutting him out." Sue drew in a deep breath, then asked, "Is this about his old girlfriend being back in town?"

"Sure, that's part of it," Hannah admitted readily. "She's so vibrant and alive. I hate reminding Luke that I could have cancer again at any moment."

"Sweetie, I doubt anyone is more aware of that than he is. He loves you. Let him show that by supporting you."

Sue's frank talk finally registered with her.

"Thank you," Hannah said softly. "You always have known how to cut through my garbage."

"Happy to oblige. If you need me with you next week, let me know. Otherwise, I'm going to assume that you've come to your senses and brought your husband to New York. If the two of you don't come by to see the baby, though, I'm going to be very angry."

"We'll be there," Hannah said, smiling finally. "It'll be fun to see you so totally gaga. You're going to spoil that baby rotten."

"Absolutely," Sue said unrepentantly. "I'm going to leave it to her father to straighten her out."

Laughing, Hannah hung up, turned out the lights and headed slowly upstairs.

In the bedroom, she went to Luke's side of the bed and sat on the edge. "I'm sorry," she said quietly. "I'll call and make a reservation for you first thing in the morning."

He sat up. "Thank you. What changed your mind? Or do I even need to ask. You called Sue, didn't you?"

"The voice of reason," she said wryly. "Yes, I did. Do you mind that she can get through to me, when you can't?"

"I don't mind anything or anyone as long as it gets us on track," he told her. "I love you so much, Hannah. It kills me to think you don't get that, that somehow I'm not showing you how important you are."

"It's not about anything you do or don't do. It's about me. I think the cancer took a toll on more than my body. It sapped me of my self-confidence. I'll try harder to fight these doubts and insecurities that wash over me."

Luke pulled her down beside him. "And I'll be right here whenever you need to be reminded that I'm always going to be in your corner."

She settled into his arms, and for the first time since she'd made her flight and hotel reservation, she felt at peace.

Ten

Seth spent a lot of time lying awake, staring at the ceiling after leaving Abby's. He'd seen her in a totally different light tonight after that council meeting that hadn't gone her way. He'd detected unanticipated vulnerabilities. He'd also identified in new ways with her desire to make a fresh start in Seaview Key. Wasn't that exactly why he was here, too? To put the past behind him?

In a way that made the attraction he felt toward her more dangerous than ever. If she became too approachable, too human, how was he supposed to keep his defenses in place? And those defenses—the ones that kept him from acting on his already confessed desire to sleep with her—could be all that stood between him and unbearable pain, a pain he knew all too well.

He thought back to his feelings for Cara Sanchez. She'd been so blasted strong in the face of battle. She'd seen atrocities no woman—or man, for that matter—should ever have to witness, yet there had been a sweetness about her that had spoken to him. She'd been one of the most optimistic people he'd ever known, one of the funniest. To be able to share laughter with someone at the end of a day filled with horrendous crises had been a gift.

When she'd been killed by a suicide bomber while he'd been on a mission to rescue some injured soldiers who'd been ambushed, he'd been devastated. He'd blamed himself for not being there to protect her, though the truth was, had he been there, rather than in the air in a helicopter, he'd have been killed, too. When he'd called Luke to tell him what had happened, berating himself for failing Cara, Luke had tried to hammer it home that what he was feeling was survivor's guilt, but Seth simply couldn't accept it. Surely there would have been something he could have done.

After that his emotions had closed down. Even though he hadn't been there during the attack, he'd seen enough to know the carnage it would have caused. And no matter how he'd pleaded, his commander had refused to let him view Cara's body. Even now he wasn't sure which was worse, to have seen what remained of the woman he'd loved, or to have his reality-fueled imagination supply the details.

He broke out in a cold sweat just thinking about that day, about coming back to a base that had been partially shattered by an extremist, a guard who'd turned on the American troops he was supposed to be aiding.

The images in his head brought back the anguish, the fury that had overtaken him when he'd realized Cara was gone. He'd lost his mind for a time, wanted to kill the remaining guards to retaliate for the one who'd betrayed them all. Luke's calls and emails had kept him sane, reminding him that Cara wouldn't have sought revenge. She'd known the risks and chosen to be there, had believed the mission to be worthy of the sacrifice. She'd been a hero among many heroes.

With his dream of coming back to the States, marrying Cara and having a family no longer viable, he'd reenlisted and gone back to Afghanistan, where he'd focused a hundred percent on his job, numbed himself to his emotions. Then he'd gotten out of the army and come here.

In an attempt to drive out the memories, Seth got up and made a pot of strong coffee designed to keep him wide awake, because if the images were vivid when he was alert, they were worse when he was sleeping. He'd awakened in a cold sweat more than once, screams echoing in his head.

He took his cup of coffee and went outside. There was a chill in the night air that made him shiver. He gazed up at the stars in the inky sky.

"Are you up there, baby?" he asked, not for the first time. "You're still in my heart, you know."

But there was another woman pushing Cara aside these days, another woman whom he sensed had the ability to sneak into his heart and put him at risk for more pain. The excuses he'd dreamed up to keep distance between them—some valid, some perhaps ridiculous—were all that kept his heart whole.

"I'm not sure I can take that chance," he murmured to himself.

Sure you can.

The voice in his head almost seemed real and so, so familiar. It was Cara's, sweet and softly accented.

You're the bravest man I know.

"Not anymore," he argued with this ghost from the past.

Don't sell yourself short. I'll be disappointed if you don't do enough living for both of us.

With the soft whisper of a sigh against his cheek, she was gone. He knew that when he suddenly felt more at peace than he had in a while.

That didn't mean he was ready for all the complications that Abby represented, he told himself staunchly, but there was no denying the tiny crack in the shield around his heart. He wondered how long it would be before the crack that Cara had started would widen enough to let Abby in.

"You sleep okay last night?" Grandma Jenny asked as she piled a plate with food the next morning.

Seth noticed she'd fixed eggs, bacon, biscuits, all of his favorites.

"Sure," he said.

"Really? Then what were you doing out on the porch for half the night?"

He sighed. Of course she'd caught him. She slept lightly and checked on sounds in the night.

"I was just thinking through a few things," he said.

"How to keep Abby at arm's length?" she guessed.

He chewed his food slowly to put off answering, then managed a suitably bemused tone—or so he thought. "Why would you ask that?"

She merely rolled her eyes. "Do you really need me to spell it out for you? You've been manufacturing all sorts of excuses to avoid her, yet every time I turn around you're right there with her. I think I know a man who's struggling with his emotions when I see one."

"You saw Abby after that meeting last night," he said. "She was totally down. She needed support."

"I was there. So was Jack. You could have come on back here and left us to cheer her up," she said reasonably, then gave him a sly look. “Or didn’t you trust us to be suitably supportive?”

“I’m sure you would have done an outstanding job,” he said, flushing under her scrutiny. “I just figured I could hang out and help, too.”

“Any special distractions you used once you got her home?” she asked.

There was no mistaking the knowing glint in her eyes.

“Of course not,” he said with indignation, well aware of what she was really asking. “I don’t take advantage of vulnerable women.”

She had the audacity to laugh at that. “Whatever you need to tell yourself.”

“I am not having this conversation with you of all people. If you think you get to dig around in my personal business, then it really is time for me to get my own place. With Kelsey and Jeff due home later today, it’s past time, anyway.”

She waved off the threat. “Oh, settle down. I’m just saying you and Abby are two adults who might have a whole lot to offer each other. Seems a crying shame not to take advantage of the opportunity.”

“Would you be so eager for this if you weren’t worried about her having designs on Luke?”

She faltered a little at that. “Okay, maybe that was a consideration at first, but I don’t see the same sparks flying between those two that I do between you and Abby. That’s reassured me I don’t have anything to fear for Hannah’s marriage.”

“I’m glad you recognize that,” he said, thinking it would keep things around here on a more even keel, especially if she could convince Hannah of the same thing.

She gave him a pointed look. “Now I can focus on you,” she told him cheerfully.

The remark sent a shiver of dread down Seth’s spine.

“You need a woman in your life,” she continued. “I’ve been saying that since you got to town. Now fate seems to have brought one and plunked her down in front of you. The way I see it you shouldn’t spit in destiny’s eye.”

Despite his discomfort, Seth couldn’t help laughing. “A very persuasive argument,” he said. “I’ll take it under consideration. I surely wouldn’t want to ignore all this sage advice.”

She gave a little nod of satisfaction. “Good enough, but I’ll have more to say if I don’t see signs of progress.”

“Oh, I can believe that,” Seth said.

Heaven help him!

“Knock, knock!”

Hannah heard her daughter’s voice and immediately abandoned her computer and headed downstairs. Of all the interruptions she’d had recently, this was the most welcome.

“Kelsey, you’re back!” she called out excitedly. “Do you have my precious grandbaby with you?”

“Do you think I’d dare come by without her?” Kelsey replied, a grin on her face as Hannah reached the bottom of the staircase.

The baby held out her arms toward Hannah, a grin splitting her face. “Ga’ma,” she said, straining toward her.

Hannah reached for Isabella and held her close. “How are you, my sweet little angel? I’ve missed you.” She glanced at Kelsey, saw the color in her cheeks and the shine in her eyes. She looked rested and relaxed. "Looks as if the vacation did you a world of good. No problems with the in-laws?"

Kelsey made a face. "Jeff's folks were so gaga over their granddaughter, they didn't have time to make a fuss with us for dropping out of school. Of course, that didn't stop them from making at least one valiant pitch for us to return to Stanford to finish. Frankly, I think that was more about getting Isabella closer to them than it was about college."

"Still, it is something you should think about at some point," Hannah said, drawing a frown. "Okay, okay. I know you're perfectly content running Seaview Inn, but what about Jeff?"

"Jeff has sold two more software programs since he's been here. He doesn't need a degree from Stanford to make his mark in the tech world. We're both doing what we love, Mom. Give it a rest."

Hannah immediately backed off. She should know by now that her strong-willed daughter and doting son-in-law had worked through how they wanted to spend their future. She should be grateful they wanted to be right here, especially with her first grandchild. No matter what she said, she'd be brokenhearted if they went back to California.

"Have you had lunch? Can I fix you something?"

"Just some iced tea," Kelsey replied. "Then I need to get the baby down for a nap. Between all the excitement of new people and new places and jet lag from the red-eye flight last night, Bella's schedule is totally out of whack."

When they were in the kitchen and the baby was in the portable playpen Hannah kept on hand along with several toys, Kelsey looked over the rim of her glass and inquired casually, "So what's this I hear about Luke's old flame being back in town?"

Hannah frowned. What had her grandmother been thinking when she'd told Kelsey about that? "It's no big deal," she assured her daughter. "Abby and I were best friends back then. I'm hoping we can be again. She's actually been very supportive. She's assured me she has no designs on Luke, and I have no reason not to believe her."

"Well, you'll have to excuse me if I keep a close eye on her. I need to see that for myself," Kelsey said protectively.

"I don't suppose your grandmother also mentioned that Abby might have something going on with Seth," Hannah said.

Kelsey looked surprised. "But isn't he a lot younger?"

"A few years, sure. What's the big deal?"

"It just seems weird, that's all."

Hannah chuckled. "You did know that sooner or later he'd meet someone, right?"

"Well, of course," Kelsey said indignantly. "He deserves to be happy. I'm just not sure he needs some cougar chasing after him."

"Wait till you meet Abby. She's not like that," Hannah said. "I think any chasing is pretty mutual."

"If you say so." Kelsey's expression sobered. "How are you feeling?" she asked. "I know your tests are coming up. Are you okay?"

"I haven't found any new lumps, if that's what you're asking."

"I was thinking about your outlook. I know how

panicky you get. Having this Abby turn up can't be helping."

Hannah hated that she hadn't kept her worries from her daughter. She squeezed Kelsey's hand. "I have everything in perspective, I promise."

"Then you're a lot more evolved than I've been giving you credit for," Kelsey said. "If some old flame of Jeff's came around, I'd want to cut out her heart."

"No, you wouldn't," Hannah chided. "You'd keep an open mind. That's what I'm doing."

Just then the baby whimpered before letting out a full-blown squall.

"Oops!" Kelsey said, jumping up to get her. "Looks as if it's past nap time."

With Isabella in her arms and still crying, Kelsey bent down and gave Hannah a kiss. "Love you. We'll see you soon. I'm going to call Grandpa and invite him over for Sunday dinner in a couple of weeks. Is that okay with you?"

Hannah hesitated for only an instant. Her relationship with her father, who'd abandoned her at a young age, was still evolving, but he wanted desperately to make amends. And, she was forced to admit, he'd been trying hard to be a good grandfather to Kelsey.

"Sure," she said, trying to hide any evidence of reluctance. "It'll be good to see him."

Kelsey gave her a long look. "Try to work on being more convincing, Mom. He's trying."

"I know that. Now, give Jeff a hug for me," Hannah told her. "I'm glad you're home."

"Me, too. I couldn't wait to get back." A beaming smile spread across her face. "Do you have any idea how much I love it here?"

Since she'd given up a college degree to stay in Seaview Key, Hannah had some idea. "You're so lucky to have figured out what's right for you at such a young age."

"I'm the luckiest," Kelsey confirmed.

Hannah stood in the doorway as they left. Kelsey settled the baby into her car seat, then got behind the wheel. She waved as they drove away.

As many regrets as she'd had when Kelsey had turned up here, pregnant and determined not to go back to college, she couldn't deny that her daughter was happy. After years of being on their own, just the two of them, in New York, they were now surrounded by family. And wasn't that the most important thing of all? How had she ever lost sight of that?

Abby strolled into The Fish Tale precisely at twelve-thirty, trying to look as if her arrival in the middle of Grandma Jenny's lunch with the mayor were completely coincidental. She even managed to feign surprise when Jenny beckoned her over.

"Abby, why don't you join us?" Jenny said, ignoring Sandra Whittier's suddenly down-turned mouth. "Sandra, you know Abby, of course. You knew her parents, too, I imagine."

Sandra nodded. Her sour expression made it plain she recognized that she'd been set up.

When Abby had pulled up a chair, the mayor scowled at Jenny. "Nothing you have to say is going to convince me to change my mind about this," she told them, her tone unyielding. "Blue Heron Cove is a bad idea and I'll go right on opposing it."

Abby drew in a deep breath and fought for calm. She

remembered everything Seth had said the night before. "Would you mind telling me why?"

Sandra looked startled by the direct question. Or maybe she was more taken aback by the lack of animosity behind it.

"You've been gone a long time, Abby. What do you know about our population?"

"That most people have lived here for years. That some of them have struggled to make a living." She looked the mayor in the eye. "That's one reason I want to do this. I think it will help the economy out here. There will be construction jobs, at least for the next year or two. The owners of these new houses will spend money in the restaurants and businesses."

"Tourists are coming to do that now, and they're not making this island too expensive for people to go on living here," Sandra countered. "We have a lot of folks living on fixed incomes. Taxes go up, they could be chased off."

"Taxes could go down," Abby argued. "Because the value of these properties will be higher than average, the owners will be contributing more to the tax base."

"And expecting more in return."

It was exactly as Seth had predicted, Abby thought, discouraged. How could she possibly prove that the mayor's fears were unfounded?

Jenny had been silent up to now, but she frowned at the mayor. "Why all the negativity, Sandra? Can't you see any of the positives in this? Have you spoken to any of the business owners in town to see how they feel? They're your constituents, too."

For a moment, Sandra looked disconcerted, but then her jaw set. "Someone has to look out for the retirees and the families of the fishermen who started Seaview Key," she insisted. "I intend to be that someone."

"But this could be your chance to make a real difference in this community, to take Seaview Key forward," Jenny protested. "We've been stuck in the same rut for years."

"You've made a nice living in that rut, haven't you?" the mayor retorted. "Why do you suddenly need more?"

"Because I look around and see potential," Jenny told her. "I don't want Seaview Key to change too much, any more than you do. What Abby is proposing seems like the perfect compromise, a compromise whose time has come. Seems to me there are three possibilities. This community can grow in a reasonable way. It can be overwhelmed by some other developer who comes along and isn't sensitive to our way of life here. Or it can die."

"We're hardly at risk of dying," the mayor protested.

"You're wrong," Jenny said flatly. "Young people won't stick around if there are no opportunities here. We're already seeing that, Sandra. We're increasingly a community of seniors on fixed incomes, just as you said. That's a surefire path to dying a slow death."

"What about your own great-granddaughter?" Sandra retorted. "She's chosen to settle right here with her husband and baby."

"Kelsey's an exception to the rule," Jenny granted. "She loves Seaview Inn and the history of the island. The inn can provide a decent income for her. Her husband has the kind of work he's able to do anywhere. Most of our young people don't have that same opportunity. They'll take their talents to someplace where they'll be appreciated, where they can establish businesses that will thrive or work for companies that can pay them well."

She sat back and let her words sink in. Abby fell silent, as well. Her heart dipped when Sandra eventually stood up.

"I'll think about what you said," she conceded grudgingly, then scowled at Jenny. "And out of respect for our long friendship, I won't hold it against you that you got me here under false pretenses."

Jenny grinned, clearly unrepentant. "What false pretenses? I promised you lunch. I'm buying. You got exactly what I said you'd get."

Abby had to swallow a laugh at Sandra's expression. Slowly a smile tugged at the older woman's lips.

"I just wish I'd ordered the steak," she grumbled. "That salad was the cheapest thing on the menu."

Jenny patted the seat beside her. "It's not too late. Sit back down and order it. I'll have one, too."

Sandra merely shook her head. "Another time. If I stay now, heaven knows what you'll try to talk me into."

Once she'd gone, Abby looked at Jenny. "Well, what do you think? Did I get through to her? Did you?"

"Hard to say," Jenny admitted. "She's a stubborn one, but she does have the best interests of Seaview Key at heart. She loves this community as much as I do. I have to believe she'll do the right thing."

"Who do we tackle next?" Abby inquired, eager to continue this campaign to win over the dissenters.

"Hold your horses," Jenny recommended. "Let's see how this plays out. If Sandra comes around, we may not have any more convincing to do. There's such a thing as overselling, you know."

"How are we supposed to know if we need to do more?"

"Jack will hear things," Jenny said confidently. "He'll fill us in on whether the tide's turned. And we have plenty of time."

"But the next meeting is in December," Abby protested.

"It's *supposed* to be in December," Jenny corrected. "We haven't had a December meeting in years. Somebody always moves to postpone it till January."

"They didn't say anything about that at the meeting last night."

"Of course not. But I can just about guarantee someone will float the idea of a postponement, and next thing you know there will be a sign posted down at city hall."

"Isn't that illegal? Shouldn't they vote on something like that in public?" Abby asked.

Jenny merely lifted a brow. "You going to tell Sandra she doesn't know how to run things?"

Abby sighed. "I suppose that wouldn't go over very well," she said dryly.

Jenny nodded approvingly. "Now you're getting the picture. Sometimes you have to recognize where you are and how things work, then bite your tongue."

Abby suspected she was going to wind up biting right through hers before all was said and done.

Eleven

"How'd things go with the mayor today?" Seth asked Abby when he dropped by that evening.

He was starting to accept the fact that he couldn't seem to stay away from her. These visits were going to turn into a nightly ritual, unless he developed a lot more willpower than he currently had…or unless she banished him. This whole friends-first policy was working for now, but it was incredibly hard on his libido. He sensed her frustration from time to time, as well. That didn't mean it wasn't the smart way to go.

"I got a lesson in patience and in small-town politics," she told him. "Apparently this project is going to be a lot more challenging than I thought, and I'm not just talking about winning over the mayor."

He laughed at the hint of annoyance in her voice. "Not so good at being patient?"

"Or at playing games," she said. "I can't imagine why I thought this would be easier than taking on all the city's regulations in Pensacola." She glanced over at him. "Did I mention that there were a number of people who wanted me to open a second restaurant there?"

He shook his head, wondering why she hadn't seized the opportunity. It sounded like the perfect fit to him. "But you said no. Why?" He thought the answer might reveal a bit more about the woman she wanted to become.

"As egotistical as I know it sounds, I envisioned myself rushing back to Seaview Key to save the day," she said, a wry note in her voice. "I was expecting enthusiasm and cooperation. Silly me."

Seth regarded her worriedly. "You're not throwing in the towel, are you?"

"Not a chance," she said with reassuring determination. "I may have been egotistical, but I'm also stubborn. That looks as if it will serve me well right now."

"That's good, then. And enough serious talk for now." He stood up and held out his hand. "Why don't you go for a walk with me? I'll ply you with ice cream. You'll feel better."

She lifted a brow. "Haven't you noticed that the temperature has taken a nosedive? It's not an ice cream kind of night."

"Bet I can keep you warm," he taunted.

She looked startled by his lighthearted banter. "Is that a test of some kind?"

"Could be," he admitted, keeping his tone innocent. "You afraid?"

"Of you?" she inquired. "Hardly. We've established you're all talk."

"Then maybe we should skip the ice cream and head back to my place," he suggested.

A smile tugged at her lips. "Isn't your place Seaview Inn? Do you really want all those interested onlookers around when you're trying to seduce me?" she inquired, taunting him right back in a way that kept his pulse racing. "I heard Hannah's daughter and son-in-law got home today."

Seth winced. He'd actually forgotten about that. Kelsey's return especially definitely put a damper on that plan. She wouldn't hesitate to get up in his business if she disapproved of his relationship with the woman who'd once been involved with her mom's husband. He'd discovered the young woman had absolutely no ability to censor herself, something she'd obviously inherited from Grandma Jenny. Boundaries were a foreign concept to both of them.

"We could stay here," he suggested, "that is, if you have any hot chocolate on the premises. Or we could make Irish coffee."

Abby caught his gaze and held it. Heat turned the cool evening air into something that felt a lot more like a sauna.

"Ice cream is sounding better and better," she said, her voice choked.

"Or does it just sound safer?" he inquired quietly, then asked, "Now who's all talk?" Aware that the dangerous game they were playing was close to destroying their friends-only pact, he once more held out his hand. "Come on, Abby. Let's walk into town."

"I'll grab a jacket," she said.

He had a hunch she needed a few minutes to collect herself more than she needed a coat. Good, he thought, smiling. It was exactly the effect he'd been hoping for. If she was going to accuse him of being all talk, he wanted to make sure it was the sort of talk that would keep her off-kilter. After all, she might as well be in the same rocky boat he was in—wanting something and scared to death to reach for it.

* * *

"I was wondering when I'd finally see you in here," the woman behind the counter at Flavors said when Abby walked in with Seth.

Abby searched her brain, but simply couldn't come up with a name. She studied the dark brown hair that curled wildly, the crystal-blue eyes and plump figure and not a single memory came to mind. She flushed with embarrassment.

"You don't recognize me, do you?" the woman prodded genially. "Mary Margaret Connors. I sat in front of you in just about every class."

Abby suddenly recalled a scrawny girl who'd worn thick glasses and barely said a word. She couldn't reconcile that image with the effervescent woman in front of her.

"I'm so sorry," Abby apologized. "It's been a very long time."

"Plus I was a nerd, so we didn't exactly hang out," Mary Margaret said without any hint of censure. "Welcome to Flavors."

Abby glanced around and mentally compared the bright, cheerful decor of today with the drab, dark interior of the beachfront ice cream parlor she'd remembered. "Didn't your parents run this back then?"

"My mom did," Mary Margaret confirmed. "I took over a few years back. I renovated and brought the place into this century and started making my own ice cream. By the way, I just go by Mary now, Mary Whittier. I married Sandra Whittier's grandson, Kyle."

Abby flinched. "Then I imagine you've been hearing quite a lot about me lately."

"Oh, yeah," Mary confirmed, her eyes twinkling.

"Kyle and I have both been trying to sell Sandra on your plans, but she's stubborn as the dickens. Just give it time. There are plenty of people on your side. Businesspeople in town know this is a real good shot at improving the economy."

"Abby's not the patient kind," Seth chimed in.

Mary chuckled. "If you're going to survive life around here, you'll have to be." She gestured toward the freezer display of ice creams. "I know what Seth wants. He always gets a double scoop of the praline. How about you? What can I get you? The mango gelato is real popular."

"Then I'll have that, just a single scoop," Abby said.

Once they'd been served, Mary headed toward a back room. "Just holler if you need something," she told them. "I'm experimenting with a new flavor. The last batch was disgusting, but I'm determined to figure it out."

When Abby and Seth had taken seats by the window looking out toward the beach, Abby took her first taste of the gelato. "Oh, sweet heaven!" she murmured. "This is amazing. Who would have thought there'd be anything this fabulous created right here?"

"I hear a couple of the specialty stores on the mainland have begged Mary to mass-produce some of her tropical flavors of gelato for their stores. She's refused. She says she'd rather draw tourists out here if they want to taste it."

"Interesting," Abby said, momentarily forgetting about her gelato as she considered what Seth was saying. "I wonder why Sandra didn't mention anything about Mary when we were at lunch. Clearly her granddaughter-in-law is an example of a young person who's not only stayed here, but is doing her part to build the economy. She was certainly doing her best to try to contradict Jenny's characterization of Seaview Key being in danger of dying. Mary and this business should have been a prime example."

"Maybe she didn't want the two of you in cahoots," Seth suggested. "You seem to be like-minded. And Kyle's a good guy. He took over his father's bait-and-tackle store. He's found a way to expand it by setting up a website and selling to fishermen all over the country."

"So obviously not everyone on Seaview Key or even in the mayor's own family is living in the Dark Ages," Abby said thoughtfully.

"Change is coming out here," Seth agreed. "It just has to find its own pace. It can't be rushed."

Abby nodded. "That's just another way of telling me I have to learn patience."

"Exactly."

She savored another spoonful of the gelato, then leaned toward Seth. "So, if I have to wait before taking the next step with Blue Heron Cove, what shall I do to occupy myself?" she inquired, giving him a lingering look.

He grinned. "There's the fish fry," he suggested innocently.

"Under control," she assured him.

"We'll need another fund-raiser of some kind."

"Also under control. I sent out letters today seeking contributions for a silent auction. Any other ideas?"

"I thought you still had a lot to do to get your house in shape."

She noted that he was starting to sound a little desperate, since they both knew exactly the sort of distraction she really had in mind. Or thought she did. While a fling held a lot of appeal, she had a hunch starting something with Seth would quickly turn complicated. It was another slow and steady race, the very kind that made her a little crazy.

"Painting's next," she agreed without much enthusiasm, "but I need to take a trip to the mainland to find what I need for that."

"You want some company for that?" he asked. "I have a day off coming to me."

"And you're willing to go shopping with me?" she asked, surprised.

"You'll be going to some big box store with paint and tools," he reminded her. "Very manly. It's not as if you want to go lingerie shopping." He grinned. "Though that could be fun, too."

Abby could feel the heat climbing into her cheeks as she imagined modeling some lacy confections for Seth's approval. Sweet heaven! She really did have to shift mental gears around this man. She tried picturing Marshall anywhere near a lingerie store, but the image wouldn't come. Seth, however? Oh yeah!

"I think we'll stick to the hardware store this time," she told him a little too breathlessly.

He leaned closer. "Sweetheart, you do realize the image of you holding a hammer is probably just as effective a turn-on as you in lace, right?"

She swallowed hard at the glint in his eyes. "Oh?"

He sat back and shrugged. "What can I say? You're an attractive woman. You get to me. Add in some tools and you're every guy's dream. If you hopped on a riding mower in shorts and a tank top, I'd probably follow you anywhere."

Abby blinked at that. "Then it's a good thing we've both vowed not to give in to temptation," she said, her voice faintly choked.

"I don't recall that," he claimed, though the twinkle in his eyes said otherwise.

"Then thank goodness I'm here to remind you," she said sternly. "Casual. No expectations. That's what we decided."

He shook his head, feigning bewilderment. "Nope. No memory of that."

"Your testosterone must be interfering with your brain waves," she suggested.

He laughed. "Could be. That seems to happen a lot when I'm with you."

Striving to act cool, calm and collected, she patted his hand. "Bear with it. Maybe it will pass."

His expression suddenly sobered and his gaze caught hers. "As smart and sensible as it might be, I don't see that happening," he said softly.

She thought she heard a faint note of regret in his voice. That was just about the only thing that kept her from seizing the moment and dragging him straight back to her bed, where they both so clearly wanted to be.

"Since Marcia's out of the woods, would you mind if I take tomorrow off?" Seth asked Luke. "Could you handle any squad calls that are too tricky for Doug and Scott?"

The two men had taken their EMT training, but still didn't have a lot of on-the-job experience since major emergency calls in Seaview Key were rare.

"That'll work," Luke said at once. "You need to sneak in a couple of days off before I go to New York with Hannah next week." He studied Seth. "Any particular plans?"

"I thought I'd go over to the mainland with Abby. She wants to pick out paint for her house. I can pick up a few supplies for the rescue squad, too. We're low on bandages, gauze and a few other things."

Luke smiled. "Sounds very domestic. Shouldn't you be taking her someplace for a romantic dinner, instead?"

Seth shook his head. "We've established some ground rules," he said. "I laid them out there one night in a move of sheer desperation, but she's apparently taken them to heart."

Luke laughed. "Ground rules, huh? Designed to delay gratification? That's a surefire way to fuel the fire."

"I was thinking they'd slow things down," Seth argued.

"But, of course, the opposite's happened. You're both chomping at the bit to get naked."

Seth sighed. "You have no idea."

"Oh, I have some idea," Luke said. "Hannah and I took our sweet time getting together, too. It was the smart, rational thing to do. We agreed. Drove me flat-out crazy." His gaze narrowed. "Of course, I pretty much knew where we were headed. How about you?"

"I have no idea," Seth admitted. "I still have a lot of reservations about getting involved with anyone. A relationship with Abby seems even more complicated."

"Then you're smart to give it time. She says she's here to stay. So, I hope, are you. It's not the place to be making a mistake it'll be hard to live with in such a small community."

"I don't feel smart," Seth said. "I feel frustrated."

"Get used to it, buddy."

Seth frowned at his friend's unmistakable amusement. "I'm so glad I can provide you with some entertainment. How's Hannah, by the way? Is she freaking out over this trip to New York?"

Luke's expression sobered. "Yes, though she tries to hide it from me. She's terrible at it, though."

"Do you know if she filled Abby in on what's going on?"

"She did. I think Abby was very supportive."

"She wants their friendship back. What can we do to encourage that?"

"Stay out of it," Luke recommended. "If I start pushing for it, Hannah will only question my motives."

"What about me? It'll be a lot easier on us, if Hannah's not regarding Abby with suspicion. Maybe there's something I can do to encourage a reconciliation."

"If you get tight with Abby, anything you push for is likely to be suspect, too," Luke told him. "This will all work out eventually."

"Boy, patience seems to be a consistent theme around Seaview Key," Seth said in frustration.

"You have no idea," Luke responded. "Welcome to a slow-paced lifestyle, my friend."

Seth sighed. It was what he'd claimed to want. Now he just had to figure out how to live with it.

On the trip to the mainland, Seth took care of his errands first, then drove to the nearest big box store for paint and supplies. He figured he was in for a long morning. Not that he'd ever gone shopping for paint with a woman before, but he couldn't imagine that Abby had come with specific ideas in mind.

He should have known better. This was the most organized woman he'd ever met, after all.

She gravitated toward the displays, her eyes lit up. She immediately reached for a pale sage-green paint chip. "This is beautiful," she said. "So soothing. Don't you think so?"

"Sure," Seth said, more interested in the sparkle in her eyes than the paint color.

"Good. I'll probably need three gallons of this for the living room and dining room. Could you have them mix it, while I finish choosing?"

He blinked. "That's it? You're not going to weigh a dozen other colors? There must be a bunch of other paint chips similar to this."

"Why would I? This one's perfect." She shooed him along to find a sales clerk.

Ten minutes later she joined them with paint chips for the bedrooms and both bathrooms, plus the trim. Even the clerk looked impressed.

"Now here's a woman who knows her own mind," he said to Seth. "You're a lucky man. I've seen some guys trail around after their wives for hours, finally pick out a paint and then turn right around and return it the next day."

"That could still happen," Seth said direly, envisioning a trip back to the same store tomorrow.

The clerk shook his head. "Not this time. If I see you in here again, it will be for something besides paint."

Seth might have made him a bet, but Abby was regarding them both with an expression that suggested she wasn't entirely happy about Seth's doubts.

After they'd loaded up the car, he turned to her. "That went a lot more quickly than I'd imagined it would."

She gave him a wry look. "So I gathered."

"How about lunch? We have time before the ferry heads back."

"Lunch sounds good," she said at once. "There's a restaurant I've heard a lot about. I wrote down the address in case we had time. Would that be okay with you?"

"Sure," Seth said, trying to imagine what sort of expensive gourmet restaurant would entice her. He reminded himself it didn't matter. That's what credit cards were for, though his rarely came out of his wallet. He'd always been a pay-as-you-go guy, the exact opposite of his sister Laura.

He set the GPS in the car, following directions that took them to a small, nondescript strip mall. He turned to Abby. "You sure this is the right place?"

She nodded and gestured toward a tiny restaurant at the far end, her eyes alight. "There it is."

He blinked at the sign on the door. It looked to him like a small Mexican grocery store. Since she seemed confident, he shrugged and pulled into a parking space out front. At least it wasn't going to break the bank, that was for sure.

Inside, the heady aroma of spices made his mouth start to water. Although the front of the place was filled with Mexican specialty items, he spotted a few tables in back and a doorway that led onto a small patio with bright fuchsia bougainvillea covering the high privacy fence. Mexican pottery filled with more colorful plants lined the walkways that wound between the tables. It was tiny but utterly charming.

As soon as they were seated, a waiter hurried over

with menus. Abby waved them off. "What do you recommend?" she asked. "What are your specialties?"

His eyes lit up. "You trust me to select," he suggested. "You will be pleased."

"Perfect," she told him, then turned to Seth. "Does that work for you?"

Given the smells emanating from the kitchen as they'd passed through, he was more than willing to go along with it. "Absolutely," he said, earning a delighted smile from their server.

He brought them ice-cold Mexican beers while they waited, then served two hot plates filled with enchiladas, beans, rice and guacamole.

Seth had eaten his share of Mexican food and this looked no different than most. Then he took his first forkful of the succulent stuffed enchiladas and nearly groaned with pleasure.

There was heat and smokiness in the spices and the tenderest beef he'd ever tasted.

"How on earth did you know about this place?" he asked Abby, whose eyes were actually closed as she savored her own first bite.

"I read about it in a guidebook to out-of-the-way restaurants worth finding. Several friends who were visiting the area tried it and raved. They were absolutely right. This food is incredible." She grinned at Seth. "We have to come back. I want to try everything."

The server overheard them and beamed proudly. "I'm so glad you're enjoying it," he said. "My family began this business ten years ago."

"You own it?" Abby asked. "Why haven't you considered expanding?"

"We like this location," he said simply. "We're able

to keep our overhead low, so it helps to keep our prices affordable. There's an immigrant population nearby that relies on us for spices and other items hard to find elsewhere. We might draw fewer tourists, but they leave happy. And we do well enough. Word of mouth keeps us busy."

"I'm not sure I'm going to tell another soul," Abby said. "I want to be able to get a table whenever I come."

He laughed at that. "For you, beautiful *señorita,* I will always find room."

After they'd shared a creamy flan for dessert and had their coffee, Abby spoke with the owner again. She thanked him profusely for the meal and his hospitality.

"We'll be back. I promise you that."

"*Gracias.* I will look forward to it," he told her.

In the car, Seth glanced over at her contented expression. "Is that all it takes to make you happy? A great meal?"

She turned to him. "It's not the only thing, but it certainly is an excellent start. Thank you for bringing me here."

"It was my pleasure. It's one of the best meals I've had in a long time." He winked at her. "The company was pretty good, too."

And better than either of those things, in some ways, was the reassurance that Abby didn't require candlelight, champagne and filets mignons to be happy. Perhaps they were more alike than Seth had realized. Another crack appeared in his defenses.

Back on Seaview Key, Abby invited Seth to stay for iced tea. When they were settled on the porch, a deep sense of contentment stole over her. There was only one thing nagging at her about an otherwise perfect day.

"Seth?"

"Yes?" he murmured, his eyes half-closed as he rocked slowly beside her.

"Why did you seem so surprised by the restaurant I chose? I know it was kind of out-of-the-way, but it was more than that, wasn't it?"

He nodded. "I was expecting you to choose something fancy," he admitted.

"And expensive?" she asked, beginning to see the problem.

"Okay, yes," he admitted. "You owned an expensive restaurant. You're obviously used to gourmet food."

"I'm used to *good* food," she corrected. "And I don't think I've had anything much better than what we had today. Fancy has its place, but so does excellent regional or ethnic cooking." She studied him for a long time, then asked, "We've touched on this before, but I have to ask again. Should I be worried that there seems to be some reverse snobbery going on here?"

To her regret, he sighed, all but confirming her impression.

"I'm working on it," he admitted. "I haven't run across many women like you."

"Good thing or bad?" she asked.

"I'm actually beginning to see it in a much more positive light," he admitted.

"I'm not going to apologize for having money or for the life I've led," she told him. "I worked hard. I earned whatever success has come my way."

"I wouldn't want you to apologize for that. I just have to figure out how a guy like me fits in."

She smiled at that. "There's always room for a good guy in my world," she told him. "In any world. I think you bring a lot to the table."

"Oh?" he said, as if he was unsure of what those attributes might be.

She studied him intently. "You really don't know, do you? I don't think I've ever known a man as decent, kind and generous as you or as sexy and funny, who didn't know his own value. I've known a lot of men with less to offer who have hugely overblown egos." She allowed herself a thorough once-over, then grinned. "I have to admit you're a lot more attractive."

She expected the usual cocky, masculine grin in response, but instead he simply seemed to relax. He actually looked as if he'd needed the reassurance.

Amazing, she thought. All that appeal and he was unaware of it. That's when she realized just how much trouble she was in, because in that moment, it was no longer about an attraction that wouldn't quit. In that instant, she fell just a little bit in love.

Twelve

Abby looked up to find Hannah standing in the doorway, trying hard to smother a laugh apparently.

"What?" Abby inquired testily.

"I'm amazed any paint is actually on the walls," Hannah said. "Looks to me as if most of it is on you. You'd make a good partner for the Incredible Hulk now. Isn't he the giant green guy or is that the Green Hornet? Or maybe I'm thinking of the Jolly Green Giant."

"Ha-ha," Abby said. "It's been a long time since I've painted anything. It's taken a while to get the hang of it."

"Maybe you should have asked Seth for his help," Hannah suggested slyly.

"If you're trying to figure out what's going on with us, just ask," Abby grumbled. "He was more than willing to help, but I wanted to do this on my own."

"Another part of the reinvention of Abby Miller?" Hannah asked.

"Something like that." She gave Hannah a stern look. "If you promise to stop making fun of me, I'll invite you in for iced tea. I even have fresh blueberry scones. I've been feeling domestic."

Hannah immediately held up her hands in a gesture of surrender and plastered a serious expression on her face. "Not even a chuckle," she promised.

"Go on in the kitchen," Abby suggested. "Let me at least get some of the paint off my hands and face and I'll be right there."

"I'll pour the tea," Hannah said.

By the time Abby joined her, Hannah had also found the scones and warmed them in the oven. Her mouth was full, her eyes twinkling.

"Sorry," she mumbled. "I couldn't wait."

Abby laughed. "So, what brings you by this morning. Isn't this your usual writing time?"

"I sent off the latest manuscript yesterday, so I'm suffering from postpartum letdown today. I decided to see what you were up to and to issue an invitation."

Abby regarded her with surprise. "I haven't even reciprocated for the last dinner," she said.

"Not a problem," Hannah said. "This is for Thanksgiving. As hard as it is for me to believe since it's still hot as Hades around here, Thanksgiving is only two weeks away. I'm trying to get all the details under control before I head to New York later this week."

Abby thought she detected fear behind the casually spoken words. "Your tests?"

Hannah nodded.

"How long will you be gone?"

"Just two nights, but with the weekend in there, it will be a few days after that before I know all the results."

"How are you doing with that? The waiting, I mean. I already know you're worried about the tests."

Hannah's expression turned wry. "You'd think I'd be used to it, but I'm not."

"Luke's going along?"

Hannah nodded. "At first I told him he didn't have to, but it was pointed out to me that I wasn't protecting him or being brave. I was just shutting him out."

"Sounds like sensible advice," Abby said.

"I can always count on my friend Sue for that," she said, then hesitated before adding, "The way I used to count on you."

It was hard to tell if her tone reflected more nostalgia or bitterness, but Abby chose not to let the way the words hurt reflect in her response. "You can count on me again, Hannah," Abby said, though even as she uttered the reassurance, she knew that gaining Hannah's trust was going to be a process. Her words alone would never be quite enough.

"One of these days I hope you'll test that," she added.

"Baby steps," Hannah responded. "I hope you understand. It's not as if you did anything wrong back then. But watching you and Luke, it hurt. Nobody's fault, of course, but that didn't lessen the way it felt at eighteen."

"Of course I understand," Abby said, aware of how painful it must have been and the fear—albeit an unwarranted fear—that it could be repeated. "And thank you for wanting to include me on Thanksgiving."

Hannah smiled. "It was my idea, but I also had a hunch that Seth would spend the meal in a funk if you weren't at the table."

Abby grinned. "I'd like to think so, too."

"I can't wait to see for myself how things have changed since the two of you came for dinner," Hannah admitted. "And Kelsey is anxious to meet you. I should also warn you that my father will be there with his wife, as well as my half-brother and his family."

Abby regarded her with shock. "What? When did you find your father? I thought he hadn't been in touch for years."

Her stunned reaction only deepened as Hannah described the letters she'd found hidden away in her mother's dresser, Luke's efforts to locate Clayton Dixon, only to find him less than an hour away on the mainland, and the awkward reunion that had paved the way for establishing a new relationship.

"Kelsey is absolutely thrilled to have more extended family here and I'm trying to make peace with the past," Hannah told her. "Things weren't the way I thought. He never abandoned me, not the way I believed he had. He tried to keep in touch."

"I can't believe your mother and grandmother hid the truth from you," Abby said.

"It was complicated," Hannah conceded. "A lot more complicated than I could have understood as a child."

"What about after you grew up?"

Hannah shrugged. "They thought they were doing what was best. Grandma Jenny concedes now that it was a mistake, but their intentions were good. I've managed to accept that. There's not much point in holding a grudge now."

"But he has this whole other family?"

"My half-brother is a great guy," Hannah said. "I've enjoyed getting to know him and his family. My stepmother, who set events in motion back then, is a piece of work, but I've even come to accept that she wasn't reacting rationally back then."

"That's all very evolved of you. I'd want to rip her hair out."

"It was my dad who had the affair and got her pregnant," Hannah said. "That gave her the ammunition she used to try to blackmail him into marrying her."

The story got more outrageous by the minute. "Hold on," Abby said. "She actually blackmailed him?"

Hannah nodded. "She threatened to go after Seaview Inn. Of course, she didn't know that it was in my grandmother's name. She'd never have gotten her hands on it. I guess my dad was torn. He thought the only way to keep her from causing trouble was to give in and keep her away from us. Or maybe he actually loved her and that was just the excuse he needed to make the break from my mom and me."

Abby sat back in amazement. "Wow!"

Hannah chuckled at her reaction. "Yeah, that was pretty much my response when I finally had all the pieces of the puzzle."

"And this wife of his is coming for Thanksgiving dinner, too?"

"Yes." Hannah grinned. "Have I scared you off?"

"Not a chance. This may be the most fascinating Thanksgiving dinner I've been to in years. I've spent most of the holidays in recent years at the restaurant on the fringes of a few bizarre family celebrations, but this will be the first time I've been in the middle of one."

Hannah gave her a long look. "You do see that this may be your first real test of whether you're serious about being friends again," she said. "If you can survive this, I'll have no choice but to give you a chance."

"I'm definitely up for the challenge," Abby told her.

She set her glass of tea on the table and leaned forward, taking Hannah's hand in hers and giving it a squeeze. "And if there's anything you need before, during or after this trip to New York, just ask, okay? I know you have the support of your friend in New York, but I'm right here, even if all you need to do is come over here to scream your head off where Luke and the rest of the family won't hear you."

Tears welled in Hannah's eyes at the offer. "Don't be surprised if I take you up on that." She wiped her eyes, then stood. "I'd better run. I have lots to do before we leave."

"What can I bring for dinner on Thanksgiving?" Abby asked.

"Just yourself. Between me, Grandma Jenny and Kelsey, the food's under control."

"I could bake a pecan pie or two, the kind my mama used to make."

Hannah's eyes lit up. "I wouldn't say no to that. I'll see you then."

"Or sooner, if you need me," Abby reminded her.

She watched Hannah walk away and sighed. She regretted so much that there wasn't more she could do to make the next few days easier for her old friend. Looking skyward, she murmured, "God, please let her be okay."

Maybe prayers were the best thing she had to offer.

Seth showed up at Abby's prepared to help with the painting, only to walk into a living room that smelled of fresh paint. The floors had been polished and the furniture was back in place. Abby stood back while he surveyed the room, a self-satisfied expression on her face.

"More evidence of what an overachiever you are," he commented. "It looks good."

He stepped closer and spotted a few specks of paint she'd missed on her forehead. He rubbed at them with his finger. "Did you leave that there so I'd know you did the work yourself?"

Abby laughed. "Hardly. There was a lot of paint on me. I was bound to leave some behind, though I tried really hard to scrub it all off."

He surveyed her. "I don't see any more. Want me to conduct a more thorough inspection? Maybe hop in the shower with you and give you a thorough washing myself?"

"You wish. What I really want is a fish dinner."

"Absolutely," he said. She deserved that and more after what she'd accomplished today.

"You sure I look presentable enough to be seen in public?"

He lifted a brow. "You fishing for compliments? I didn't think that was your style."

"Every woman could use the occasional compliment," she chided. "I'm no exception."

"Then let me assure you that you look as beautiful as ever. Now grab a jacket and let's head to the restaurant before I start getting other ideas."

"To hear you tell it, you always have other ideas," she retorted.

Seth laughed. "I do at that, so give me some credit for my amazing restraint."

"I don't know. It's beginning to take a toll on me."

"Me, too, sweetheart. Me, too."

He noticed that she looked exceptionally pleased to hear that. This game to see which of them would fold first had probably been a bad idea. The stakes seemed to be climbing every time they got together.

At The Fish Tale, Seth and Abby found all the booths taken, so they took seats at the bar. Jack immediately served cold beers, then took their orders.

"You been painting?" he asked Abby.

She flushed and whirled on Seth. "You told me all the paint was gone," she accused.

Jack looked bewildered. "I just heard a rumor earlier that you'd been tackling that house of yours on your own."

Abby sat back, looking embarrassed. "Sorry. I have been, but I managed to paint myself almost as thoroughly as the living room. I'm a little sensitive about that."

Jack frowned at Seth. "What's wrong with you? Why weren't you over there helping?"

"Hey, I volunteered. She has an independent streak. She wanted to prove something."

Jack shook his head. "My Greta pulled that on me a time or two."

"How'd you handle it?" Seth asked.

"I ignored her and pitched in, anyway. She scowled a lot but things got done a lot faster. Even she couldn't deny that. She even thanked me once."

Seth glanced at Abby. "That might not be the best approach with my friend here."

She nodded approvingly. "Smart man. However," she began with obvious reluctance, "if you offered again, I might be willing to let you help with the bedrooms."

Seth caught her gaze. "Painting, you mean?"

Jack swallowed a guffaw, then quickly turned away.

Abby frowned at Seth's teasing. "Yes, painting,

though I'm suddenly having second thoughts about that."

"Let the man help," Jack recommended, giving her a wink. "It hurts our egos to think we're not needed."

"Seth's ego seems just fine to me," Abby commented.

"Nope, it's seriously wounded," Seth claimed.

Abby merely rolled her eyes. "Then the guest room is all yours," she soothed.

"Not your room?" he asked.

She barely managed to conceal the grin tugging at her lips. "I thought we'd agreed that room was off-limits."

Jack's face turned red. "I'll go get your meals," he said, backing away.

"Now you've gone and embarrassed him," Seth said.

"Me? You're the one who kept poking away at all this talk about bedrooms. You seem a little obsessed."

Seth held her gaze, then released a sigh. "I think maybe I am," he admitted.

It was definitely worrisome.

It had been days since Seth had heard anything from either of his sisters. Crazy him, he'd assumed that meant they'd worked things out. Instead, he found legal papers seeking his presence for a deposition back home. It appeared Laura was going ahead with her lawsuit.

He punched in her number on his cell phone. "Why are you dragging me into this?" he demanded when Laura answered. "You already know what I'm going to say. I'm not going to be on your side. Didn't you tell your attorney that?"

"He says he can make you a hostile witness," she claimed defensively.

"So he can get me to say what? That Meredith is the wrong person to be handling the estate? She's not. That you're responsible enough to handle your own inheritance? You're not. Stop this nonsense, Laura, before it gets out of hand and the only people with any money are the lawyers."

"I don't know what else to do," she lamented. "I have to have that money, Seth. I'm in trouble and Meredith won't help."

He calmed down enough to hear the genuine panic in her voice. "What do you mean you're in real trouble?"

"I can't pay these credit card bills. I'm barely making rent and utilities. I've thought about trying to get a second job, but then I won't have any time for Jason."

Alarm bells went off. "Are you and Jason seeing each other again?"

"Not really, but I keep hoping he'll change his mind," she admitted.

"Oh, Laura, don't count on that," he said gently. "As for those bills, see a credit counselor. Maybe he can help you work things out."

"Meredith could solve it all with the stroke of a pen," she countered bitterly.

"Until the next time."

"There won't be a next time," she promised. "I've learned my lesson. I'm determined to prove that to you, Meredith and to Jason."

"Honey, I think your ex-husband might be a lost cause," he dared to suggest.

"Don't say that," she pleaded, crying.

"It's time to face facts," Seth said. "He gave you plenty of chances to fix things and you kept right on spending."

"It was an addiction," she said. "Seriously. Like drugs or something."

"But you're cured now?" Seth asked skeptically.

"I am. I see how messed up my life was because of all that shopping. I had closets filled with stuff I didn't need or even want. It was crazy."

Seth could hardly disagree with that. He wanted to believe she'd honestly changed, but how could he? All of her husband's threats and pleas hadn't forced her to get control of her spending habit. Why should he believe her now?

"These credit card bills of yours," he began. "How recent are the charges?"

Silence greeted the question. "What do you mean?" she asked in a small voice.

"It's an easy question. Are these old charges or recent ones?"

"I've bought a few things recently," she admitted. "Just things I needed to fix up my new apartment and to look good for work."

"You didn't have enough furniture in that huge house you insisted Jason buy for you?"

"It was all wrong for the apartment," she responded defensively.

"And the clothes, when we've already established that you had a closet filled with things you hadn't worn?" he asked wearily.

"They were either too casual or too fancy for work," she claimed.

"How much have you spent in, say, the last month, Laura?"

"A thousand dollars, maybe a little more," she revealed eventually.

"How much more?"

"Okay, closer to three thousand."

Seth heaved a sigh. "And you think that's proof you've changed? Does your attorney agree? If he does, you need a new attorney, one who's not just ripping you off."

Laura began crying in earnest. "Seth, please, talk to Meredith. There's plenty to pay these bills with enough left for me to start over."

"Start over doing what? Going shopping? Sorry, I can't do that. And you need to have this request for a deposition withdrawn, understood? I'm not being dragged into the middle of this. And you're just throwing good money after bad, if you keep pursuing it."

"I hate you," she shouted as he hung up.

Seth closed his eyes. Yeah, he got that. If there had been even a tiny hint that his sister had really mended her ways and was trying to get her life back on track, he'd have paid her blasted bills himself. How could he, though, when she clearly wasn't even trying, just looking for an easy way out of the mess she'd gotten herself into. He shook his head and sympathized with his parents just a little. Tough love really was a pain.

Abby noticed that Seth was awfully quiet when he showed up to help her finish painting. He was brooding about something, but she wasn't entirely sure whether it was her place to pry.

She put him to work in the guest room, then returned to the master bedroom to finish in there. The fact that he didn't complain or utter even a single taunting remark about that was more proof of his lousy mood.

She finished the trim, cleaned up her brushes and

took a shower, while he kept right on working, his silence deafening.

Once she was cleaned up, she popped a homemade lasagna into the oven, then went into the guest room.

"Dinner will be ready soon, if you want to wash up."

"Sure," he said. "I'm almost done in here."

She stood in the doorway, hands on hips when he didn't even turn to look at her.

"Okay, that's it. Put down the brush right now."

He finally glanced her way, his expression startled. "What?"

"You've been fretting about something since you got here. I swore I wasn't going to pry, but I've changed my mind. I want to know what's going on. Did something happen with a patient today?"

His expression shut down even more, something she hadn't thought possible.

"No, nothing like that."

"Then what?"

"I'm not going to dump my problems on you," he said stiffly.

"You already have. You're here, but you'd clearly rather be somewhere else. Talk to me."

He finally met her gaze. "You'll regret asking," he warned.

Abby frowned. "Why would you say that? We're friends. If something's worrying you, maybe I can help. At the very least I can be a sounding board."

"But we're the kind of friends who joke around, maybe flirt a little."

She had never been more insulted in her life. "If that really is all you believe is going on between us, maybe you should leave."

He seemed genuinely startled. "You want me to go?"

"If you think our relationship is that shallow, then yes, I do."

He stood there, the paintbrush in his hands dripping onto the drop cloth on the floor, looking so thoroughly bewildered that Abby almost took pity on him and retracted her words. Instead, she bit her tongue and waited to see what he would do. She sensed this was a real turning point for them. Either something of substance would evolve or the game would end.

He finally nodded. "Let me clean up and I'll join you on the porch."

"Is this the sort of conversation that could use a glass of beer or wine?" she asked. "Or will iced tea do?"

He smiled ever-so-slightly. "Tea will do."

Abby rocked as she waited for him on the porch. When he came outside, he sat in the chair next to hers, but for once he didn't set the rocker into motion.

"I had a conversation with one of my sisters earlier," he finally blurted. "It didn't go well."

"I see," she said, though that didn't explain much. "Everything okay back home?"

"Hardly." He took a deep breath and in halting, frustrated words explained the situation. "So here I am, caught in the middle. I feel like a heel for not helping Laura out, either by lending her some money or siding with her against our older sister, but I know neither of those solutions is really the answer."

"It sounds to me as if you took the only stance you could," Abby told him.

"Then why do I feel so lousy?"

"Because you're a good guy. You love your sister and

want her to straighten out her life, but you can't make that happen, Seth. It's up to her."

"She is right about one thing. The inheritance could get her out of this financial mess."

"And then what?" Abby asked reasonably. "It seems to me your parents knew what they were doing."

"Yeah, I think so, too," he admitted. "That doesn't make it any easier to see her hurting." He glanced at Abby. "Thank you."

"For what?"

"Listening, I guess. Not making me feel like a louse for not bailing her out."

"What you did took guts," she told him. "It would have been easy to give in, then turn your back on the consequences. You're trying to help. So were your parents, even though it sounds as if they were at least partly responsible for Laura's attitude toward money. Your older sister must feel terrible, too."

"Meredith's a wreck," he acknowledged. "She's ready to cave in, let Laura have the money and call it a day."

"But that wouldn't be the end of it. It sounds as if Laura needs help with her problem. She's right. It probably is an addiction. She wouldn't be the first woman—or man, for that matter—to go wild with money. And I suspect she's far from the first to have it cost her a marriage."

She studied Seth for a minute. "Does all this have something to do with why you're so sensitive to financial stuff with me?"

"Sure," he said at once. "Having money can be great, but it can also change people. My parents were driven to stash away what to them seemed like a small fortune so they could leave behind something for the three of us. I didn't want or need some nice inheritance. I'd have preferred it if they were around more. Meredith gets what they sacrificed and appreciates it, but not Laura. She just feels entitled."

Abby frowned. "And you see me in whom? Your folks? Laura?" Neither was particularly flattering.

"No way," he said fervently. "But at first, I wasn't so sure how having money had affected you. It made me skittish, no question about it."

"And now?"

He smiled. "I've discovered that you may be the most sensible, grounded woman I know."

"Thank you for saying that. I didn't always have money, Seth. I've told you that. I don't think having it has changed me. I certainly don't want it to. And if you're worried about whether I'm anything like your sister, you can go inside and check my closets."

"Aren't they in that room that we've agreed is off-limits?" he teased, lightening up for the first time since the sensitive conversation had begun.

"I'll make an exception for this," she told him, chuckling. "But I can tell you what you'll find. They're half-empty. I have a few designer things because they were expected with the restaurant clientele, but you'll mostly find things just like this." She gestured toward the jeans and T-shirt she'd put on after her shower.

"Good to know," he said, his eyes darkening with desire as he took a lingering survey. "You look great, by the way. My kind of woman."

Abby allowed herself a smile at that. It was the sweetest, most promising thing he'd ever said to her. Maybe they were finally edging toward that relationship of substance she'd hardly dared to imagine. She couldn't help wondering, though, how many more hurdles they'd have to face before Seth acted on the unmistakable desire that was always simmering between them. Or what it would take to allay his deep-rooted fear that her money would somehow come between them.

Thirteen

By Saturday Abby knew that Hannah and Luke had to be back from their trip to New York, but she'd heard no news about how the cancer screenings had gone. It was one more reminder that she and Hannah weren't back on their old footing, not like the days when they'd been on the phone a half dozen times a day to share confidences about everything going on in their lives.

She debated barging in on Hannah and pushing for answers, but that didn't seem wise. Hannah had to come to her.

But, Abby argued with herself, what if the news had been bad and she needed support, but couldn't bring herself to ask for it? She tried reminding herself that it was unlikely that Hannah even had the results yet, but surely she'd developed instincts about how things had gone.

"I'm at a loss," she told Seth when she met him for Sunday lunch at The Fish Tale. Grandma Jenny, Hannah and Luke, and Kelsey and her husband had begged off this week, according to Seth. She found that even more worrisome. "Has Luke said anything? Were the test results bad?"

"He hasn't said a word to me. They may not even know the results yet."

"And I don't suppose you've thought to ask," she said with frustration.

"I figured Luke would tell me whatever he wanted me to know," he said.

"Of course you did." It was a typically male attitude, she thought irritably. Even she subscribed to it on occasion, but not when it came to something this important.

Seth frowned. "If you're really worried about Hannah, go by to see her."

"We're not exactly there yet," Abby admitted.

"Thanksgiving's later this week. You'll see her then," he reminded her.

"That's hardly the right occasion to get into the state of her health. From what she told me, Thanksgiving dinner is bound to be chaotic."

"Then I don't know what to tell you," he said, clearly giving up any attempt at a solution and apparently tired of the topic.

She regarded him with amusement. "It's a good thing you have lots of other things going for you, because you're not being real helpful right now."

"Hey, I'm a guy. I don't meddle. That was my best attempt at being supportive."

Abby shook her head. "And it was a pitiful one," she chided. "You're Luke's friend and I know you're a compassionate man. What you did for Ella Mae demonstrated that. I also know you care about Hannah. This situation should be on your radar."

"It is on my radar. I'm worried about her, too," he

insisted. "But there's this whole other layer to your worrying. It's all wrapped up in the dynamics of your relationship. You're feeling left out. Hannah's silence reminds you that things aren't back to normal between you."

Abby stared at him with surprise. "I might be forced to take it all back. Apparently you do have a sensitive bone in your body. Decent insight, too."

Seth laughed. "Thank you for that high, if grudging praise."

"I always give credit where credit's due," she said, then decided a change of subject was definitely in order, since this one was going nowhere. "Now let's talk about you. Anything new from your sisters?"

His expression immediately turned sour. "Still warring," he said tersely.

"Oh, Seth, I'm sorry. What about the deposition? Did Laura withdraw that request?"

He shook his head. "Looks as if I'll have to do it, though I've told the attorney it will have to be done down here. With my job, I can't get away to go there. He seems perfectly happy to spend my sister's money flying down to Florida for a couple of days far away from the cold weather, even though I was very clear that it was unlikely I'd say anything that might be helpful to Laura's case."

"Shouldn't that tell Laura something?"

"It should, but it hasn't," he said with a sigh of regret. "Let's talk about something else. How about the fish fry? How's that coming?"

Abby smiled for the first time since they'd sat down. There was lots of good news to impart on that front.

"Between Jenny and Ella Mae and this competitive

thing they have going, tickets are almost sold out and it's not even December."

Seth whistled. "Amazing."

"Isn't it? And the fish fry's not till January. Lesley Ann and Jack suggested we might want to hold a second one, since tourists haven't even had a crack at the tickets yet. The fishermen are apparently agreeable."

"You going to go for it?"

"Are *we* going to go for it?" she corrected. "You're part of the decision-making team."

"One with absolutely no opinion about this," he replied. "You're the expert."

"I think we should do it," she said. "There's almost no overhead since the fishermen are donating their catches and a couple of the women's groups from churches on the island are supplying the rest of the food at no cost. The printer on the mainland donated the flyers, too, so everything we make is pure profit."

"How'd you talk the printer into that?"

She grinned. "Turned on my Southern charm."

"So he didn't stand a chance," Seth concluded.

"I'd like to think it was more about his compassionate nature and recognition of what a worthy cause this is." She grinned. "And the bonus that he grew up out here."

"Aha! The secret weapon," Seth said. "How'd you know that?"

"His mom tipped me off," she admitted.

He lifted a brow. "And that silent auction thing? Has the same technique worked for that?"

"As a matter of fact, donations have been pouring in," she said happily.

"No arm-twisting involved?"

"Oh, maybe a little here and there," she confessed. "Some of the fancier shops on the mainland expect that."

"Fancy, as in expensive?"

She nodded. "I was able to persuade a jewelry store in Naples to donate a watch and a few boutiques to give us gift certificates."

He regarded her with suspicion. "I don't suppose you were giving your own credit card a workout at the same time, were you?"

"Only for things I'd have bought anyway," she admitted. "That's how it works. As soon as they see the upside business potential, they tend to hand over whatever I've asked for." She frowned at his expression. "This isn't the same as Laura, Seth. It's all for a good cause."

"It just seems like another way that you're subsidizing all this without actually writing another big check," he said.

"No, it's leveraging relationships. If I'm a valued customer, then the store owners want me to be happy. And, again, don't lose sight of the goal. This boat could be the difference between life and death for residents out here."

He sat back, his expression resigned. "True, but it seems you've been doing most of the work. Where do I fit in?"

"When we start doing media for the second fish fry and the silent auction," she said at once. "I want Hannah to make sure all the newspapers and TV stations talk to you about the importance of acquiring this rescue boat."

She chuckled when he cringed. "Camera shy? Don't be. You're articulate and gorgeous. Every single woman on the mainland will flock out here just to get a glimpse of you." She paused as another idea struck. "Maybe we should include a bachelor auction, too. By combining that, the second fish fry and the silent auction into one big, easily promoted event, we'll come awfully close to making our goal."

"Bachelor auction?" he asked warily. "Are you thinking I'll parade down some runway and let women bid on me?"

Abby nodded. "You and a few other men."

He was shaking his head before she had the words out. "Not a chance," he said.

"Oh, come on. It could be fun."

His gaze narrowed. "You wouldn't mind a bunch of women ogling me and throwing their money around to get a date with me?"

She hesitated. "Would I be jealous? Is that what you're asking?"

He nodded, an annoying smirk on his face.

Abby thought about the scenario he'd described. She'd actually hate it, but then she reminded herself it was for a good cause. Besides, speaking of leverage and relationships, Seth didn't need to know how much it would bother her.

"No reason to be jealous," she told him. "We're friends. No benefits. Those were the rules."

He looked taken aback by the reminder. That smirk turned to a frown. "Okay, then, if it won't bother you, I'm in."

Check and checkmate, Abby thought, regretting her impulsive idea. Too late to change her mind now. She'd just have to suck it up and pretend she didn't care if some beautiful, sexy young honey won a date with him.

"This is going to be great," she said with feigned enthusiasm.

"And you think it will put us over our goal? You're actually telling me we could pay for this boat by the end of January?" he asked incredulously.

Seth's evident astonishment pleased her. "I can't be a hundred percent sure, but it looks that way." She grinned at him. "Told you I knew what I was doing."

He shook his head. "I can't believe it."

"Well, it's possible we might need one more event in February," she cautioned. "But I really doubt it."

"And then our job will be done," he said, holding her gaze.

Abby almost thought she heard regret in his voice. "I thought you'd be happier."

"I'm thrilled about the boat," he said at once.

"But?"

"I thought there'd be more to do."

She finally thought she understood what was bothering him. "You do know that finishing up this project doesn't have to mean the end of us spending time together," she said carefully. "At least not if we don't want it to. How much time have we really spent working together on the fund-raisers, anyway?"

He seemed taken aback that she was being so direct. "We agreed," he began, but Abby cut him off.

"What we agreed was that we'd play it casual while we were working on the fund-raisers and see where things led." She looked him in the eye. "I like where things have been leading. What about you?"

"I like where we are, too," he admitted.

"Then is there some reason we need to quit spending time together just because the excuse Luke gave us has come to an end? Or are you worried that you'll fall for whoever wins you in the auction?"

"Not likely," he said, dismissing the possibility.

She held his gaze. "Of course, if we do keep seeing each other, we might be forced to admit that all these get-togethers of ours have actually been personal all along," she said.

Seth looked momentarily startled, then chuckled. "I think that ship pretty much sailed a while back."

A grin spread across Abby's face at his acknowledgment of the truth. "I'm relieved you saw that, too."

"There are still a lot of reasons we should probably be cautious," he warned.

"Small-town gossip?" she suggested.

"And the fact that I have a lot of emotional baggage," he admitted.

She laughed at that. "Don't we all? Come on, Seth. Let's not get too far ahead of ourselves. The one-day-at-a-time philosophy we adopted from the get-go can still apply. I'm not so ancient that I see time slipping away. I'm in no rush."

He looked momentarily relieved by her words, but then an unsettled expression crossed his face.

"What?" she asked.

"Where do you see this going, Abby? All joking aside."

"I haven't asked myself that," she claimed.

"To bed or down the aisle?" he pressed.

"Either. Both. I have no idea. What about you? Have you given the future any consideration?"

"The ending I see scares me to death," he admitted.

"Why?"

He hesitated for a long time. "Because the last time I felt this way about anyone, it didn't end well," he revealed eventually.

"You broke up?"

He shook his head. "She was a nurse in a combat zone. She was killed by a suicide bomber."

Shocked, Abby immediately reached for his hand. "Seth, I am so, so sorry. I can't imagine the kind of pain that caused you."

"That's what I meant about baggage, Abby." He held her gaze. "Can you understand why I might not want to risk ever feeling anything like that again? Falling in love is great. Being in love is fantastic. Having your heart ripped out? Not so much."

She swallowed hard against the tide of dismay that washed over her, but nodded. There were a lot of complications for which there might be easy solutions. This wasn't one of them. In fact, there might be no solution for this sort of fear at all and she understood now that it was at the root of all those other excuses he'd been throwing out there to keep distance between them.

Abby stayed awake most of the night debating whether she had any right at all to speak to Luke about what Seth had revealed to her earlier in the day. He knew Seth better than anyone. He would have some idea if Seth was ever likely to be capable of putting that tragic past behind him.

In the end she counted on her old friendship with Luke to get him to open up with her. Hadn't he been the one to give her and Seth a shove toward each other by making them co-chairs of these fund-raising efforts? He owed her some answers.

It was late on a chilly, rainy morning when she stopped

by the clinic. She was relieved to find the waiting room deserted.

"Is Dr. Stevens available?" she asked the receptionist.

"You're Abby Miller, right?" the young woman asked, her expression guarded.

Abby nodded, wondering about the reaction. She studied the young woman, but though she looked vaguely familiar, Abby was certain they'd never crossed paths before.

"Is this a medical emergency of some kind?"

Abby shook her head. "No, it's personal."

The woman frowned at her response, but she pressed a button on the intercom and announced to Luke that Abby was waiting. There was an edge to her voice that made no sense to Abby.

The door to the treatment area opened almost at once and Luke waved her back, scowling at the receptionist as he did so. Abby watched the exchange with confusion.

"What did I miss out there?" she asked him.

"My regular receptionist is off sick today. That's Hannah's daughter, Kelsey. She clearly knows our history and her suspicions are on high alert."

Abby was immediately filled with regret. "I am so sorry. I had no idea. I'm sure it didn't help that I told her I was here for personal reasons."

Luke frowned. "Probably not." He sat down behind his desk. "So, what does bring you by?"

"Seth, as a matter of fact." She gave Luke a rueful look. "He filled me in on what happened with his last girlfriend."

"Then you know that Cara was killed," Luke said. "What is it you're trying to find out?"

"I'm asking you as his friend and mine, if you think that's something he's ever going to get past."

To her surprise a smile tugged at Luke's lips. "Are you asking simply as a concerned friend of Seth's or is something more going on with the two of you?"

"Something more," she said, then amended, "Maybe."

"You used to be more certain of things, Abby."

"I've never been in a situation quite like this before," she responded. "I didn't expect to be in so deep with someone I've known such a short time."

"You do know that the person you should be talking to about this is Seth."

"I do know that. I just wanted your insights. You've known him a long time. Surely you have a sense about whether this is something he'll ever forget."

"Forget, no," Luke said candidly. "Move beyond? I certainly hope so."

The words were barely out of his mouth when the door to his office burst open and Hannah stepped inside, her expression unapologetic.

"What sort of personal mission brought you by to see my husband?" she asked heatedly, her gaze on Abby.

"Hold on," Luke said at once, crossing the room to put his arm around Hannah's shoulders. His voice calm, he added, "I assume we can thank Kelsey for getting you over here, but you've got this all wrong, Hannah. There is nothing personal going on between me and Abby. You know that."

"She's here, isn't she? Behind a closed door."

Abby winced at the hurt behind Hannah's words. It didn't matter that her reaction was unreasonable. This was a consequence of this visit she definitely hadn't anticipated.

In an attempt to set Hannah's mind at ease, she explained, "I came to speak to Luke about Seth. I had questions that I thought an old friend could answer."

Hannah looked toward Luke, clearly seeking confirmation. He gave her a reassuring nod.

Abby added her own firm declaration. "That's the honest-to-God truth, Hannah. I'm sorry if you thought otherwise." She stood up. "Obviously I shouldn't have come."

Hannah seemed to wilt at that. "This was about Seth?"

"And Cara," Luke confirmed.

The mention of Cara seemed to convince her as nothing else had. Hannah sank into a chair and covered her face, which was flaming now not with anger, but unmistakable embarrassment.

"I'm sorry, Abby," she whispered when she finally dared to meet Abby's gaze. "I should never have barged in here like this. I'm an insecure idiot." She turned to Luke. "Forgive me."

"You don't need to shoulder all the blame," he told her, glancing toward Kelsey who was hovering in the doorway, her protective gaze focused on Hannah. "Your insecurities were obviously fueled by your daughter."

"You're absolutely right, Luke. I owe all of you an apology," Kelsey said, her expression chagrined.

"I appreciate that you were willing to fill in on short notice, but obviously that was a bad idea," Luke said, clearly not ready to let her off the hook. "What goes on around here is supposed to be confidential, no matter what extenuating circumstances you might think you see."

"I know that," Kelsey said, sounding miserable. "Mom, Luke, I am so, so sorry. What I did was completely wrong." Her gaze shifted to Abby. "And again, I owe you an apology, too, for misjudging you. This was obviously not the way for us to meet."

"You thought you were protecting your mom. I get it," Abby said. She regarded them all hopefully. "Maybe we can put this behind us once and for all. All of it. I didn't come back to Seaview Key to cause trouble."

Luke looked to Hannah. "Can you accept that now? You have to let this go."

Hannah nodded at once, then gave Abby a look filled with regret. "You'll still be at the house for Thanksgiving on Thursday, won't you? Don't let this keep you away. I swear I'll be sane by then."

"Me, too," Kelsey promised.

Abby drew in a deep breath. As hurtful as the past few minutes had been, she wanted her old friend back in her life. That meant not letting something like this get in the way.

"If you want me there, I'll be there," she said. "We'll forget this ever happened." She glanced at Luke. "All of it. I'm sorry for putting you in an uncomfortable position by asking about Seth. It won't happen again."

"No problem," Luke responded.

A faint grin tugged at Hannah's lips. "Or you could come to me. I probably know Seth almost as well as he does."

"I appreciate the offer, but I think my belated instinct is correct," Abby told her. "Just as your husband suggested earlier, the next time I have questions, I'll go right to the source."

It might take longer to ferret out information Seth didn't want to share, but it was far less likely to cause all this drama.

Seth realized that Luke was studying him curiously. "What?" he demanded. "Did I forget to shave or something?"

Luke shook his head. "You told Abby about Cara."

"Just the basics," Seth said. "How'd you find out?"

"She came to me to see if I'd fill in the blanks," Luke told him.

Seth sighed. "I probably should be furious about that, but I guess I'm not surprised. I told her how Cara's death affected me, then I clammed up."

"What surprises me is that you got into it at all," Luke told him. "You usually avoid any reference to Cara."

"It was fair warning," Seth said. "I owed Abby that."

"Because the two of you are getting serious or because you're not and she is?"

Seth sorted through the options Luke had suggested, then shrugged. "It's not that easy to explain."

"Okay, maybe this is none of my business, but since Abby came to me and since you're my friend, I'm making it my business. Be careful, Seth. I don't want to see either one of you get hurt."

"That's certainly the goal," Seth agreed.

"But emotions have a way of getting out of hand before you know it and then things can get messy in a hurry."

Seth frowned at him. "I thought you were all for Abby and me hanging out. You are the one who pushed us together and then pushed me to stop obsessing about the whole money thing. The more time I spend with her, the better I like her. You were right. Having money doesn't define her. She's an incredible woman."

Luke flushed. "Pushing you together might not have been one of my wisest moments," he conceded. "I was thinking a casual fling. Seems now that things are getting a lot more complicated."

"You were advocating a fling between me and your old girlfriend?" Seth asked incredulously. "That's a little weird, don't you think? Shouldn't you have more respect for her? Or was that just a convenient way for you to get Hannah off your case?"

"I have plenty of respect for Abby and, yes, I figured it would calm Hannah down to know Abby was involved with you. I just didn't give it much thought beyond that. Now I have."

"And?"

"I'm worried."

"You don't need to worry about me."

"And Abby? Do I need to worry about her?"

"Abby and I have been honest with each other from the beginning," Seth said defensively.

Luke actually smiled at that. "I hate to tell you this, pal, but as important as honesty is in a relationship, it can only accomplish so much. After that, you have to own any emotional damage you might unintentionally cause."

Seth sighed. Down deep he knew that.

"Abby and I are on the same page," he insisted.

"I guess I'll have to take your word for that," Luke responded, but there was no mistaking the worry that continued to darken his eyes.

Unfortunately Seth didn't have anything more to say that might reassure him. He wasn't even a hundred percent convinced himself.

Fourteen

The house was filled with all the familiar scents of Thanksgiving. The turkey was roasting in the oven. The celery and onions for the stuffing were being sautéed in butter on the stove. Two pumpkin pies were cooling on the counter. Hannah looked around and sighed. It was all coming together nicely.

"You're looking mighty pleased with yourself," Grandma Jenny commented.

"I have a lot to be thankful for this year," Hannah told her. "I got word late yesterday that I passed all those tests with flying colors. My editor loves the new book. My husband loves me. And I have my whole family coming here today to celebrate the holiday."

"Where does Abby fit in? Are you counting her being back in Seaview Key as one of those blessings?"

Hannah sighed. "That's still a work in progress," she said, then admitted, "I had a setback the other day."

"Kelsey told me," her grandmother said. "She was furious with herself for causing you unnecessary worry."

"She wouldn't have been able to do that if I'd truly gotten past all of my insecurities and suspicions," Hannah said. "But today is all about being thankful, and I am going to focus on that. I'm going to be especially grateful that my husband isn't fed up with my doubts."

Just then Luke's children, Nate and Gracie, bounded into the kitchen. Smiling at their exuberance, Hannah added, "And that these two are spending a little time with us."

Gracie immediately sidled closer and gave her a hug.

"I'm starving," Nate announced. "When do we get to eat?"

Hannah grinned. Nate was always starving, and he knew very well that Grandma Jenny almost always had cookies to offer.

"Not for another couple of hours," Hannah told him. "And you are not spoiling that appetite of yours with cookies." She aimed a warning look at her grandmother to make sure she got that message, too.

"I told him that," Gracie said.

Nate's gaze landed on the pies. "What about pie? I love pumpkin pie." He looked pleadingly at Grandma Jenny. "They smell really good. I bet you baked them."

"I did," she confirmed. "And you'll enjoy the pie all the more after dinner."

Gracie grinned, clearly pleased that her little brother's attempts to wheedle pie from Grandma Jenny had been thwarted.

"Is the table set?" Hannah asked her.

Gracie rolled her eyes. "I did my part," she said. "Then I fixed everything Nate did wrong."

"Well, there are going to be a lot of people here," Nate complained. "I got confused with all those forks and spoons. And how come everybody has two glasses? What's that for?"

"Water for everyone. Wine for the adults," Hannah explained.

"But there were two glasses at *every* place," he said. "That's what Hannah said."

"I thought you kids might want soda for this special occasion," Hannah told him.

Nate's eyes widened. Sodas were a rare treat, at least when they were visiting their health-conscious dad. "Seriously?"

"Seriously," Hannah confirmed, fighting a smile. "And I appreciate that you tried to get everything set up right in the dining room. Why don't you find your dad? I think he's got the parade on TV. Maybe he'll go outside and throw a football around with you."

"Cool!" Nate said, scampering off after taking one last longing look at the pie.

"What can I do?" Gracie asked. "I want to help."

"Then come over here with me," Grandma Jenny told her. "You can help me put the marshmallows on top of the sweet potatoes."

Gracie's eyes lit up. "Yum! That's my favorite part of Thanksgiving dinner."

"Mine, too," Hannah said. "And I still can't make the sweet potatoes the way Grandma Jenny does. Maybe you'll learn her secret and then they can be your specialty every year."

"I can do that," Gracie said confidently.

Hannah smiled at the two of them, side by side at the counter. Gracie was almost as tall as Grandma Jenny and every bit as talkative. She marveled at how well they got along and how Gracie had finally adapted to this new family that had evolved after her parents' divorce. She was no longer the sullen, difficult, resentful girl who'd first come to Seaview Key. She was back to that sunny disposition Luke had despaired of ever seeing again.

Luke stuck his head in the kitchen, observed the incredibly domestic scene and smiled. "I'm going outside with Nate. Shout if you need me."

"Everything's under control thanks to Grandma Jenny and Gracie," Hannah assured him.

"I see Abby parking," he reported from the doorway. "Should I send her inside?"

Hannah took a deep breath. "Absolutely. She's bringing pecan pies. See if she needs any help with them."

She noted that her grandmother was watching her closely. "You have to stop doing that," she warned. "I'm fine."

To prove it, she plastered a warm smile on her face and went to the door to greet Abby. As she neared, Hannah reached for the pies.

"It's okay," Abby said. "I have hot pads to carry them. They're just out of the oven. I got a later start today than I'd planned."

"Ooh, that aroma is amazing," Hannah said. "You've obviously mastered your mom's recipe."

Grandma Jenny turned with her own welcoming smile. "Those pecan pies of hers were always the hit of the Christmas bazaar at church. I can't wait to taste yours."

"I can't promise they'll live up to hers, but they're close, I think," Abby said. "She had a knack with the crusts that I'm still working on."

"Well, these look perfect," Jenny told her. "But if you need any more coaching, come over one day. I bake pies every few days at the inn."

Abby looked startled by the offer. A pleased smile spread across her face. “If you really mean that, I’ll take you up on it.”

She set the pecan pies on the racks that Hannah had set out, then caught sight of Gracie. “Well, hello, there. You must be Gracie. Your dad has told me about you. I’m Abby.”

“She’s a very old friend of your dad’s and mine,” Hannah said. “She’s just moved back to Seaview Key.”

Interest sparked in Gracie’s eyes. “You knew my dad when he was little?”

“Sure, but we got to be good friends when we were in high school,” Abby said. “He, Hannah and I were together all the time.”

Gracie frowned. “Hannah says they didn’t date back then. Did you date him?”

Abby glanced at Hannah, then nodded.

Gracie seemed to be absorbing that news, but to Hannah’s relief she didn’t ask any more probing questions. To be sure that the topic died, she glanced at Abby. “You said you got a late start. Any particular reason, a late night for example?”

“Not the way you’re thinking,” Abby replied, laughing.

Before Hannah could probe any further, there was a tap on the back door that caught their attention. A blush immediately tinted Abby’s cheeks with a telltale glow. Though she started to take a step in Seth’s direction, Gracie was already racing for the door. Abby stood back and watched.

“Seth!” Gracie exclaimed, throwing herself at him. “I missed you.”

A grin spread across his face as he lifted her in the

air. "Hey, short stuff. How are you doing?" He gave an exaggerated groan as he set her down. "You're almost too big for me to keep doing that."

"I've grown another inch since I was here last summer," she announced excitedly. "I'm almost as tall as my mom. And it's only fourteen more months till I'm a teenager."

That particular countdown had begun a full two years before her thirteenth birthday, Hannah recalled. Shortly after she'd set eyes on Seth, as a matter of fact. The child had suddenly been determined to grow up fast.

Seth shook his head at Gracie's announcement. "Not possible," he insisted.

"Really," Gracie said.

"Don't be too anxious to grow up," he advised. "You'll have a lot more responsibilities."

"But I'll be able to date," she reported excitedly. "Mom said."

"And what did your dad say?" Seth asked.

Gracie hesitated before responding to Seth. "I don't think he liked the idea."

A massive understatement, Hannah thought, recalling Luke's vehement reaction. Fortunately he'd held off on his tirade until after Gracie had gone to bed, so his daughter had missed the profanity. Though Hannah hadn't been around when he'd spoken to his ex-wife, she imagined the woman had gotten an earful about allowing a thirteen-year-old to date.

Hannah glanced at Abby and noted that she was fascinated by the exchange, or maybe it was just Seth's arrival that had captivated her. At just that moment, he glanced over Gracie's head and gave Abby a wink.

"Hello to you, too."

"Where's your contribution to dinner?" she teased. "I brought pies."

"I brought myself," he said as if she were crazy to suggest anything more was needed. "Oh, and there are bottles of wine in the car," he added, as if they were an afterthought.

He held Abby's gaze. "I forgot all about them. Want to give me a hand?"

"Sure," she said eagerly.

Hannah watched them go, amused by Seth's clever maneuvering to get Abby to himself. She had a hunch that wine had been deliberately left behind.

Unfortunately his best attempt was thwarted when Gracie bounced out the door after them.

"Oh, boy," Grandma Jenny said. "Those two are going to be in competition for his attention all day."

"Seth knows Gracie has a crush on him," Hannah said. "He'll be careful not to hurt her feelings. I give him a lot of credit for how sweet he is with her."

"Do you think Abby will mind sharing his affections?"

Hannah laughed. "I don't think she's going to feel threatened, if that's what you're asking." She hesitated, thinking about something she thought she'd seen on Abby's face just now. "Did you notice anything when she was watching Seth with Gracie?"

"You mean that longing in her expression?" Jenny asked perceptively.

"Exactly. I think she really missed out on having kids."

"Which makes you luckier than she is," her grandmother commented. "Something else for you to remember."

Hannah laughed at the pointed reminder. "Yes, ma'am. Today is all about gratitude."

Her grandmother nodded, looking satisfied. "I'm just saying."

Seth gave Abby a frustrated look as they collected the bottles of wine from the car, Gracie right there to give them a hand. Though he adored Luke's daughter and would never do a thing to hurt her feelings, he'd hoped for a moment alone with Abby.

Maybe it was just as well, though. He was likely to bring up the incident in Luke's office, and today definitely wasn't the day to insert Cara into the conversation.

Back in the kitchen, Hannah apparently sensed his frustration, though, because she sent Gracie outside with a message for Luke. Seth doubted it would be a long reprieve, but it did allow him to pull Abby aside for a moment.

"Everything going okay?" he asked. "With you and Hannah?"

"Almost like old times," she said, a hint of amazement in her voice. "After the other day, I wasn't sure what to expect."

Seth was surprised that she'd introduced the subject. "You mean your visit to Luke's office?"

Her expression turned rueful. "I figured you'd already heard about it. Luke's the kind of up-front guy who'd be into full disclosure."

"Actually I heard it from several directions," he said. "Kelsey gave me her side of the story, too. And, as you might imagine, Jenny had an opinion, as well."

"I'm sorry for trying to pry," she told him. "If I had questions about you and Cara, I should have come to you."

"I didn't exactly leave the door open," he admitted. "How about this? One of these days we'll spend a quiet evening at your place and I'll tell you anything you want to know."

She looked surprised by the offer. "But I know how hard it is for you to talk about her," she protested.

"Maybe it's time I did, though," he admitted. "Sometimes keeping things bottled up inside is the worst thing you can possibly do."

"Do you talk about her with Luke?"

"Not if I can help it, at least not since my first calls to him after she died," he said. "And believe me, he hasn't been shy about trying to get me to spill my guts since I got here. I just didn't see the point. Talk's not going to change what happened."

"But you will talk to me?" she said, clearly confused. "Why?"

"Because I'm the one who made what happened this huge barrier between us and the future. You probably deserve to hear the whole story."

"Only if and when you're ready to tell me."

He could see that she really meant that, that she would wait as long as it took. Amazingly, that made it easier for him to face the prospect of opening up an old wound, one that had changed his life, quite possibly forever.

* * *

With the arrival of Kelsey, Jeff and their precious baby girl, along with Hannah's father and his family, the house was as crowded and chaotic as Hannah had predicted. Abby stood on the sidelines and watched the dynamics of all these people who shared so much history—good and bad—as they interacted on such an important family occasion.

As usual, she found herself gravitating toward the baby. "She's so beautiful," she told Kelsey.

"Isabella is gorgeous, but she's a real handful," Kelsey responded. "I don't suppose you'd want to hold her so I can help Mom in the kitchen."

Abby could feel the smile spreading across her face. It wasn't all about the prospect of holding the baby, but Kelsey's trusting overture. She sensed that fences really were being mended.

"I'd love to," she told her eagerly.

Abby found an empty chair, no mean feat in the crowded house, and settled down with Isabella in her arms. In moments, Seth was by her side.

"There you are again with another borrowed baby," he teased.

"I can't seem to resist," she said.

His expression sobered. "You're such a natural, I'm surprised you never had a houseful of kids of your own."

She considered blowing off the comment with an innocuous response, but couldn't bring herself to do it. If she was expecting candor from him, then she had to be willing to expose her own emotions and the painful events that had shaped her life.

"I'm surprised, too," she said softly, not even attempting to hide her regrets.

"There's a story there, isn't there?"

She nodded. "I think it belongs on that list of things we need to talk about when we're having that quiet evening alone. It's certainly not a topic for here and now."

He nodded, but he brushed a comforting hand over her head, then allowed the caress to linger on her cheek. "I'm sorry."

Abby regarded him with surprise. "For what?"

"For whatever happened that hurt you so deeply."

She immediately blinked back tears at the tenderness in his voice. "I'm not going to think about that today," she told him. "We're counting blessings today, and my life is filled with them."

"Mine, too," he said. "I'm starting to think you belong at the top of the list." He winked then. "Now I need to find Gracie. I promised her I'd play a game with her before dinner."

Abby grinned. "Then you should definitely track her down. That little girl is one of your biggest admirers. Come to think of it, you have a lot of them around here today."

He held her gaze. "Including you?"

"Afraid so," she said. "It must be such a curse to be so popular."

"It is a struggle," he said with a self-deprecating grin. "But I try not to let it get me down."

Abby laughed. "What a guy!"

She might be teasing, but the truth was, he was the most amazing man she'd met in a very long time.

Given all the past history and tensions among the various attendees at Hannah's Thanksgiving dinner, Seth had expected a stressful atmosphere. Amazingly, though, whatever issues there were seemed to have been put aside for the day.

He found himself in the den with Luke, his son, Nate, and Hannah's father and half-brother after a meal that had left them all stuffed and content. The football game was on TV and their commentary on the plays was far livelier than that of the announcers, thanks to their diverse views on the two teams playing. Even Nate at only nine had strong opinions and the knowledge to back them up.

Seth thought back to the last time he'd shared a Thanksgiving dinner with his own family. There'd been no detente that day. Laura and her husband were already feuding after barely a year of marriage. Meredith's workaholic husband had spent most of the afternoon outside on his cell phone. Seth had hung out in the kitchen with his mother for a time, but watching her take the prepared meal she'd ordered from a local grocery store out of its containers had only depressed him.

"Are we ever going to eat?" his father had grumbled. "I have a report due at work tomorrow. I need to get back to it."

So much for joy and family togetherness, Seth had thought, finally electing to go for a walk to get away from the tense atmosphere. Sadly, it had been the last time they'd all been together for a holiday.

By Christmas he'd been on his first tour in Iraq, and by the following Thanksgiving, his parents were gone, killed when a small plane taking them to a business convention had gone down in a storm. An official investigation had revealed they should never have taken off in such terrible weather conditions, but Seth hadn't been the least bit surprised that his impatient father, a licensed pilot, had taken off anyway.

Abby's touch as she sat on the arm of his chair snapped him back to the present.

"Where were you just then?" she asked, looking worried.

"Thinking about what a disaster today could have been, given all the undercurrents among the folks here."

She nodded. "I've been pleasantly surprised by the genuine happiness I'm feeling in the air. Despite everything, people seem to be getting along. Things are even different between Hannah and me. For the first time, I'm really hopeful."

"That's great."

"She told me the test results were good," Abby added. "I'm so happy for her."

"Maybe that explains a lot," Seth said. "Not knowing would stress anyone out. Now that she knows she's cancer-free, she can let herself relax. The world must seem like a brighter place."

"I wonder if anyone who's had cancer can ever fully relax," Abby responded.

"I hope so," Seth said. "At least until it's time for the next round of tests. Did she say when those will be?"

"Not for a year," Abby said. "That's a good sign, too. The doctors have had her coming back every six months up to now."

"Luke must be relieved, too," Seth said. "He doesn't say much, but I know he panics almost as much as Hannah does. He just tries not to show it around her."

"They're really good for each other, don't you think so?" Abby said.

"I do. Remember, I was with Luke overseas when his

wife sent an email telling him she wanted a divorce so she could marry the man who'd been his partner in his medical practice back in Atlanta. Talk about a lousy bit of timing. It sent him to a very dark place. I honestly worried for a time if he'd start getting reckless and put his life at risk, or at more risk than we already were."

Abby's eyes widened at that. "I had no idea. Nobody told me that's how his marriage ended. How horrible! No wonder he came here instead of going back to Atlanta."

"Add in the injury that kept him in rehab for months and Seaview Key was exactly what he needed," Seth agreed. "God knows, I could feel the healing powers of this place when I got here. It's a great place to get your perspective back and remember the things that matter."

"Exactly what I'm hoping for," Abby said.

"Is it working for you?" he asked curiously. "I'm still not seeing that laid-back Abby you swore you were aiming for."

"Hey, I've been hanging out at the house redecorating, haven't I? I haven't been down at town hall every day pestering them about my permits for Blue Heron Cove. Jenny even convinced me to hold back from insisting on another meeting with the mayor and avoiding her two cronies altogether, at least for the time being. The old Abby would have been in their faces by now."

Seth smiled at that. "Okay, then, definitely a new you."

"Well, a work in progress, anyway," she said.

Hannah appeared in the doorway to the den just then. "Okay, people, anyone who wants pie has to come and get it."

"In a minute," Luke promised distractedly, his attention focused on the TV.

"Yeah, it's not quite half-time," her father said.

Hannah directed a frustrated look at both of them. "Ten minutes," she declared. "Or the pies are going in the garbage."

Nate jumped up, alarm on his face. "I'm coming right now," he said. "I've been waiting and waiting for pie."

Hannah grinned at him. "Good boy!"

"Seth and I are coming now, too," Abby said, tugging on his hand.

Seth cast one last look toward the TV and shrugged. "The game's lopsided, anyway. I don't have a dog in that fight. My team's not even on the field."

Hannah nodded approvingly. "Two more appreciative people. Thank you. Luke Stevens!"

He finally glanced her way. "Yes, dear."

"Pie—now!"

Clayton Dixon chuckled and looked toward Hannah's half-brother. "I guess those are our marching orders, too." He stood up and pressed a fatherly kiss on Hannah's cheek. "Dinner was real good, honey."

Hannah looked momentarily startled by the compliment. "Thank you," she said, a pleased expression spreading across her face.

"It looks as if she hasn't experienced many compliments from her father," Seth said.

"I've known Hannah for a very long time," Abby said, then confided, "This is the first time I've ever laid eyes on her dad."

"You're kidding me!"

"Nope. He left home when she was young and she didn't hear from him until Luke tracked him down a year or so ago," Abby said. "Hannah says she found letters he'd sent, but her mom and Jenny had kept them from her."

Seth didn't even try to hide his astonishment. "I can't believe Jenny would do something like that."

"Neither could I," Abby said. "Looks as if all is forgiven now, though."

Seth glanced down at her. "It's been a day full of surprises, hasn't it?"

She nodded. "The best kind of surprises."

As they reached the dining room, Gracie edged closer to Seth. "Can I sit next to you for dessert?"

He grinned at her. "You bet."

"But I get to sit on the other side," Abby said, a teasing glint in her eyes.

Gracie gave her a long look, then asked, "Are you his girlfriend? I mean for real?"

Seth held his breath as he waited to hear how Abby would answer. She leaned down to whisper in Gracie's ear, her voice so quiet, he couldn't hear what she said. He gave her a questioning look, especially when Gracie giggled.

"What did you tell her?" he asked Abby when Gracie ran ahead to hold their seats at the crowded table.

Abby grinned. "That I thought maybe she had the inside track on that."

"You're willing to take a backseat to an eleven-year-old?"

She shrugged. "She did see you first."

"Are you telling me I have to break that little girl's heart before you'll consider being my girlfriend for real?"

Abby faltered at that. "I don't think I realized that was an option."

"I'm beginning to think I might not have any choice," he told her. She was definitely sneaking past his defenses in ways he'd never anticipated.

Fifteen

Abby had been talking to a contractor about the Blue Heron Cove project for several months. Troy Hall had been eager to take on the construction work she'd described and had been impressed with the architectural plans she'd shown him for the development.

When he called on the Monday after Thanksgiving, though, his outlook had changed.

"I'm hearing from a few people that you're not likely to get those permits anytime soon," he told Abby.

"What people?" she asked, distraught not only by what he was saying, but by the fact that the news had reached him. Had someone deliberately set out to sabotage the project by scaring Troy off?

"Trust me, they're reliable sources," he said. "I can't wait around, Abby. I have to keep my guys working. We'll be wrapping up our current job before the holidays. Construction's been picking up and I've had other offers. I put them off as long as I could, but if things over there aren't going to get under way anytime soon, I need to move on. Work is work, you know what I'm saying?"

"Troy, you have to bear with me a little longer," Abby pleaded. "You're the man I trust to see that these houses are built right. You understand my environmental concerns better than anyone."

"Believe me, I want to work with you. Seaview Key is beautiful. I love the scope of the project and all the care you're taking to protect the island from over-development and to do as little damage as possible to the environment."

His enthusiasm sounded sincere, but so did his frustration.

"If this drags on much longer, it doesn't make sense for me to wait around," he said. "I've heard that the mayor is dead set against the project and that she has allies."

Abby could hardly deny that. Instead, she requested, "Can you give me till tomorrow to see what I can work out?" She had to work to keep a note of desperation from her voice. She didn't want to start over from scratch trying to find someone else with Troy's credentials and passion for protecting a fragile ecosystem.

"The way I hear it, there's not even a council meeting scheduled till after the first of the year, and there's no guarantee you'll win even then," he protested.

"Tomorrow," she repeated, determined not to lose this chance to hire the very best man to handle the project. "Please, Troy."

"Okay, end of the day tomorrow," he agreed finally. "That's the best I can do."

When she'd hung up, she stared at the phone. What on earth was she supposed to do between now and tomorrow to get this development moving? And why had no one told her that the December meeting she'd been counting on had been officially canceled? At least she could start with that.

She reached for the phone, then stopped herself. This was a conversation she needed to have face-to-face. She finished dressing and headed for Seaview Inn. She had a hunch Jenny would have at least some of the answers she needed, and would understand the crisis she was suddenly facing. Maybe she'd even have some thoughts on ways that Abby could keep this whole project from falling apart.

At Seaview Inn, she discovered the front door standing wide open and a few strangers on the porch. Obviously the winter tourist season had begun.

Inside in the foyer, she found Kelsey decorating a huge Christmas tree. The wonderfully fresh, woodsy aroma of the live tree filled the air.

"Getting an early start on the holiday season?" Abby asked.

Kelsey smiled. "From the time I was a kid, I always wanted to rush it. Now that I'm at the inn, I have the perfect excuse. People seem to love the holiday atmosphere, even if it is right after Thanksgiving."

Abby nodded toward the porch. "And you have guests already?"

"The Johnsons. They come every year at this time for a whole month. They like celebrating Christmas here with their family."

"I don't blame them," Abby told her.

She sniffed the air again, then glanced toward the kitchen. "Is Grandma Jenny baking sugar cookies?"

"Indeed, she is. Just one more sign that the holidays are around the corner. Did you come to see her? Mom's in there helping out. To be honest, she's probably just getting in the way, but nobody dares to tell her that."

Abby laughed. "I'm sure I'll be in the way, too, but I do need to see Jenny."

"Watch out. If there's any indication at all that you can put some frosting on those cookies, you'll be drafted."

"That actually sounds like fun."

She walked into the large kitchen just in time to overhear Jenny scolding Hannah.

"You're making a mess of those. Why don't you just sit there and talk to me?"

"I came over to help," Hannah protested. "You grumbled all day yesterday about how much baking you had to do."

"There's help and then there's real help," Jenny countered. She spotted Abby. "What about you? Any skill in the cookie-decorating department?"

"None that's been tested," Abby claimed. "But I'm willing to try." She glanced over Hannah's shoulder, then quipped, "I can't do any worse now, can I?"

"Sure, trust her, even though she's totally untested," Hannah grumbled, but she was grinning at Abby when she said it.

Abby sat at the kitchen table and watched closely as Jenny showed her what to do. "And wait until the cookies are cool before you start," she warned. "Hannah's too impatient."

"Yes, ma'am," Abby said dutifully.

As Jenny went back to putting another batch of cookies into the oven, she glanced at Abby. "I don't imagine you showed up just to help out."

"No, this is just an unexpected bonus for me," Abby

told her, then explained about the call she'd had. "Troy's the best possible contractor for building these houses and I'm about to lose him. Is he right? Has the December meeting been canceled?"

Jenny and Hannah exchanged a look that told the story.

"It has been," Abby guessed, sighing. "You warned me about possible delays."

"I tried to," Jenny agreed.

"The December meeting is almost always called off," Hannah added, backing up Jenny's earlier warning. "Everybody's too busy to be bothered, and usually there's nothing urgent on the agenda."

"Well, Blue Heron Cove is urgent," Abby protested.

"To you, not to Sandra," Jenny said. "I imagine the official notice will be in the local paper when it comes out this week."

"What am I supposed to do now?" Abby asked, trying not to give in to defeat. "Just wait till January? Is there any chance at all I could make sure this meeting happens on schedule?"

"Not unless you're willing to risk having the vote not turn out in your favor. You don't have enough people on your side yet," Jenny said realistically. "My advice is to be patient."

"I don't see that you have any choice," Hannah agreed. "Welcome to small-town life."

"And if I lose my contractor?"

"Even if he takes another job, he'll be free eventually, won't he?" Jenny asked.

"Or you could find somebody else," Hannah suggested. "He's not the only contractor in the whole state of Florida, after all."

"But he is the one who came to me highly recommended because he's willing to work around environmental issues in a responsible way." She shook her head. "Blast it! I just hadn't counted on this."

She looked at the other two women. "Am I beating my head against a brick wall if I keep fighting for this project? Tell me the truth."

"Absolutely not!" Jenny insisted. "This is too important to Seaview Key for you to give up now."

"She's right," Hannah said. "I think you'll pull it off. You just have to be patient."

"Do you recall that being among my virtues?" Abby asked in frustration.

Hannah chuckled. "Not exactly. Maybe this will be good practice for you."

Abby sighed. Between this delay and Seth's reluctance to get involved with her in a meaningful way, it seemed her patience was getting a real workout.

When Abby got back to her cottage, she threw a couple of pillows across the living room, but that did nothing to relieve the frustration she was feeling. She thought of the one remaining project that needed to be completed—the master bathroom. She'd intended to leave that renovation to a professional, but suddenly the idea of ripping out tiles and maybe even smashing up the old tub with a sledgehammer held a tremendous amount of appeal. She was pretty sure she'd seen one in the toolshed out back.

An hour later, she'd made a pretty impressive mess out of the bathroom and was feeling marginally better. Her muscles ached, her back hurt and perspiration was coating her skin. Still, she looked around at the debris with satisfaction.

"Taking out your frustration on the bathroom?" a voice inquired from behind her.

Abby turned to find Seth, a grin spreading across his face.

"You don't want to mess with me in the mood I'm in," she warned.

"Certainly not with that sledgehammer in your hands," he agreed. "Can you take a break?"

She sighed. "I'm more than ready for one, to tell you the truth." She set aside the heavy tool, took one last look at the mess and followed Seth into the kitchen. He immediately headed for the refrigerator and poured two glasses of iced tea.

"I assume this was brought on by your conversation with Jenny and Hannah earlier," he said. "They told me about the possibility you could lose the services of the contractor you wanted."

"I'm still not reconciled to that," she said. "But I haven't come up with a single way to get him to postpone making a decision to move on. I promised I'd get back to him before the end of the day tomorrow."

"So, no chance of stalling for a little more time?"

She shook her head. "He was adamant. And I can't blame him. He wants his guys on the job, not waiting around, especially with Christmas around the corner. They need to know they'll be working and will have money to pay the holiday bills."

"Okay, let's think about this," Seth suggested. "But let's do it on the porch, where there's a breeze."

Abby joined him outside. She dropped into a rocker

and sighed. She had to admit, it felt awfully good to be off her feet.

To her surprise, rather than sitting, Seth moved behind her and put his hands on her bare shoulders and began to massage the taut muscles there. She closed her eyes and sighed.

"Keep doing that and I will follow you anywhere," she murmured, barely containing a moan of pure pleasure.

"Not going anywhere, but good to know," he said, laughing. "I'm beginning to figure out all the paths that lead to your heart."

His words caused a hitch in her breath. As a man who'd declared that they had no long-term future, he had to stop saying things like that. It left her hopeful, which was exactly opposite of what he'd claimed to want—a relationship with no expectations.

"Let's focus on how you can make your contractor change his mind," Seth said after several blissful minutes of his deft hands working out the kinks in her shoulders.

"If I'm being honest, I'm not sure it's fair for me to even try," Abby admitted. "I can't guarantee that this project will ever happen."

"It's going to happen," Seth said confidently. "If you don't believe that with everything in you, then you might as well give up. Are you willing to do that?"

"No," she said, but the response sounded weary and unconvincing even to her.

"Excuse me?" Seth prodded.

She smiled at his cheerleading attempt. "No!" she said more emphatically.

"Okay, then, how about this? What if you suggest he

take on something short-term, something he can wrap up by, say, spring? That would give you time to get all these ducks over here lined up in a nice, neat row, but it wouldn't delay the start of the project by much, if at all."

"I suppose that could work," she said. "He didn't say whether these other offers were for big developments or single homes." A thought suddenly discouraged her. "I'm pretty sure, though, that he only takes on bigger jobs."

"Still, it's worth asking about," Seth insisted. "If he's really interested in doing Blue Heron Cove, surely there's a compromise that would put his guys to work in the short-term and allow him to do this in a few months. If it were me and this project appealed to me, I'd work it out with you, rather than losing the opportunity to another contractor."

"I hope you're right," Abby said. Though she was unconvinced, she did feel marginally more optimistic.

"Call him now," Seth urged.

She glanced up at him. "I'm not sure I'm ready to hear his answer."

"Which is why it's better to get it over with while I'm around to cheer you up if it doesn't go your way."

Intrigued, she smiled. "You think you can pull that off?"

He held her gaze. "I'm willing to try."

Eager to put him to the test, if not to get a rejection from Troy, Abby pulled her cell phone out of her pocket and made the call. Using her most persuasive attitude, she told him she was convinced that the project would move forward, that she had the support of some key movers and shakers, and that he was the only man for the job.

"You're the man I trust to do this right," she said. "Isn't there some way we can compromise, Troy? Isn't one of those other offers on the table enough to keep your men employed, but not so long-term that it would prevent you from getting to Blue Heron Cove by spring?"

"You told me you wanted to start by the first of the year," he reminded her.

"Well, obviously I was overly optimistic. I'm learning to adjust to the way things work here. If you'll give me a commitment to start this spring, I'll make sure everything's ready to go on this end. If I don't think I can pull it off, I swear I'll give you plenty of notice so you can move on and accept another offer."

He hesitated for such a long time that she thought he was going to turn her down. Instead, he said, "That's fair enough."

Abby felt relief flood through her. "You'll do it?"

"I'll do it," he confirmed. "I never wanted to back out on you, Abby. Blue Heron Cove's going to be special. I just felt I had to do what made economic sense for my crew."

"I totally understand," she assured him.

"You'll give me a heads-up sooner, rather than later, if things start to fall apart over there? I need your commitment on that."

"You have my word," she said.

"Good enough. You're a good negotiator, Abby. You pushed all the right buttons."

She laughed. "I'll pass the compliment along to my coach," she said, glancing up at Seth when she said it. "He's standing here looking very pleased with himself."

Troy chuckled. "You'll have to introduce me. A few

hours ago, I wouldn't have given two cents that you'd come up with anything to convince me to hang in here."

"Talk to you soon," she said. "I'll keep you updated as things move along."

"Looking forward to it."

She hung up, then stood up. "You're a genius," she told Seth.

"He agreed?"

"He agreed," she confirmed. "You gave me the win-win idea and the confidence to sell it to him."

Seth pulled her into his arms and twirled her around. "I guess that makes us a pretty good team."

She looked into his eyes. "I certainly think so."

And with each and every example of their compatibility, she fell a little more deeply in love. She studied Seth's expression and wondered if he felt the same way. If so, it must scare him to death. Right this second, though, he looked every bit as thrilled as she felt.

"This calls for a celebration," Seth announced as he set Abby back on her feet. "Dinner? Ice cream? What do you feel like?"

Abby gave him a rueful look. "I feel like a shower and I just had a terrible thought."

He frowned. "What's that? I thought the news was all good."

"Oh, the news was great," she confirmed. "But I just destroyed the only shower in this house."

He stared at her dismayed expression and started laughing. "The other bathroom doesn't have a shower or a tub?"

She shook her head. "Just a sink and toilet." She moaned. "What was I thinking?"

"Isn't there an outdoor shower out back?"

She frowned at the suggestion. "Sure, for rinsing off when people come back from a swim and are still in their bathing suits. It's not meant for scrubbing from head to toe, which is what I need."

"Why not? There's water, isn't there? Grab a towel and a bar of soap."

She scowled at the suggestion. "There's no privacy, Seth."

He laughed. "I'll hold up a blanket. No passerby will see you. I promise."

"What about you?"

"I won't peek," he insisted, though the temptation might very well kill him. "Cross my heart."

She regarded him skeptically. "Cross your heart?"

"Absolutely. Or you could grab some clothes and come back to Seaview Inn and use the shower in my room. I would remain safely downstairs." Another test of his willpower, though one he was more likely to pass with Jenny, Kelsey and an inn full of other people around.

"I think I like that idea better," she said. "Give me a couple of minutes to get a few things together."

"Maybe you should consider staying over there till you can get a plumber in here to finish the renovations," he suggested.

"The inn's not full?"

He shook his head. "I think Kelsey said there were open rooms for another week or so. Worst-case scenario, you could share mine."

Even as the impulsive words came out of his mouth, he flinched. Bad idea! A really bad idea, in fact. That would be the absolute end of any pretense that they weren't involved. Even if he never laid a hand on her—

which was unlikely enough—the entire world would believe they'd become a couple.

"Why do you suddenly look so panicky?" Abby asked, her expression knowing. "Scared you won't be able to resist me?"

"I *know* I won't be able to resist you," Seth confirmed. "Which makes that idea insane."

"Insane?" she questioned. "Or dangerous?"

"Is there a difference?"

"I can't say for sure," she said. "But I'm suddenly very interested in finding out. I'll pack a bag."

Seth swallowed hard as she headed inside. What the heck had just happened here? He'd suddenly lost control of the entire situation. Or maybe what he really feared was that he was losing control of his heart.

"I'd like a room for a few nights," Abby told Kelsey when she and Seth got to Seaview Inn.

Kelsey studied the two of them curiously. "Something happen over at your house?" she asked Abby. "You didn't set fire to it, did you? You weren't in such a good mood when you left here earlier."

"Nothing like that," Abby said, laughing. "But I did get a little overzealous with a sledgehammer."

Kelsey's shocked reaction had her quickly adding, "I gutted the only fully equipped bathroom."

Kelsey chuckled at that. "I imagine that has something to do with that situation you discussed with Mom and Grandma Jenny earlier. They told me about what was going on with your contractor. Were you able to resolve the problem?"

"Thanks to a suggestion from Seth, I was," she said. "But not till after I went on my destructive rampage.

Seth took one look at the mess and suggested I should probably stay here till I can get the plumber in to install new fixtures and do the rest of the renovations."

"I'm surprised he didn't invite you to move in with him," Kelsey said, her gaze on Seth. "How come you let that opportunity slip through your fingers?"

Seth scowled at the question.

"Oh, he did," Abby confided. "Sort of."

"Huh?" Kelsey said.

"Never mind. I'll just take my own room, if one's available."

"Sure," Kelsey confirmed. "A word of warning, though. We're sold out starting in about ten days. Do you think your repairs will be completed by then?"

Abby nodded. "If I have to lay the tile myself," she told her.

"Then we're good," Kelsey said.

Abby handed over her credit card, then glanced at Seth. "You must be feeling relieved about now."

"Relieved?"

"No sharing necessary," she explained.

"Looks to me like he's disappointed," Kelsey commented. "What about it, Seth? Want me to suddenly discover we have a full house now?"

"Just give the woman a room," he grumbled. "I'll carry her bag up."

Kelsey laughed. "You won't have to go far. Lucky for you, the room right next door to yours is available. Pretty convenient, huh?"

Seth shook his head. "I hope you two are enjoying yourselves." He gave Abby a warning look. "Remember that conversation we had about dangerous situations? You're playing with one right now."

Abby trembled under his heated gaze. The prospect of testing Seth's limits suddenly held a whole lot of appeal. Just as Kelsey had said, how convenient that she wouldn't have to go far to do it.

Sixteen

Seth could hear Abby moving around in the room next door to his and felt his willpower crumbling.

"You're not going over there," he admonished himself. "Not tonight. Not tomorrow. Not the entire time she's there."

And please, God, let that not be for long. He vowed to call the plumber himself first thing in the morning and offer all sorts of incentives for him to get that bathroom at Abby's whipped back into shape in record time. *He'd* go over and lay the new tiles, if it came to that. Maybe he could even install the new tub, though he had no experience doing such a thing. Desperate times called for desperate measures. This was one of those times.

He heard a tap on the door and cast a frantic glance in that direction. The second tap, however, came not on the door to the hallway, but on a door he hadn't really paid attention to before. It apparently connected his room to Abby's. *Blast it all,* he thought, staring at it in dismay. *Now what?*

"Seth, are you in there? I'm ready to go out to dinner if you are."

Dinner, he thought with relief. *Thank goodness!* He jumped up and opened the door.

Unfortunately, though Abby was, indeed, dressed, she was wearing some slinky little dress that barely skimmed over her curves. She looked sophisticated and hot. Very, very hot. Take-me-to-bed hot. He swallowed hard. How was he supposed to go on resisting her—protecting his already wounded heart—if she looked so blasted sexy?

"Aren't you going to freeze in that?" he asked in a choked voice.

She held up a jacket. "I'll be fine." She met his gaze, then held it for several endless beats. "And you keep telling me you're up to the task of keeping me warm," she added, her voice a soft caress. "I'm not worried."

Well, *he* was worried. The game was getting wildly out of hand. Sex with Abby he could handle. Falling in love, which seemed to go right along with it, spelled disaster, and all of his many excuses were wearing very, very thin.

"Let's go," he said, closing the connecting door, then locking it firmly.

As they exited his room together, they ran straight into Grandma Jenny in the hallway. Her eyes glinted with amusement.

"Kelsey told me you were staying here, Abby. I wondered how long you'd be in your own room."

"She is not staying in my room," Seth blurted. "She just came over to tell me she was ready to go to dinner."

Jenny actually laughed. "Did I ask for an explanation?"

"No, but I thought you should know," Seth said, then

added emphatically, "There is nothing going on. Absolutely nothing."

Jenny glanced at Abby, who looked almost as amused as she did. "He sounds guilty."

"Doesn't he?" Abby said. "I wonder why that is."

"Why, indeed?" Jenny replied.

Seth looked from one woman to the other, then headed for the stairs. He had a hunch if he opened his mouth in his own defense one more time, he'd only dig a deeper hole for himself. This one was plenty deep enough.

Seth was so quiet at dinner that Abby began to worry that she'd pushed him too far, with a little unanticipated, but welcome assistance from Kelsey and Grandma Jenny.

"You okay?" she asked eventually.

"Of course."

"We were just teasing, you know."

"Oh, believe me, I got that." He looked her in the eye. "How much longer am I supposed to hold out before this gets out of hand?"

"Out of hand? That's an interesting way to put it. We are two consenting adults who are obviously attracted to each other, Seth. What's your definition of *out of hand* in those circumstances?"

"I've warned you," he began.

"That you'll never fall in love again," she said solemnly. "Yes, you've mentioned that."

"You don't seem to be taking me seriously."

"I have heard every word you've said," she contradicted. "I've taken them to heart. There are no misunderstandings, Seth."

He frowned. "Then why do I have the feeling that you're deliberately testing my limits?"

She smiled at that. "Because it's so much fun to see you squirm," she confessed. "Flirting with you is more entertaining than anything that's happened to me in a long time. You make me feel sexy, desirable."

"Well, of course you're sexy and desirable," he said as if she ought to be aware of that.

"Marshall didn't think so."

Seth looked satisfyingly incredulous. "Seriously?"

"Not after the first couple of years," she admitted. She'd often wondered if that was because he'd feared intimacy might lead to a pregnancy he refused to confess he didn't want.

"We've already established that your ex-husband was a jerk," Seth said.

Abby smiled. "Yes, you've mentioned your opinion before."

Again, that incredulous look passed over his face. "You don't agree?"

"Sure, in some areas, he was, but in general he was a good guy, Seth. I don't want you to get the wrong impression. He just wasn't the right man for me."

He shook his head. "You're a lot more forgiving than you ought to be."

"It hardly makes sense to hold a grudge at this point. I'm just saying that you make me feel things I haven't felt in a long time." She leveled a look into his eyes. "And I consider that to be a very good thing."

"Even if the end result leads to disaster?" he asked.

"It can only do that if we're not honest with each other," she told him. "So far, you've been brutally honest with me. I promise I have no long-term expectations."

To her surprise he looked more disappointed than

reassured. "That doesn't seem to be setting your mind at ease the way I thought it would," she told him.

"Yeah, I know. I can't explain it, either," he said, looking charmingly bewildered.

Abby hid a smile. "Okay, let's look at this. We have fun together, right?"

"Sure."

"We tend to look at the world the same way."

"Agreed."

"There's some kind of chemistry thing going on."

"Hard to deny that," he said. "Where are you going with this?"

"Just trying to say that from my perspective, it's all good. I didn't come to Seaview Key hoping to fall madly in love and settle down for the rest of my life. My marriage wasn't great. We've established that. I'm no more eager to repeat the experience than you are to have your heart broken again. Seems to me that puts us in the same place emotionally, or close to it."

Seth frowned. "You don't see yourself getting married again?"

"If the right man comes along, sure," she said, then amended, "Probably. I suppose it depends."

"On what?" he inquired curiously.

"Whether making that commitment feels like the right thing for both of us. I'm not opposed to living with someone at this stage of my life. I don't need a piece of paper to make it legal."

Seth regarded her as if she'd suddenly grown two heads. "Women don't think like that."

Abby's lips curved. "Really? It's how I think."

"But all women want happily ever after," he insisted.

"All women want a man who loves and respects them and makes them deliriously happy," she corrected.

"Isn't that the same thing?"

She shook her head. "It doesn't require a marriage license."

He continued to look skeptical.

"You still disagree," she concluded.

"Sure. Despite some of the examples I've been around, I believe in marriage. I always wanted to share my life with someone, have a family."

"But now you don't," she reminded him softly. "At least what you've been telling me is that the pain of losing Cara was so huge that you'd never risk loving anyone that deeply again."

Seth sat back. "That is what I've been saying," he agreed.

"And I've been taking you at your word."

He frowned at that. "So, what? This stuff you're saying is what you think I want to hear, not what you believe?"

"Oh, no. I believe it," she said. "I'm not saying it just so I don't scare you to death. I'm trying to get you to see that every relationship doesn't have to lead to the altar to be strong or committed."

"But if two people are committed to each other, with or without saying the vows, there's just as much pain involved if it all falls apart."

She held his gaze. "So light and casual is the only way to go for you?"

"I guess, yes," he said, then shook his head. "No, that's all wrong, too."

Abby hid a smile. "You seem to be having a little trouble sorting out where you stand."

"Tell me about it," he said dryly. "Most women would have listened to this and run for the hills by now. It's obvious how messed up I am."

"I imagine that's what you were hoping for with me, too," she said, then shrugged. "I'm not most women."

"Boy, is that the truth," he murmured.

It seemed to Abby that he didn't sound entirely happy about it.

Seth was so completely confused by the words that had come out of his mouth, he couldn't imagine why Abby hadn't laughed her head off right before walking out on him. He'd been so sure he had a grip on what he did and didn't want in terms of a relationship. Casual was one thing. Committed was something else entirely. He might yearn for what Luke and Hannah had, even Kelsey and Jeff with little Isabella, but he didn't think he could ever do committed again. So, why had he argued so passionately in favor of it?

Was it because Abby clearly was not a casual sort of woman? No matter how forcefully she tried to make it seem that she was willing to go with the flow, he thought he knew her better than that. She was the kind of woman who deserved forever, who should be living in a house filled with kids and a doting husband. She ought to be with a man who wasn't scared out of his wits every minute that something terrible would strike and rip their world all apart.

Imagining a future with Abby, seeing her with a child in her arms as she had been on Thanksgiving with Isabella and on other occasions with Lesley Ann's son, A.J., reminded Seth that she'd promised to fill him in on why she'd never had kids of her own.

Could that have anything at all to do with this crazy stance she'd just taken against marriage?

Though they'd fallen silent over their meal, as soon as their desserts came, Seth looked her in the eye. "On Thanksgiving you said you'd tell me why there are no kids in your life. Didn't you want them?"

She blinked at the apparently unexpected question. "What made you go there?" she asked.

"I'm trying to figure out what makes you tick. Something tells me this could be the key. Am I wrong?"

She was silent for a long time before she said, "Not entirely."

"Then you did want children?"

"More than anything," she confessed, tears gathering in her eyes.

Seth almost regretted bringing the subject up, but those tears told him they needed to get into this. "What happened?" He frowned. "You didn't lose a child, did you? Or have a miscarriage?"

She shook her head. "It just didn't happen. I never got pregnant."

He recognized that there was a world of hurt behind those words. "So, you were sterile?"

She shrugged. "I don't know. I was never tested. Neither was my husband."

"I don't understand. Didn't you want to know why?"

"Of course I did," she said heatedly. "I pleaded with Marshall. I even set up an appointment with fertility experts. He refused to go and didn't want me going, either."

Seth regarded her with shock. In this day and age when answers to most things could be figured out with proper testing, who wouldn't want the clarity?

"Why on earth not?" he asked.

"You know he was a minister. All he'd tell me was that we'd have a child if that was God's will. If I didn't get pregnant, then that was God's will, too."

"And you accepted that?"

"What choice did I have? Sure, I could have gone on my own and been tested, but then what? If I wasn't the problem, was I supposed to throw that in his face?"

"You would have known," Seth argued.

"Things were tense enough as it was. And it wouldn't have changed anything."

"Did you discuss adoption?"

She gave him a rueful look. "He wasn't interested in that, either. Frankly, that was the final straw for me. It told me we were never going to be on the same page about the future. I think the congregation was enough family for him. I wanted more. And once again, Marshall's needs were the only ones that counted."

"So you divorced him," he concluded.

"Not right away," she conceded. "It took me a while to accept that this good and decent man I'd married was really quite selfish and domineering, that I was losing myself trying to keep him happy."

Seth reached for her hand. "I really am sorry, Abby. You didn't deserve to be treated like that."

"No, I didn't," she said. "I see that now. And I know I allowed it to continue for way too long, more than likely well past the time when I'd ever be able to have a child of my own."

"Women still have babies in their early forties," Seth said.

"It's possible, but there are a lot more risks," she agreed.

"And you're not willing to take the risks?"

"It's not that. First, I'd have to meet the right man. I'm not interested in sperm donation or sex with random strangers. And with every year that passes a pregnancy becomes more unlikely."

Somewhere deep inside a part of him wanted to say, "Ask me. I'll have a baby with you." He fought the impulse. As amazing as it would be to share a child with her, he couldn't imagine doing it without marriage, without commitment for the long-term. He wasn't there yet. He wasn't sure he'd ever be there.

Abby leaned forward and regarded him earnestly. "Can you see why I'm more interested in a partnership, in genuine caring, than I am in risking another marriage like the one I had? I want to be with a man who sees value in the woman I am, who encourages me to reach for the unexpected, who makes me laugh and appreciate life in all its craziness."

"And I make you laugh?"

"You do."

"And I appreciate you for the extraordinary woman you are," he said, beginning to understand.

"You seem to."

"So that's enough for you?"

"For now," she confirmed. "I've said it before, Seth. I love spending time with you. Today, for instance, was just about perfect."

Other than a few moments of apparently unnecessary panic, Seth had to agree. It had been a good day. Maybe that was enough for now. If they concentrated on making every day as good as it could be, maybe every tomorrow would take care of itself.

He glanced across the table and saw the smile on Abby's face.

"How about it?" she asked. "You ready to go with the flow?"

"It might never work out," he warned.

"That's a given," she said. "Come to think of it, that's life."

He drew in a deep breath and decided taking the risk was worth it. "Okay, then. I'm all in."

"No more talk of heartbreak and imminent disaster?" she teased.

"I'll do my best," he promised.

"Not good enough. You have to put those things out of your head and live in the moment."

"You're asking an awful lot," he complained.

"But just think of the rewards."

"Rewards?" he repeated, intrigued.

"Just wait and see," she taunted. "You won't be disappointed."

"I'll hold you to that," he said, his blood suddenly pumping a little faster at the promise he saw in her eyes.

Even though he'd just agreed to a go-with-the-flow approach with no demands or expectations, Seth had the feeling that he'd just jumped feet-first into forever.

Despite his commitment to live in the moment, Seth couldn't seem to silence the occasional dire warnings about heartbreak and disaster. Abby got into the habit of putting a finger to his lips to silence him.

For the most part, though, she could see the effort he made to put aside his reservations and get into the spirit of this new approach to their relationship. For several days after their heart-to-heart conversation, things were almost perfect. Abby hadn't laughed this much in a very long time. Who knew that outrageous flirting could be so much fun?

Of course, the fact that Seth seemed determined not to take advantage of any of the openings she was leaving for him was getting under her skin, especially with only that connecting door between their rooms separating them. One of these days she was going to lose control and burst through that door in the middle of the night and climb right into his bed and have her wicked way with him.

"The man is making me crazy," she admitted to Hannah one afternoon when they were alone on the porch at the inn, sharing iced tea and friendly conversation. It was almost like old times, which encouraged Abby to confide her frustrations about the pace of her relationship with Seth.

"So you lied to him when you said you weren't looking for anything more than here and now?" Hannah asked.

"No," Abby insisted. "That much was true. I just want more intimacy here and now."

Hannah laughed at her frustration. "Isn't it awfully soon to think about getting involved with someone? The ink's barely dry on your divorce papers. And no matter what you claim, if you and Seth have sex, you will be involved with him."

"Marshall and I were separated for a long time before those papers were even filed," Abby responded. In fact, even when they'd been living under the same roof, the separation between her and Marshall had been insurmountable for months.

"Okay, let's forget that nonsense you spouted to Seth

in an attempt to settle his nerves. Are you looking for a fling with Seth or something more permanent? Be honest," Hannah commanded.

Abby gave the question a moment of serious thought. Before she could reply, though, Hannah continued.

"It sounds to me as if you're just ready to cut loose and have some fun," she told Abby. "And while there are plenty of men who'd be eager to take you up on that, I don't think Seth is one of them. Underneath all that teasing is a decent guy who's looking for happily ever after, whether he's ready to admit it or not. I can feel it when he's hanging out with Luke and me. He wants what we have. I see it in his eyes when Kelsey and Jeff are around."

"Seriously? I don't see that," Abby said, struck by Hannah's perceptions. They contradicted everything Seth himself had claimed.

"Maybe you don't want to see it," Hannah suggested.

"I swear I'm just going by what he's told me."

"He's lying to himself," Hannah declared convincingly. "That's what men do when they're afraid to give in to their emotions."

As much as she'd wanted to believe that, too, at one time, Abby found it hard to accept. "He sounded pretty sure of himself."

"So it's okay with you if this never goes any further than a fun flirtation or maybe an affair?" Hannah asked. "That doesn't sound like you, either."

"I need it to be me," Abby told her. "I need to be where Seth is."

"Interested in a fling and nothing more?"

"Exactly." Abby sighed. "Look, I do know that there

could be all sorts of complications with having a fling, especially here in Seaview Key."

"More to the point, I think there are complications to having a fling with a man like Seth," Hannah said. "He's capable of loving deeply, Abby. That's what he had with Cara. It's what he deserves again. So do you. Neither of you should be settling for less, no matter what you tell yourselves."

Abby was forced to admit that her friend had a point. A man who'd loved, heart and soul, shouldn't resign himself to a meaningless affair. She deserved better, too.

But the timing for a serious relationship for either of them was clearly all wrong. Seth was still clinging to his grief. She was still wounded from her disaster of a marriage.

"Do you think Seth will ever truly get over losing Cara?"

"First I think he has to get over the guilt," Hannah replied. "People keep calling him a hero for all the rescues he made, the people he saved. He can only see the one person who was lost, the woman he loved and wasn't there for. A man like Seth doesn't get over something like that. I'm guessing that he keeps things light as a defense mechanism. He doesn't want to have his heart ripped out for a second time."

She gave Abby a hard look. "You might want to think about that, if you're just playing games. Since you brought this up, I have to tell you what I believe. You and Seth could be on the brink of something amazing. But if that's not what you're really after, if all you want is this go-with-the-flow craziness you mentioned, then back off, Abby, before Seth takes a real risk with his heart and winds up hurt."

The somber note in Hannah's voice gave Abby pause. Was she playing games? Or were these feelings Seth stirred in her real, something they could build on? From time to time, she'd labeled them as love, but could she trust that? Sometimes infatuation and lust got all twisted up and felt like more than they really were.

Since Abby honestly couldn't answer Hannah's question, she realized she should indeed take a step back. She needed to figure out what was really going on in her heart before she and Seth took things to another level.

Seth came home after a long day with half a dozen minor emergencies and a long visit with Ella Mae. He was looking forward to a shower, then dinner with Abby. It was the pattern they'd established since that first night she'd spent at Seaview Inn.

When he tapped on the connecting door between their rooms, though, she didn't answer. He frowned, glancing at his watch. She should have been back from Christmas shopping on the mainland long before now. That's what she'd told him she intended to do today.

He went downstairs and found Grandma Jenny in the kitchen looking through her recipe file. He gave her a peck on the cheek and peered over her shoulder.

"Chicken and dumplings? It smells fantastic!"

"Seemed like the sort of comfort food you might find appealing," she said.

Seth frowned at something he thought he heard in her voice. "Why would I need comfort food?"

"Because Abby moved out this afternoon," she said. She gave him a worried look. "You didn't know?"

"I knocked on her door just now and she didn't answer," he admitted. "But I had no idea she was heading back to her place today. Are the bathroom renovations finished?"

"I have no idea. She came back from shopping right after lunchtime. She and Hannah spent an hour or two out on the porch and next thing I knew, Abby was checking out."

"Did they have some sort of argument?"

"Not that I could tell. She looked a little pale, but otherwise she seemed just fine. Hannah never said a word, either. In fact, I think she helped Abby take her things back to her place."

"That doesn't make sense," Seth said. "I'd better go over there."

"If you're not back by the time I have the chicken and dumplings on the table, I'll save you some."

"Thanks."

Seth took his time walking up the beach toward Abby's. He couldn't begin to imagine what might have happened between the time he'd kissed her goodbye this morning and midafternoon that would have sent her scurrying home. He had few doubts, though, that it must have something to do with him.

Unfortunately when he got to Abby's, the house was dark and her car was gone. He glanced inside, spotted a couple of suitcases sitting in the middle of the living room and concluded she hadn't left town for good. That, at least, was something.

He walked to The Fish Tale next, but Lesley Ann told him Abby hadn't been in.

Was she hiding out at Luke and Hannah's? he wondered. And if so, why?

Back at Seaview Inn, he was about to get in his car and drive over there, when it occurred to him that wherever Abby was, she didn't want to be found, at least not by him. Otherwise, she'd have left a note in his room or a message on his phone.

As frustrating as it was to give up without answers, he made himself go inside.

"Any luck?" Jenny asked.

He shook his head. "I wish to heaven I had some idea what's going on with her. What could have changed since this morning?"

"You won't know till you talk to her," Jenny said, then gave him a hard look. "Don't wait too long to do that, either."

"I just went looking for her," he protested.

"You can't have searched very hard. This island's not that big. If you'd really looked, you could have found her. That tells me you gave up."

"I didn't give up. I just decided to give her a little space, since it's evident that's what she wants."

"And that's killing you, isn't it?"

"I'm not overjoyed," he agreed.

"Well, just be sure your pride doesn't get in the way of doing what's best for your heart," she advised. "Now sit down and try this recipe. It's been years since I've made it."

Seth sat down and tasted the chicken and dumplings, then smiled. "You haven't lost your touch. As comfort foods go, this is pretty darn good."

"Not good enough to wipe those worries out of your head, I imagine."

He smiled at the suggestion. "It's going to take more than excellent chicken and fluffy dumplings to do that."

"When you figure out why that is, I'm guessing it will go a long way toward telling you what your next step ought to be."

"Am I supposed to get that?" he grumbled.

"Just give it some thought," she said and patted his shoulder. "It'll come to you."

"Since you clearly have some idea of what I should be doing, why not just tell me?"

She winked at him. "What would be the fun of that?"

If anybody had asked, Seth would have told them there was nothing fun about any of this. As hard as he'd been working to protect himself from pain, it had apparently been for naught.

Seventeen

Abby had seen Seth approaching her cottage from the window of her darkened bedroom. She'd held her breath as he'd knocked on the door, then sighed with relief when he finally walked away.

She wasn't ready to see him yet. She had a lot of things to figure out before she spent any more time with him. While she might not need to know if what she felt for him really was love, she certainly needed to know if she was truly ready to settle for less than a lifetime commitment. Hannah had made her see that games could be fun, but could also be emotionally dangerous.

She unpacked her bags, poured herself a glass of tea, then grabbed a light blanket and settled into a rocker on the porch. She could hear the soothing sound of gentle waves washing onshore, the occasional call of a bird. It was peaceful and serene, just what she'd been hoping for when she'd come home.

Inside her head, however, her thoughts continued to be in turmoil. If only she'd met Seth a few months from now when she'd truly had time to figure out who she was these days. If only they'd met when he'd had time to put aside the grief that still consumed him. If only he were older or she were younger. If only, if only… Unfortunately there were too many things that couldn't be changed, important things that couldn't be dismissed so easily.

But even as she struggled to put things in perspective, to examine her innermost thoughts, she kept remembering things he'd said to challenge her, comments that had made her laugh, flirtatious remarks that had made her blush or made her pulse race. And remembering those things made her smile. And in so many ways, more importantly, they made her feel alive and hopeful for the first time in ages.

"Why couldn't this have been less complicated?" she murmured aloud, the question fueled by regret.

Most likely because they weren't untested teenagers the way she and Luke had been. Things had seemed so simple back then, at least until the time came for the hard decisions about going their separate ways for college and into the future.

Instead, she and Seth had met when they both carried enough emotional baggage to be charged extra when they flew. Adults had history that couldn't be ignored. They'd also formed habits and discovered needs they wanted fulfilled. Merging lives at that stage required patience, understanding, determination and compromise. Did she possess any of those qualities?

Patience? Well, hers was definitely questionable, she concluded candidly.

Understanding? She tried to listen and be empathetic, so that probably fell into her plus column.

Determination? Unquestionably that was her best trait, at least among the four.

The ability to compromise? Wasn't that what she'd done a million and one times with Marshall? Wasn't that what she'd vowed never to do again, at least to the extent that she lost herself in the process? How was she to reconcile that promise to herself with the reality that every relationship required compromise to succeed?

The honest assessment left her as confused as ever, and more exhausted. She sighed, folded the blanket and took her empty glass inside. Maybe if she slept on all this, she'd awaken in the morning with the right answers clear as crystal.

First, though, she had to fall asleep. Sadly, sleep turned out to be just as elusive as those answers she was seeking.

Since nothing had magically changed overnight and Abby awoke as confused as ever, she buried herself in work. By midmorning she'd made dozens of calls, organized her notes for the fish fries and the silent auction, then drew up what she hoped was a persuasive new presentation to show to the mayor and subsequently to the council when they finally held their next meeting after the first of the year.

What she needed, though, was an ally, someone who knew the mayor and believed in the project. Since Grandma Jenny had already played her trump card by getting Abby and Sandra at the same table for lunch, maybe it was time to seek out additional support. She headed to Flavors.

Behind the counter, Mary's expression brightened when Abby walked in. "You back for more ice cream?"

"More ice cream and some company, if you have the time," Abby said.

"Mornings in here are slow except at the height of the tourist season," Mary told her. "And this time of year, everyone's already worrying about gaining weight over the holidays from all the parties and family celebrations. They don't eat a lot of ice cream on top of that."

"Wouldn't that make it the perfect time to take a vacation?" Abby asked.

Mary laughed. "There are no vacations when you run a business like this. I can't just shut the door and walk away, even for a few weeks. As soon as I do, someone wants five gallons of some special flavor for a party and I hear about it if I'm not around to provide it. It's not worth the aggravation. A small business thrives on word-of-mouth and excellent customer service."

"Sounds like a good way to drive yourself into an early grave," Abby told her as Mary set a bowl of mango gelato in front of her, then pulled out a chair and sat down. "You're not having any?"

Mary shook her head. "Look at me," she said, patting her generous hips. "I learned a long time ago that eating my own ice cream was a surefire way to pack on extra pounds. I'm still taking off what I gained before that lesson sank in. I may not be able to get around the occasional taste test when I'm experimenting, but I've cut out any more than that."

"Will it bother you to watch me devour this?" Abby asked. "It really is amazing."

"That's what I like to hear," Mary said. "I live for compliments. They're almost as satisfying as a bowlful of ice cream." She studied Abby curiously. "Did you stop by for more ice cream or would I be safe in guessing you want to talk about Blue Heron Cove?"

"Good guess," Abby confirmed. She filled her in

on the most recent complication with the contractor. "I don't have a lot of wiggle room. If things drag on past that January council meeting, I'll lose the best man for the job. Any thoughts on how I can assure that doesn't happen?"

"Aside from tying up Sandra and stuffing her in a closet, you mean?" Mary asked, a glint of amusement in her eyes.

"I've ruled that out," Abby told her, laughing. "Though it has been quite a temptation the past few days."

"Mind if I call Kyle and get him over here? He's her precious grandson, after all. She listens to him when not another soul on the planet can get through to her."

"I'll take advice from anyone at this point," Abby said. "He backs this project, right?"

"Sure. He's as eager for economic development in Seaview Key as I am." She pulled out her cell phone, made the call, then sat back. "He's on his way. While we wait, why don't you tell me what's going on with you and the hottest newcomer to Seaview Key in years?"

Abby blushed at the direct question. "Seth and I are just friends," she said in what she hoped was her most convincing tone.

Mary regarded her with disbelief. "And here I used to think you were smart," she said, shaking her head with dismay. "Please tell me you are not going to let him get away."

"We're friends," Abby repeated.

Mary shook her head. "Ignoring all those sparks is a crying shame," she lamented. "Who's holding out, if you don't mind me asking? It sure didn't seem like it was Seth. He never took his eyes off you the night you were in here. You looked pretty smitten yourself." She sighed. "Or maybe I'm so used to watching the teenagers come in here with stars in their eyes that I see romance everywhere I look these days. If I misjudged the situation, I apologize."

"It's complicated," Abby responded.

Apparently her choice of words gave away her own ambivalence. Mary's eyes lit up. "I knew it. Those sparks never lie."

Fortunately before she could pursue it, her husband came in. Abby recognized Kyle immediately, even though he was balding now and wore glasses. Hard to imagine there'd been a time when he'd been the star on the high school baseball team and had girls chasing after him. He dropped an affectionate kiss on his wife's cheek, went behind the counter and scooped up a dish of dark-chocolate-mint ice cream, then joined them at the table.

"You all having a strategy session?" he asked as he spooned ice cream into his mouth.

"We were waiting for you to do that," Mary told him, then glanced pointedly at the spoon in his hand. "If you'll stop eating long enough to give us your insights."

"Baby, you make ice cream this good, I'm going to eat it whenever I get the chance," he retorted, but he did set down his spoon and turn to Abby. "What can I do to help? I know Gran is dead set against Blue Heron Cove."

Abby's heart sank at the certainty in his voice. "Can you think of any way to change her mind?"

"I've already used my most persuasive arguments to no avail," he told her. "Once that woman sets her mind to something, it's like trying to carve Mount Rushmore with a pocketknife. A waste of time and energy."

"He has tried, though," Mary confirmed. "Which

brings me back to stuffing her in a closet until the vote is over." She grinned at Kyle. "Sorry, hon, but it's what she deserves for being stubborn."

"To be honest, I don't entirely disagree," he admitted. He paused, his expression turning thoughtful. "There could be a better approach."

Abby immediately sat up a little straighter. "Tell me. I'm ready to try anything."

"I just got to thinking, is there anyplace over on the mainland that might be comparable to what you're planning for Blue Heron Cove?"

"You mean a small enclave of homes that have been built so they don't impact too much on the environment?" Abby asked slowly, liking where she thought he was going with this.

"Exactly."

"I'm not all that familiar with Naples or some of the other communities on the coast, but I'll bet my contractor could help me out. This sort of project is what he likes to do and he has a reputation for being good at it. He didn't take me to see his past work, but I read about it."

"Find the very best example he has to offer and take Gran to see it," Kyle recommended. "Or if you think she'll balk at going with you—"

"She will," Mary said with certainty. "When she mentions Abby at all, she makes it sound as if her sole mission is to destroy Seaview Key. Abby's not going to be able to persuade her the sky is blue." She glanced apologetically at Abby. "Sorry, hon, but it's the truth."

Kyle nodded. "More than likely," he agreed. "That doesn't mean we can't take Gran on an outing one day, let her do a little Christmas shopping, feed her a nice lunch, then when she's feeling all mellow, we just happen to drive by to see something that resembles what Blue Heron Cove could be."

Mary's eyes were sparkling now. "And that is why I married you, you wonderfully sneaky man. It's a fantastic idea! Your grandmother's been chomping at the bit to get over to the mainland to shop." She turned to Abby. "She doesn't like the traffic over there, so she relies on us to take her."

"It really is the perfect idea," Abby agreed. "I'll get on it this afternoon. As soon as I have some options, I'll get the information to you. I may run over first to check them out myself so I can guide you to the one that's closest to my vision."

Despite her enthusiasm, she hesitated for just a second. "Before we go to all this trouble, do you both agree that getting Sandra on board is the key? I shouldn't be trying to win over the men who voted with her, so she's just outnumbered?"

"It'll never happen," Mary said. "How those two keep getting reelected is beyond me, but they'll never go against her."

"They're reelected because nobody has bothered running against them," Kyle said. "And, no, I don't think you should be the first." He grinned at Abby. "It's an ongoing debate. In the interest of family harmony, I've been discouraging her from getting mixed up in local politics, at least until my grandmother gets out. The thought of those two butting heads in public gives me heartburn."

"It could definitely make family meals awkward," Abby said, smiling.

Mary waved off the comment. "They're not exactly

a picnic as it is. I might not run against one of these old fuddy-duddies, but I don't keep my mouth shut."

Abby laughed at Kyle's resigned expression.

"That would be hoping for too much," he said dryly.

"You knew I had a mouth on me when you married me," Mary retorted.

"I know, but I overlooked it because you make the best ice cream in the state," he said. "Now, I've got to run. Nice seeing you again, Abby."

"Great to see you, too, Kyle. And thanks for the help."

"Don't thank me yet. Let's see if it works."

Abby was hopeful that it would, but even if it didn't, she was grateful for having found two more people in Seaview Key who might become real friends.

Seth sighed when a call came in from Ella Mae. Though he'd seen her recently, it had just been a drop-in to say hello. She hadn't called for a paramedic since she'd started selling tickets for the fund-raiser. He'd been congratulating himself on devising a plan to keep her busy and to keep her mind off of every little ache and pain.

To his surprise, when he reached her house, she was on the porch waiting for him. There was a healthy glow in her cheeks.

"What's up?" he asked as he joined her. "You feeling okay?"

"No better or worse than usual," she said. "I just figured since you already think my only complaint is boredom, I might as well take advantage of that and call for company."

He regarded her with shock. "Ella Mae, if you want

visitors, including me, all you have to do is issue an invitation. You don't need to call 9-1-1."

"It seemed like the only surefire way to get you here," she said, shrugging off his dismay.

"Do I need to remind you that I dropped by just the other day to say hello?"

"That was then," she said blithely.

He shook his head. "What am I going to do with you?"

"Given my age and overall health, it's not something you'll need to concern yourself with forever," she replied tartly. "Now, tell me what's going on with you and Abby. You managed to dodge every question I asked the other day."

"Maybe because my private life isn't your concern."

The look she gave him was withering. "I expected to see more signs of progress by now."

"Progress?"

"Don't you dare try to pretend you're not interested in her," she said. "Or to tell me she doesn't feel the same way. I saw the handwriting on the wall at that press conference."

"And what makes you so sure there hasn't been any progress since then?"

"I hear things," she said. "And what I'm hearing about the two of you is dead silence. It's discouraging."

"Maybe you should stop using the Seaview Key grapevine as your news source," he suggested.

"Unless you're going to sit there and tell me that Jenny doesn't know what she's talking about, I think we can agree that my source is reliable."

This kept getting worse and worse, not that it was much of a surprise. "You and Jenny have been discussing my relationship with Abby?" he asked, hoping his tone would suggest that he found that objectionable.

"Well, we certainly don't spend all our time talking about ticket sales for that fish fry," she replied. "And just so you know, if I don't like what I'm hearing from you, my next call will be to Abby."

"When did you turn into such a meddler?"

"When you dragged me out of my peaceful existence," she said, then grinned. "Told you that you should have left well enough alone."

"So this is payback?"

"I don't look at it like that," she insisted. "I'm just giving you a push in the direction you ought to be smart enough to go on your own."

Seth sighed. "Thanks for the interest, but maybe you should stay out of this, Ella Mae. It's complicated."

"You like her, am I right?"

"Of course."

"And she's attracted to you, no question about that."

"I suppose," he acknowledged reluctantly.

"Then I don't see the complication."

"Trust me, there are a boatload of them."

She shook her head, her expression filled with pity. "Spoken like a man desperate for excuses."

Seth stared at her. The woman was more perceptive than he'd given her credit for being. Since he couldn't really defend himself, he said, "Leave it alone, Ella Mae. I'm begging you."

She smiled. "I'll give your request some thought," she promised. "But I'm an old lady. I might forget."

"You don't forget anything unless it's convenient," he accused.

"If you understand that, then you're duly warned," she said, laughing.

Seth walked away with the distinct impression that his fate was no longer in his own hands. And maybe that would be a blessing. He sure wasn't doing too well handling it on his own.

That night Seth lay awake, thinking over what Ella Mae had said about making excuses. As he considered that possibility for perhaps the hundredth time, it dawned on him that for the first time in a couple of years the woman on his mind nonstop wasn't Cara Sanchez. He hadn't had the nightmare about the day she'd died in a while now, either.

Abby had taken over his thoughts lately, made him start to yearn for a future he'd all but given up on having.

And yet they were so blasted wrong for each other, or so he kept telling himself. The other day Luke had essentially accused him of focusing too much on money, and he had a feeling his friend had gotten it right… again. What Luke had said came awfully darn close to mirroring Ella Mae's opinion that he was drumming up excuses to avoid getting entangled with a woman who could leave him with a broken heart. It was annoying how Luke—and even a comparative stranger like Ella Mae—saw things in Seth that he didn't want to acknowledge.

Impulsively, he reached for his cell phone and hit speed dial. When Abby answered, her voice husky with sleep, he felt a moment's guilt, right along with enough heat to set his sheets on fire.

"I thought you were a night owl," he said lightly. "I'm sorry if I woke you."

"It's okay," she murmured. "I must have dozed off while I was reading."

"Then you're not in bed yet?"

"No. Why?"

"I was thinking about coming over, if it's not too late."

She hesitated for so long he thought she might refuse.

"Abby?" he prodded. "What do you think? Are you up for company? Or are you still hiding out from me?"

"I wasn't hiding out," she claimed.

Seth didn't call her on the blatant lie, but waited until she sighed.

"Okay, maybe I was," she said.

"So, is it okay if I come over or not?"

"Sure," she said at last.

"That's good, then. I'll be there in a few minutes."

"Seth, wait."

"What?" he asked, holding his breath. Now that he'd made up his mind, he didn't think he could bear it if she told him not to come.

"Are you sure?"

The question was proof enough that she knew exactly what he'd had in mind when he called, that he was ready to put an end to this impasse they'd reached. Whether she'd intended it or not, she'd given him just enough time to realize he didn't want to live without her, at least for tonight.

"Are you?" he countered.

"I'm sure," she said, but there was an uncertain hitch in her voice.

"Abby, this doesn't have to happen. It could be a huge mistake."

"I don't think so," she said. "At least not for me. How about you?"

"I wish to hell I knew. I just know I need to be there tonight, with you."

"Then no more talk about mistakes or regrets, okay?"

Regrets hadn't even crossed his mind, not until now. He had a hunch he'd have a boatload of them by morning. But the thought of her there, waiting, outweighed them.

"On my way," he said.

The soft click of the phone as she disconnected told him she'd be ready.

"Oh my gosh! Oh my gosh!" Abby muttered, racing around her bedroom, gathering up the clothes she'd left scattered everywhere. Neatness had never been one of her virtues. She vowed on the spot to change that, especially if surprise visits like this one were ever to become commonplace.

She whipped off the flannel pajamas she'd been wearing and tore through her lingerie drawer in search of something sexier, then decided the pale blue negligee was too obvious. She covered it with a thick terrycloth robe that would have been suitable for receiving the most judgmental visitor.

But when Seth arrived, took one long look at her and sealed his mouth over hers, what she wore hardly mattered. In less time than she could count, she wasn't wearing anything at all.

Eighteen

Abby fell back against the pillows and tried to catch her breath. Just the sight of Seth had been stealing her breath for weeks now, but that was nothing compared to this. Boy-howdy, when this man finally let himself go, he held nothing back.

She glanced in his direction, took in the glorious view of his beautiful body stretched out beside her. She propped herself on an elbow and studied him, aware that a smile was forming on his lips, even though his eyes remained closed.

"Don't look smug," she said, nudging him.

"Smug was the last thing on my mind," he said. "I was simply enjoying the experience of being ogled."

"How did you know I was ogling you?"

His smile spread. "Lucky guess, but that indignation in your voice is a clear giveaway."

"Not amusing," Abby declared.

"Would it make you feel better if I swear to you that I was just wondering why the heck we took so long to get here?"

"Marginally," she told him. "And I'd have to say that

mature, rational thought probably played an important role in our delayed gratification. We had a lot of very good reasons for taking our time."

He frowned at her answer. "Are you suggesting this was an immature, irrational thing here tonight?"

She thought about the question. "Maybe a little impulsive," she responded carefully. "I mean we've been resisting for ages and suddenly, out of the blue, here we are." She held his gaze. "Why is that?"

"Because I came to my senses," he suggested.

"What sort of an epiphany did you have today?" she inquired curiously.

"It has been brought to my attention that I've been making excuses to avoid getting involved with you," he said. He glanced at her. "And the truth was, we were already involved. No matter how many sane, logical reasons I came up with for keeping you at arm's length, it couldn't stop the inevitable."

"The inevitable?"

"Tonight," he said, his hand stroking her hip. "This."

Abby shivered at the touch, but made herself say, "Maybe we should talk about those sane, logical reasons of yours."

"Now?" he asked, propping himself on an elbow to look directly into her eyes. "You want to rehash them now?"

"I think we should," she replied. "I want to know what's changed. If anything."

"Okay, if you insist," he said. "First, there's the fact that you have more money than me."

She nodded. "That hasn't changed."

"But I've come to accept it."

He glanced over at her, doing a thorough survey that had her skin heating.

"You're older than me," he said, continuing to list the arguments he'd had for not getting any closer. "Though frankly that one didn't amount to much."

Abby smiled, relieved.

"Seaview Key is gossip central," he added.

"Little question about that."

He shrugged. "Doesn't seem to matter. I think we can weather a little talk."

"Is that it?"

"No, here's the biggie, that I wasn't sure I could go through another loss that hurt as much as losing Cara. I've been protecting myself from the kind of emotional pain I went through when she died. I think I saw from the beginning that a relationship with you had the capacity to destroy me."

Abby wasn't at all surprised by anything he'd said. They'd talked about all of his concerns at one time or another. She did think she had a perspective on that last one that he hadn't considered.

"You know, Seth, you're not the only one who'd be hurt if things don't work out."

His startled expression told her it had been all about him. He'd never once considered how she might feel if they took a chance and failed. "You don't think I'd get hurt if you dumped me?" she pressed him.

"I'm a self-absorbed guy. It was all about me," he claimed in an apparent effort to make light of it.

"I'm serious, Seth. I could get hurt, too."

"Are you saying now you're the one who thinks this is a bad idea?"

"Not at all. Rather I've weighed the risks and think

what we have is worth taking the chance. What happened to you today to suddenly wipe out all that caution?"

"I realized that Luke and Ella Mae—"

Abby's eyes widened. "Ella Mae?"

"I told you that woman has too much time on her hands. Now she's using it to dissect my personal life," he lamented.

Abby laughed at his expression. "That must have hurt."

"Actually it got me to thinking about whether I'd be any worse off if we got together and it didn't work than I would be if I gave up before we even got started."

"And you concluded you didn't want to miss out on the moment," she said.

"Something like that," he agreed. "I should warn you that I'm still confused."

"Welcome to the club. Why do you think I was hiding out? And, yes, I admit it. That's exactly what I was doing. Anyway, I think we all fret over whether we're making the right decision, especially when it comes to getting intimate with someone and putting our hearts on the line."

"You, too?"

"Of course, me, too," she said. "I've been trying to convince myself I'd be happy with a wild, carefree fling, because I figured that's all you'd ever go for."

He gave her a penetrating look. "And?"

"Even though I wanted to recapture my wild and carefree youth when I came back to Seaview Key, I'm not sure I'm cut out for a meaningless fling. Sorry."

"Don't be sorry," he said, caressing her cheek. "I

think that particular ship has sailed. There was nothing meaningless about what happened here tonight."

Abby's breath caught at his words.

"It's too soon for promises," he warned. "And there are a lot of things we both need to sort through, but being with you is the best thing that's happened to me in a very long time." He held her gaze. "And it's about a whole lot more than the sex, which was pretty spectacular."

She smiled at his heartfelt assurance. "It was, wasn't it?"

She wanted to ask where they went from here, but it already sounded as if he were no more certain of that than she was. Better not to press for answers he might not have, especially when she wasn't sure of what she wanted to hear.

Maybe she wasn't a live-in-the-moment kind of woman, not yet, anyway. But if every moment could be as glorious as the ones they'd just shared, it wouldn't be such a bad way to live.

Seth woke at dawn, expecting to feel a certain amount of awkwardness about being in Abby's bed. It had been a long time since he'd wanted to wake up next to a woman. He'd become a master at finding an excuse to go home after sex, no matter how satisfying the act itself might have been. That he was still here said a lot about how deep his feelings for Abby were. It was time to stop denying that much at least. He'd put up a valiant, if foolhardy fight, and lost. He was in love with her, no question about it.

She shifted closer, her arm across his stomach, her head settling into the curve of his shoulder. He smiled at the trust she'd placed in him. She was something, all right. He brushed a hand down her back before letting it come to rest on her hip. She stirred at his touch.

"Hmmm," she murmured.

"You awake?" he asked softly.

"Getting there," she replied, her breath feathering across his chest.

"Any thoughts about morning sex?" he asked, his body already responding to her closeness.

He could feel her lips curve against his bare skin.

"I'm in favor of it," she told him. "It appears you are, as well."

He laughed. "You noticed, huh?"

"Hard to miss." She pulled him on top of her. "We could be in trouble, Seth."

"Oh?"

"It's possible I'll never get enough of you."

"Then isn't it a wonderful coincidence, that I'll never get enough of you, either. Now come here and let me show you."

It was an hour before they left her bed, showered and then wandered into the kitchen.

Abby made coffee while he pulled eggs, butter and juice from the refrigerator. For two people who'd never shared a morning routine, they functioned in perfect harmony. Seth couldn't help wondering if that ought to scare him to death, the fact that they clicked on so many levels.

He glanced over to see Abby regarding him with amusement.

"Was that panic that just flitted across your face?" she teased.

"Not panic," he insisted. "Just a momentary qualm."

"It's breakfast, Seth. There's not a minister in sight."

The comment made him laugh, just as she'd clearly intended.

"You have to admit, we do this part surprisingly well."

"I don't know about your breakfast skills, but I've been making coffee every morning for a lot of years long before you were in my life."

"Okay, I'm overreacting," he conceded. "But it does feel awfully domestic."

"And you're scared of domestic?" she asked, eyes sparkling. "Then I promise not to suggest you vacuum, while I dust."

He frowned at her teasing. "Point taken."

She gestured toward the table. "Sit down for a minute."

"But I was about to scramble the eggs," he protested, gesturing toward the eggs he'd cracked into a bowl.

"They'll still be there." She handed him a cup of coffee, then pulled out a chair and sat down facing him. "Here's the one thing I have figured out. This only gets as complicated as we want it to be."

He drew in a deep, calming breath, knowing she was right. No one controlled their destiny except for the two of them. "Fair enough."

"Frankly, I take it as a good sign that this feels so easy and right," she said. "It's been a long time since I've had a morning-after situation that didn't involve my husband, but I seem to recall that things can be awkward."

"That's been my experience, too," Seth acknowledged, then frowned. "Exactly how long has it been since you've been with anyone other than Marshall?"

"He and I were married for twelve years and dated for a couple of years before that, so let's see," she said. "That would make it about fifteen years ago, maybe longer."

Seth regarded her with astonishment. "Between him and Luke?"

She shrugged. "I didn't have a lot of time for dating. And I almost never slept with men I saw only a few times. There was one semi-serious relationship in there."

"So for all this talk about flings, you don't have a track record with such a thing, do you?"

"Not so much. Do you?"

"Well, more than you do," he admitted. "I've made an effort to get Cara out of my head, but it's never really worked, so I gave up on it."

She held his gaze. "Is she out of your head now?"

He saw the worry in her eyes and reached for her hand. "Cara had nothing to do with last night, Abby. That was all about you and me. So is this."

She nodded, a smile touching her lips. "Good to know."

"So, can I get back to scrambling those eggs?"

"Go for it," she said. "I'll make the toast."

As they finished working in the tight space, they brushed hands, bumped hips. Each time, Seth found himself smiling. Suddenly domestic bliss took on a whole new and pretty satisfying meaning.

As soon as Seth had left for work, Abby took a second cup of coffee onto the porch and settled into a rocker. She couldn't seem to stop the smile that spread across her face.

"I know that expression," Hannah said, appearing around the corner of the house. "Something's happened between you and Seth." She grinned. "Finally!"

Abby feigned a scowl. "If I'm that easy to read, I'd better not leave the house today."

"I just know you too well," Hannah said. "Is there more coffee?"

"Help yourself," Abby said, not budging.

When Hannah returned and sat down, she glanced Abby's way. "It feels kind of like old times, doesn't it?"

Abby nodded. "I was so afraid we wouldn't get this back."

"Me, too."

"So, what brings you by this morning?"

"I was at loose ends," Hannah admitted. "It happens right after I turn in a book, especially if I'm not entirely sure what I want to work on next."

"Are you happy with this new career?" Abby asked her. "From everything I've heard, you worked nonstop in New York. This must be a very different pace for you."

"You have no idea," Hannah replied. "And at first I kept feeling as if I was wasting huge amounts of time, but then a very wise person pointed out that part of the creative process is allowing ideas time to simmer."

"Was that wise person your editor?"

"No, it was Luke. I think it was a self-serving response to keep me calm and serene, but he was right. It makes sense."

Abby studied the contentment on her friend's face. "Can I ask you something?"

Hannah glanced her way. "Sure, why not?"

"It's personal. I just wondered if we're there yet."

"No way to know till you ask your question. Try me."

"Have you given any thought to having another child?"

"You mean with Luke," Hannah said, stating the obvious. While she appeared to be considering her response, tears welled up in her eyes, spilled down her cheeks. She swiped at them impatiently.

"I'm sorry," Abby said at once. "I shouldn't have asked."

"No, it's okay. Really. Sure, I've thought about it, but between my age and the cancer, it seems like a far-fetched dream."

"Does Luke agree? He is a doctor. He could probably say if it's far-fetched."

Rather than replying directly to Abby's question, Hannah asked, "What brought this on? Are you wondering if it's too late for you to have a baby? And is that because Seth is younger and you think he's going to want children?"

Abby nodded. "It is a consideration."

"Has he given any indication that not having a child would be a deal breaker?"

"Absolutely not. In fact, if that subject came up, it would probably terrify him." She thought of his panicky reaction to how smoothly they'd managed to prepare breakfast together. "He thinks things are moving too fast as it is."

"So this is about you," Hannah concluded. "You want a baby."

Abby nodded. "I'd pretty much given up hope, but suddenly it's all I think about. There just might be a man in my life at least in the short-term, which was something I definitely hadn't anticipated. I can't help wondering if maybe it's not too late."

"See a doctor," Hannah recommended. "Luke might have some thoughts, but an obstetrician who specializes in high-risk pregnancy would be even better."

"High risk?" Abby echoed, daunted by the phrase.

"Given your age, I'm sure that's how they'd classify it," Hannah explained. "But before you panic, I should tell you that my friend Sue in New York just had her first baby at our age. She handled the pregnancy with flying colors, but the doctors did keep a close eye on her. And if the 'high risk' label scares you, just imagine what they'd pin on me." She shook her head. "Not in the cards for me, I'm afraid. And I do have Kelsey and little Isabella. Luke has Gracie and Nate. We're good."

"No regrets, then?" Abby pressed.

"Sure," Hannah conceded. "But I can accept the situation and be grateful for what we do have." She studied Abby. "Are you going to pursue this?"

Abby drew in a deep breath, then nodded. "I think I should at least know my options in case the subject comes up with Seth."

And if children were out of the question for her, she needed to prepare herself for the possibility that it very well might be a deal breaker for Seth. Of course, they were a long way from having that discussion. If she was being totally honest with herself, she was forced to admit it might never come up at all.

After last night, though, and this morning, she found herself hoping against hope that it would.

A few days later, to keep herself from dwelling too much on her relationship with Seth and all of the unanswered questions about where they might be headed, Abby headed into town after lunch to do a little shopping at the boutiques on Main Street. Though business wasn't as brisk as it would be in another month or so when tourists piled in, the shops were all decorated for Christmas and filled with browsing locals.

She was holding up two sweaters she thought might be perfect for Hannah when she heard a familiar voice from across the shop. Choosing the pale blue sweater, she headed for the register. Her arrival had an expression of distaste spreading across the mayor's face.

"You!" she said as if Abby were her avowed enemy. "I imagine I have you to thank for that stunt my grandson pulled on me yesterday."

Barb Vitale, the shop owner, winced at Sandra's words. "Sorry," she mouthed to Abby.

Abby directed a smile at her, then faced Sandra. "What stunt would that be?"

"Kyle drove miles out of our way to show me a bunch of houses that he claimed were just like what you're proposing for Blue Heron Cove. We missed the ferry home because of it and had to wait for the last one. We didn't get back here till after midnight. It was a colossal waste of time for all of us."

"That was hardly Abby's fault," Barb dared to suggest. "What were the houses like?"

"Nice enough, I suppose," Sandra said with a sniff. "They were well suited for the mainland. Out here, they'd be an eyesore."

Abby was stunned by her claim. "An eyesore? In what way? I saw those houses myself. They were beautiful. They were built so they complemented the natural landscape. They were on big lots, surrounded by mature trees."

"That's all well and good," Sandra said. "But they're too big. It would make everything else out here look like a slum."

Barb regarded her with shock. "That's awfully harsh, Sandra. There are some lovely homes here, including yours." Her eyes widened with sudden understanding. "Oh my gosh, that's it, isn't it? Your family home has always been the showplace of Seaview Key. You'd lose that distinction if these homes are built. That's what you're really afraid of, isn't it?"

As soon as Barb said the words, Abby knew she'd gotten it exactly right. The indignant flush on the mayor's cheeks confirmed it. Abby was about to try to reassure her, even though words failed her, but Barb had more on her mind.

"How selfish can you be?" Barb demanded. "This isn't about what's best for you personally, Sandra. It's about what's best for Seaview Key. Businesses here are suffering. The tax base needs to be bigger if we're to add on needed services. Just think about how hard it was to scrape together the money to pay Seth Landry to put together our own rescue squad. I know for a fact we're paying him a pittance compared to what he could get anywhere else."

"We found the money, didn't we?" Sandra replied. "We've always managed to do right by our residents."

"But think how much more we could do for the seniors, for instance, if we had a bigger tax base," Barb said.

Since Barb was making the case for her, Abby stood by and watched Sandra's face for her reactions. Her expressions were every bit as telling as her words. It was evident she was running out of arguments in the face of the store owner's clear thinking.

"Will you feel the same way when you can no longer afford to live out here?" Sandra finally inquired with a huff.

Once again she'd fallen back into the same old fear-based rut. Abby sighed. If Sandra insisted on using fear to stir public sentiment against Blue Heron Cove, it was going to be hard to fight her. She had to try, though.

"If these homes hold their value as I think they will," Abby responded quietly, "and contribute to the tax base, taxes may well go down for most locals. I'm going to make sure people understand that."

"You can certainly try," Sandra replied. She set her collection of merchandise on the counter. "I've lost all interest in shopping today."

She turned and walked out without a backward glance.

Abby faced the store owner apologetically. "I'm so sorry I cost you that sale."

"Not your fault," Barb said. "I'm surprised you didn't walk out the minute she went on the attack."

"I keep hoping I can get through to her. For a minute there I thought you might accomplish what I haven't been able to."

"It was worth a shot," Barb said. "Sorry the results weren't better." She grinned at Abby. "Were you really behind that little excursion Kyle and Mary took her on yesterday?"

Abby nodded. "It was Kyle's idea. I found a few projects that seemed comparable to Blue Heron Cove, took a look at them and decided this one would wow her."

She sighed. "I guess I was overly optimistic. It seems to have had the opposite effect."

"Only because she's stubborn. It's past time for someone to replace her as mayor, but nobody else wants the job. Overall, she's been dedicated and loyal, but she doesn't have a lot of vision."

"Who does?" Abby asked.

"Well, you, for one," Barb said. "I could get behind a campaign for you to replace her."

Abby smiled at her enthusiasm. "No way. For one thing, as long as this development is on the agenda, I'd have a huge conflict of interest. Down the road? I guess we'll see."

Barb lifted her cup of coffee. "Then here's to down the road."

On her way home, Abby stopped by Flavors. As soon as the customers had left, she smiled at Mary. "I gather our plan backfired."

"Big-time," Mary conceded with a sigh. "Sandra figured out right away what we were up to and pitched a merry fit. She even told off Kyle, who'd never heard a harsh word cross her lips in all these years, at least not directed at him."

Abby winced. "Sorry."

"Not your fault. At least he now sees what the rest of us see, that she's not a misunderstood saint."

"Someone just suggested to her that what she really objects to is that these houses will outshine the Whittier family home. Is that possible?"

Mary's expression turned thoughtful. "You know, I never even considered that, but it makes sense. She takes an awful lot of pride in her founding family status.

Being on the Christmas tour of historic homes every year means a lot to her. She acts like the island's benevolent grande dame for a night. You should see her all dressed up as she greets everyone at the front door. The tour's next week. You should come with Kyle and me. It's a command performance for us."

"And have her cut you both out of the will?" Abby asked wryly.

Mary waved off the worry. "Not that big a deal, believe me."

"Well, I'll definitely consider going, but I think I'd better show up on my own. You all don't deserve the aggravation. You've done enough to try to help me." She studied Mary. "What do you think will be accomplished if I do go?"

"Maybe it'll give you some ideas about how you can preserve what she cherishes—that house—and still do what needs to be done with Blue Heron Cove."

Abby could see how it might actually help. In fact, there was an idea in there that could work. If she pushed to make the Whittier home an official historic landmark, would that be enough to appeal to Sandra's ego? Would she be reassured that her family's place in the island's history would be preserved forever? And would that be enough to get her past her objections to Blue Heron Cove?

Only one way to find out, Abby concluded. She'd start looking into the possibilities first thing in the morning.

Nineteen

Filled with trepidation, Seth walked into the kitchen at Seaview Inn at the end of the day. He'd never missed breakfast at the inn before this morning. He couldn't help wondering what sort of aggravation he had in store.

Fortunately, Grandma Jenny was nowhere in sight. Kelsey, however, turned from the stove and grinned at him, her expression all too knowing. Before she could say whatever was on her mind, Isabella cried out from her high chair, holding her arms out toward Seth. He seized on the opportunity to distract her mom like the lifeline it was.

"How's my favorite girl?" he asked, scooping the baby into his arms. She gurgled with delight, a mile-wide smile on her face.

"Favorite, huh?" Kelsey said. "Does Abby know she has competition?"

"Abby?" he repeated innocently. "No idea what you're talking about."

"Then you didn't stay at her place last night?" Kelsey asked skeptically. "You certainly weren't here."

"And how do you know that?"

"Because Jeff went to your room to see if you wanted to join us for a game of Scrabble. No answer. And you hadn't come in by the time we went to bed."

"I could have come in later," he suggested.

She leveled a look straight into his eyes. He'd seen that same penetrating look a time or two from Grandma Jenny, and from Hannah, for that matter. Must be a family trait, the ability to make people squirm.

"Did you?" Kelsey asked. A smile tugged at her lips. "And before you decide to fib to me, you need to know that my next question will be about why you missed breakfast this morning."

"Has it occurred to you that guests might not appreciate this kind of interrogation?" he grumbled.

She waved off the question. "You're not a guest. You're family. That makes you fair game."

"And *that* gives me even more incentive to find my own place," he told her.

"Why bother," she retorted, "when it's entirely likely you and Abby will be moving in together someday soon?"

A little shiver that might have been anticipation—or panic—washed over him. "How did you make the leap to that conclusion simply from the fact that I may or may not have spent the night elsewhere last night? For all you know I could have been on the mainland with a patient. I might have missed the last ferry back."

"Were you?"

Seth sighed. "No."

Kelsey grinned happily. "So things really are heating up with Abby? That's great news."

"I thought you disapproved."

"That was before I got to know her and before I realized that you were the key to keeping her away from Luke."

"So you see this as a means to an end for your purposes," he surmised. "It's not my welfare that concerns you at all? Or Abby's?"

"That's not entirely true," she said, trying to take Isabella from him so she could feed her. The baby clung to him for dear life, screaming at a level that could have registered her objections all the way over on the mainland. She wrapped her fists around clumps of Seth's hair and held tight.

Kelsey frowned at her daughter and tried to pry her fingers loose. In pain, but impressed by Isabella's strength, Seth waved Kelsey off. "Let me, please."

"Hey, sweetheart," he coaxed, slowly freeing her grip on his hair and shifting her in his arms so he could look into her sweet little tear-streaked face. "Dinnertime, okay? Mama has your favorite." He glanced at the jar of carrots and made a face. "At least she has something healthy. Yum!"

Isabella didn't look convinced, but she allowed him to settle her back in her high chair. She regarded him with a look of betrayal and once more held out her arms.

"Dinner first," Seth told her, as Kelsey lifted a spoonful of carrots toward her.

Isabella batted the carrots away. Kelsey started to get up, but Seth put a hand on her shoulder. "Concentrate on getting that into her. I'll clean up."

Double-teaming Isabella, they finally managed to get her fed. Kelsey handed her a bottle and she leaned back, contented at last, her big eyes still following Seth every time he moved.

"Now, let's get back to you," Kelsey said, turning to Seth.

"Let's not. I've got places to go and things to do."

"You're not staying for dinner?"

"Not tonight," he said. He had no idea where he was going to eat, but it wouldn't be here.

"Interesting," Kelsey said. "Last night, MIA. Breakfast, MIA. And now out to dinner with no admitted destination. I think I'm detecting a pattern."

"Whatever pattern you think you're seeing, keep it to yourself. I've had about as much aggravation as I can take for one day," he said as he walked out the back door.

"You do know it's only because we care," she called after him.

Yeah, he got that. But right this second, he could do with a little less caring and a lot more privacy.

Though Seth wanted nothing more than to head directly to Abby's, if only because she would commiserate with him over the grief Kelsey had subjected him to just now, he talked himself out of it. If he kept showing up there, it would just add to the mountain of evidence people seemed to be gathering already that he and Abby were a couple.

Instead, he went to Flavors. It was another unseasonably warm night and ice cream held a lot more appeal than dinner. When he walked in the door, Mary greeted him with a smile.

"You just missed Abby," she told him.

So, yet again, someone was assuming that would

matter to him. It did, but did everybody have to hop on that particular bandwagon at once? It was starting to freak him out.

"Did she come in for more ice cream? I knew she'd be hooked."

"Actually she came by because she'd heard the plan we'd devised to win over Sandra had backfired."

Seth's heart sank. "What plan was that?"

Mary filled him in as she scooped up his usual praline ice cream and handed him the cup. "It should have worked, too," she lamented. "Those houses over in Naples were beautiful, everything we could possibly want to see out here."

"Abby must have been disappointed," he said.

Mary's expression turned thoughtful. "Actually she seemed to take it better than I'd expected. I got the feeling she has something else up her sleeve. She didn't say a word about it, but she left here looking pretty determined." She gave him a sly look. "Maybe you should check it out. Could be she's just good at hiding her feelings and would love a shoulder to cry on."

Before Seth could say whether he'd drop in or not, Mary scooped some of the mango gelato into a carton and put on a lid. "Take this by. It's on the house."

With the pint container already filled, Seth couldn't very well decline. Besides, this gave him the perfect excuse to do what he'd been wanting to do all day, anyway: see Abby again without having to acknowledge to anyone—even himself—that he couldn't stay away. He might have acknowledged to himself that he was down for the count, but the whole blasted world didn't have to know it.

"Yours is on the house, too," Mary said, shooing him toward the door.

"You seem awfully anxious to see that Abby's doing okay."

"Truthfully, I'm worried she'll get so sick of Sandra and the politics in this town that she'll pack up and leave. That would be a crying shame, you know what I mean?"

Seth knew exactly what she meant, and the thought of Abby going anywhere before they could figure out where they were headed as a couple made his heart ache. He gave Mary a wave and left Flavors, determined to do everything in his power to keep Abby right here in Seaview Key.

Ever since she'd gotten home, Abby had been online researching how to get the Whittier home onto the National Register of Historic Places or even onto some Florida equivalent that would assure the home's place in local history.

She didn't have access to enough information to fill out any forms herself, but she printed out everything to pass along to Kyle and Mary. She'd just printed the last document, when Seth tapped on the front door, then held up a container of ice cream.

She beckoned for him to come in.

"You're bringing bribes now? Didn't you think I'd let you in if you came empty-handed?"

He laughed. "I was hoping that my charming self would be enough, but Mary had other ideas. She thought you might be feeling blue, so she sent more of that mango gelato you liked so much."

Abby sighed. "Then I assume she told you what happened with Sandra and our grand scheme."

Seth nodded. "Want me to scoop this up?"

She shook her head. "I'm good right now. Put it in the freezer for later, unless you want some."

"I just had a double scoop of praline in a cup on the walk over here," he admitted. "Dinner, as a matter of fact."

She frowned at that. "That's not exactly a healthy meal. I have some pasta I made with tomatoes and fresh basil. There's plenty left over. Interested?"

"It sounds good, especially if you have grated Parmesan cheese."

"Of course I do. And it's fresh, too, not in one of those boxes."

"What a woman!"

"Don't get too excited. For someone who owned a restaurant, I have a surprisingly limited repertoire in my own kitchen. What I do, though, I try to do well."

Abby led the way into the kitchen and took the leftover pasta from the refrigerator. "You realize this won't be as good reheated as it was when I made it."

He grinned at her. "Stop making excuses. I'm so hungry, I could eat cardboard."

She put the pasta into a pan to warm, then regarded him closely. "I thought you usually ate dinner at the inn, at least when you don't have other plans."

"Tonight's menu included too many questions about where I spent the night," he admitted.

Abby chuckled. "Ah, Grandma Jenny was on a quest, was she?"

"Not Grandma Jenny. She wasn't even around. This was Kelsey. That was embarrassing enough. I didn't stick around to see what might be on Jenny's mind."

"You do realize they're only the tip of the iceberg,

right? If we keep seeing each other, there will be questions and looks and speculation everywhere we go."

"We could just hole up right here," he suggested hopefully.

Abby laughed. "I know this house seems as if it's hidden away, but trust me, on Seaview Key nothing is off-limits to prying eyes."

He sighed. "Yeah, I was afraid of that."

"There's always the mainland," she suggested. "No one over there knows us or cares what we're up to."

She was only joking, but Seth immediately stilled, a frown settling on his face. "What?" she said.

"Are you thinking about leaving Seaview Key?" he asked.

"Of course not," she said at once. "I was teasing. Why?"

"It was something Mary said. She was afraid if you got too discouraged, you'd take off."

She studied him intently. "And that would bother you?"

"Well, sure it would," he said irritably. "We're just getting started. I know that I've predicted all along that we might not last, but I was hoping for more than a one-night stand."

Abby thought she heard real worry in his voice. She turned the heat off under the pasta and slipped onto his lap, linking her hands behind his neck. "How about a two-night stand?" she suggested quietly.

He smiled at that. "Not enough."

"Three?"

"Better."

"You want to go for broke?" she asked. "See how long a run we can have?"

"That sounds more like it," he agreed. "How about you?"

"Just what I was hoping you'd say," she agreed, lowering her head and touching her lips to his.

The kiss was so sweet, the heat so immediate that dinner no longer seemed to be on Seth's mind. As for Abby, she couldn't think at all.

It was after midnight when the grumbling of his stomach reminded Seth that he was hungry for more than the woman beside him. He tried to slip out of the bed, but Abby's whimpered protest kept him in place.

"Don't go," she murmured.

"I was just going to the kitchen to heat up that pasta."

Her eyes blinked open and she was suddenly wide-awake. "Oh, Seth, it's probably a congealed mess by now," she said apologetically. "I'll fix you something else."

"I can make a sandwich or something," he protested. "You stay right here."

She looked as if she wanted to argue, but then she sighed and stretched, drawing his attention straight to the expanse of well-toned skin exposed by the suggestive drape of the sheet. He blinked and looked away. If he focused on Abby, he'd never get out of this room.

She smiled, obviously sensing his struggle. "You won't take off, will you?"

"Not a chance," he promised. "Try to stay awake till I get back."

"I might be fighting a losing battle," she said. "But feel free to wake me."

Seth nodded and headed for the kitchen. The pasta truly was an unappetizing mess, so he fixed himself a thick ham-and-cheese sandwich on sourdough bread, then even grilled it. As he finished the last bite, he congratulated himself for not having lost his skill at making the best grilled cheese he'd ever tasted.

In the bedroom doorway, he hesitated, noting that Abby had snuggled deeper under the covers and was sound asleep. While crawling back into bed with her and taking advantage of her invitation to wake her held a lot of appeal, so did the prospect of going back to the inn. A night in his own bed might save him from another awkward cross-examination. It would also help him to reclaim some of the emotional distance that made him feel safe, as if he were still in control of his life.

He jotted a note—"See you tomorrow. Love, Seth"—and left it on the nightstand, then headed back to Seaview Inn.

Only when he was stretched out in his own bed did he acknowledge that what he'd done was a self-protective act of cowardice. He was still hedging his bets where Abby was concerned. As long as he could walk away, even for a few hours, as long as he could sleep without her beside him, he could tell himself that his heart wasn't in danger.

The reality, though, was that he'd already lost it. That note he'd left? *Love, Seth.* It pretty much gave him away.

Abby woke to a lonely bed and a note that said far too little. Impulsively, she picked up her cell phone and dialed Seth's number.

"Did you get scared?" she asked bluntly.

Rather than a direct answer, he said, "You were sleeping so soundly, I didn't want to wake you."

"Very thoughtful," she commended him. "Did you get scared?"

She heard him sigh and knew she'd hit the nail on the head.

"Okay, yes, I had a momentary twinge of panic," he admitted eventually. "But it wasn't so much about us."

"Oh?"

"It was more about avoiding another one of those inquisitions over here," he insisted.

He made it sound like a credible excuse, but Abby wasn't buying it. "I find it hard to imagine that a woman in her eighties and a girl in her twenties can scare a big, tough ex-soldier like you."

"Have you met those two? Those in-your-face reporters on *60 Minutes* are pussycats by comparison."

Abby laughed. "You just have to learn avoidance techniques," she said. "Dodge and weave. Isn't that something they taught you in basic training?"

"That's a technique for avoiding gunfire. It has nothing to do with evading a direct question from a female who's staring you straight in the eye and all but daring you to lie. I swear that's almost as intimidating as facing down the enemy. It creeps me out."

"You need to toughen up, big guy. Come back over here for breakfast and I'll give you some tips," she suggested. "Besides, I owe you a decent meal."

"Not your fault that I never got that pasta," he reminded her. "And the sandwich I made myself later was pretty darn good, if I do say so myself."

"So, you didn't starve," she agreed. "But that was hours ago and you know what they say—breakfast is the most important meal of the day. If you don't have it with me, you'll have to sit across the table from Jenny and Kelsey. Now you tell me which of us is less likely to give you grief."

Seth laughed. "Definitely a valid point," he said, but he didn't sound a hundred percent convinced.

"What's worrying you now?" Abby asked.

"If I take off again this morning, don't you think it'll just cause more speculation?"

"It might, which is exactly why I'll be coaching you on the best way to head off these inquiries."

She hesitated, then made what she considered to be the perfect, devious suggestion guaranteed to get him to her place. "Or," she began innocently, "I could send Hannah over to help you out. I'll bet she taught some of her clients how to get around tough questions. And she certainly has plenty of experience at evading Jenny's prying."

"I think Hannah will have enough tough questions of her own for me," Seth said. "Let's leave her out of it. Give me a half hour and I'll be there. Make the coffee very, very strong."

"Done," she said at once, satisfied with her progress in learning which buttons to push.

As soon as she'd hung up, she showered, pulled on clean clothes and headed for the kitchen, wondering what she'd find after Seth's late-night snack attack.

To her surprise, the kitchen was spotless. The dishes had been washed and put away. The counters were clean and the coffeepot had been filled to a level that promised Seth's desired strength. It was already plugged in, which made her wonder if he'd intended to come back this morning all along.

She found herself grinning as she flipped the switch to turn on the coffeemaker.

She searched the kitchen until she discovered her mother's old waffle iron in the back of the pantry. Then she made the batter for waffles while it heated. She set the table, poured the juice and was on her second cup of coffee when Seth arrived. He had a handful of daisies in his hand. She laughed when she saw the roots still clinging to some of them.

"Please tell me you did not yank those out of Jenny's garden," she said.

He shrugged. "I figured she'd give me a pass this once. She's a big fan of the romantic gesture."

"Good luck with that. She's also very protective of her flower beds."

Seth chuckled. "And that's why these didn't come out of the flower beds. I yanked them out of a container on the steps, then hid the container."

Abby stared at him. "You didn't."

"I did," he confirmed, looking pleased with his own ingenuity.

"In that case I'm very glad I decided to fix you waffles this morning," she said. "You deserve a really fabulous last meal."

Seth looked vaguely alarmed by her comment, then shrugged it off. "She loves me," he insisted.

"I sure hope you're right."

"What about you?" he asked, holding out the flowers. "Do these get me points with you?"

"You don't need any more points with me," she told him, moving closer. "You had me the day you rescued me and let me kiss you."

"Yeah, I was pretty much lost that day, too," he said, setting the daisies in the sink and looping his arms around her waist.

"Seriously?" she asked, surprised by the admission.

"Come on. There was a beautiful, sexy, half-drowned woman in my arms and she was kissing the stuffing out of me. It would have taken a much tougher man than I am to resist."

She leaned back and met his gaze. "So you did kiss me back? I didn't imagine that?"

"Afraid so," he said. "Do you think less of me now for taking advantage of you in such a vulnerable moment?"

"I think we can agree that whatever happened was mutual," she said, relieved to know that she hadn't made a complete fool of herself that morning. She grinned. "And maybe we should never speak of it again."

"I don't know," he protested. "I sure don't want to forget those moments."

"I doubt that's an option," she conceded. "But I'd like to think we can keep on topping that morning."

Seth laughed. "Now there's a goal I can definitely get behind."

Abby nodded, pleased. Every goal they shared brought them one step closer to an intimacy that might have the potential to last. At least that's what she increasingly found herself hoping.

Twenty

When his cell phone rang, Seth had just returned home after taking a patient to the hospital over on the mainland. He answered without bothering to check the caller ID.

"Hey, Seth," Laura's ex-husband said. "How are you?"

"I'm doing okay, Jason. How about you?" he asked cautiously. Though he and Jason had remained in touch after the divorce, it wasn't as if they were pals. There had to be something going on for him to be calling now. "Is everything okay?"

"Have you spoken to Laura recently?"

"More than I've wanted to, frankly," he replied.

Jason's chuckle suggested he was in the same place. "Did she mention that she wants us to get back together?"

"She did," Seth admitted. Even though he thought he knew the answer, he asked, "How do you feel about that?"

"I love her, man, but I can't go back there," Jason replied wearily. "I'm still trying to clean up the financial mess we were in before the divorce."

"I'm sorry."

"She says she's changed, that once she gets the money from your parents' estate, she'll pay off all the old bills. She seems to think the slate will be wiped clean if she does that and we can start over."

"She's said something similar to me," Seth said.

"Do you believe her?"

Seth heard the hopeful note in Jason's voice, but he couldn't make himself lie, not even for his sister. "No," he said quietly. "I asked a lot of questions, Jason. The answers weren't reassuring."

His former brother-in-law sighed. "That's pretty much what I figured. I liked your parents, but bless 'em, they raised Laura to expect a certain lifestyle. I couldn't give her that before, but she spent like I could. I'm never going to be rich, and that's what she needs, no matter what she claims about learning to economize."

"I wish it weren't that way," Seth told him honestly. "But I think you're right."

"Thanks for being honest with me. I knew you would be. And I needed a reality check. I was about ready to take a chance on going down that path again. I guess sometimes love's just not enough."

"In some situations, it's not," Seth said. "Sorry, pal. If it's any consolation, I do think she loves you. I just don't know if she's capable of changing."

He sure as heck hadn't seen any evidence of it and with Laura's attorney due in town tomorrow, it was yet more proof that she was always going to take the easy way out. And once that inheritance was gone, assuming a long-shot victory in her case against Meredith, what then? Seth didn't even want to think about what the future might hold for her. But he couldn't help believing that Jason was better off being out of it. How sad was it that two of the people who loved her the most had no faith in her?

Seth's conversation with his former brother-in-law depressed him. It was a stark reminder that love didn't always triumph, especially when two people were in such different places financially. He couldn't help once again comparing that to his relationship with Abby. Doubts he thought he'd put to rest resurfaced.

Not that Abby frittered away money the way Laura had, or lived a lavish lifestyle, but was there any guarantee that she wouldn't? Like Jason, he was and always would be a blue-collar kind of guy, not rich, but bringing in enough to pay the bills and support his family. At least as long as one of them wasn't throwing money down the drain.

Though the past few weeks had reassured him about Abby's priorities in life and that their financial differences weren't so important, Jason's distress ate away at Seth's conviction that Abby and his sister were nothing alike. Maybe he was as oblivious as Jason had been. He wanted to believe in Abby just as Jason had obviously once believed in what he had with Laura. Was that faith blinding him to a very real problem that could crop up down the road? Had his initial worries been based on some reality he'd recently chosen to ignore? How long had he known Abby, really? And how good was his judgment? It was a well-known fact that lust could impair common sense. It made him a little crazy that all this was cropping up in his head again just when things between them had started feeling right.

He was still in that dark place when Laura's attorney turned up at Seaview Inn the next morning to take his deposition. Seth had to admit the guy was skilled at trying to twist Seth's words to suit the case he was trying to build. After the first few questions, though, Seth had had enough.

Scowling at the man in his expensive sportswear, Seth said, "You can play whatever games you want to play. That's what my sister is paying you to do, but you need to hear me." He directed his words to the cell phone camera which was video recording the interview. "My parents knew exactly what they were doing when they left Meredith in charge of the estate. Laura is financially irresponsible. Any lawyer worth his salt is going to be able to look up her credit card statements and her credit rating to prove that. They'll be able to put her ex-husband on the stand to talk about why their marriage ended and the debt he's still trying to clear up. You drag me in to testify and I'll support Meredith a hundred percent."

The lawyer looked momentarily taken aback by his vehemence. "But you haven't been living close by for a long time. How reliable can your testimony possibly be?"

"So you intend to discredit me? Go for it. I doubt it will hurt Meredith's case, but it sure as heck won't do anything to help Laura. Now, if we're done wasting time here, I have things to do."

He stood up and walked away, leaving the obviously stunned attorney to stare after him. He headed straight into town and into The Fish Tale.

Lesley Ann took one look at his face and gestured toward a booth. "I'll bring you a beer."

Seth shook his head. Alcohol wasn't the answer. "Just coffee will do."

"And some company? Abby's back there. Her mood doesn't look much better than yours. Maybe you can cheer each other up."

Abby was the last person he wanted to see right this second, but Seth headed her way just the same. Standing beside her booth, he announced, "I'm probably lousy company."

She smiled at his declaration. "Me, too." She gestured toward the seat. "Sit down, anyway. We can just scowl at each other and save the rest of the world from having to deal with either one of us."

Lesley Ann brought his coffee, then discreetly left them alone.

As Seth took his first sip of coffee, he caught Abby studying him.

"Laura's lawyer was just here," he said, answering her unspoken question.

"Ah," she murmured. "And it didn't go well?"

"Not for him," he said. "And it reminded me of what a mess people can manage to make of their lives even when they're in love with each other."

"So the conversation sent you right back to that ominous place in which all relationships end in disasters of one sort or another," she guessed.

He shrugged. "Something like that. Add in a depressing conversation with Laura's ex-husband, and I'm in a foul mood. What about you? You're not looking all that cheery this morning, either."

"Troy called. He's got an offer that trumps mine, a project that's ready to move forward right after the first of the year and is too alluring to pass up. He says he regrets having to bail on me, but it doesn't make sense to turn this offer down when there's been no progress with Blue Heron Cove."

Seth frowned. "I thought he gave you time to try to get that January council vote to go in your favor."

"He promised to try," she said. "I can't blame him, though. If this opportunity were just some ordinary house or even a cookie-cutter housing development, I think he would wait. Apparently, though, it's Blue Heron Cove on steroids, not just a half dozen homes the way I'm planning, but a couple of dozen on acre lots with every environmental precaution to be taken. The houses will be loaded with energy-saving everything, plus a ton of custom carpentry."

"So, it'll be as green as Blue Heron Cove, but bigger," Seth concluded.

She nodded. "How can I blame him for choosing a sure thing that's exactly the kind of project he loves? It's not as if I could sign him to a binding contract at this point. We just had an agreement to work together if Blue Heron Cove happens. And because this other project is so big, it'll keep him tied up way too long for me to wait around until he's free."

Seth couldn't miss how the news had deflated her. "I'm sorry, Abby. I know you were counting on him. So, what now?" He held his breath, half expecting her to announce she'd be throwing in the towel.

"I keep fighting to get the approval I need from the council," she said with surprising determination. "And, in the meantime, I look for another possible contractor. Troy had some suggestions. Of course, the truth is, no matter how good they are, they won't be as good as he is."

She met Seth's gaze, her expression knowing. "You were expecting me to give up, weren't you?"

"I was afraid you might."

"Not in my nature," she told him. "Not without a fight. Let that be a lesson to you, Seth. I won't walk away from you without giving it my all, either."

He smiled at the fierce declaration. "Good to know." Especially when he'd spent the past couple of days filled with all these renewed doubts. If she could hang in there and ignore the odds against them, how could he possibly do any less?

To distract herself from Troy's defection and from Seth's uncertainties, Abby decided to plan a Christmas party. It had been a long time since she'd had a chance to throw a holiday event for herself. In recent years she'd organized dozens of private parties at the restaurant and a dozen or more in the church's parish hall for the congregation, but Marshall had always said the Christmas season was too demanding to open their home to guests.

She wrote out a guest list and a menu, then called Seth.

"I need you," she announced when he answered.

"Really?" he said, a smile in his voice. "Should I even ask about the hint of desperation I hear in your voice or should I just rush right over there?"

"No need to rush. I'll meet you at the Christmas tree lot," she said.

"Ah," he said, not even trying to hide his disappointment. "It's my brute strength you're after."

"Yes, but your charming company is quite a bonus." She paused, then asked, "You are back to your charming self, right?"

"Mostly," he told her. "And I'll try to keep your priorities in mind while I nurse my wounded ego," he said. "How soon do you need me and my muscles over there?"

"Fifteen minutes," she suggested. "Will that work?"

"Sure. Shall I borrow Luke's truck?"

"Probably a good idea."

Abby drove her car to the tree lot, as well, even though it was within walking distance. For what she had in mind, she had a hunch they'd need the pickup and her trunk.

Walker Smith greeted her as she walked onto the lot. "Heard you were back in town," he said. "I can still remember you coming here with your folks when you were just a girl. You always wanted the biggest tree on the lot."

She laughed. "I still do," she told the man who'd always borne a striking resemblance to Santa Claus with his white beard and oversize belly. Not that Walker exploited that. He determinedly refused to wear so much as a red hat, much less the rest of the costume. Today he was wearing a blue Hawaiian shirt with a startlingly bright pattern of pink hibiscus blooms.

Abby drew in a deep breath, loving the aroma of pine and Fraser fir that evoked Christmas in a way nothing else could. "It smells so wonderful I could stay right here all day," she told him.

"Just got a delivery of fresh trees this morning," Walker said. "There's plenty of holly, too."

"What about garlands? Or do I need to buy greens and make my own?"

"My wife's been making garlands from the branches we've trimmed," he told her and gestured toward a display. He gave her a wink. "And there's plenty of mistletoe, too."

Seth arrived just in time to overhear that. "Point me toward the mistletoe," he said.

Walker shook his head, his expression sorrowful. "Now, I took you for a man who wouldn't need help stealing a kiss from time to time. You've disappointed me."

Abby laughed. "Next he'll be telling you he's shy," she said. "Don't believe him."

Seth grinned at her. "Okay, fill me in. Why are we here?"

"It's not to buy a car," Abby retorted.

Seth groaned. "I figured out that much. A tree, then. Have you had a chance to pick one out?"

"I'm thinking I could use three," Abby said.

He blinked at that. "Three?"

"Three big ones," she confirmed. "Enormous, in fact. One for the living room and two for each side of the porch. Then I need garland for the railings." She smiled at him. "And mistletoe for over the front door."

"How about the bedroom door?" Seth inquired.

She held his gaze. "Do you really think you'll need mistletoe at that point?"

Walker held up his hands and backed away, his cheeks bright red. "Too much information," he declared.

Seth laughed. "Now you've gone and done it. It'll be all over Seaview Key by nightfall that I have an open invitation into your bedroom."

Abby stared at him. "That is not what I said."

"Doesn't matter what you said. What matters is the spin Walker's going to be putting on it the first chance he gets."

Sadly, he was probably right, Abby concluded. "I can't worry about what people are saying."

"Even if it means they'll think less of you? Don't you want a spotless reputation when you go before council again?"

"Seth, the reality of life is that no one's reputation is spotless. We've all made our share of mistakes."

She frowned at her own choice of words. "Not that you and I are a mistake," she added hurriedly. "I just meant that everyone's reputation could be picked apart by small-minded individuals. I'm sure there are a few people with long memories who disapproved of my relationship with Luke years ago. A few of them probably still wonder if I'm here to stir up trouble for him and Hannah. Thankfully Hannah's no longer among them, and she's the one who counts."

"Duly noted," he said. "Now let's get serious about those trees. Have you made your choices yet? What about these three right here?"

"Are you kidding? I can't just point and take whatever's handy," she scoffed. "This is serious business. We have to stand each tree up, shake out the branches, check out the shape, make sure the needles are still fresh."

Seth sighed. "We're making a morning of it, then?"

"At least," she said.

"And if I get an emergency call?"

She chuckled at the hopeful note in his voice. "I'll probably still be here when you get back."

"I was afraid of that." He reached for the closest tree, stood it upright and gave it a shake.

"Nope," she said at once.

"What's wrong with it?" he asked. "Just so I can try to get a grasp on your standards."

"Too short, for one thing."

"Even for the porch?"

"Yes, even for the porch," she said. "Besides, there's a big hole on that side."

"Couldn't you turn that side toward the wall or something?"

She patted his cheek. "We're looking for perfection, okay? There are lots to choose from. Let's not settle just yet."

He sighed. "Got it. And you'll know it when you see it, so I should keep my opinions to myself."

"That's the spirit," she said, then gestured toward another tree. "Try that one."

Walker had returned just in time to overhear the exchange. He winked at Seth. "Better you than me, my friend. I have a thermos of coffee over there if you need an energy boost. Her dad and I could tell a lot of fish tales while this one was choosing trees back in the day, and she was barely knee-high to a tadpole at the time."

"I'll keep that in mind," Seth said, looking resigned as he shook out the next tree's branches. "Well?"

"Not bad," Abby told him. "It's a maybe."

"But too soon to be a sure thing," he concluded.

"Now you're catching on."

It took two hours to find the perfect trees, even on a comparatively small Christmas tree lot. By the time Abby had added sufficient garland and that package of mistletoe, even she was exhausted.

"I'll stop by The Fish Tale and pick up lunch," she offered. "Then meet you back at the house."

Seth's gaze narrowed. "That ought to take you just long enough for me to unload the trees, am I right?"

She laughed. "Almost exactly," she acknowledged. "But lunch will come with dessert."

He caught her gaze. "There's only one dessert I can think of that would satisfy a man who's worked this hard," he said.

"Something tells me it's not apple pie that you have in mind," she teased.

"Not even close," he agreed. "Though a little whipped cream might come in handy."

Abby spotted the twinkle in his eyes and nodded. "I'll see what I can do."

For an instant Seth looked taken aback. "Maybe you'd better stick to ordering the pie. I'd hate to think what conclusion Lesley Ann might jump to if you order whipped cream to go."

"Exactly the correct conclusion, I imagine," Abby replied. "But I'll get some pie to go along with it just to save your sterling reputation."

Seth nodded approvingly. "And the pie won't go to waste. It'll be great after we've finished the whipped cream."

"I like the way you think."

"I'm so glad you're aware that I'm good for lots of things besides toting Christmas trees," he said dryly.

She gave him a thorough survey that had his cheeks turning pink and her pulse racing. "I can definitely vouch for that," she said. In fact she got a little breathless just thinking about a few of his skills.

It took a lot longer to get the trees in place and the decorations on them than Abby had probably intended, Seth thought as they finally finished up around midnight. They'd spent a good amount of that time in her bed.

Now the only lights in the living room were on the

tree and they were curled up next to each other on the sofa with mugs of hot chocolate. Christmas music was playing in the background to set the mood, although Seth was far more interested in romance than holiday cheer. He couldn't get over the fact that no matter how much time he spent with Abby, he always wanted more. And when he was with her, he was able to shove any lingering doubts right out of his head.

"This is nice," he murmured as she snuggled into his side, her eyes closed.

"It is," she agreed. "It was another one of those perfect days, nothing at all like the day I'd been anticipating this morning. How about you?"

"Definitely not what I figured the day had in store," he replied. "Luke's been grumbling about getting all of the rescue squad's paperwork up-to-date. There's nothing I hate more than sitting at a computer filling in blanks."

Abby stirred and studied his face. "Is Luke going to be furious that it didn't get done?"

"Maybe."

"And that doesn't worry you?"

"I'm the one whose head will be on the chopping block if the reports aren't ready for the budget hearings in January."

Abby frowned. "Seth, why didn't you say something? You don't need to blow off work just because I could use your help."

"Stop it. I'd rather spend the day with you anytime, and it's not as if the meeting is tomorrow. I have weeks to pull these numbers together." He held her gaze. "Given how I feel about irresponsibility, do you think I'd have put this off if the timing were critical?"

"You're sure?"

"I'm sure," he said. He waited until she'd settled her head back on his shoulder before asking, "Now maybe you can tell me why you suddenly went into party-planning mode?"

"I love the holidays," she replied.

"And?"

"Does there have to be more to it than that?"

"There doesn't have to be, but I think maybe there is."

She was quiet for a long time, so long that he thought she might not answer.

When she finally spoke, her voice was low. "I used to love Christmas," she said. "It was my favorite time of the year."

"I think I got that when you went a little nuts picking out the trees," he said. "Walker pretty much confirmed that your obsession with perfection goes way back. But why are you talking in the past tense?"

"Because for too many years the holidays started to feel like work. The restaurant was crazy with private parties. It was great for the bottom line, but I could barely catch my breath. And of course at the church there was something going on every minute. Marshall expected me to be there for every choir performance, for the Christmas pageant, and, of course, for every service. Then there was the Christmas bazaar and the annual party for the women's guild. By January first I wanted to crawl into bed, pull up the covers and sleep for a month, but then the decorations had to come down at the restaurant and at the church. It was just too much."

"So today was all about recapturing the way Christmas used to be," he concluded. He allowed himself a smile, though he hoped she wouldn't notice. "In that case, wouldn't one tree have been enough?"

"Not when I intend to throw the most spectacular Christmas party I've been to in years, just for people I like."

He finally got it. "Not for strangers. Not for your husband's congregation. Not out of duty or obligation."

"Exactly. This is going to be just for fun, a real celebration of the holiday spirit, the sort of party my parents used to throw for all their friends."

"Have you picked a date?"

"I'm thinking about Saturday," she said. "Or do you think that's too little notice?"

"What I think is that it's the same night as the holiday house tour," he reminded her. "You know that's Sandra's moment of glory. Aren't you supposed to be going to pay your respects?"

Abby groaned. "I'd forgotten." Her expression brightened. "Okay, I'll have my party the next Saturday."

"The town tree-lighting ceremony," he said. "And before you suggest the following week, that's when the stores have their big Christmas open houses."

She regarded him with frustration. "Suggestions, please."

"Pick a Friday night or do a Sunday afternoon open house," he suggested, then grinned. "Or resign yourself to having just one appreciative guest, me, for any night you choose. I'm pretty sure I can keep you entertained so you won't even miss having no one else here." He grinned at her. "I'll bring presents."

"An intriguing thought," she agreed. "But I'm having a party with my friends. I like the idea of a Sunday open house. It'll be less formal." She grinned at him.

"Do you think it would be tacky if I happened to leave the architectural drawings for Blue Heron Cove laying around in plain sight?"

"Not tacky, but maybe a little obvious."

She nodded. "I can live with being obvious. I think I'll invite everyone for next Sunday. And in a display of genuine holiday spirit, I might even include Sandra and her two pals on the council."

"In that case, I'll bring along a first-aid kit, just in case things get out of hand."

"Not amusing," she chided, then sighed. "But probably a very good idea."

Twenty-One

The Whittier family home was surrounded by lush landscaping, including flowering hibiscus and bougainvillea that draped over a low wall around the property, covering it with bright purple color. Elegant royal palms, outlined with hundreds of twinkling white lights, lined the driveway in a display more suited to a mansion in Palm Beach or Naples than the tiny island community, but it was beautiful just the same.

Abby glanced at Seth. "If this is any indication, Sandra has definitely gone all out."

He smiled. "Wait till you go inside. I came last year with Luke and Hannah. I swear it looked to me as if she'd hired somebody from one of those fancy lifestyle magazines to decorate. I doubt a speck of dust would have had the nerve to try to sneak in."

The house itself wasn't all that impressive in terms of size, Abby decided after they parked along the edge of the driveway to walk the rest of the way. It had been built up off the ground with amazing forethought, given its age. Most early builders in the region hadn't been as conscious of hurricanes and storm surges as people—and insurance companies—were these days. A screened-in porch wrapped around the entire house. Garlands of lighted greenery accented every inch of it. In the distance, waves from the waters of the Gulf of Mexico lapped against the shore.

As it turned out, the exterior was deceptive. The house was much roomier inside than it had appeared and, as Seth had predicted, it had been tastefully decorated with crystal bowls filled with fragrant greens, lots of sparkling white lights and a massive tree in the foyer that dwarfed even Abby's carefully chosen trees. Every square inch of it was covered with lights and delicate glass antique ornaments.

Sandra stood just inside the door greeting guests—locals and tourists alike—as if this were a private party, rather than the grand finale of the historic homes tour. Her eyes widened when she recognized Abby.

Abby held out her hand, leaving Sandra little choice but to take it. "Your home truly is lovely," Abby told her. "I can see why you're so proud of it."

Sandra blinked at the apparent sincerity behind the compliment. "Thank you."

"You know," Abby continued. "I've been looking into how you might get it onto a registry of historic homes. Would you be interested in that?"

Now Sandra was actually gaping, and Seth was fighting to hide a smile. Abby recognized that she had finally seized on the one thing that might actually sway the woman to regard her with more favor.

"Do you think that's possible?" Sandra asked her, sounding a little breathless.

"Seaview Key has historic significance as a fishing village, and yours is one of the only homes to survive so many decades," Abby said. "I do think it's possible. I can share the information with you, if you like. I've already printed out the forms. I'm having an open house at my place tomorrow. I'd love to have you join us. I can give you everything then. Please say you'll come."

Though she looked taken aback, Sandra also looked intrigued. "I imagine Kyle and Mary will be coming, is that right?"

Abby nodded.

"I suppose I could come along with them." She hesitated, then added, "Thank you." Her tone was much warmer now than it had been when they'd first spoken.

"No problem at all," Abby said. "I'll look forward to seeing you. Now I've taken up enough of your time. There are a lot of people hoping to speak to you."

She quickly moved on, Seth right beside her. She didn't stop until she'd reached the dining room where there was a huge crystal punch bowl with some sort of holiday punch along with trays of bite-size appetizers and Christmas cookies. She accepted a glass of punch, then risked a glance at Seth.

"That went well," she said.

"What just happened?" he asked, looking a little dazed. "I actually thought for a minute that Sandra was going to throw her arms around you and officially welcome you home to Seaview Key."

Abby laughed. "I stumbled onto her soft spot," she admitted. "Someone pointed out to me how much she loves this house. They suggested having the loveliest home on Seaview Key matters to her, and that the homes I'm proposing for Blue Heron Cove might be a threat to that. It got me to thinking that maybe a historic landmark designation might pacify her."

Seth shook his head. "You're amazing. A little sneaky, but amazing."

She shrugged. "More like desperate. I need her support. Without it, I'll never get this project off the ground."

"You could do other things," he suggested. "You could open a restaurant, for instance."

"Been there, done that," she said, dismissing the possibility. "It's exhausting." Besides, she'd come home looking for new challenges and ways to make a difference. Opening a restaurant, especially one that would be in competition with good friends like Jack and Lesley Ann, would feel wrong.

"Well, assuming you do get the approvals for Blue Heron Cove, that won't keep you occupied forever. What then?" Seth asked.

Abby shrugged. "I'll cross that bridge when I come to it. Maybe I'll just sit on my porch with a good book and sip sweet tea."

Seth looked skeptical. "You've mentioned that sort of scenario before. I don't see it. What I do see is you getting bored without a challenge and deciding to take off for a city where there's more to do."

"Been there and done that, too." She held his gaze with a steady look, aware that he was seeking reassurance. "This is the lifestyle I want now, Seth. I want to be part of a community. Maybe I'll volunteer at the library or mentor some kids at the school. I think that could be incredibly rewarding."

"You'd be good at that," he agreed, his expression thoughtful. "But would it fill that empty place inside you?"

She sighed at the direct hit. "I honestly don't know, but it's worth a shot."

There were a lot of changes she could control for her future. Having the child she so desperately wanted? That one was probably out of reach. Surely, though, there had to be some way to fill that terrible empty space that even Seth recognized as being too important to ignore.

That, however, was too deep a topic for tonight and this occasion. Instead, she took his hand. "Let's mingle," she suggested.

"I thought one triumph for the night would be enough," he teased. "You out to conquer the entire community?"

"Nope. From this moment on, we're just here to have fun. I see Kyle and Mary over there. Let's say hello."

As she and Seth spoke to the people they knew for the next hour, Abby was aware of Sandra's gaze on her from time to time. The mayor managed a smile whenever Abby caught her eye, but mostly she seemed conflicted about the fact that the woman she'd so evidently considered an enemy might be giving her a shot at the enduring respect she so desperately wanted for her family's place in the history of Seaview Key.

Abby was aware, too, of how many speculative looks were directed toward her and Seth. If anyone in town had been unaware that they were close prior to tonight, they weren't any longer. She couldn't help wondering if that would come back to haunt them.

If Seth had marveled at Abby's clever tactic with Sandra the night before and the inroads she'd made with the mayor and with everyone she spoke to, it was nothing compared to his awe as he watched her handle the crowds that descended on her cottage Sunday afternoon.

Though he had no idea when or how she'd managed

it, trays of food kept magically appearing, each appetizer more delicious than the one before. Abby was everywhere at once, greeting people at the door, mingling with guests, cuddling Isabella or A.J. who gurgled with delight at the sight of her.

Though she'd left the Blue Heron Cove plans in plain sight, he never saw her pointing them out to anyone, not even to Sandra. The mayor had arrived a few minutes earlier with Mary and Kyle, looking uncertain of her welcome, even though she'd been issued a warm, personal invitation. Abby spent extra time with her explaining the paperwork she'd found to obtain the historic designation, but never once drawing attention to Blue Heron Cove.

Kyle's face lit up when he realized what Abby had done. "This is amazing, Abby. Grandmother, this is just the sort of thing you've always hoped for."

"I know," Sandra admitted, an unmistakable tear in her eyes. "If this truly happens, Abby, I'll owe you."

"You don't owe me a thing," Abby assured her.

A twinkle replaced the tear. "Not even my vote on your project?"

Abby smiled. "Not even that, though I'd certainly be grateful if you'd reconsider your stance." She held the mayor's gaze and added, "Not because of what I've done for you, but based on what Blue Heron Cove might mean for the community."

There was a pause as her words sank in. Sandra studied her with a considering look, then said, "I'm starting to like you, Abby."

"Well, it's about time you saw what the rest of us have seen all along," Grandma Jenny declared when she overheard her. Seizing on the moment, she linked an arm through Sandra's. "I always knew you'd come to your senses. You're too smart to let a wonderful opportunity slip away."

Seth watched the two older women wander off and turned to Abby. Right now she looked the way he'd felt watching her in action the night before—a little dazed.

"Do you think she might be leaning my way?"

"It sure sounded that way to me," he confirmed. "Think you can relax and enjoy your own party now?"

A smile broke across her face. "I believe I can."

Just then Luke and Hannah arrived. Hannah caught her expression and asked, "Okay, what's that smile all about?"

"It seems like Sandra might be coming around on Blue Heron Cove," Abby told her.

"Good for you!" Hannah said enthusiastically.

"I was just about to get a couple of glasses of champagne to celebrate," Seth said. "Luke, do you want to come with me?"

"Sure," Luke said, following him to the table that had been set up as a bar with soft drinks, wine and champagne.

As they poured the champagne, Luke studied him worriedly. "You and Abby seem to be getting close. I noticed it last night at the open house. Today's it's even more evident that you're acting like a couple."

Seth frowned. "I thought that's what you wanted."

"Only if it's serious," Luke said. "Is it?"

"We're taking things one day at a time," Seth replied.

"Last time we talked, you had a lot of doubts. Any of those get resolved?"

"Some of them," Seth responded. "Most of them, actually, at least when I'm being rational. Why the third degree, Luke?"

"Because the look I saw in Abby's eyes just now suggests she's no longer thinking of this as some casual fling. What about you?"

"I told you, we haven't pinned labels on what's going on. I'm happy. She's happy. That's enough for us for now."

Luke shook his head. "Not buying it. Abby's the kind of woman who wants forever, Seth. It's what she deserves."

"You're awfully protective of her all of a sudden. Why is that? Are you compensating for some sort of leftover feelings you have for her?"

"That's ridiculous," Luke said indignantly. "We're friends. Old friends. I don't want to see her get hurt, any more than I want to see you hurt again."

"Well, I appreciate your concern, but it's all good. I think Abby agrees, but you'd have to ask her to find out for sure."

"Let me just ask you one more thing and then I'll butt out," Luke promised. "What happens if this all blows up? Have you given a single thought to that? It's not as if you can get lost or simply move on in a town the size of Seaview Key. You'll be running into each other everywhere you look."

Seth hesitated, aware that Luke was right. Still, he managed to keep a carefree note in his voice when he claimed, "We're adults. We can deal with it."

His answer clearly didn't appease Luke.

"You're delusional, if you believe that, pal. Seems to me the only question will be which one of you takes off. I'd hate for this community to lose either one of you."

Before Seth could utter what could only be another upbeat lie not even he believed, Luke took the champagne and went in search of his wife and Abby. Seth gulped down his own champagne, refilled the glass and then followed.

When he found the group again, Abby gave him a questioning look. He forced a smile, but he had a hunch it didn't go very far in convincing anyone that his mood hadn't turned decidedly sour and that Luke was more than likely the one responsible.

When the last of the guests had left, Abby kicked off her shoes and padded barefoot into the kitchen, where she found Seth up to his elbows in sudsy dishwater.

"So this is where you disappeared to," she said, nudging him aside with a hip while she tried to take over. "You dry," she said.

He leveled a forbidding look into her eyes. "You sit. I'll wash *and* dry. You've been working for days to make this party a success. Seems to me you must have exceeded your wildest expectations. I think everyone from Seaview Key was here at one time or another. There's not a single crumb of food left and the recycling bin is filled with empty champagne and wine bottles."

Abby smiled as she settled onto a chair and put her feet onto the seat of another chair. "It was a pretty great party, if I do say so myself. I had fun. How about you? You seemed to be having fun, too, at least until you and Luke got into it about something. What was that about?"

Seth winced. "You noticed, huh? I was hoping you hadn't."

"I'm nothing if not observant, particularly when two men I know pretty well come back from fetching drinks with matching scowls in place. What was the argument about?"

"I wouldn't describe it as an argument," Seth said, clearly choosing his words a little too carefully. "Luke's worried we're not thinking clearly."

"About what?"

"Us."

Abby stared at him. "What do you think?" she asked eventually.

"I think we both know what we're doing." He frowned. "How about you? You don't look quite as certain of that as I thought you would."

"No, no," she said quickly, "I like where we are, too. We agreed—"

Seth cut her off. "Maybe what we agreed to no longer applies. At least for you."

Abby hesitated, not willing to risk starting an argument of their own. Nor did she want to reveal feelings that might destroy what they currently had.

"Abby, it's okay if you've changed your mind," Seth said, evidently interpreting her silence as an indication that he was right. "I may not have a lot of experience, but I do know relationships are fluid."

"But things haven't changed for you, have they?" she asked. "You're still not ready for anything serious, am I right?"

"Are you ready for serious?" he asked, turning the tables on her.

Abby recognized the tactic as one he'd likely use if he honestly wasn't sure how he felt these days. That uncertainty meant it would be wise to hedge her own bets.

"Casual's been fun," she admitted, trying to keep any hint of longing from her voice. "It's easy. I'm okay with it. It would be crazy to expect anything more so soon." She rambled on with similar disclaimers, hoping to reassure him. She had a hunch she'd gone a little overboard, especially with Seth watching her so intently.

Abby could tell how badly Seth wanted to believe her. That expression convinced her she was right to skirt the truth, though she probably should have done it with one convincing lie.

"That's quite a defense of the casual fling," he commented dryly.

"I meant every word," she insisted.

"And we both know that serious is something else entirely," he responded, watching her closely, his gaze intense. "It can lead to heartbreak."

"And neither one of us wants that," she said more firmly. Who could possibly argue with that?

"Absolutely not."

She nodded. "Then it's all good."

He tossed aside the dish towel and moved toward her. "It's all good," he agreed.

Abby stood and moved into his open arms. For now—for this minute—she had everything she needed. Hopefully she could continue to convince herself that it was enough.

"What is going on between those two?" Luke asked Hannah over a light snack after leaving Abby's open house. Neither of them were interested in an actual meal after all the hors d'oeuvres they'd consumed. "They certainly were behaving as if they were a couple at the party. They were practically finishing each other's sentences."

Hannah chuckled. "You sound as if that's a crime. We do it all the time."

"But we *are* a couple," he said. "Seth claims they're keeping things light. He swears neither of them has any expectations, as if that's even humanly possible. Have you spoken to Abby? What's she saying?"

"That she's having the time of her life, that she's never been happier," Hannah said. "I'm taking that at face value. Why can't you?"

"Because it's wrong," Luke grumbled. "That's not who they are. Abby should be with someone who respects and loves her, who's ready to make a commitment."

Hannah frowned at him. "You seem awfully concerned about her."

"She's our friend. Of course I'm concerned. Aren't you?"

"I'm thinking she knows her own mind," Hannah said. "She told me she's not ready for anything more serious."

"And you believed her?"

"No reason not to," she said.

"I thought you of all people would be eager to see this thing between her and Seth get to the next level," he said.

Hannah stilled. She knew exactly what he was implying. "So I won't feel insecure anymore?" she asked.

Luke looked as if he regretted going there, but he nodded. "I thought you'd be reassured by now, but I can still see how tense you are whenever we're all together."

"I'm handling it," she said tightly, wishing she were completely free of doubts. Mostly she was, but every once in a while one stray bit of insecurity would creep into her head. She had no idea how to turn off her mind and keep it from giving in to fear. "Abby and I are getting close again. I have to trust her. And I'm not going to disrespect what you and I have by doubting you, either."

Luke actually grinned at that. "Brave words. Are you there yet?"

She frowned at him. "I'm working on it. And the last thing I want is to see Abby jump into something she's not ready for just to keep me from freaking out."

"What about Seth? Have you given any thought to his feelings? This limbo isn't good for him. When Cara died, you weren't around. I was still in rehab, but I could hear the pain in his voice. Even after he came here, that pain was still visible whenever I looked into his eyes. For a while there, he was a shadow of the man I'd known in Iraq. I worried about him, Hannah. I know in my gut that one of the reasons he decided to settle here was because he didn't expect to find anyone to take her place. He figured Seaview Key would be the ideal place to put his heart on ice."

Hannah frowned. "If you knew that, I'm surprised you encouraged him to stay. Why didn't you push him to find someone who could make him happy?"

"Because men don't butt in like that," he claimed.

She laughed. "As if," she commented wryly. "You've done plenty of butting in. You just didn't expect him to fall for Abby," she said. "Your old girlfriend."

"That is not what I'm worried about," Luke insisted. "I'm worried because they're lying to themselves and to each other. He's falling in love with her."

Hannah's spirits perked up. "You really think so?"

"Of course he is," Luke said with certainty. "But she's keeping him at arm's length because she thinks it's what he wants. He's trying to go along with it, claiming it's what he wants, too. If one of them doesn't break the stalemate, they're both going to be miserable. That seems like a crying shame to me."

"Maybe they're telling the truth," Hannah argued. "Maybe it only seemed like they had this instantaneous deep connection. Maybe they're smart to accept what they have as some kind of temporary chemistry, a part of the healing process they both need to go through."

Luke shook his head. "I thought women were supposed to be the romantics. Come on, Hannah. You know better."

She sighed. "Yeah, I do. And I feel bad for him. For her, too, for that matter."

"Then talk to Abby. If she's not serious about him, encourage her to end it."

"Absolutely not. If you feel that strongly that they're messing it up, talk to Seth."

"I did talk to Seth," he said in frustration. "He wasn't listening."

"Then leave it alone," she advised. "Otherwise the one who loses might be you."

Luke sighed. "They're our friends. I can't just ignore what I see happening. I'll talk to Abby myself. Maybe I can get through to her. She's not half as hardheaded as Seth is."

Hannah smiled. "That's what you think, but fine. Go for it. Just don't be surprised if she tells you to mind your own business. That's what I'd do if I were in her shoes."

Twenty-Two

Christmas day dawned bright and clear with a slight nip in the air. Abby snuggled more deeply under the covers and a little closer to the man in bed next to her.

"Merry Christmas," Seth whispered in her ear.

She smiled and rolled over. "Merry Christmas to you, too. What time is it? We're supposed to be at Seaview Inn early if we want to see Isabella open her presents."

"You do realize she's just going to be tearing at paper and playing with the boxes, right? She's not old enough to understand all the commotion."

She nudged him with an elbow. "I want to be there. She may not be big enough to understand about Santa or the true meaning of Christmas, but she's going to look so cute when she sees all the presents and the lights on the tree."

"And you need to be a part of that, don't you?" he said knowingly.

"Sure," she said, seeing no reason to pretend otherwise. "I may never experience it with a child or grandchild of my own."

"Then let's get moving. I happen to know for a fact

that Isabella never sleeps much past seven in the morning and it's almost that now. Jenny will probably have a batch of cinnamon rolls coming out of the oven any minute to tide us over till after the presents are opened."

They showered and dressed quickly, then headed for the inn. Luke and Hannah arrived at the same time, laden down with even more brightly wrapped packages than Abby.

"Thank you so much for including me this morning," Abby said, giving Hannah a hug. "I think I may be more excited than I used to be as a kid."

"I doubt that," Hannah replied. "Even as a teenager, I think you stayed up half the night watching out the window for Santa."

"I did not," Abby protested, but she was grinning. "I stayed awake watching old Christmas movies. That's my story and I'm sticking to it."

Hannah turned to Seth. "I'm telling you, she never gave up on Santa."

"No, what I've never given up on is the magic of the season," Abby corrected. "Now let's go inside before we miss Isabella's reaction to everything."

She didn't have to say that twice. Luke held the door and they all trooped inside just in time to see Kelsey and Jeff coming down the stairs with Isabella in Jeff's arms. She was wearing Christmas pajamas with feet and had a red bow in her tousled hair. Her eyes were bright with excitement, but no more so than Kelsey's.

"Jeff, let me have her," Kelsey said. "You go in and turn on the lights on the tree."

"I've already done that," Jenny announced, coming out of the kitchen with a plate piled high with fragrant cinnamon buns. "Coffee's ready if anyone wants it. I've set the pot up in the living room. Cups are there, too."

Hannah hurried into the living room to add the gifts she and Luke had brought to the pile under the tree. Abby followed with hers. Then Kelsey brought Isabella into the room, while Jeff snapped pictures as her eyes widened with delight.

"Me, me, me," she shouted with glee, pointing at all the packages.

Kelsey laughed. "No, my little princess. Not all of them are for you."

"Just most of them," Jeff said, shaking his head. "We need to have another baby before we spoil her rotten."

Kelsey gave him a withering look. "I'm still getting used to the fact that we have Isabella. Let's not rush things."

Jeff grinned at her. "I'm just saying it's the smart thing to do for our daughter's sake."

Abby chuckled at his tactics and leaned over to Seth. "Want to bet Kelsey's at least pregnant by this time next year? Jeff is a very persuasive guy and she clearly adores him."

Seth studied her with a surprisingly concerned expression. "Are you envious?"

"Of course not," she insisted, then sighed. "Okay, maybe a little."

"One of these days we probably need to talk about that," he said.

Unsettled by the offhand remark, Abby was about to reply, when he squeezed her shoulder. "Not today." He nodded toward Luke who was watching them a little too intently, worry etched on his face.

"I'll talk to him," Abby offered. "I'll get him to back off."

"But not today," Seth said again. "The show's about to begin."

Jeff set Isabella down amid a sea of packages. He and Kelsey sat beside her.

"Which one first, baby girl?" Kelsey asked. She picked up a large box wrapped in bright red paper with Santa figures all over it. "How about this one?"

She put Isabella's tiny hand on an edge of the paper and showed her how to tear it. One good rip exposed the doll inside. "Baby?" Isabella said excitedly, getting into the spirit of it and ripping at the paper with more determination. Kelsey helped her to get the doll from the box and put it in her arms.

"That doll is almost as big as she is," Jenny said, laughing.

"It's the one she wanted," Kelsey said defensively.

"No, it's the one *you* wanted," Jeff corrected, chuckling. "I was with you at the store, remember? You couldn't take your eyes off of it. Isabella wasn't even with us."

"Oh, so what if it is?" Kelsey grumbled. "I didn't have dolls when I was little."

Hannah regarded her with amusement. "And why was that?"

Kelsey shrugged. "I had a thing for fire engines," she admitted.

"And?" Hannah coached.

"I shoved the one doll Mom gave me down the stairwell in our apartment building in her baby carriage. Mom concluded I wasn't interested."

"Fortunately you've turned into a much better mother these days," Hannah teased her.

With her new doll in her arms, Isabella lost interest in the rest of her presents, so Kelsey and Jeff passed out packages to everyone else in the room.

Ignoring her own presents, Abby waited expectantly as the others opened the gifts she'd chosen for them. She'd tried so hard to get it exactly right. She'd found a soft cashmere throw for Jenny to use on the porch on cool nights, a first-edition copy of *Little Women* for Hannah, fishing tackle for Luke who'd been claiming that he wanted to spend more time out on the water in his old rowboat, and for Seth a fancy waterproof watch.

"Do you like it?" she asked worriedly when he didn't say anything.

"It's incredible," he said slowly. He lifted a troubled gaze to meet hers. "But I can't accept this, Abby. It's too much."

Everyone in the room had fallen silent at the comment. Luke looked on, his expression concerned, as they all sat silently awaiting her response.

"Seth, you've done so much for me," she said quietly, her heart in her throat. "I just wanted to get you something special."

If anything, his expression seemed even more miserable. "And you did. The watch is amazing."

"Then please, keep it," she said.

He shook his head, closed the box and handed it back. "I can't."

He stood up and left the room, leaving her feeling humiliated in front of their friends. She looked to Hannah. "I don't understand. What did I do wrong?"

It was Jenny who came to sit beside her. She gave her hand a squeeze. "You didn't do anything wrong," she said firmly. "It's his pride."

"What does his pride have to do with me giving him something special for Christmas?"

"Admittedly, I have no idea what a watch like that costs," Jenny began.

"A couple of thousand," Jeff chimed in, oblivious to the glare Kelsey directed his way.

Abby winced at the accuracy of the statement. "So what? It's a watch. It's practical."

"So is a fifty-dollar watch," Luke said. "You know how sensitive Seth is about money, Abby. You were throwing yours in his face."

"Which is not at all what she intended to do," Jenny said with certainty, frowning at Luke.

Abby finally began to see that what she'd meant as a special gesture had just reminded Seth of the financial differences between them, differences she thought they'd put behind them. What on earth had she been thinking?

"I need to talk to him," she said. "I'm sorry for ruining the morning."

"Nonsense," Jenny said. "Nothing is ruined. You and Seth have your talk, then come back in here for breakfast. Hannah, Kelsey and I will have it on the table in a half hour."

"I should help with that," Abby protested.

"Three of us in the kitchen is more than enough," Hannah said. "Talk to Seth and get this settled, so you can enjoy the rest of the day."

Abby nodded. She picked up her cup and Seth's, freshened them with hot coffee, then headed outside. When she didn't find him on the porch, she crossed the street to the water. She found him standing down at the edge of the beach.

"It's cool out here. I thought you might like something hot," she said, handing him the coffee.

He accepted it, then met her gaze. "I don't deserve it, you know."

"What, me being nice to you?"

He nodded. "I was rude back there."

"A little," she acknowledged. "But I think I finally understand why. I didn't mean to upset you or to throw my money in your face. I just knew you didn't have a waterproof watch, so I found one I liked and bought it."

"And then I behaved like a fool." He regarded her with genuine regret. "I know you're not like my sister. I do. But something like this, coming right in the middle of that ongoing battle, scares me."

She touched a hand to his cheek. "I get why you reacted the way you did. It's okay if you want me to take the watch back, but I hope you'll change your mind."

"Why is it so important to you that I keep it?"

She forced a grin. "Well, for one thing I had it engraved. I'm not sure they'll be able to find another man named Seth to buy it."

He chuckled at last. "In that case, maybe I'd better keep it. A watch that amazing certainly shouldn't go to waste."

"Only if you can forget what it cost and focus on the fact that I was trying to do something nice for you." She held his gaze. "I do get why you're sensitive about this. I imagine it's the kind of impulsive, over-the-top thing Laura might have done."

He nodded. "It's exactly the sort of thing she would have done. I hate to even think about what her January credit card bills must be like."

"Here's the difference," Abby said. "I pay off my

bills every single month, Seth. There are no mounting interest fees, no late fees. I don't buy what I can't afford to pay for."

"I know that should reassure me, but it just reminds me that you're loaded and I'm not."

She regarded him wearily. "And I can't change that," she said. "I can only tell you that it doesn't matter to me. I wish it didn't seem to matter way too much to you."

She turned to go back to the house. She'd made it halfway across the sand when he called out to her. She faced him.

"I'm sorry," he said, walking toward her. "This is my problem. It's not yours."

"It *is* mine," she corrected. "Because I care about you and I can see this is going to be a problem between us unless you can find a way to accept the situation."

"Will it be enough for you if I promise that I'll try?" He held her gaze, his expression filled with remorse. "I promise, Abby. I've had the occasional freak-out, but I actually thought I'd made pretty good progress till I opened that present just now."

She smiled and linked her arm through his. "Then let's leave it at that, at least for today. Now let's go join the others before they eat all the food. I've been looking forward to a huge Christmas breakfast for days now."

"Not until I give you this," he said, reaching into his pocket and pulling out a small package awkwardly wrapped in bright red paper with a silver bow.

Abby's hand shook as she accepted the gift.

"It's not extravagant," he apologized.

"Seth, I don't need extravagant. Honestly. You chose this for me and I'll treasure it, even if it's a pencil holder for my desk."

He smiled at that. "Given the size of the box, I think it's a safe bet that it's not a pencil holder. Go ahead. Open it."

Eager now, she ripped off the paper with as much enthusiasm as Isabella. The jeweler's box in her hand had her blinking with surprise.

When she flipped the lid, she found a silver charm bracelet to which a single charm had been added, a blue heron. Tears filled her eyes. "Oh, Seth, it's perfect," she whispered. "You couldn't have found anything that would mean more to me."

"I thought it was something I could add to," he said. "You really like it?"

"I love it. Help me put it on."

When the clasp had been fastened, she held the bracelet up to let the sunlight bounce off the silver. Then she stood on tiptoe and kissed him thoroughly.

"Merry Christmas," she said softly.

"Merry Christmas, Abby. I hope it's the first of many we share."

"I hope so, too." And now, in this moment of hard-won rapport, a little of the magic had returned.

Once the holidays were behind them, Abby turned her full attention to the fish fry and to the council vote on Blue Heron Cove. She was counting on both being successful.

Thanks to the efforts of Jenny and Ella Mae, the sold-out fish fry was a rousing success. Everyone who attended actually bought tickets for the follow-up event in February, anxious to be part of the fund-raising effort for the rescue boat and for a chance to bid on the exciting gifts Abby had assembled for the silent auction.

"We're sold out again," Ella Mae announced happily as the organizers relaxed at the end of the event.

"And you sold the most tickets," Jenny reported. "I don't know how you did it."

"Fear and awe," Ella Mae said contentedly.

"Well, all I know is that you'll be on every committee for every event on this island from here on out," Jenny told her. "There will be no more hiding out in seclusion at home, is that understood?"

Ella Mae turned an accusing look on Seth. "I warned you about this. Now look what you've done."

He laughed. "Oh, don't even try to pretend you haven't had fun. You've enjoyed every minute of reconnecting with some of your old students and making new friends. I know because you haven't been pestering me every few days."

"Don't be smug, young man," she grumbled. "Or that can change. In fact, I'm feeling a little under the weather right now."

Seth merely rolled his eyes. "Your cheeks are glowing. Your eyes are bright. You look just fine to me."

"You don't know everything. Where's Luke? I want a real doctor to confirm that diagnosis."

Abby caught an odd expression pass over Seth's face. She pulled him aside. "Are you okay? She was just teasing. You do know that, right?"

"Sure," he said. "Take a walk with me, okay? Or are you too exhausted?"

"I'm fine."

After they'd walked for a few minutes, she turned to him. "Okay, tell me why Ella Mae's comment seemed to bother you so much."

"It didn't bother me exactly. It's just that she said something that I've been thinking about lately."

"About not being a real doctor?"

He nodded, then glanced over at her. "Maybe I should think about going to medical school."

Abby felt a twinge of excitement. "Are you serious? Is that something you really want to do?"

"Maybe," he said. "I never really gave it much thought before. I was so anxious to get away from home, I just took the training for being a paramedic, then joined the military. With the money from my parents' estate, I could take the time now and go to medical school."

A troubling thought occurred to her. "And then what? Seaview Key probably doesn't need two doctors."

"It might, if one of them specialized in pediatrics," he said thoughtfully. "Sure, Luke handles all of it now, but I think the island could use a specialist. I don't need to get rich from medicine. As long as I'm making a decent living, it's all good." He studied her. "What do you think, honestly?"

"I think if it's something you really, really want, you should go for it," she said without hesitation. "But, Seth, if you're doing this for some other reason, then you need to give it more thought. It's a big commitment. You'd need med school, an internship, a residency. All of that takes time."

"I know how long it would take," he said irritably. "I still think it makes sense for me. What other reason could there be?"

Abby was terrified of voicing her real concern, that he was doing it because he thought it would put the two of them on a more equal footing. "Does it have anything to do with me?" she asked carefully.

"Absolutely not," he insisted. "I've been giving this some thought for a while now. Even before you came to town, I was considering doing something more with my training."

Relieved, she nodded. "Then go for it."

"It would mean being away at medical school for a long time," he said. "I'd try to get into Florida or Florida State."

"They're not so far away," she said. "It might be kind of fun to go to college football games again."

"So you're with me on this?" he asked, studying her closely.

"A hundred percent. We can make it work, Seth, at least if you want to make it work. If you're looking for an excuse to take off on me, just say the word."

He looked genuinely shocked by her words. "Not a chance," he said at once. "In fact, one of the reasons I've been struggling with the idea recently is because I don't want to walk away from what we have."

"You're sure?" she pressed.

He caressed her cheek. "I can't deny that meeting you got me to thinking more seriously about all of this. I want to be the kind of man who makes you proud."

Her heart sank at that. "But Seth you do make me proud. You're a wonderful man already. Otherwise, I would never have fallen for you."

A spark lit his eyes. "You've fallen for me?"

"Oh, don't act so surprised. Didn't I kiss the stuffing out of you on the day we met?"

"Maybe a little," he said with a grin. "But there were extenuating circumstances."

She stood on tiptoe and kissed him again, thoroughly enough that he couldn't mistake her enthusiasm. When she finally stepped back, a little breathless, she said, "No extenuating circumstances that time."

"So it's okay if I start believing this just might get serious?" he asked.

"I think it's definitely a safe bet," she admitted. "It's probably time to stop denying what everyone else can plainly see. Casual's not really working for us."

Amazingly, the admission didn't give her a single qualm. They might not know exactly where they were headed yet, but she was almost a hundred percent sure they were going in the same direction. And whatever might lie ahead, she didn't feel any sense of urgency to get there, not when the route itself was so thoroughly intriguing.

Abby slept late the morning after the fish fry. Seth had crawled out of bed at dawn to go for a run and then take his shift with the rescue squad.

After her shower, she poured herself a cup of the coffee he'd made before he left the house and went onto the porch to enjoy the morning. She was smiling when Luke came around the corner of the house, a frown on his face.

"You look gloomy," she told him. "What's up? I thought you'd be thrilled at how well yesterday's fish fry went. The next one will bring in enough to pay off the last installment on that rescue boat."

"I know. That's great," he said.

"Such enthusiasm. I'm all aglow."

He scowled. "I'm not here about the blasted boat. I'm worried about you."

"About me? Why? My life is just about perfect these days."

"Is it really?"

"Sure. I'm pretty confident Sandra's going to vote in favor of Blue Heron Cove. The work to get that boat is almost done. I've been reconnecting with old friends."

"And Seth? Where does he fit in?"

"We're good," she said, aware of where he was headed. "But if that scowl on your face is anything to go by, you disagree."

She listened patiently to Luke as he stumbled through what appeared to be a lecture on the way she was mistreating Seth. She couldn't believe there was any truth to what he was telling her, that Seth needed a real commitment from her, not some kind of game. She was pretty sure they'd already resolved all of that.

"Excuse me? You don't know what you're talking about. Seth and I have been totally honest with each other."

"Do you know that he's considering going away to medical school?"

"We talked about it," she said. "If it's something he wants, I'm all for it."

"He never once mentioned medical school until you turned up. He's using it as an excuse to get away from this crazy situation you all are in."

"I worried about the same thing at first," she said, clearly surprising Luke. "He says that's not the case and I believe him. He told me he was considering it before I even turned up here. I think it may have more to do with his admiration for you than it does with me."

Luke looked skeptical. "That's certainly a convenient

theory for you. You don't have to take responsibility for driving him away."

She stared at Luke incredulously. "Exactly how am I driving him away?"

"Because you won't commit to the future we both know he wants. The same future I suspect you want, as a matter of fact."

"Luke, you're crazy," she said with certainty. "Our relationship is every man's dream, an undemanding woman with no expectations. Seth seems happy enough to me. You're worrying about nothing."

"He thinks he's giving you what you want," Luke argued. "Is he? I never thought you'd be satisfied with some crazy no-strings fling. Am I wrong about that?"

"What we have is more than that," she corrected. "Just because we're not rushing into a major commitment doesn't mean we're not heading in that direction. And you're out of line for butting into this. It's between Seth and me."

"Okay, fine. I'll back off, but before I do, I'll tell you what scares me. I'm convinced the two of you are going to ruin a good thing because neither one of you has the guts to ask for what you really want."

He leveled a look into her eyes. "That's all I'm saying, Abby. Don't wait too long to be honest. Universities are jam-packed with young women who'd be eager to get serious with a man like Seth."

Shaken by what he'd said, she watched him go, then reached for her cell phone.

"How fast can you get over here?" she asked Seth. When he'd replied that he ought to be able to make it there in a half hour, she said, "Make it five minutes, okay?"

It wasn't the first time one or the other of them had communicated a sense of urgency, but if Luke was right about any of this, it might be the last time such a call was necessary. Maybe it was time to take her foot off the brakes and go for what she wanted full-throttle.

Of course, if Luke had gotten it all wrong, then she was about to wind up with a very large portion of egg on her face.

Twenty-Three

Seth's blood was pumping as he drove over to Abby's. Though there'd been other calls like this one, he'd sensed something different in her voice this morning. He cut the ten-minute drive down to four minutes.

Even so, she'd apparently had enough time to set out wine and light candles, even though it was the middle of the morning. Something was definitely up, he concluded.

"Special occasion?" he asked, eyeing the romantic ambiance with confusion.

"That depends," she said. "We need to talk."

He picked up a glass of wine and took a long sip. "That's never good."

She chuckled. "Talking hasn't been our first priority for a while, has it? Maybe that's been a mistake."

Seth took another gulp of the wine. If it was one of those expensive bottles, it was definitely wasted on him. Thank goodness he wasn't on duty this morning, because it appeared he wouldn't be in any condition to take a call if she didn't get to the point soon.

"I thought we were doing okay these days," he said.

"So why are you suddenly talking about mistakes?" Before she could reply, the answer dawned on him. "You've been talking to Luke, haven't you?"

She nodded. "He was here a little while ago. I thought he was way off the mark for the most part, but he did get me to thinking about something."

Seth regarded her worriedly. He knew Luke had reservations about the two of them. Had he somehow convinced Abby to end it?

"Are you breaking up with me?" he asked her.

A smile tugged at her lips, her very alluring lips.

"To the contrary," she said, holding his gaze. "I'm thinking I should tell you how I really feel for a change."

"I thought you were being honest with me all along," he said. "Didn't we have a heart-to-heart on Christmas, and again the other day after the fish fry?"

"I was definitely being honest on both occasions," she agreed, then amended, "Up to a point."

Seth frowned. "How does that work?"

"I told you how I felt, or at least what I thought you wanted to hear, and then I got scared."

"Of what?"

"Losing you if I got too serious. I mean, we were all about easy, right? No complications. No demands. Moving forward, maybe, but at a snail's pace?"

"That is what we agreed," Seth said. "But we've also acknowledged that it's starting to get serious. Is that the part that's bothering you? Isn't it true?"

"Oh, it's true," she said. "The serious part, anyway. But I'm not just getting there. I *am* there. Pretending otherwise isn't working for me anymore. I want complications, Seth. I want a commitment. I might even want forever." She gazed directly into his eyes. There was a hint of fear in hers. "I hope you can deal with that."

For the first time since he'd arrived, Seth released the breath that had seemed caught in his throat. "So, if I were to go for broke right here and now and propose, if I were to ask you to marry me, you might say yes? Even though there's medical school to get through?"

"That's just one of those complications I was talking about. It's not a deal breaker," she said, smiling.

She leveled a lingering look into his eyes that had his hand shaking so badly he had to set the wineglass on the table to keep from spilling the wine all over the place.

"Seth," she said quietly. "Maybe you ought to try that proposal on me. If you really want to, that is."

He swallowed hard and tried to wrap his mind around what she was saying. For so long now he'd been so sure he'd never take another chance on love, but the irony was, without even realizing it, he already had. The risky part was in the past. All he had to do was utter the words and he could have everything he'd thought was lost to him.

"I love you," he said, his gaze locked with hers. "I didn't go looking for love. I didn't expect it. But here you are."

"Here I am," she echoed, moving closer and placing a hand against his cheek.

"Want to make it for a lifetime?" he asked.

Tears welled in her eyes and spilled down her cheeks, but her eyes were shining, which he considered a good sign.

"There's nothing I want more," she said.

And then she was in his arms and neither of them

needed words to communicate what they wanted. Their hearts were totally in sync.

Even though everything he'd ever imagined was within reach, Seth couldn't help thinking of the obstacles.

"What if Blue Heron Cove doesn't get approved?"

"Then I'll come live in some dinky little apartment near campus and cook for you while you study," she said without hesitation.

He smiled at the image. "You'd be satisfied with a dinky little apartment?"

She glanced around at the small house she'd turned into a home. "I might have to spruce it up a little," she conceded. "But we'd have this to come home to."

He searched her face. "So, this is it for you? Seaview Key is home? No reservations?"

"Not a one," she told him. "As long as you're here, I'm home. I never told you this but that contractor I wanted tried to convince me to work with him, rather than pursuing Blue Heron Cove. He thought we'd make a good team."

Seth felt his heart stumble. "Why didn't you say something? It sounds as if it would have been a great opportunity."

"Because Seaview Key is what I want. You're what I want. I don't have a single doubt about either of those things."

Relief flowed through him. "That's good, then."

She hesitated for a minute, worry etched on her brow. "Seth, we're not entirely crazy for thinking we can make this work, are we?"

"I certainly don't think we are. Did Luke suggest otherwise?"

"No, actually I think this was exactly what he was hoping for when he came over here. He seemed to think we'd gotten way off track by not admitting what we really wanted."

Seth smiled. "I'll have to thank him one of these days. Not right away, of course. He's already entirely too smug about thinking he knows what's best for me."

"That's what good friends do," she reminded him.

"Then I'll thank him sooner rather than later," Seth said, pulling her into his arms. "But not just now. I have much better things in mind."

And he set out to prove it.

There was one thing Abby wanted to do before she and Seth walked down the aisle. It was the one thing that might change their plans. She made an appointment with a fertility expert on the mainland, then made the trip over on the ferry on her own.

After the examination and several tests, she sat across from the doctor in her sunny office and waited for the verdict.

"I'm not seeing anything obvious to explain why you haven't gotten pregnant in the past," she told Abby. "We'll have to wait for the test results to know definitively whether there's a problem."

"And if nothing turns up, it would be okay for me to try?" Abby asked, her heart in her throat. "It's not too late?"

"A pregnancy at your age would be high risk," she replied candidly, "but not out of the question. You seem to be in excellent health overall, so as long as you get good prenatal care, follow directions and are prepared for the possibility of bed rest at some point, I think it would be safe to try. You'd want to consider amniocentesis to be sure there are no abnormalities, but we can discuss that when the time comes. Let's get the results of these tests first, then see where we are."

Abby nodded, trying hard not to let her excitement get ahead of the results that would be the true test of what might be possible. "Thank you so much."

"I'll be in touch as soon as I know more," the doctor promised. "May I ask, is there some reason this is so important to you? Your patient questionnaire indicates you're divorced."

Abby couldn't stop the smile that broke across her face. "I'm engaged, actually. We both want children. I just don't want to get his hopes up if it's not likely we'll have them."

"Then we'll both hope for the best," the doctor told her.

When Abby got back to Seaview Key, she found herself stopping by Hannah's. When her friend opened the door, she regarded Abby with concern.

"Is everything okay? You look a little shaken."

"I saw a fertility expert today," she admitted.

Hannah's eyes widened. "Come on in. I'll pour tea."

They settled at the kitchen table with glasses of iced tea and a plate of homemade oatmeal raisin cookies.

Abby bit into a cookie, then grinned. "Jenny's," she guessed.

"Of course. Mine are more like hockey pucks." She studied Abby closely. "Why the sudden decision to visit a doctor?"

"Can you keep a secret?"

Hannah chuckled. "How many of yours are still locked away in my head?"

"Okay, crazy question," Abby conceded. "It's just

that Seth and I don't want word to get out just yet. We're engaged."

Hannah's eyes lit up. "Oh, sweetie, that's fantastic. But why the secrecy?"

"We both want to savor it for a little bit," Abby admitted, then shrugged. "And we don't want Luke to get all smug and take credit for nudging us in the right direction."

Hannah laughed. "Yeah, I can see why you'd want to avoid that. My husband does love being right. And here I told him not to meddle."

"Well, he did meddle and it worked," Abby said. "Anyway, after Seth and I decided to get married, I started thinking that maybe it wasn't too late to try for a baby."

"How does he feel about that, especially with this whole medical school thing I hear he's considering?"

"That's the thing, I didn't want to say anything to him until I knew if a pregnancy was even possible."

"But what if he sees it as a huge obstacle to his plans?" Hannah asked worriedly.

"There's no reason it has to be," Abby said defensively. "We're not two young kids. We've both juggled a lot of balls in the air in our lives. And we have financial resources."

"Yours," Hannah reminded her. "We both know how he'd feel about relying on your money."

"Well, it will be *our* money when we're married," Abby said defensively.

Hannah merely lifted a brow.

"Well, that's how I'm going to think of it," Abby said. She hesitated, then asked, "Do you think I'm nuts?"

Hannah smiled. "For what? Wanting to marry Seth?

Absolutely not. For wanting a baby? Of course not. But I'm not the one whose feelings count."

"I will talk to Seth," Abby promised. "But only after I hear from the doctor. There's no point in getting his hopes up or fighting about this, if there's no chance I'll get pregnant." She regarded Hannah hopefully. "Right?"

"I suppose so, though I've learned the hard way that being open and honest always pays off in marriage. Secrets, even innocent ones, tend to get all twisted around and out of proportion."

Abby sighed. "You're probably right. If the opportunity presents itself before I hear from the doctor, I'll fill Seth in. Now I think I'll go home and fix something amazing for dinner."

"You do that and it sounds to me as if opportunity will be knocking," Hannah suggested.

"I'm not sure I hear it," Abby told her.

"Well, listen more closely," Hannah advised.

Abby hugged her hard. "Thanks for listening."

"Anytime," Hannah said. "And I'll add this secret to that data bank in my head."

As Abby drove home, she realized that for the very first time, she truly felt as if she and Hannah had recaptured the friendship she'd been so afraid might be lost forever. Everything had felt totally right about sharing this secret with a woman she'd known almost her entire life.

There was something on Abby's mind, but for the life of him, Seth couldn't figure out what it was. She wasn't talking. He assumed it had something to do with the vote on Blue Heron Cove that was coming up tonight.

With its potential to impact Abby's future, that would make anyone tense.

"Are you nervous about the vote?" Seth asked her over breakfast.

"A little," she admitted.

"Any idea about how Sandra will vote?"

"She's called a couple of times to ask questions," Abby said. "I couldn't tell which way she was leaning, though. Jenny's tried to pry it out of her, but Sandra's been tight-lipped. Jack says her cohorts haven't said a word when they've been by The Fish Tale for beers. He guesses Sandra hasn't told them how to vote yet."

"You do know that no matter how this vote goes, we're going to be just fine," he said.

She smiled at that. "Of course we are. Totally separate issue."

"And after the vote, we're announcing our engagement," he continued. "This secrecy thing is for the birds. I've almost blurted it out to Luke half a dozen times. Even Ella Mae knows something's up. She's called me over there twice in the past week without even bothering to pretend she doesn't feel well. She just asks a bunch of prying questions, then kicks me out when she doesn't like my evasive answers."

Abby chuckled. "You really like her, don't you?"

"Sure. I told you before she reminds me of my grandmother."

"Speaking of your family," she began pointedly, "what have you heard from Meredith or Laura?"

Seth stiffened. "Nothing, which should be a relief, but it isn't. It scares me to death."

"Are you thinking they've had it out and put each other in the hospital?"

"It's not out of the realm of possibility," he admitted. "I should call and see what's going on."

"What about Laura's lawyer? Any word from him?"

"No. I think my deposition discouraged him."

"Well, I hope that situation gets resolved. I want them here for our wedding."

Seth stared at her incredulously. "You want my sisters in the same room for our wedding?"

"I insist on it," she said.

"Boy, you really must love me even more than I imagined to be willing to take that risk."

Abby laughed. "I love you plenty. Now, you'd better get out of here and work your shift. I may need your shoulder to cry on at that council meeting tonight."

"I'll be there," he promised.

Though he still wasn't satisfied that he knew what was really on Abby's mind, he could tell he wasn't likely to get any straight answers until she was ready to reveal them.

On his way to work, he called Meredith, hoping to put his mind at ease on that front, anyway.

"Hey, Seth," she said wearily. "I've been meaning to call you."

"And yet you haven't," he said. "How are things between you and Laura?"

"Surprisingly calm," she admitted. "No threatening calls in days now. No pleading. I'm a little worried she's dreaming up some new sneak attack. Have you spoken to her?"

"Nope. I didn't even hear from her over the holidays. She's my next call."

"Well, let me know if you find out anything."

"Will do. Everything else okay?"

"If I could get this particular albatross off my back, my life would be great," she said.

"One way or another, it will be over soon," he assured her. "If Laura's attorney has his way, he'll have a court date this month."

"So I hear," she said. "Love you."

"You, too," he told her. He disconnected, then called Laura. To his astonishment, it was Jason who picked up.

"Hi, Seth," his ex-brother-in-law said.

"Hey, pal. What are you doing answering Laura's phone or do I even want to know?"

"We've kind of made peace," Jason admitted.

"You're kidding me!"

"It's true."

"When did this happen?"

"Christmas day," Jason told him. "She showed up at my place with a handful of credit card statements. Every one of them had zero balances. She said that was my gift."

"Where'd she get the money to pay them off?" Seth asked suspiciously.

"That was my first question," Jason admitted. "She sold her car."

Seth didn't even try to hide his astonishment. "But she loved that Jaguar."

"I know," Jason said. "She said she loved me more."

"So, what's she driving?"

"A used VW," Jason said. "She says it's cute and that it gets good gas mileage."

"She actually knows what kind of mileage it gets?" Seth asked incredulously.

"I know. It blew my mind, too. You probably think I'm nuts to give her another chance, but she's really trying."

"No," Seth told him. "I'm actually happy for you. I hope she sticks to it this time."

"All I know is that she stood right in front of me and cut up her credit cards," Jason said.

"All of them?"

"Every one," Jason confirmed. "Believe me, I checked. She's out of the shower now. Want to speak to her?"

"Sure," Seth said. "Good luck, pal. I mean that."

"Thanks. Here's Laura."

"Hi," she said hesitantly.

"I am so proud of you," Seth said. "What finally got through to you?"

"The lawyer told me what you'd said. I know it was nothing you hadn't said before, but he explained that he was starting to see that I didn't stand a chance of winning. He asked me if I hadn't lost enough without paying him a fortune just to lose in court. I guess I needed to hear it from an objective outsider, or maybe even more from someone I was paying to be on my side. I weighed winning against getting Jason back. It was no contest."

"How come you haven't told Meredith you're dropping the suit?"

She hesitated, then admitted, "I don't want to listen to her gloating."

"Laura, she's not going to gloat, any more than I am. We've both always wanted what's best for you. Sounds to me as if you finally have it."

She laughed. "I really do, don't I? Who knew I didn't need all that stuff to be over the moon? All I need is Jason. Now, tell me about you."

"Do you realize this is the first time you've asked about what's going on in my life in months?"

"I know. I know. Selfish me. But I'm asking now."

Seth filled her in on his plans to marry Abby. "She wants you and Meredith at the wedding. Jason, too."

"I can't speak for our big sister, but Jason and I will be there. I want to meet this woman who was smart enough to grab the second best man on the planet."

Seth laughed. "Meaning Jason tops the list, I assume."

"Of course."

"Abby might take exception to that, but you two can battle it out when you meet. See you soon."

"How soon? When is this wedding?"

"Soon, if I have my way. I'll keep you posted."

He drew in a deep breath after he'd hung up. Knowing that Laura and Jason had worked things out was a huge relief. Not only was he happy for the two of them, but it reassured him that even complex differences could be resolved if two people worked at it with open hearts.

Abby's presentation to the council was much more succinct this time. She figured there was very little to add to what she'd already told them, collectively and, in Sandra's case, individually.

She sat back down next to Seth, who took her hand in his. Luke and Hannah were seated on her other side, along with Jenny, Kelsey and Jeff. Jack Ferguson and Lesley Ann were beside Seth. Mary and Kyle Whittier were beside them. It was an impressive show of support that didn't go unnoticed by anyone on the council, least of all the mayor.

"I've had some time to think about Abby's proposal," Sandra said to her fellow council members and the audience. "The concerns I had about the changes this would bring to Seaview Key have been resolved, at least in my mind. I see the benefits and those outweigh any disadvantages I perceived. I think this community can handle a development of this limited scope, that it would be a boon to our economy. I'm prepared to vote. Is there a motion for approval?"

"So moved," one of the original supporters said.

"Second," another backer added.

Abby held her breath as the vote was taken. Sandra called on her two backers before casting her own vote, then smiled as she added her own "Yea" to make it unanimous in favor of proceeding.

Seth turned to Abby and kissed her soundly. "Congratulations!"

Abby was immediately surrounded by well-wishers.

"Drinks are on me at The Fish Tale," Jack said. "I'll see you all there."

As the crowd filtered out, Abby noticed that there were messages on her cell phone, which she'd turned off earlier and forgotten about.

"I'd better check these," she told Seth. "You want to go on ahead?"

He shook his head. "I'll wait."

She listened to a couple of messages that were routine, then realized that the next one was from the doctor she'd seen. Heart pounding, she listened to it.

"Oh my God," she murmured, then played it again. No, she concluded, she hadn't misheard.

"What?" Seth asked. "Are you okay? What's going on?"

She handed him the cell phone. "Listen," she whispered. "Then tell me if I heard it right."

As his jaw dropped and his eyes widened, she knew there'd been no mistake. He stared at her.

"You're pregnant?" he whispered.

"Apparently so," she said, her astonishment mirroring his.

"You saw a doctor?"

"I went to see a fertility expert to see if I could get pregnant. She ran some tests. I had no idea I might already be pregnant. It must have been really early because she missed it in the exam, too." She stared into Seth's eyes. "Are you okay with this?"

He laughed. "I've never been more okay with anything in my life," he told her, picking her up and twirling her around.

Just then Luke and Hannah walked back, regarding them curiously.

"Everything okay?" Hannah asked.

"We're having a baby," Abby blurted.

"And getting married," Seth added hurriedly. "But not in that order. We're getting married first. I'm thinking tomorrow would be good. Or the next day."

Luke laughed, then slapped Seth on the back. "Boy, once the two of you get with the program, you don't waste any time, do you?"

Hannah nudged him with an elbow. "No gloating."

"Hey, who's gloating? I'm just happy they saw the light."

"He's gloating," Seth said. "But you know what? I don't care." He grinned at Luke. "Are you interested in being the best man?"

"I'm there," Luke confirmed.

Abby turned to Hannah. "And you? Matron of honor?"

Hannah's smile was almost as wide as the one Abby

could feel on her own face. "Done," she said at once. "Anything you need, you can count on me."

"Just make sure I don't trip going down the aisle," Abby said.

"Church wedding?" Hannah asked. "Town hall?"

Abby glanced at Seth, who clearly guessed exactly what she was thinking. He nodded.

"Seaview Inn, if it's okay with Grandma Jenny," Abby said.

"That's perfect!" Hannah said. "She'll be thrilled."

And for Abby, it would be proof at last that she was well and truly home for good.

Epilogue

Seth stood nervously beside Luke in the living room at Seaview Inn. Christmas decorations had been replaced with huge bowls of fresh spring flowers. Only a few guests had gathered, including his sisters, Jason, Jeff, Jack Ferguson and Lesley Ann. Grandma Jenny and Ella Mae sat in places of honor in the front row of chairs set up for the service.

Recorded music announced the start of the ceremony. Seth looked toward the foyer, then grinned as Isabella toddled unsteadily into the room clinging to Kelsey's hand and tossing fistfuls of flower petals in her path. When she caught sight of her dad, she let out a scream and headed in his direction.

Then came Hannah, wearing a deep blue silk dress that shimmered like the sea at night.

Seth's breath caught in his throat as Abby stepped into view, wearing a simple cream silk sheath and carrying a bouquet of daisies as a tribute to the day he'd brought her flowers stolen from one of Jenny's containers. As she reached his side, he leaned close.

"Did you steal those?"

She laughed. "Nope, Grandma Jenny gave them to me of her own free will. She seemed to think they might have some special significance."

"And I thought I'd gotten away with it," Seth said, then turned to face Sandra, who'd agreed to conduct the ceremony.

When it came time for their vows, Seth looked into Abby's eyes and saw everything he'd ever dreamed of. "You are my future and my hope for all that's good," he told her. "Whatever comes our way, we're strong enough to face it together. If there's heartache, I promise there will be joy. If there's tension, I promise to balance that with laughter. Above all, there will be love." He held her gaze. "Never-ending love."

Instinctively Abby's free hand went to her stomach and stayed there. With her other hand, she clung to his. "You have given me everything I ever wanted," she said. "My dreams are coming true because of you and this life we're pledging to build together. You are my heart and my future. You and our family will always be the most important things in my life. I love you, Seth, today and forever."

They exchanged rings and Sandra pronounced them husband and wife. Seth looked into the face of this woman who'd taught him that love was possible, even after heartbreak.

"I love you," he said as he leaned down to kiss her.

And in that kiss he proved that what had happened on the beach all those weeks ago was no fluke. Abby could still—and always would—take his breath away!

* * * * *